MITTELEUROPA

Vienna, the capital of the Austro-Hungarian Empire, but in a world in which the First World War did not take place: a man disappears. Ludwig Pechstein, of the Pechstein Security and Investigations Agency, is asked to investigate. The trail leads to gruesome secret government chemical warfare research programmes, a land commune in Switzerland, smugglers of avant-garde art, political radicals in the East End of London, and a Zionist colony in German Central Africa.

MITTELEUROPA

A NOVEL

KURTIS SUNDAY

Front cover images:
Photograph of Gustav Nagel, *Naturmensch* and *Lebensreformer*, who
spent time at Monte Verità, Ascona, Switzerland,
taken by Louis Held, circa 1900.
Packet of Sphinx cigarettes,
manufactured by Jasmatzi AG, Dresden.
Graphic of woman with globe is from
Élisée Reclus's six-volume *L'Homme et la Terre* (1905–1908).

Map: Global telegraph network, 1903.
Carte générale des grandes communications télégraphiques du monde, 1903.
Map reproduction courtesy of the Norman B. Leventhal Map &
Education Center at the Boston Public Library.

Strange how blind people are! They are horrified by the torture chambers of the Middle Ages, but their arsenals fill them with pride!

— Bertha von Suttner
Die Waffen nieder!, 1889

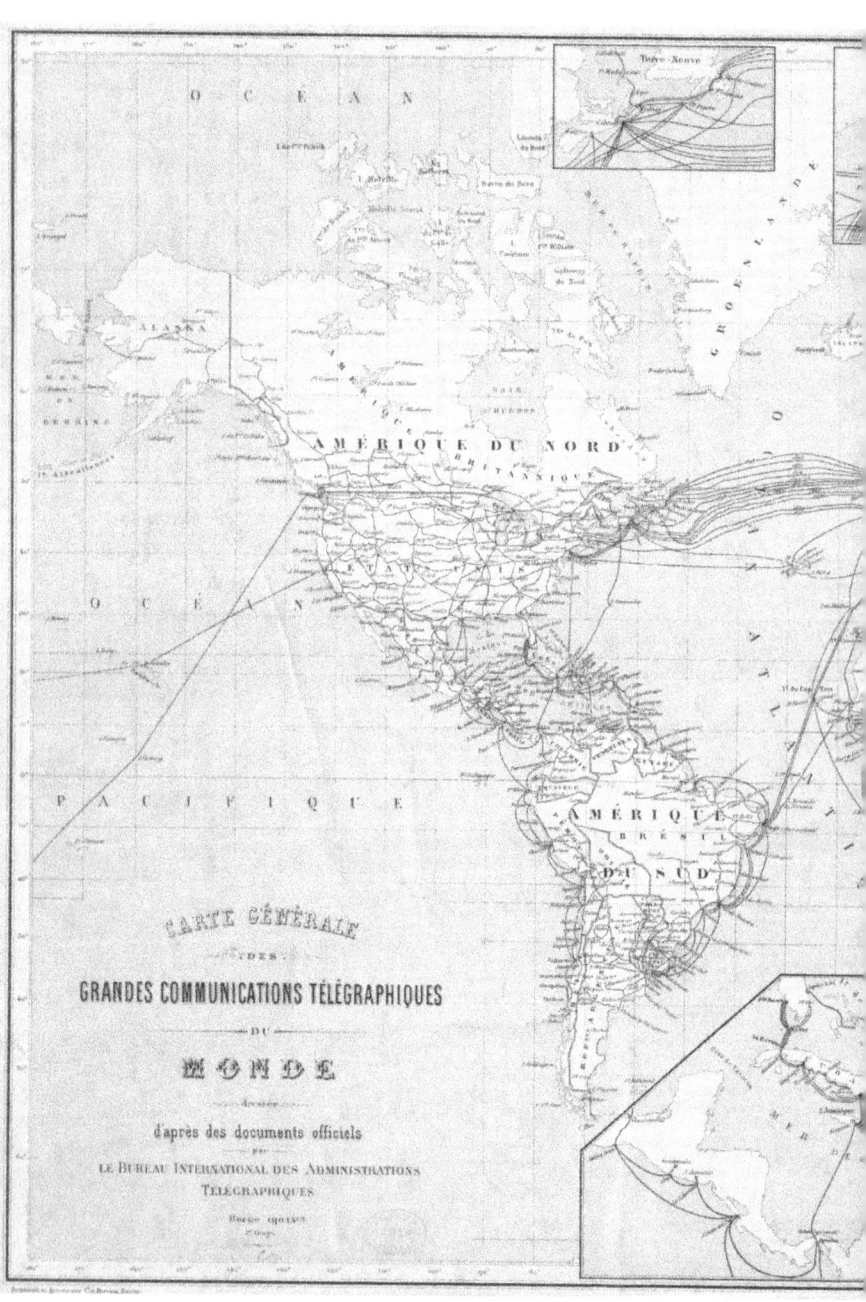

CARTE GÉNÉRALE

DES

GRANDES COMMUNICATIONS TÉLÉGRAPHIQUES

DU

MONDE

dressée

d'après des documents officiels

par

LE BUREAU INTERNATIONAL DES ADMINISTRATIONS

TÉLÉGRAPHIQUES

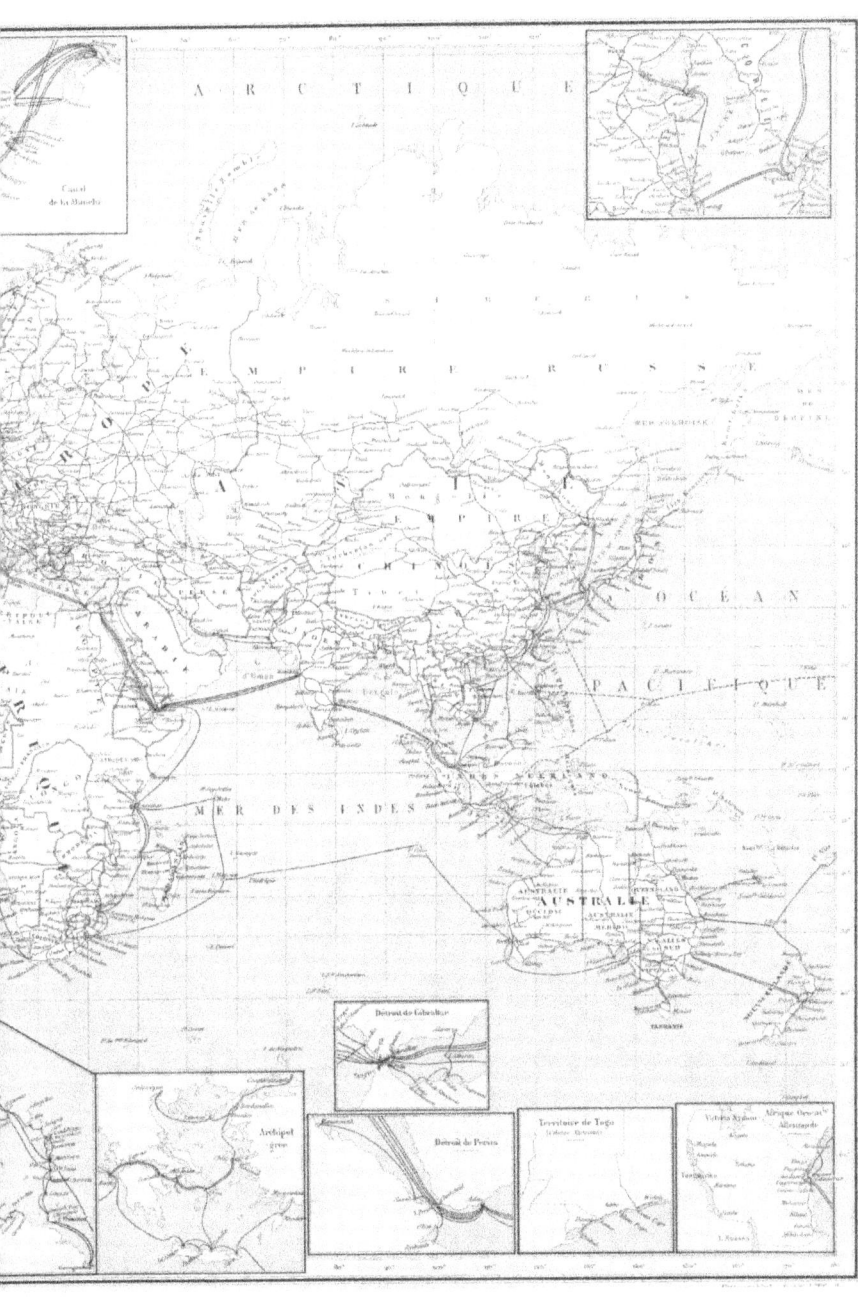

A R C T I Q U E

Canal
de la Manche

E M P I R E   R U S S E

MER DE BOCHOTSK

ARABIE

EMPIRE
CHINOIS

O C É A N

P A C I F I Q U E

MER DES INDES

AUSTRALIE

Détroit de Gibraltar

Archipel
grec

Détroit de Perrin

Territoire de Togo

Victoria Nyanza   Afrique Orientale
Allemande

Futurism

Historically, Futurism or the Futurist art movement is identified with Fascism, but in fact it had both leftist and anti-Fascist supporters. In 1924 the socialists, communists and anarchists walked out of the Milan Futurist Congress. However, in the alternative timeline of *Mitteleuropa*, the word *Futurist* comes to be applied to modern art in general and to speculative literature, and *futurist* (lower case 'f') to forward-looking utopian political ideas.

1914

1

'The double agent is the prince of spies,' said Konrad Wartenheim. Which, of course, Saaldeck knew was not his real name, but then neither was 'Saaldeck' Saaldeck's real name.

Wartenheim inserted a new eyepiece into the telescope, looked through the viewer, and carefully aimed the telescope high into the night sky.

Saaldeck had had many clandestine meetings with men – and not a few women – who led secret lives over the last decade, in workingmen's bars, in museums, in parks, in nondescript bourgeois suburbs, in proletarian tenements, down backstreets at night. But Wartenheim's chosen location for this rendezvous was unexpected: an idyllic cottage in the foothills of the Austrian Alps. The typed note he had received, accompanied by a key, had instructed him to take the 18:25 train to Spittal an der Drau and disembark at Mühldorf. Just outside the railway station entrance he would find a grey gentleman's Bianchi bicycle; the key was to the bicycle's security lock. There had been a neatly drawn sketch map showing him the route to the cottage, which he would recognise from the wooden sign at the gate: Knabenkraut, the name of some sort of orchid. It had taken him about an hour to get there. In the July evening light and the warm air, the countryside had smelled of freshly cut hay and cowpats, as if all was right with the world. He had arrived as dusk was descending and the bats were coming out. Wartenheim had been in the garden, setting up an expensive-looking metre-long telescope on a tripod.

Now the sky had been dark for about an hour and the stellar expanse of the Milky Way was clearly visible above them in the moonless sky.

'Take a look,' Wartenheim said.

Saaldeck removed his eyeglasses and put his eye to the telescope's rubber-rimmed eyepiece, and suddenly he was looking at countless twinkling points of light, stars upon stars, as if countless granules of sparkling sugar had been cast casually across an infinite black velvet void.

'How far away do you think they are?' Wartenheim asked him.

'A long way.'

'Tens to hundreds of light years,' Wartenheim said. 'And a light year is—'

'I know what a light year is.'

'Not a few astronomers believe that many of all those stars have planets orbiting them, just like our sun has. And some believe that the Milky Way is not the only galaxy, that some of the nebulae may also be galaxies in their own right …'

'… and such is the backdrop against which we play out our human stratagems,' Saaldeck added.

He removed his eye from the eyepiece and looked at Wartenheim – or rather, at the man who called himself Wartenheim – and wondered, not for the first time, if the man were *genuine* – if what he hinted were his motivations really were his motivations. The envelopes of banknotes and the various *real forged* blank identification documents Wartenheim had provided him with, no questions asked, over the last few years, had proved to be real enough – and extremely useful; and Saaldeck had no scruples about spying on one bourgeois state for another, as long as it served the Cause.

Later, sitting in front of the cast-iron wood stove – which was packed with fresh logs but not alight – Wartenheim asked him what he thought about spiritualism, if anything.

'I'm a materialist,' Saaldeck said. 'I don't think anything

about spiritualism.'

'But you have beliefs, strong beliefs. Beliefs are hardly material things.'

Saaldeck took another sip from his glass of Welschriesling and thought for a moment.

'Consciousness emerges out of the material substance of the world. Rationality emerges out of consciousness, imperfectly at first, but slowly it becomes more rational – more precise … or, rather, less imprecise – as it analyses the material world out of which it has evolved. My beliefs, as you call them, are simply part of that process. The new replaces the old in biological evolution. In the evolution of human society, the same process is at work. The mindless chaos of nature is gradually tamed. New economic and social orders replace the old. My beliefs are merely part of that process of nature transcending itself, manifested as the will to simply replace an inefficient and misery-inducing economic and social system with a more rational one.'

'With a little help from the misery-inducing system you wish to destroy.'

'Modes of life produce contradictions,' Saaldeck said. 'Those contradictions eventually destroy the modes of life that produced them …'

'… and make room for new modes of life to develop.'

'Something like that.'

Wartenheim, who was in his fifties, was perhaps twenty years older than Saaldeck. He was a man formed by the last century, Saaldeck thought, a century that had spawned the seeds of the ideas that would in time, inevitably, destroy the economic and social order that that century had given birth to. It often surprised him that the men of Wartenheim's generation – and social class, a class that was changing the world like no other class before it had, transforming a world of farms and villages into a world of industries and metropolises – could not see that the world of the nineteenth century would also pass. All they needed to do was to look around them. Everywhere the new was consigning the old to the dustbin of the past. The very air of the twentieth century radiated change.

'Why do you ask?' Saaldeck asked.

'What you think of spiritualism?'

'Yes.'

'I wasn't trying to be morbid,' Wartenheim said, lighting his pipe again, 'but it just seems to me that things are more inexplicable … than, when you think about it, we are usually in the habit of thinking them to be. We – and I do believe that we're essentially spiritual beings; it's the spiritual part of us, our minds, that perceives the world of matter, gives it reality – suddenly appear in the world, pop into it as it were, and never really know what we really are. Then, in the blink of an eye, we're ageing men staring oblivion in the face. Somehow, it just does not seem to add up.'

'We awake, we live, we fall asleep again,' Saaldeck said. He thought of saying something about imagining anything else was nothing but bourgeois sentimentalism but refrained.

'An ultimatum was delivered to the Serbian ambassador a few days ago,' Wartenheim said, changing the subject. 'It hasn't been made public to the press yet but it will leak out eventually. Though, by now, there isn't a chancellery in Europe that doesn't know the details of it. The diplomatic telegraph wires have been buzzing. It'll all probably blow over, no doubt … this time. Alliances are dangerous. You did get a return ticket?'

'Yes.'

'Good. It's probably overdoing it a bit but better safe than sorry. Not being a local, you might be remembered at the station if you bought a ticket there. If you leave at sunrise, there'll only be a few souls about.'

Again, Saaldeck wondered why Wartenheim had not arranged this meeting at some suitably discreet location in Vienna, instead of going through the rigmarole of dragging him all the way out here. A stranger in the countryside stood out like a sore thumb. It had hardly been to show him the wonders of the Milky Way. He could have asked, but he doubted he would have got a straightforward answer.

'The device I mentioned,' Wartenheim said. 'I'd better show you how it works now. Then you can hit the hay.'

'Do you have an alarm clock?' Saaldeck asked.

'The neighbours have a cockerel. Always crows at the crack of dawn. Loud enough to wake the dead.'

Wartenheim then got up, went over to a half-empty bookshelf, and took down a cardboard Lendvay & Schwarcz shoebox, placed it on the low table between them, and opened it.

2

'… a one-donkey town in some God-forsaken ex-Ottoman bailiwick. Sarajevo and the events that followed was the death knell for the world that came into being when Wellington put Boney in his place and ushered in a century of peace – among the civilised nations of Europe at any rate – during which, for the most part, wars were relatively limited and brief.'

Quentin Youghal had the weathered face of an old India hand. His Anglo-Irish accent filled the Waugh House library, now serving as a briefing room for the War Office's newly set up and innocuously named Government Scientific Research Establishment.

His audience consisted of twenty or so men, most of them in army or navy uniform, the rest in grey civil service suits. The curtains – the windows opened onto the stately home's landscaped garden – were drawn, and the overhead electric lamp was on. Youghal gave Constance Cohen, who was fiddling with the new Ensign electric lantern slide projector, a near-imperceptible nod. A moment later the room was plunged into semi-darkness and electric light from the lantern-projector beamed the following words onto the white canvas screen:

SCIENCE IN THE SERVICE OF EMPIRE

'The list of scientific inventions that have changed the face of military conflict is long,' Youghal continued. 'The mathematics of ballistic trajectories. The exploding shell. The gun we have *and they have not*.' For a moment he wasn't sure if they had got the joke. 'The Maxim gun. Belloc,' he explained. 'But the relationship between soldier and scientist has not always been a cosy one. The scientist, if the truth be told, is sort of poet in a way, but a poet whose imagining subjects itself to the laws of matter, the laws of the real world of fact and hard edges. The soldier is by nature a conservative man, a man with his boots on the ground, who values traditions and customs – a man willing to lay down his life to preserve them. He is a man of the barracks and the field, not of the rarefied lecture hall, nor at home among retorts and Bunsen burners. He is a man who values the tried and tested. For at the end of the day, it is his life and the lives of the men he leads that are risked in the heat of battle. His is a fine balancing act between what he knows to work and the possible. When the use of rifled cannon was first proposed during the American Civil War, the Northern generals were sceptical, but the rifled cannon won the war. The trusty smooth-bore cannon, that steadfast of the artillery for centuries, became a museum artefact overnight. Just as wind-powered wooden ships of the line gave way to the steam-powered ironclad, and the ironclad in its turn gave way to the oil-powered dreadnought. Now previously unconceivable weapons of war are on the horizon.

'But enough of quasi-philosophical speculations. Though I'm damned sure our opposite numbers at the Kaiser Wilhelm Institute indulge in them as well, given the Teutonic's renowned proclivity for constructing metaphysical castles in the clouds, despite his tendency to what I suppose one could call a sort of plod-footedness.' His audience laughed, always a good sign. 'But our Teuton also possesses no mean technical ability. Which we ignore at our peril. Next slide, Miss Cohen.'

The lantern-projector mechanism clicked twice and a new image appeared on the screen: a sepia-toned photograph of a cigar-shaped airship floating above a chocolate-box southern English landscape. Attached to the underneath of the vessel was what looked like a full-sized railway passenger car with a propeller protruding from the rear

'His Majesty's Airship the *Beowulf*,' Youghal pronounced. He'd considered calling it the *Eye of Shiva* – Owen-Sykes, being an old India hand like himself, might have appreciated the reference to the 'destroyer of worlds' – but he was not sure anyone else would. 'The dreadnaught will rule the seas of the twentieth century, but airships like the *Beowulf* will rule its skies.'

'Does this thing actually exist?' a gravelly voice shot out of the semi-darkness. Youghal immediately recognised it as belonging to Owen-Sykes, who, with the rank of Brigadier-General, was the most senior military man present. And a man, Beardsley had informed him, who wielded considerable influence in the upper echelons of the War Office. His wife was reputed to be a bit of suffragist.

'No, Brigadier-General, the *Beowulf* does not yet exist,' Youghal replied. 'What you see here is a manipulated photograph – *doctored* is the technical term, I believe.' This received a few guffaws. 'It is an image of things to come. The envelope – that's the cigar-shaped balloon containing the lifting gas – is that of a real airship or dirigible, but the gondola ...' – he indicated the railway-carriage under construction with a long wooden pointer – '... as it's called, is a photograph of a real railway passenger car, and the propeller is an aëroplane propeller, enlarged, of course. So yes, the photograph is a work of the imagination. But it is not a mere fantasy. Think of what you see here as a blueprint, an *aide imaginaire*, or a back-of-an-envelope drawing, if you like.' That got another few laughs. 'There are details to work out, details wherein, as we say, the devil has his abode. But for the moment I just want you to keep this vision in mind: a fleet of these magnificent vessels cruising the heavens, wrathful sky-gods above the armies of our enemies, safely out of range of gunfire ... and also well out of range of any aëroplane. The altitude record for any lighter-than-air craft, you might like to know, is not in fact held by Herr Zeppelin, but by our very own Messrs Coxwell and Glaisher. Their coal-gas hot-air balloon, the *Mammoth*, reached over thirty-five thousand feet. In 1863.'

Youghal paused for a moment, long enough to become aware of the summer-world sounds filtering in from the garden outside. Clouds of pipe and cigar smoke hung slowly swirling in the light of the lantern-projector beam. At times, whenever he did these 'shows', he felt a bit like some Viennese mesmerist. The slide lantern had a hypnotic effect, and it made men more receptive than they normally were. Owen-Sykes seemed satisfied with his reply.

'A fleet of these aërial dreadnoughts could drop all sorts of conventional explosives. Incendiary bombs. Impact bombs. Grenades of various types. But all these armaments are heavy – and heaviness and airships are unhappy bedfellows. The number of airships required to deliver even a small fraction of the destructive power that a conventional artillery barrage can deliver, or even that of half a dozen of today's large guns, would simply be too many to make it a practical option. And aëroplanes can carry little more than their own weight. The Italians have flown many bombing raids against the Turks in their North African colonies using dirigibles. However – and it's a significant *however* – their airships cost more to manufacture than the damage they actually cause. The reason: they use conventional bombs.'

There were other technical problems too of course – no shortage of them – but this was neither the time not the place to go into them. In time, he was sure, they were all amenable to some sort of solution. The least of them was that the latest aëroplanes could now reach altitudes of eight thousand feet. The Frenchman Garros had reached something like eighteen thousand feet. Hydrogen was about as flammable and explosive as you get – and airships were hardly difficult targets. But, in theory at least, hydrogen could be replaced with hot air or even helium.

'The solution to this problem,' he continued, 'is … Miss Cohen?'

The next image appeared: a cross-sectional engineering drawing of a canister of some sort. It had a coned tip, facing downwards; two fin-like protuberances; two internal compartments, one labelled CHEMICAL A and the other labelled

CHEMICAL B; and there was a small mechanical device in the coned tip labelled DETONATOR.

'The aërial gas-bomb,' he announced, 'is the weapon of the future, the weapon that will preserve our empire against the barbarian hordes.' He had not quite intended to say that. It had just slipped out. After all, one had to admit that Germany's claim to *Kulturnation*-hood was hardly without merit. But, he noted with satisfaction, the comment had evoked more than a few hearty laughs. He restrained himself from mentioning that, according to the intelligence reports Beardsley had shown him, Haber and his men at the Kaiser Wilhelm Institute were far ahead of them in the development of gas weaponry.

'Each of the compartments contains a different chemical.' He indicated the two compartments with the pointer. 'Both chemicals are in themselves harmless. But …' – he indicated the detonator mechanism – '… here, at the bottom, in the tip of the shell, there a small explosive charge which ignites when the shell makes contact with its target. Which in this case, is a rather large target, the proverbial barn door so to speak, namely the ground onto which the aërial gas-bomb is dropped – and, needless to say, from a great height. The fin-like protuberances guide the bomb to its destination, like the fletching on an arrow.'

He did not say that any bomb or shell dropped from a height would more than likely bury itself in the ground by the sheer force of its impact: Newton's second law and all that. An aluminium casing, or even one of plywood, would reduce the weight, but hardly significantly. The scientists had considered the possibility of using some sort of barometric trigger, one that would trigger the detonator at, say, thirty, or even sixty, feet, but the air pressure difference between the Earth's surface and sixty feet above it was miniscule. However, a bomb with a small parachute that opened, even by means of a simple timer at, say, five hundred feet above the surface, leaving the bomb to slowly drift down, was a possible solution to the problem.

'Miss Cohen.'

The next image showed an imaginary aërial gas-bomb hitting the ground and exploding.

'The detonator explosion needs to be finely controlled – though some sort of mechanical device might also do the trick, perhaps even with greater precision. The barrier between the two compartments containing the chemicals A and B disintegrates, and the two chemicals react with each other to rapidly produce a gas. The mounting pressure blows off the top of the canister, allowing the gas – considerable quantities of it – to be released into the surrounding environment. The effective blast radius, or rather gassing radius, is considerably greater than that of a conventional artillery shell.'

The next image was a coloured-in pen and ink drawing of the type and style churned out by illustrators of *The Times* and the *Daily Telegraph*. It showed an infantry column – obviously not British, nor German for that matter; their demeanour was far too slovenly – and a lance-bearing regiment cavalry scattering in all directions, attempting to escape a cloud of bright yellow-green, almost luminescent, fog.

'Chlorine gas, which is a sort of yellow-green colour, can cause death by asphyxiation within minutes. Heavier than air, it stays pretty much at ground level – exactly where we want it. Though we are also investigating a number of other compounds in Mother Nature's chemistry set, which could also be suitable for the purpose.

'A gas-bomb has a lethality radius several factors greater than the blast radius produced by a conventional exploding shell. And gas lingers, for hours at times. In short, one gets more bang per farthing, puffs per ounce. Which makes the gas-bomb the ideal bomb to be dropped from airships, or even from aëroplanes.

'Favourable weather conditions are of course essential. Operating from the air means, however, that these can be chosen almost at leisure. Wind, gentlemen, is the goblin in the detail here. We need the wind to deliver our gas. But too much wind and our gas disperses too swiftly. A doldrum and it just hangs in the air with minimum effect. A gentle summer zephyr is ideal. Our airship fleet can simply hover among the clouds out of range of enemy guns until the opportune moment. Gas shells or gas canisters delivered by artillery or any other sort of mortar would require proximity to their target – a proximity which could be problematic should the direction of the wind change, which, as you Senior Service Jack Tars will know, it is wont to do at times. Delivering the gas by the relatively simple method of releasing it from cylinders and letting it drift toward the enemy would require even greater proximity to him, and, consequently, would be even more problematic if things went wrong, as they are prone to on occasion. *Homo proponit, sed Deus disponit* – Man proposes, God disposes – as they say.'

His attempt at erudite wit, contrary to his expectation, did not even induce a snigger. Usually not a good sign, but perhaps – it was impossible to make out any facial expressions in the semi-darkness – his listeners were simply so impressed by the scenario he was laying out before them that they had missed his attempt at levity.

'But by delivering our gas from the air,' he continued in a more serious tone, 'this simply ceases to be a problem. Our bombs can be dropped at any location near to the enemy's position – *to the right of them, to the left of them, and behind them*, to sort of quote Tennyson – regardless of whether he is on the march, dug in somewhere, in a fortress, or holed up in a village or a town, or even a large city. The wind will simply deliver our package to wherever we wish.

'However, to reach the altitudes at which airships are invulnerable, electric engines will need to be used. But that is something which the scientists are working on.' Which was not without its problems, but anything to do with electricity always went down well. 'The wars of the future, gentlemen, will be fought by soldiers, seamen *and* men of science.'

The applause was polite rather than enthusiastic.

The curtains were drawn open again, letting fresh air and August daylight into the smoke-filled room. He hadn't expected to bring the house down. Most new ideas were dead ends. And, even when they were not, led with disconcerting frequency to unanticipated outcomes. Alexander Graham Bell had imagined his telephones would be used to pipe arias from concert halls into people's homes; but Electrophone – with its piped theatre, music-hall shows, news reports, and church services on Sundays – hadn't managed to sign up more than a couple of thousand subscribers – while millions of person-to-person telephones were made every day. But the purpose of these briefings was to expose at least some of the members of the various experimental weapons research committees to a broad overview of the outer reaches of the military-scientific imagination. 'Open their minds, Quentin,' the Beardsley had said. 'Let some twentieth-century air clear the cobwebs from their nineteenth-century brains.' Though, if truth be told, Waugh House was a mere sideshow. The money being spent on the research facility was a drop in the proverbial ocean in comparison to the vast sums being poured into the dreadnought programme and the Vickers diesel-electric submarine programme.

A young army officer raised his hand.

'Yes,' Youghal said.

'Is not the use of chemical and poisonous weapons forbidden by the Convention? Not that I'm a lawyer but gas is rather—'

'Not quite cricket?' Youghal suggested.

'Yes, rather.'

Youghal glanced across at Owen-Sykes. The old warhorse's grey eyes were looking at him intently. He was waiting to see how he would respond to the obvious point; a point no small number of hymn-singing politicians were bound to make.

'Strictly speaking, you are correct,' Youghal replied, addressing the young officer directly, vaguely wondering what type of man he might be, whether – to use the fox-hunting expression – he had been blooded. The memory of his own blooding decades ago, on a frosty winter morning in the Wicklow hills, surfaced unannounced from this memory: the barking hounds, the limp corpse of the dead fox, the red coats and the horses, and his clerical-collared father ... The man had that unblooded air about him. But maybe he had seen some action, in Afghanistan or the Sudan or some other hotspot. It was hard to tell a lot of the time. He'd met enough blooded warriors who still seemed to wallow in a *Boy's Own Paper* attitude to it all. Even Owen-Sykes retained more than a bit of that *Boy's Own*-ishness under his old warhorse exterior.

'The Hague Convention,' Youghal continued, resisting the temptation to suggest that when push came to shove, and backs were up against the wall, that hallowed document would not be worth the paper it was written on, 'does say something along those lines. But it does not forbid the manufacture or the possession of chemical weapons. Neither does it forbid research or preparation for defending oneself against such weapons. Moot points of course, but points that I am very confident that our opposite numbers in the Kaiser Wilhelm Institute will be perfectly aware of, and whose attitudes to the Convention – I think we can safely assume – will be ruthlessly Germanic. The bow and arrow – with its capacity to kill at a distance, without looking the enemy in the eye, and silently – was once no doubt considered not cricket. But who thinks that today? Was Agincourt not quite cricket? I think not. We need to prepare for all eventualities. The other fellow is doing so. That's the simple logic of it.' Youghal noted with some satisfaction that Owen-Sykes seemed to approve of his reply. 'Mister Dickens, one of our top scientists, will now perform a little experiment for us.'

1918

3

Anja Jensen searched for a word to describe the brown-stained cranium on the trestle table. *Chthonic* came to mind. There was a hole in the rear of the cranium, rough-edged, as if it had been punctured with an ice pick, though most probably it had been made with some ancient weapon. She vaguely remembered somebody saying that there were daylight truths and the truths of the night. Pascal perhaps.

'Well, it's definitely not Piltdown.' Heinrich Weber said. He was a big, bespectacled man and, in the light from the tent's paraffin lamp, looked even more Buddha-like than he usually did. 'Early mediæval perhaps.'

When Crnjanski – a grey-haired gentle giant of a man who'd beaten Weber at chess twice, to Weber's amusement, though he had not played him a third time – had found the skull, Weber had had the men lower a ladder down into the pit and had climbed down to personally extract it from the packed soil, insisting that Anja Jensen photograph him several times with her Kodak Box as he did so.

'Male,' Weber added, pointing out the brow ridges 'The cranium of a female usually has a smoother frontal lobe.'

'And what would we see if we had Mr Wells's time machine, Herr Professor?' Anja asked him half-jokingly.

She had a lilting Danish-German accent.

'Man red in tooth and claw, Fraulein Jensen,' he replied, also jokingly, but in a more serious tone. 'A man being done to death by another man, perhaps.'

The night sky, occasionally criss-crossed by the fluttering shape of a bat, was visible through the open tent flaps. Despite the brightness of the near-full moon, a planet, either Jupiter or Saturn, and some stars were clearly visible above the moonlit shapes of the hills.

He offered her a Sobranie from his silver-plated cigarette case with the two-headed Habsburg eagle engraved on its lid. She took one and he struck a match and lit it for her. The aroma of the expensive Russian tobacco filled the warm air.

'Progress is only possible if one faces up to our primitive past,' he added, 'and transcends it.'

Could anyone ever look upon a human skull again and not think of Darwin, she wondered. Weber was a believer in progress. As was she: what reasoning modern woman could not believe in progress and its necessity. But he was not, he liked to think, one of those dewy-eyed technological utopians.

'A thousand years ago,' he said, 'poor Yorick here – another random discovery upon which we build theoretical edifices that purport to explain the past – had his head smashed in. And while I would not suggest that the Middle Ages lacked its moral sensibilities, I doubt that poor Yorick's untimely demise ruffled the feathers of the consciences of his contemporaries overmuch.'

She found herself again becoming aware of his physicality. Buddha meditates upon Yorick, she thought. Though she doubted if his habit of announcing that half the jokes he told were ones he made up himself quite fitted the Buddha archetype.

'Today nobody would fail to see such a brutal act,' he added, 'assuming our speculations as to the nature of poor Yorick's demise are correct, for what it was: a brutal act. Except perhaps a heathen native of the Bismarck Archipelago. And the motor of the civilisation is science now. The society of the future will be run by men of science. Religion has had its day.'

'A society run by doctors,' she suggested, quoting a phrase

she had read somewhere once.

Weber opened his notebook. He was never without a stiff-covered notebook of some kind and his Penkala fountain pen. It was as if he feared the world would somehow fade away unless he constantly wrote notes, which he took as compulsively as he smoked. Though his carnality, she had discovered – and, surprising herself, had indulged in on more than one occasion – seemed to be an appetite that needed only occasional, and brief, sating.

She decided it was time to go.

As she made her way back to her tent along the edge of the site, she lingered and gazed over the maze of trenches and pits they had dug over the summer, their stark contours visible in the moonlight.

The German-speaking valley dwellers called the place Das Grab, the grave. Local legend had it that the original mound was the sleeping place of a mythic emperor who, when the time was ripe, would one day reawaken and usher in a thousand-year utopian *Reich*. The upper archaeological layers contained the remnants of an early mediæval manor. Deeper down were the remains of a Romano-Germanic settlement, but also possibly a small villa surrounded by various other smaller buildings geometrically laid out – as opposed to the more haphazard layout of the mediæval buildings which had been constructed on its ruins centuries later. A portion of a tiled Romano-Germanic floor – half a square metre of a black-and-white checkerboard mosaic – was surprisingly intact. They had found the remains of pots, some glazed, and some amphoræ fragments. Deeper still was evidence of a Celtic Iron Age site; and beneath that was what Weber believed might be a pre-Celtic Bronze Age settlement. A story of increasing complexity and then a decline into lesser complexity – what Weber called one of those 'setbacks' on the onward march of civilisation.

Further up the valley were the ivy-covered remnants of a late mediæval Gothick church. Its outline, clearly visible in the moonlight, was reminiscent of one of Casper David Friedrich's painted ruins. A carved-stone Gothick window frame was still intact in one of the walls. But the church had nothing to do with the early mediæval settlement. Two centuries, Weber calculated, give or take a few decades, separated them. The Middle Ages had lasted a long time, seven centuries if you dated them from Charlemagne to when Columbus sailed the ocean blue. Which was three centuries longer than the time which had since passed.

The further excavations Weber intended would no doubt determine a good approximate age for the Yorick cranium. It could well be a thousand years old, twenty to fifteen lifetimes, perhaps thirty generations. Anja tried to visualise the ghosts of human figures spanning thirty generations: a milkmaid, a blacksmith, a woman at a spinning wheel, a knight in chainmail, a wandering preacher hawking indulgences, a mercenary in chequered hose from the Thirty Years War leaning on a pike … She tried to imagine herself strapped into Wells's time machine, tumbling back through the centuries as if they were minutes, the faces of dead generations appearing and disappearing as rapidly as the faces in a flipped-though photograph album, and then eventually finding herself – when? – staring at the face of a being of whom one could definitively say: this face is not human.

From somewhere, far off in the moonlit darkness, among the black shadows of the wooded hills that enclosed the valley, a shrill præternatural cry cut through the nocturnal silence. A vixen, she supposed.

***

The next morning Weber insisted on taking her to the village railway station in the pony and trap, her bicycle – the latest Orion – tied securely on the back. For most of the last two months she'd worn loose-fitting corduroy cycling trousers; but now, returning to the world of bourgeois civilisation, she was wearing a dress.

The sun-drenched platform was deserted except for the

stationmaster in his gold-braided uniform watering the potted geraniums outside the station office. The Habsburg yellow-and-black and the green-white-red-crested Hungarian tricolour hung limply at half-mast on their poles by the signal box. She gave her suitcase and bicycle to the station porter and purchased a copy of the *Neuer Wiener Telegraf* at the kiosk.

'The unexpected twists and turns of history,' Weber said, referring to the newspaper's black-bordered front page.

'Yes, indeed,' she said.

Moments later they heard the locomotive and saw its plume of white steam rising into the July sky. They shook hands and when she presented her cheek for him to kiss, he did so with more formality than she had expected.

She found a compartment occupied solely by a bearded young Orthodox Jew with the long curly sidelocks of his persuasion and wearing a coal-black *kapoteh* longcoat. He tipped his wide-brimmed black hat to her in a muted salute as she took a seat.

As the train pulled out of the station, she caught a glimpse of Weber on the platform timidly waving her off. It reminded her of the way people waved at strangers on passing ships. She returned his farewell with equal timidity, experiencing a momentary and unexpected shyness. They had been intimate a few times over the summer, engaged in mutual, awkward, semi-clothed caresses. 'Muscular,' he'd said she was, and she supposed she was. She felt a twinge of shame at the memory of the encounters – Christian shame? – and glanced at the young Jew opposite, his head stuck in a cheap-looking novel.

A few minutes later the train was steaming across the flat floor of the valley. Looking out the window at the passing landscape, she caught a glimpse of her reflection in the window glass: her straight brown-blond hair – and her face – and for a moment wondered how women, and men, had imagined themselves before there were mirrors, though, of course, they would have sometimes seen reflections of themselves in pools of water.

She observed the vegetation growing along the side of the railway tracks as they sped on: red poppies, a tall yellow-flowering plant she didn't know the name of, fern-like grasses, purple-bulbed thistles, plants that seemed to thrive in gravel. Rail-side plants all seemed to have something intangible in common, whether they grew along the railway tracks of the North German Plain or along those of Italian hills. Maybe it was that they were all colonisers, Darwinian pioneers who had found virgin land in which to thrive, a thin strip of man-made desert, a man-made ... she searched for the word ... *Lebensraum* perhaps?

The front page of the *Telegraf* was devoted to reports on the preparations for the state funeral, which was expected to be attended by all the emperors – the German Kaiser, the Czar and the British King-Emperor, each to follow the hearse in black electric automobiles – and all of Europe's reigning monarchs. She looked through the other pages. The Italians had carried out another aëroplane bombing raid against an Ottoman island in the Aegean; an opinion piece by Benito Mussolini, the editor of *Avanti,* condemned it. There was a report on anti-Jewish riots in Odessa, and a whole page on the final official handover in Brussels by bankrupt Portugal of her African colonies to the Germans and the British. But the German Kaiser's attempt to purchase lands in Palestine for a Jewish colony had fallen through, the Young Turks having proved stubbornly reticent to parting with the Holy Land. There'd been another suffragette bomb in London, this time at the Stock Exchange; some shootings in Ireland; and plans for the Antwerp Olympics were being finalised.

Her work at Das Grab had gone well. She had typed up Weber's article for the *Archäologisch-epigraphische Mitteilungen* on her portable Blickensderfer and edited it – or rather rewritten it, though she'd diplomatically called it 'tidying it up'. She had also now completed the set of ink and pencil sketches of the site and of various finds, including the Yorick cranium, and shot more than half a dozen rolls of Kodak film, some of which, with a bit of luck, should be usable.

She lit a Waldorf and decided to do the crossword puzzle.

***

She arrived at the Südbahnhof late that afternoon and ordered a horse cab to take her to her apartment on the Zedlitzgasse. The Viennese sky was blue and cloudless and the trees in full summer foliage but the streets were near-deserted, as if a deadly epidemic was raging silently in the city, driving half its inhabitants indoors out of fear of contagion. The public buildings, the schools and the university had shut, as had the shops, coffee houses and beer gardens. Black pennants hung limply from balconies all along the Prinz-Rudolf-Alleé. The electric trams and trolleybuses were decked in black. The policemen and Vienna's army of uniformed civil servants were wearing black armbands. Even the horses seemed to be trotting at a more respectful pace, as if they too sensed the solemnity that hung over the imperial capital in the hot July air.

***

When she set off the next morning to the Girardigasse to see Dolfi, the sky was again blue and cloudless, and the atmosphere of the streets as muted as it had been the day before.

The queue outside Stephansdom, the twelfth-century Gothick edifice where the two emperors were lying in state before the high altar, stretched all around Stephansplatz. The morning newspapers had been full of how, all week, the citizenry had been silently filing past the open caskets. A bald, middle-aged man was being carried on a stretcher to a row of horse-drawn Red Cross ambulances, his grey bowler and walking stick lying upon his chest as if he were a fallen knight being borne to his interment. Groups of uniformed children, under the auspices of their schoolmasters and mistresses, were laying wreaths all along the buttressed southern wall of the mediæval edifice. Three cinematographers, their bulky camera mounted on a tripod, were capturing the moment in silent black and white for eternity or, she thought, for as long as celluloid film lasts.

The death of Franz Joseph had hardly been unanticipated. The

man had been in his eighties. The grey-whiskered patriarch –
he'd reigned for near three-quarters of a century – in his
countless flamboyant dress uniforms had stared out from
portraits on walls across the empire from seemingly time
immemorial. But that, four days later, the Crown Prince Franz
Ferdinand himself, the new uncrowned emperor, who had only
been in his mid-fifties, should drop dead while struggling with
his morning boiled egg seemed like a perverse prank of the
Fates. But they said he had never properly recovered from his
Sarajevo injuries. Franz Ferdinand was far from being a
handsome faerie-tale prince embodying the hopes of the
empire's nations, but he had been hailed for the few short days
that he'd reigned as a steady hand at the helm of the state. He
had never been an inspiring man, despite his occasional
speeches about his dreams of a 'United States of Greater
Austria'. But the almost slapstick assassination attempt four
years earlier, almost to the day, had suddenly transformed his
public image. There'd been endless articles about how the sang-
froid he and the Archduchess, his beloved Soph, had displayed
as they were being shot at and bombed by Serbian terrorists
embodied the spirit that made the empire what it was.

**

The rimless eyeglasses Donnerstag wore magnified his yellow-
brown round eyes and gave him a distinctly owlish look, despite
his crane-like nose, lanky limbs and claw-like fingers. He was
dressed, as always, in his invariably shabby customs officer's
uniform. How he managed to hold onto his post despite his
perpetual unshaven slovenliness – she'd more than once seen
him cycle back from wherever he worked inspecting ships that
sailed up the Danube – was a bit of a mystery to her, as was his
ability to seemingly get himself extended periods of leave. The
Imperial Customs Service was generally fastidious regarding
the appearance of its officials. There was a bit of the John
Calvin in him – he neither smoked nor drank – though now and
again he did turn up bearing such relatively exotic luxuries as

Palestinian oranges and Turkish coffee acquired, presumably, during the inspection of some ship or other. Once, he'd turned up with a squirrel-sized monkey of some sort which he'd given to a girlfriend of Polanyi's, who'd dressed it in a multicoloured jacket and trousers, kept it on a lead and carried it around on her shoulder.

'A lemonade?' he suggested.

The apartment consisted of two large rooms, with an in-apartment lavatory. Dolfi had one of the rooms and the Donnerstag the other. While Donnerstag fetched her a glass of lemonade from the small kitchen at the end of the hallway, she examined his tightly packed bookshelf under his ridiculous cuckoo clock. There must have been near a hundred volumes, most of them second-hand, picked up in the numerous *Antiquariate* around Vienna that specialised in occult and the esoteric lore. There was an open copy of a full, unabridged edition of Fraser's *The Golden Bough* on the table. But apart from the books, the room had a distinctly spartan air about it. The walls were bare except for a large, faded and kitschy oil painting of a stag on a rocky outcrop gazing over a forested Alpine ravine; and his iron-framed bed, which did not seem long enough for him.

'So, you got my letter,' he said when he returned.

'No,' she said, sipping the surprisingly cool lemonade. He'd never written to her before.

'I posted it on Monday. Too late obviously. I should have sent a telegram.'

'A telegram?' she said.

'Dolfi's disappeared,' he said. 'I haven't seen him since the day after I got back from Ascona.'

'You mean he has gone somewhere?' she said.

'But I have no idea where. He didn't leave a note or say anything.'

She paused for a moment to think.

'But you saw him when you came back?'

'Only that evening, and the next morning.'

Dolfi had not written to her for several weeks – but there was nothing unusual about that,

'So how long exactly has he been gone?'

'It's nearly a week now.'

She tried to think if that were unusual. Dolfi could be unpredictable in his habits. And Donnerstag was prone to over-imagining things.

'There was something …' he said. 'It might be of some significance. But then again it might not.'

She waited for him to explain.

'A couple of days after he went missing somebody called. A woman.'

'Looking for Dolfi?'

'She left her card.'

'And why might that be of some significance?

'Just a feeling.'

He fumbled around in some papers on a small table by the hat-and-coat stand behind the door and retrieved a simply printed visiting card. She read the name: Sigrid Xavier Kupfer, printed in purple Latin lettering. Neither the name nor the address meant anything to her.

'Smallish woman. Red-haired.' Donnerstag said. 'I've seen her a couple of times at the Ottoman.'

The New Ottoman Bazaar was a coffee house, decorated in a sort of Orientalist Jugendstil style, where a lot of the Girardigasse crowd met.

'Can I see his room?' she said.

Dolfi's 'den', as he called it, was in semi-darkness. Donnerstag opened the shutters to let some daylight in, and left her alone. Her brother's desk was a clutter of papers. He earned his crust translating scientific and scholarly English, American and French texts. A thick English–German dictionary lay open beside his Urania typewriter. But the rest of the room was tidy, the bed neatly made – he disliked domestic disorder. The only unfamiliar item she noticed was the unframed oil painting of three Expressionist female nudes sunbathing on a verdant hill overlooking an expanse of summer sea. She wondered where he had got it from.

For some reason – she could never remember why exactly – she decided to look through the drawers in Dolfi's desk. There was their grandfather's artillery corps revolver pistol – from the Second Schleswig War, or so he claimed. She picked it up for a moment and felt the heavy latent power of the thing. Their father had shown them how to use it, how to activate and deactivate the safety catch. They'd practised shooting at tin cans at the bottom of the garden one winter. They'd been about sixteen at the time. There had been snow on the ground. He had *shuffled off his mortal coil* – as Dolfi referred to it – about two years ago. A sudden death. The funeral service in the Nolde Lutheran village church in Schleswig had even been curiously cathartic. She had felt strangely distant from it all, like an anthropologist observing the funeral rites of an exotic tribe. The small family house in Schleswig-Holstein had had to be auctioned off to pay debts. What remained was a trust fund that provided them with independent incomes that just about paid their rents. Their mother – a faded sepia oval photographic image of a young woman posing in a white dress and large floral hat in a photographic studio somewhere in the past – had died giving birth to them. There was a small box of the special pinfire bullets the pistol used. But there was also something else: a curious metallic cylinder, with rows of letters aligned along its axis. The device consisted of a stack of rotatable steel discs – twenty in all – on an axle; by rotating the aluminium discs, the letters on their rims could be rotated into various combinations. It reminded her of one of those combination padlocks – but it was not a lock, more likely some sort of puzzle-toy, a mechanical crossword puzzle of some sort. She rummaged a bit more but there was nothing at all out of the ordinary. Just the usual: stationary, notebooks, a tin of Agfa cinematographic film. Then suddenly, again for no reason she could verbalise, she knew that something was wrong.

***

Several weeks later Anja found herself talking to Ludwig Pechstein. The detective was a studious-looking man, in his early forties, with greying-hair and a small thin moustache that gave him a vaguely oriental look. His office was quiet except for, every now and again, the hiss of a document cylinder being sucked through the pipes of the building's pneumatic post system.

'The work of a private investigator,' he said after she had told him that Dolfi had been missing for several weeks, 'contrary to how it's depicted in detective novels, is pretty mundane. Footwork for the most part. Ninety or so percent of it consists of making enquiries, of asking around … which I presume you have already done?'

'I have talked to everyone who knows him,' she said. 'And to everyone I know who knows him.'

Weber had recommended Pechstein. 'Give Ludwig Pechstein a try,' he'd said. 'Of the Pechstein Security and Investigations Agency. He's the brother of Werner Pechstein, who runs it, and who likes to think of it a sort of *mitteleuropäische* version of the American Pinkerton's. Ludwig's not exactly Sherlock Holmes, but he's a reliable sort. Handles missing persons. Runaway black sheep, elopers and the like. I can have a word with him if you like.'

'No stones left unturned?' Pechstein asked, adjusting his rimless eyeglasses and looking at the list she had given him of everyone she knew of in Vienna who knew her brother.

The list had been Weber's idea.

'None that I can think of,' she said.

She appeared remarkably calm, Pechstein could not help thinking, considering what she must have been through over the last few weeks, and was still no doubt going through. He'd had experiences of enough missing-persons cases to know the devastating effect that the sudden disappearance of someone could have on those close to them.

'People don't simply just disappear that often,' he said, 'and when they do, there is usually a fairly mundane reason for it. Not that that makes it easier to find them. It's not illegal of course, the simple act of disappearing … it's a sort of human right really … though, of course, it does cause all sorts of complications. Your brother's disappearance does seem to be a voluntary act. He may not want to be found. Can you think of anything, any reason why he might have wanted to disappear?'

'None,' she said.

'You've checked the hospitals?' he asked, looking at the photograph she had given him. The resemblance of the missing man to his twin sister was striking, though the contours of her hairless Nordic face were sterner, more masculine even, in a boyish kind of way.

'All of them,' she said.

'Weber said you had been to the police?'

'They said they would put his details on their missing-persons list.'

'As they would,' he said fatalistically.

The face of the pale, and vaguely consumptive-looking, moustached young man had the same ineffable quality that all photo-chemical images of missing loved ones seemed to have. In Italy, somebody had told him, they put photographs of the departed – twentieth-century photo-chemical death masks – onto tombstones.

'Well, the good news is that the chances are that your brother is alive and will turn up eventually,' he said. Which wasn't exactly a lie. But he had little reason to believe that was not the case. 'If anything untoward … If the police had found—'

'A body that matched his description?'

'… they would have contacted you.'

She had hazel-brown eyes. He tried to imagine what it must be like: twins, two psyches gestating together in the warm fluid of the same womb, bound together in ways he could not imagine – and then wrenched apart without warning.

'I will be honest with you,' he said. 'If you were to engage our services, all we would end up doing is what you have already done. It would be a waste of good money. And do no good. However …' he paused for a moment, and found himself for a few seconds wondering what she was like normally, before this had happened, '… there are a few things that can be done easily enough.'

'Such as?'

'An announcement in the main Vienna papers would be a good beginning. Run it for a few weeks. Have some posters printed. It's not that expensive. Maybe they can reproduce this photograph or a good likeness based on it. A few hundred copies of something about the size of a magazine page. I can recommend a company we use. They'll also paste them up in appropriate places around the city.'

'Should I offer a reward?' she asked.

'You'll get a lot of wild geese … as being led on wild-goose chases, but, yes, I would. A hundred *Kronen* at the most. Just enough to make it worth somebody's while to make the effort of contacting you. It's rather obscene, I know, to talk of money in the circumstances, but one has to be practical.'

She does not think of herself as good looking, he thought, or even attractive. She was pale-skinned but looked as if she had spent time in the sun recently. He imagined the whiteness of what he imagined to be her rather muscular body under her dress. In fact, he found her oddly attractive, though he was not sure that other men would. She was wearing neither an engagement nor a wedding ring. Inappropriate thoughts considering the circumstances, but such was the nature of the human mind, or perhaps rather the human male mind. It was pathetic really, but, he supposed, biology was biology.

Later, after she had left, he decided that a contemplative Sphinx was required – 'a Buddhist smoke' as Binswanger would have called it. Outside his office window the evening was drawing in. The trees on the Naglergasse had already begun to shed their leaves. Twilight in autumn … Then, on an impulse – he wasn't sure why – he decided to telephone Binswanger.

He cranked up the device and rang the number from memory.

The telephonist took a few minutes to put him through.

'Would it be possible to meet sometime this week?' Pechstein said, almost shouting into the mouthpiece, a habit which he knew was unnecessary. 'There's something I'd like to discuss with you.'

'That sounds almost official,' Binswanger's crackly, disembodied voice replied.

'It's just that something interesting has come up,' Pechstein replied.

'I'm intrigued. You know it is possible to have a conversation over the telephone. I do it all the time. It's what a telephone is for. It's not just a way of sending spoken telegrams.' Pechstein had never been able to get used to having a conversation with somebody he could not actually see. 'You know over five hundred million telephone calls were made in the empire last year. Our telephonists are the soul of discretion – most of the time – if that's your concern.'

'It's not that. It's just—'

'No need to explain,' Binswanger's voice interrupted him. 'The usual place. One o'clock. Thursday.'

'Just the job. The schnitzel's on me.'

1919

4

The new Preßburg train crossed the cast-iron girder bridge over the Morava and entered officially into the Hungarian half of the empire. An hour or so later, after steaming through the snow-covered white-grey deep-winter landscape, it reached the Preßburg suburbs. Factories and workers' tenements passed by, drab and monotonous under the winter sky. Somebody had written graffiti on one of the gable walls of a row of tenements, in Slovak, in large white letters: BREAD AND MOVING PICTURES!

Szombathy, instantly recognisable in his Royal Hungarian Gendarmerie inspector's uniform, was waiting for Pechstein on the platform. He was a thin, short man, with steely black hair and a bushy walrus moustache.

'I thought,' he said, when the introductions and the hearty hand-shaking had been done with, 'we could go to and have a look at the spot where the corpse was washed up before delivering you to your hotel. There's plenty of daylight yet. It's only a twenty-minute drive.'

'Of course,' Pechstein agreed.

A constable, a young lad of peasant stock who didn't seem to speak much German, took charge of Pechstein's overnight valise and led the way towards the station exit.

Szombathy's automobile – the Habsburg-Hungarian coat of arms fine-stencilled onto the two rear doors – was a gleaming black Daimler. They settled themselves into the leather-upholstered rear compartment. The constable strapped Pechstein's valise to the luggage rack at the back, and hand-cranked the engine – it was a petrol-powered vehicle – and it started surprisingly quickly.

A haze of smoky fog from coal-fed heating-stoves and factory chimneys, its acrid smell detectable even with the automobile's windows shut tight against the cold, hung over the cobblestoned streets. As they headed out of the city, Pechstein caught a brief glimpse of the opera house – Preßburg was a favourite haunt of Viennese opera-goers; during the season they took the early evening train and returned at midnight – and of Halmi's famous equestrian statue of the Empress Maria Theresa.

'Nearly there now,' Szombathy said when, a kilometre or so beyond the city boundaries, they reached a potholed track that led down to the Danube.

The automobile drove over frozen puddles, its wheels crunching through the ice. They stopped at a spot overlooking a strand-like patch of the riverbank. A cold mist was drifting over the water. The river, as grey as the sky above it, was almost free of ice. Scenic desolation, Pechstein found himself thinking.

'The body was washed up right here,' Szombathy said. 'A local fisherman found it. I was called immediately. I could tell straight off that he was a gentleman ... well, let's say, of the better sort ... from his clothes and from what I suppose you could call the cut of him. Corpses, I have always found, somehow seem to retain some vestiges of social class for a while after the spirit departs, funnily enough ... I was fairly sure he was not a local. Did you know him?'

'Not in life. He was reported missing to us last September.'

Szombathy offered Pechstein one of his Turkish cigarettes and they lit up.

'Our medicus estimates that he'd been in the water for about a week,' Szombathy continued. 'The body was pretty well preserved ... the cold ... but even so, there was water damage ... But we're sure it's him.'

'He'd been already missing a few weeks before we became involved,' Pechstein said. 'We followed up the few leads we had of course ... but in the end, it was just one of those simply-vanishing-into-thin-air cases.'

'Popped out for a packet of fags and was never seen again?'

'Something like that.'

Some invisible crows cawed somewhere. A white-greyish water bird of some sort was flying across the sky, heading slowly upriver. There was a strong whiff of sewage in the air.

'How did you identify him?' Pechstein asked.

'Cigarette case. Initials and family name engraved on the inside of the lid. Silver-plated. And from the description and the copy of the rather blurred photograph Binswanger sent us. He had some papers on him but they were illegible, and two ten-*Krone* notes with some loose change in his pockets. So he wasn't robbed. There is no reason to suspect foul play. No evidence of any bruising concurrent with say ... him being hit over the head and thrown off a bridge.'

'A simple case of drowning then?' Pechstein half-suggested, half-asked.

'Yes and no,' Szombathy said.

'I don't understand.'

Szombathy flicked his cigarette butt onto the sand.

'He didn't drown. Not exactly. At least not according to our medicus. Not sure I understand the fine details of it all myself. But then necropsy-ology – if that's the word – is not an exact science. Our medicus can explain it to you far better than I possibly could. We can go there now. It's only a short drive to the Infirmary. Unless you ...'

'No, no,' Pechstein said, 'I'm fine. Let's go there.'

'Excellent,' Szombathy said as they headed back up to the waiting automobile. The constable had left the engine running and was sitting in the driving seat, reading a copy of *Nemzeti Sport*. 'She'll be expecting us. I told her we might call.'

'She,' Pechstein said, mildly surprised.

'Yes. Frau Doktor Katarína Dobrovodská. A Slovak lady. Qualified in Zurich in the late '90s.'

They reached their destination about twenty minutes later. The Preßburg Infirmary – a neo-Gothick building – looked otherworldly in the fading light. Electric lamps were already shining in some of the pointed-arched windows. Pechstein wondered if the persistence of the neo-Gothick was the expression of an unconscious desire to counteract the modern *Zeitgeist*, what the Bavarian social theorist Max Weber described as the demystification of the world. The churches were full on Sundays, and the synagogues on Saturdays, but the twentieth century no longer quite believed in the way the nineteenth century had. Though the Americans, judging from photographs he had seen of the skyscrapers of New York and Chicago, seemed more at ease with the modern world.

The building smelled of disinfectant carbolic, the odour of modern medical science. Frau Doktor Dobrovodská's consulting room was at the top of a wide, iron-banistered, spiral staircase, along a balcony that looked down on the mosaic floor of the Infirmary's atrium-entrance. She was a plump woman, in her early fifties possibly, with short blond-grey hair, and wore large, black-framed eyeglasses. Pechstein had envisioned someone taller and sterner-looking. She wore the female version of a suit jacket and had a stethoscope around her neck with the listening drum tucked into a midriff pocket.

'Did you know the deceased?' she asked him.

He told her more or less what he had told Szombathy earlier.

'The cause of death was hypothermia,' she said, 'more commonly known as exposure. That is my diagnosis.' Her German, unlike Szombathy's, was accentless, though distinctly Swiss in style. 'The man froze to death in the water. There was some water in his lungs but not enough to drown him.' She spoke with confidence. Women were often more hesitant in their opinions when venturing into masculine realms, but perhaps that was not true for the contemporary professional woman, a species of which he had only minimal experience. 'I come across cases of hypothermia a few times a year. There's no shortage of drunks – and not all of them homeless vagrants – found dead in the snow every winter. The thing about it is that there are no real tell-tale signs. They – men for the most part, though more than occasionally a woman – are simply dead. With most other causes of death there are tell-tale signs which usually come to light during a necropsy. The diagnosis is, of course, consistent with him having fallen into the Danube some evening about a week ago.'

Some evening? Pechstein wondered how she could possibly come to such a precise conclusion.

'You are wondering why I have deduced that he fell into the river at that time, rather than, say, after breakfast?'

'Well, yes,' Pechstein admitted.

'I performed a very thorough necropsy. There were no external wounds or bruises of any kind. The condition of the heart was what one would expect for a reasonably robust man of his age. Though the liver did show evidence of rather excessive alcohol consumption.'

'Standard forensic procedure these days,' Szombathy said.

The policeman was sitting beside a glass display cabinet containing half a dozen jars of what looked like various human organs suspended in formaldehyde.

'Neither was there any indication of a cerebral seizure of any kind,' she continued, 'nor any sign of burst or damaged blood vessels or the like – though of course, when it comes to the human brain one can never be sure about anything.'

Which did not explain how she had come to her conclusions regarding the time of death having been in the evening, but Pechstein was sure she would come to it. He wondered if her being so dispassionately clinical about it all – about the actual dissection of the dead body of another human being, a gory affair, to say the least – was a natural psychological defence mechanism, or a way of impressing upon him that she could be as unsentimental and as scientifically objective as any man.

'I also examined the contents of the stomach, which were in an advanced state of putrefaction, of course, but ... Well, let us say that the deceased's final meal was fairly rich.'

'Rich?' Pechstein repeated.

'Washed down with what I would describe as a rather

excessive quantity of wine and perhaps cognac,' she continued. 'There were the remains of half-digested salami, carrots and artichokes. It was not possible to test his blood for alcohol levels so long after death but I'm fairly sure that he was considerably intoxicated – drunk – when he fell into the water. Alcohol is a curse. Dipsomania is responsible for as much misery as infectious diseases. In any case, his last meal seems to have been a heavy evening meal – certainly not a breakfast – and since it was only half-digested, it would indicate that he died shortly afterwards.'

'As I said,' Szombathy added, 'no evidence of foul play, none at all. Of course, one cannot entirely rule out suicide, but there is no reason to suppose it either, and … I'm sure the family would not appreciate unfounded allegations in that regard.'

'We can go and look at the corpse now,' Dobrovodská said.

Pechstein had not expected that he would be shown the body.

'The morgue is in the basement,' she informed him.

They descended several spiral staircases and entered a maze of musty, windowless, underground passageways illuminated by overhead electric light bulbs housed in caged bulkhead fittings.

The morgue was a high-vaulted cavern. It reminded him of a drawing of the scientist's laboratory he had once seen in an illustrated edition of *Frankenstein*. There were two rows of enamelled metal cabinets in which the cadavers were stored. The two concave zinc tables – with plugless plugholes feeding pipes that emptied into channels in the tiled floor, which led to a grated drain – were where the necropsies were obviously performed. A hydrant tap and a brass-nozzled canvas hose rolled up on a drum hung on the wall beside the row of heavy-duty white ceramic washbasins, presumably so as to hose the place down after dissections. The air was so cold their breath steamed, and the smell of carbolic was almost overwhelming.

Dobrovodská slid out one of the rollered drawer-like compartments and Pechstein found himself looking at the moustache-faced man he'd been searching for. Even in death, the likeness to his twin sister was unmistakable. There was a diagonal herringbone-stitched scar across the dead man's abdomen. Pechstein had seen a few dead bodies over the course of the years. Invariably, what struck him was the utter absence of whatever it was that a living man or woman was, the metamorphosis of the once-living body into a wax-like simulacrum of what it had been in life. His rational mind told him that it was all really quite simple: a thing was alive, lived, and then simply lived no more. But another, perhaps more primitive part of his psyche told him that death was as profound a mystery as life itself.

'The poor fellow's clothes and effects are at the barracks,' Szombathy informed him.

Dobrovodská slid the naked corpse back into its metallic sepulchre and went to scrub her hands at one of the washbasins.

'An official identification will be needed,' Szombathy continued, offering Pechstein another of his Turkish cigarettes. 'By a blood relative or a spouse, or failing that, two trustworthy witnesses who knew him in life. But that can be done in Vienna. A formality, but procedure's procedure. However, if you could sign an affidavit making a provisional identification, it would smooth things along. The hospital clerk should have the appropriate forms.'

'Of course.'

'You said there was a sibling?'

'Yes,' Pechstein said. 'A sister.'

'I'll telegraph Vienna from the Gendarmerie barracks,' Szombathy said, 'and they can contact her. They'll arrange for the undertakers to collect the body from the train. He looks a bit rough now but any decent mortician will do him up nicely … I'll have one of my constables drop the clothes and effects around to your hotel this evening. We've had them laundered. All you'll need to do is sign for them.'

It began to snow lightly as they drove back through the city centre to the hotel, the slow-spiralling snowflakes magically illuminated in the beams cast by the automobile's front lanterns.

Most of the shops were still open, their display windows ablaze with electric light. Clerical workers, male and female, wrapped in winter coats and scarves, were making their way homeward. Just as the Savoy came into sight, a marching battalion of infantrymen in greatcoats and fur-trimmed hats, Mannlicher M95s over their shoulders, emerged from a side avenue and blocked their route for a couple of minutes.

'Frau Doktor Dobrovodská seems to have strong opinions on the pleasure of the vine,' Pechstein said idly, as they watched the marching men. He had no idea how well Szombathy knew the woman but he didn't have the look of an abstainer about him.

'And on other social and moral issues,' Szombathy replied. 'The good Frau Doktor can be a bit of a corset-burning harridan when she gets going, if you know what I mean.'

'Will there be a public inquest or something?'

'The public prosecutor's office does not deem one necessary,' Szombathy told him. 'A provisional death certificate – pending final identification – has been made out and signed by all the relevant authorities.'

Pechstein took his evening meal alone in the Savoy's near-empty, chandeliered dining room. The goulash was piping hot, spicy and meaty, and he was hungrier than he thought he would be. A case of the life force – or the 'libido' as psychoanalysts called it – reasserting itself in the face of its negation.

The next morning, he breakfasted under the same chandeliers – though the dining room was considerably busier. The *Prager Tagblatt* had several articles on the latest crisis in the Balkans, which he glanced over; and he felt disinclined to give the rest of the serious news much attention. But there was a photograph in the art and culture pages that caught his eye: the grainy image of a group of female workers posing in front of a row of card index cabinets. The accompanying article was about something called the Mundaneum, or the Universal Bibliographic Repertory, which was opening a German-language branch in Vienna. The Brussels Mundaneum – their international headquarters – housed several million indexed reference cards containing information on 'all fields of human knowledge'. The whole thing was the brainchild of a Belgian named Otlet, a 'pacifist' who, 'shocked by the events of July 1914', had written a book called *The End of War* in which he proposed the establishment of an international federation based on a World Charter of Human Rights, and of somebody called Henri La Fontaine, who'd won a Nobel Peace Prize in 1913 for something or other. He was just about to read a piece about the German Kaiser planning to found a Jewish colony, 'open to Jews of all nationalities', in one of Germany's new African Protektoraten, when one of the waiters informed him was required at the reception desk.

A uniformed constable had arrived with the clothes. Pechstein signed for them and was given a brown paper parcel, neatly bound with waxed twine, but – feeling it would be somewhat ghoulish to take with him back to his half-finished breakfast – he left it with the receptionist to collect after he had eaten.

Half an hour later, feeling suitably sated from the Savoy's Full Hungarian Breakfast and, thanks to the *Prager Tagblatt*, slightly less uninformed about the state of the world, he collected the parcel from the reception.

The parcel was smaller and lighter than he had expected. He had not intended to examine its contents, but if he was to be true to his private-investigator persona, he supposed he ought to take a look. When he reached his room, he slowly opened it, thinking how the clothes and the personal effects of the dead were strange things: to be handled with reverence, yet ultimately, almost shamefully, to be quietly disposed of. The freshly laundered and pressed male garments still smelled of the sweetish chemical, whatever it was, they dry-cleaned clothes with. There was also a pair of water-damaged brown leather shoes, a pocket watch on a chain and the silver-plated cigarette case Szombathy had mentioned. An unsealed police envelope contained the two ten-*Krone* notes and the loose change.

The attire of a vaguely *bohème* Viennese bourgeois male,

slightly shabby in a calculated sort of way, Pechstein thought, as he laid out the garments into some kind of order on the bed: jacket and trousers to the left; pink-striped collared shirt, tie, underpants, vest and black socks to the right; with the braces, shoes, pocket watch and cigarette case in a row beneath them. The dark brown jacket and trousers were from Gerngross's. The thin red-and-black striped necktie looked hand-sewn; perhaps it had been a gift from a female admirer or a maiden aunt. The shoes were in need of a reheeling. All in all, nothing amiss really, nothing he could see anyway. They were the clothes that several thousand men of the same social class and milieu could be seen wearing any evening in the coffee houses of Vienna, more or less. It all fitted with the imagined mental picture he had of the man. And yet … no, there was nothing amiss, nothing at all. But there was still the question of those missing months, between the time Adolf aka Dolfi Jensen had been reported missing and his cold, watery death. Had he had a secret life? It was possible. But Anja Jensen had not said anything which might suggest that had been the case. Pechstein imagined a man wandering aimlessly with no idea or memory of who he was, another victim of what the medical men called neurasthenia. In all probability what had happened was what Szombathy and Dobrovodská believed: a tragic, foolish accident, nothing more. And there was no dastardly conspiracy to distract from the grimness of it all.

***

The New Ottoman Bazaar was packed, the air thick with tobacco smoke – spiced with the more than occasional whiff of Turkish hashish – and the Gypsy fiddlers were playing a mournful melody that was vaguely audible above the polyglot din.

Sigrid Kupfer turned around and found herself face to face with the tall and handsome Siegfried Manga Bell, the last person she expected to run into. If he were an actor, he would have played a very stunning Othello. She could never afterwards remember what they had been talking about, only suddenly that he was telling her in his North German accent that Dolfi's Jensen's body had been 'found in the Danube at Preßburg'. And then it was as if he were talking to her from behind a plate-glass window. 'His sister must be going through hell,' he was saying, 'Did you know him well?' 'Yes,' she'd found herself saying, or perhaps she had merely mouthed the words; she couldn't hear her own voice. She must have gone white or something because then Bell was suddenly apologising. And she did what she always tried to do when the wrongness of the world reached out and touched her: disconnect from it.

The next day, still in what she supposed was called a state of shock, still not quite believing what Bell had told her, she bought copies of both the *Neuer Telegraf* and the *Wiener Zeitung.* She could only bring herself to open them when she was at her desk in the Mundaneum. She found the formal black-bordered death notice in seconds in the first one she opened: a block of type, a brick in a mausoleum wall of printer's ink, among all the other final farewells to spouses, mothers, siblings, parents, grandparents and dead children.

'A waste of spiritual and intellectual energy,' a voice behind her said.

It was Brockhaus, looking as dapper as ever with his English moustache, and oozing with his habitual irrepressible Panglossian optimism.

'Newspapers,' he explained. 'I try and avoid them. Not remotely possible of course in this day and age. But one tries.'

Then he noticed she was looking at the death notices.

'Somebody you were close to?' he asked.

'Once,' she said without thinking.

Through force of will she somehow managed to work through the day, and that evening she took the dust-covered, large, cardboard-backed envelope down from the top of her wardrobe. She had not told Anja Jensen about it when she'd called round that day to tell her Dolfi had 'disappeared', the day of the emperors' double funeral. She had not thought it significant, had not even thought of it. She generally avoided masses of people but, that day, lured by the opportunity to experience what the newspapers were calling 'the end of an era', she had decided to join the crowds outside the Stephansdom – Austria-Hungary's most majestic 'tomb and sepulchre of God', as Polanyi called it. The heatwave had broken early that morning; a sudden cannonade had rattled the heavens and drenched the city in a monsoon-like downpour, and it had rained intermittently for the rest of the day. She had only caught glimpses of the cortège through a sea of black umbrellas: the imperial hearses solemnly bearing the coffins down the Riemergasse towards the Capuchin Crypt, followed by the new Emperor Karl I and Europe's royalty in black automobiles, a procession of bishops, priests and altar boys, and seemingly endless cavalry regiments. Despite herself, she had been moved by the sombre pageantry of it, but then she had had enough of it and left. When she got back to her apartment in the Mahlerstraße, a distraught Anja Jensen had been waiting for her outside the house door. She had known her by sight but they had never spoken. They'd heard that Egyptian nihilist's bomb explode as they'd spoken in her cramped apartment; at the time they'd both thought it was just thunder. She had no idea of what she was going to find in the envelope but she supposed it would be more or less what Dolfi had told her: some official or semi-official letters and papers, but now rendered poignantly significant by the fact that he no longer existed in the time and space that she and the rest of the world continued to exist in. But what she found made no sense at all.

5

'The Preßburg Gendarmerie is convinced that it was an accident,' Pechstein said.

The funeral service, held at one of Vienna's handful of dour Lutheran churches and attended by a motley and rather ragtag two dozen or so mourners, had been a depressing affair. Weber had been there; the other mourners he hadn't known from Adam. Half of them gave the impression of being students, though they probably weren't. There'd been a very well-dressed and rather debonair-looking Afro-German. Then, at the cemetery, there'd been that strange long-haired figure with a nineteenth-century beard, wearing a heavy brown robe and leggings, with a shoulder-satchel, and looking uncannily and ridiculously Christ-like, or like someone doing a Christ-impersonation, who had kept his distance from the rest of the mourners, almost as if he were not really attending the ceremony. A tramp with nothing better to do than hang around cemeteries, Pechstein had thought at first, but then decided he was most probably a *Naturmensch*. Later, Weber had said he'd asked him directions to somewhere or other and that he had spoken a rather upper-class German, though with a Carpathian accent. There was also a big character in a railway workers' overcoat, fat and unshaven, standing at the back, furtively smoking, pensive-looking, a working man, sort of, but one who looked as if he somehow got by without too much of the working. Funnily enough, the priest – or the pastor, or whatever Lutherans called their intermediaries with the Almighty – spoke as if he had known Dolfi Jensen; which was a bit odd, he'd thought, for from the little that Pechstein had managed to garner about the type of man that the late Dolfi Jensen had been, he had not got the impression that he had been a church-goer, anything but in fact. The image of the varnished wooden coffin being lowered into the ground was still fresh in his mind.

'My brother was not a drunk,' Anja Jensen said.

They were in his office. Outside the window, Vienna lay under a blanket of fresh snow.

'He could have had a seizure of some kind. The Preßburg doctor said it was a possibility,' he lied. Suicide was the other unspoken possibility. But she was an intelligent woman and had surely considered that possibility.

'I don't think that whatever happened to him was an accident.'

'And what makes you think that?'

'Every nerve in my body tells me that something is wrong, that it was not a pointless accident. Call it a telepathic bond between twins if you like. If you believe in that sort of thing.'

He found himself again being intensely aware of her physical presence, of her hazel-brown eyes, her brown-blond hair, and the whiteness of her skin. Had he fallen in love with her? he wondered. Freud argued that romantic and emotional states were sanitised versions of man's animalistic sexual urges, or something like that; urges, which she too, if that was the case, being an animal herself, must also have lurking somewhere within her.

'Something like a robbery, you mean,' he said. 'Which we can rule out. He had two ten-*Krone* notes on his person when—'

'I realise that.'

'The Preßburg Gendarmerie was adamant that there was no reason to suspect foul play of any kind. Men are not generally attacked in the street and pushed into the Danube for no reason whatsoever …'

'Crimes are committed for other motives besides money,' she said.

'True,' he admitted, deciding that no argument he might come up with was likely to persuade her to abandon what he was sure any psychoanalyst would diagnose an irrational *idée fixe*, brought on by traumatic grief, a neurotic attempt to find some comfort in that age-old solace of the powerless: evil conspirators plotting evil deeds in the shadows.

She took an unsealed brown envelope from her shoulder bag and pushed it across the desk toward him. When he picked it up, he could feel it contained banknotes, and could not help thinking that money was a bit like the erotic: both seductive and shame-inducing. There were perhaps twenty freshly printed ten-*Krone* notes in it.

'An advance,' she said. 'An initial payment for your services. I want you to investigate my brother's death.'

Weber had told him she was not exactly well-off, that she and her brother half-lived from a modest trust fund of some kind; and now she would no doubt have inherited her brother's portion of it. She must have borrowed on what she was to get or somehow arranged to draw on it in advance.

'But …' he began to object.

'You probably think I am not in my right mind, a member of the weaker sex deranged by grief, the balance of my mind …'

'No, I don't. But when these things happen, it's only natural that we attempt to make some sense of them … to give them some meaning, allocate blame. Our minds are ill-equipped to deal with senseless tragedies.' Though he admitted silently to himself, she also appeared oddly calm and composed for a woman who had just buried her twenty-seven-year-old twin brother. But then, he had long suspected that the female possessed superior powers of resilience than the male. He realised he was still holding the envelope with the banknotes in it and put it down.

'Well, it's true,' she said. 'Partly. I am deranged with grief.'

He found himself making a decision, though he was not at all sure why.

'The most I can do,' he said, 'is look at the facts again, look under a few overlooked stones, if I find any, though I doubt I will. I cannot promise you anything. Personally, I am convinced it was a tragic accident.' He pushed the envelope back across the desk towards her. 'There will be no charge, not at this stage in any case.' Of course, he usually did charge for his services –

though he had not charged her for his trip to Preßburg, but then he had gone there on his own initiative; but to accept her money would reduce their relationship, or whatever it might be in the future, into a seedy business transaction, something which he instinctively knew he did not want. 'Please take your money back.'

She hesitated for a moment but then picked up the envelope and returned it to her bag.

'The chances that I will find anything ...' – he searched for a word – '... untoward ... are unlikely in the extreme. You do understand that?'

'Yes,' she said.

He offered her a Sphinx from his desktop cigarette box. She took one and he lit it for her.

'If there is more to your brother's death than meets the eye,' he continued, smoking, 'if your brother was murdered – and I think that is what you are suggesting – the obvious question is who and why. Can you think of anyone who might have wished your brother harm? I don't want to sound melodramatic, but did he have anyone whom one could describe as an enemy?'

'Not that I know of,' she said. Somehow that did not surprise him. But the fact that she had admitted it and was not speculating wildly about all sorts of scenarios on the basis of unfounded suspicions was reassuring.

'How well did you know him?' he asked. 'Really?'

'He was my twin brother.'

'Even twins, I'm sure, have private lives. There are things a man will never tell a woman, perhaps not even his twin sister. Though, of course, there are also things that a man will only reveal to a woman.'

'You are a perceptive man,' she said. 'But my brother and I were closer than, I suspect, you can imagine.'

'That list,' he said, stubbing his cigarette out in the half-full ashtray on his desk, 'the one you drew up – the one you showed me when you first came here, just after your bother disappeared – of people your brother knew. I presume you still have it?'

'Yes, I still have it.'

'Good.'

He paused for a moment before continuing.

'People are usually murdered by the people they know. The mad axe- or knife-wielding Jack the Ripper lurking in the dark alley, ready to pounce on the hapless citizen, is largely a figment of the lurid imaginations of the gentlemen of the yellow press. If your brother was murdered – an extremely big *if*, as I've said – there a reasonable chance that the name of the perpetrator would be on that list.'

He offered her another Sphinx but she declined.

'Robbery we can rule out,' he continued. 'Greed in some other form? But you yourself were the only one to benefit from his estate. I assume that is correct.'

'Yes, it is.'

'Of course, greed, as you said, is not the only passion that drives men to crime. There are other reasons. Jealousy. Envy. The desire to keep something secret. Fear. Anger. Political and religious passions. Ideas of honour. Revenge. The list is pretty endless, sadly. Can you think of any reason why someone might have wanted to harm your brother? Is there something you are not telling me?'

'I think he was involved in something. Had got involved in something, unwittingly ...'

'Something he didn't tell you about?'

'Yes,' she admitted.

'And you have no idea what this something could have been?'

'No.'

'I think,' he said, after a few moments of thought, 'we are going to have to make an assumption, a sort of working hypothesis. It may be wrong. And most likely is.'

She nodded.

'Let us presuppose there is a connection between your brother's disappearance and his death,' he continued, 'and that whatever set of circumstances – whatever he might have been involved in, or not – that led to his disappearance also led in some as yet inexplicable way to his death. The Vienna police and Preßburg Gendarmerie see no reason for thinking that may be the case, not that I think they've given it much thought. But if there is a connection … We know nothing of what happened in the three months or so after his disappearance – and, the way things stand, it's unlikely that we are going to learn anything about where he was or what he was doing in that time. Somebody may still come forward with some information, might have seen him or something, but so far nobody has – despite your newspaper announcements and your posters. I think that at this stage it's unlikely that anyone will. But the months leading up to his disappearance … perhaps we might find a clue to something there.'

There had been about thirty names on her list. The thought of tracking them all down and questioning them – on what was in all likelihood a wild-goose chase – was not a prospect that filled him with any enthusiasm. Though no doubt an anthropologist who preferred the study of Vienna's bohemian demimonde to that of the noble savages of the highlands of Kaiser-Wilhelmsland might find it fascinating.

'His apartment is still intact, I take it? It hasn't been rented to somebody else?'

'No,' she said. 'I arranged for the rent to be paid. But it's a room in an apartment, not an apartment. He shared it with a man called Donnerstag, Tobias Donnerstag. He's a customs officer.'

An odd name, he thought, Jewish perhaps. There was a book, a ridiculous one, by an Englishman, called *The Man who was Thursday* – or was it Tuesday? – in which the members of a Supreme Anarchist Council gave themselves code names of days of the week. But he doubted that this Donnerstag was a member of a supreme council of any kind.

'I should like to see it. Look through his papers and effects. I presume you have no objections.'

'None at all.'

After she had left, he lit another cigarette and watched her walk across the courtyard towards the arched exit that opened onto the Naglergasse. A light snow was falling again.

***

Pechstein let himself into the Girardigasse house with the keys
Anja Jensen had given him. The stairwell was littered with
cigarette butts, spent matches and other urban detritus. The
apartment was on the second floor. He knocked on the door
twice; nobody responded, but he had the key to that too, so he
decided to let himself in. Besides the kitchen alcove at the end
of the hallway, and the in-apartment commode, instantly
recognisable from an enamel sign on the door of a cherub
squatting on a chamber-pot, there were only two other doors.
The room on the left would be Dolfi's, she'd said.

He opened the door and went in. The room was in semi-
darkness, the half-open shutters just letting in enough light to
see by, and cold; the ceramic stove had obviously not been lit
for months. But it was larger than he had expected. Semi-
luxurious even, in the larger scheme of things, to have a room
of one's own with an in-apartment toilet. Half of Vienna had to
make do with shared stairway-toilets between floors. He
switched on the electric ceiling lamp.

He sat down in one of the two armchairs at the low round
table, took off his gloves, and decided that a Buddhist smoke
was required. There was a shiny black matchbook beside the
half-full Jugendstil ceramic ashtray. He picked it up. The words
THE CAFÉ OF ELECTRIC DELUSIONS were printed on the flap. He
tore out a match, lit his cigarette and tried to think.

There was a painting on the wall depicting three nudes in an
Edenic setting. It reminded him, vaguely, of Signac's pointillist
In the Time of Harmony – which originally, somebody had told
him, had had rather a mouthful of a title: *In the Time of Anarchy:
The Golden Age Is Not in the Past, It Is in the Future*. Though
the style, or technique, could not have been more different. The
paint had been applied with a spatula, in exuberant swathes.

There were the usual unsurprising classics on the bookshelf:
Stendhal, Fontane, Goethe, Bettina von Arnim's *Goethe's*

Correspondence with a Child and some Émile Zolas. But there
were also some examples of the New Literature: Werfel's *The
Black Mass*, and a couple of volumes by the Mann brothers.
There was also, alongside Bertha von Suttner's *Die Waffen
nieder!*, a copy of Lamszus's *The Human Slaughter-House* –
the chilling description of an imaginary future war, of armies of
millions huddled in trenches, the industries of Europe
transformed into powerhouses for the mass production of death
– more an expression of the Germanic obsession with
apocalyptic Götterdämmerungen, one hoped, than a prophecy.
Most of the rest were scientific romances. He was familiar with
two of them: Bogdanov's *Red Star*, the story of a communist
utopia on Mars whose hero had ended in up in a lunatic asylum,
and a collection of English short stories in the same vein,
entitled *The Machine Stops* after a story by the English writer
Forster, set in a future in which human beings lead isolated
existences in underground hexagonal cells, communicating
with each other by means of some kind of visual telephony.
There was also a copy of Krafft-Ebing's *Psychopathia Sexualis*.
He extracted it instinctively. Someone had written on the title
page, in blue ink: *Is this what makes everything so complicated?
S.* There were also some dictionaries, and a copy of Rudolf
Otto's *The Idea of the Holy,* which seemed rather out of place.
And a set of Reclus's *L'Homme et la Terre*.

Was this the room of a man who had been planning to
disappear, he asked himself, to severe all familiar human
contact, to vanish without a trace among the masses who walked
the earth? Or the room of a man living a *normal* life suddenly
interrupted by an unforeseen event? It was tidy enough. But was
that the result of him tidying up beforehand? Some suicides did
that. Or had he simply been the type of man who made his bed
in the mornings and washed up the crockery before going to bed
at night? But who somehow didn't get around to tidying his
desk – and emptying his ashtray on the day he disappeared?

He decided to check out the cluttered desk and see what Dolfi
Jensen might have tucked away in his drawers. There were only

a few entries in his desk diary, half of them legible, but there
was nothing that stood out. The rest of the clutter was mainly
flyers advertising various cultural events, and a couple of letters
and postcard in a bamboo letter holder. The writing on the
postcard looked familiar: *Will call Thursday. Might have some
not too badly paid work for you. S.* The same *S* who had written
in the Krafft-Ebing book most likely. There was no date, but the
faded postmark – he had to squint to make out the numerals –
was for July 1918, which was the month Dolfi Jensen had
disappeared. The letters were of no interest: a dentist's bill and
a reminder from the city library to return some books, both of
them on chemistry. Neither did the two desk drawers seem to
contain anything out of the ordinary, just the usual clerical
paraphernalia: pens, pencils, bottles of ink, typewriter ribbons,
a sheaf of carbon paper. But then – he'd nearly missed it – he
noticed a flat round tin. He was about to open it when, just in
time, he saw the word *Agfa* on the rim and realised it might
contain a reel of cinematographic film. There was no way of
knowing whether it was new, or exposed, or exposed and not
developed, so he didn't open it. People did not usually make
moving pictures of their misdeeds; but then again,
cinematographic film was not cheap – perhaps it had been used
to record something of some significance. He slipped it into the
large inside pocket of his overcoat.

   Then, in the bottom drawer, he found something else: a
strange metal cylinder, about thirty centimetres long, its entire
surface covered with rows of letters along its length. He picked
it up. It was lighter than he expected. Aluminium most likely. It
reminded him of one those Babylonian or Sumerian clay
cylinders with cuneiform symbols stamped all over them that
he'd seen photographs of in Brockhaus: otherworldly artefacts
from the alien dawn of civilisation. But it was not a solid
cylinder; rather a series of stacked rotatable discs with letters on
the rims. There was a ruler-like bar that was not moveable but
the discs could be rotated and the letters lined up against the bar.
The order of the letters seemed to be different on each disc. If

the letters had been numbers it would have made more sense; a mechanical calculator would have numbers not letters. Bizarre, he thought, and made a vague mental note of it.

There was nothing of interest in the waste paper bin.

The woodwormed wardrobe contained nothing unexpected either: some shirts, trousers, a grey felt greatcoat, a fur hat, a pair of summer sandals and a pair of boots, underwear and socks folded neatly in the bottom drawer. There was nothing on top of the wardrobe except a thick layer of dust. And nothing under the bed either, except a laundry basket with some discarded shirts and a towel in it.

He decided to have another cigarette before leaving, breathe in the atmosphere of the room a bit more. He used another match from the Café of Electric Delusions, slipping the matchbook into his pocket. And tried to think. He had found nothing that might have thrown any light on anything. But then, he had not been expecting to. There was no warm pistol smelling of cordite. No bundle of compromising letters. No brown envelope of suspicious, used banknotes. Not a clue to anything amiss in the place. Except perhaps there might be something on the reel of film. But was he missing something, he wondered, not seeing the wood from the trees? He could hear the city outside: streetcars, horses, newspaper boys hawking the evening editions and all the rest of the hum produced by the hive-like imperial metropolis as it buzzed its way, day by day, onwards into the future … without Dolfi Jensen. As it would someday, no doubt, do without Ludwig Pechstein.

'Donnerstag!' somebody was calling, somewhere in the distance.

Pechstein emerged from his reveries.

'Donnerstag! Are you in?'

The voice, a man's, and now suddenly loud, was coming from the hallway. The accent was distinctly Hungarian. Whomever it was must have let themselves into the apartment.

'Donnerstag!'

Pechstein decided to open the door and announce himself, and see who it was.

'Who the devil are you?' Polanyi said before Pechstein had his head fully out the door. Pechstein recognised him from the funeral. He was wearing the same railway workers' overcoat and had an unlit hand-rolled cigarette in his mouth. He was also carrying an open bottle of cheap Polish vodka.

'I'm a friend of the family,' Pechstein said, explaining himself rather clumsily. 'Fraulein Jensen asked me to help tidy up some loose ends. Official papers and stuff. Legal issues.'

Polanyi looked at him with what could have been contempt or merely bafflement.

'Legal issues!'

It could have been an exclamation or a question.

Pechstein decided it was better to consider it a question.

'The estates of the deceased …' he said, not quite understanding why he was even explaining himself; the man obviously wasn't Donnerstag. '… can be complicated. From a legal point of view. Probate and all that.'

Polanyi was silent for a moment, but then simply said, as if it pronouncing a great truth: '"The law is a machine that cannot move without crushing someone." Victor Hugo.'

Pechstein had never heard the quote before but didn't doubt its provenance.

'I don't like the law,' Polanyi added and left, leaving the apartment door open behind him.

The sky was fading from grey to night as Pechstein walked back to the Agency. The electric illumination was being switched on in the shops and the coffee houses. He went over what he had found out – or rather not found out – as he made his way through the winter-clad crowds. Dolfi Jensen was an intellectual man, a bit of a linguist, with a taste for fantastic literature, and, to judge from his reading matter, an interest in chemistry, sexual deviations and radical politics. Reclus was an anarchist icon, up there with Kropotkin – there'd been an article about Kropotkin's return to Russia, at the age of eighty-something and still preaching the social revolution, in the

Prager Tagblatt a few weeks back. Bogdanov was also an out and out, and still very active, revolutionist. He supposed some sort of socialism was inevitable in the long term. But a utopia inhabited by New Men and New Women, beings ruled by reason and self-discipline, was a fantasy. Bogdanov's New Men were Martians, not humans.

6

The Agency's photographic laboratory was tucked away in the back of the building. The windowless room, with its collection of lenses, mysterious optomechanical apparatuses, and bottles of solvents and fixers, was a sort of technological Aladdin's Cave. Winterkorn – in his habitual, chemical-stained, brown laboratory coat – was waiting for Pechstein when he got there.

'It's all set up for you, sir,' Winterkorn said, with an expression on his face that was halfway between a grin and a lascivious leer. 'A bit arty for my taste but then, duty is duty and schnapps is schnapps.'

'Indeed,' Pechstein said, slightly mystified, but he was disinclined to ask him what he meant.

Winterkorn had set up the cinematographic film projector on a bench in front of a white screen.

'Latest thirty-five-millimetre Mechau, electrically powered, flicker-free, double-reeled,' Winterkorn said, switching on the bench lamp and going through how the projector worked, showing Pechstein what the various buttons, switches and levers were for. 'This switch turns the electric bulb on and off. This lever here controls the direction of rotation of the film. Left for forward. Right for reverse. Dead centre for stop, which will activate the so-called fire shutter and kill the image on the screen. That way the film won't get hot. Nitrocellulose is pretty flammable. Can't be too careful with it. There is a frame viewer here …' – he indicated the small imaging lens – '… should you want to linger over a particular image.' Again, Winterkorn gave him that odd, lascivious, leering look. 'The reels stop automatically when the film runs out, but you have to switch the projector bulb off manually. Everything is loaded and ready to run. Child's play really, sir.'

'I'll figure it out,' Pechstein said.

'I'll switch the main lights off on the way out. Oh, and no smoking, sir. Absolutely *verboten*, I'm afraid.' And, with what seemed like undue haste, he was out the door, leaving Pechstein alone in semi-darkness.

He pulled out a stool from under the bench, sat down and turned the projector bulb on. He carefully moved the lever into the forward position and switched off the bench lamp. The white screen lit up, the film reels whirred into action and a title appeared on the screen: THE AGE OF AQUARIUS.

A black-and-white image appeared of the sun slowly rising over a mountainous landscape. Then, suddenly, he was looking at a dozen or so naked men and women performing a ring-a-ring-o' roses dance. The camera changed position and filmed the dancers from different perspectives, every now and again focusing in on their faces. Most of the dancers were young, in their mid-twenties, early thirties maybe – but some, of both the men and the women, were older. They each had a symbol painted on their foreheads. Off to the side, at the edge of the frame, an older man, completely bald, dressed in a long, dark-coloured robe, was playing – or mimicking playing – a lyre. It looked like they were performing a quasi-occult or magical nature-worshipping ritual of some kind. There'd been an article in *Die Aktion* a while back about 'cosmic consciousness' and nudism.

It took him a while, after first suspecting that one of the dancers might be Dolfi Jensen, to be as sure as he could be that it was in fact him, a man whom he had seen in the flesh only in death. He thought of the shell he'd seen in the Preßburg Infirmary morgue as looked at the moving image of Dolfi Jensen's living body, white and hairless, his silently laughing face half-camouflaged by a Hungarian moustache and several days of unshaven stubble. Again, the man's resemblance to his sister was striking. And again, Pechstein was both shocked and fascinated by it. Then he saw another face among the dancers that he thought he recognised: the face of a woman, in her twenties, he guessed, dark-haired, Jewish-looking even –

though he'd met enough blond-haired and light-complexioned members of the Jewish nation to know that one could rarely tell from looks. She, too, was smiling and laughing intermittently, but the smile and the laugh were those of a woman. Then recalled where he had seen her. It had been at the funeral service. She'd stood at the back of the church; and, in the cemetery afterwards, he remembered, she'd hovered at the back of the mourners as they huddled around the open grave.

The flickering images of the naked bodies, the trees, and the hills reminded him of the painting on the wall in Dolfi Jensen's room; it expressed the same innocent and erotic yearning to return to – or move forward to – an imagined Eden, the desire to burst free of the fetters of what Herr Doktor Otto Gross and his disciples would no doubt call bourgeois civilisation's stranglehold on lusty Eros, the illusion that Dionysos could be tamed by romantic love or vows of chastity. In the painting the yearning was fixed in the realm of feeling and mood, but in these ethereal black-and-white cinematographic images, accompanied by the mechanical whirring of the projector apparatus, it seemed as if it was attempting to somehow materialise itself more solidly – and in vain – into the physical world.

When the film had run about halfway, the scenes became increasingly disjointed and were often too bright or too dark, or simply out of focus. He wondered if it might be deliberate – an attempt to produce a Futurist artistic effect. The thought came to him that perhaps future generations would see this epoch of human history as a black-and-white world … But then the flickering images took on yet another quality, as if another chapter was to begin. The camera lens was focusing in and out erratically, the image sharp one moment, a washed-out blur the next, on what looked like two human figures, both naked, moving in a thicket of bushes. One of them was a man. The camera caught a fleeting image of his moustached face. It could have been Dolfi Jensen but he wasn't sure. But of the identity of the woman, who was kneeling down in front of the man, he was sure. It was the mystery woman from Jensen's funeral. She was … but the image became a blur again. The whole confused scene lasted no more than a minute. Most of the time all he could see were shaky shots of the man's pale-skinned back, half-hidden by dark-grey foliage. Then the film suddenly ended.

He turned the projector off and switched the bench lamp on. He had half-expected that the film would be of street scenes, a train leaving a station, boats sailing merrily on a lake, antics at a garden party, or something equally innocuous, certainly not something that the average Viennese magistrate would probably judge an unexpurgated work of pornography.

He decided to rewind the film and look at it again.

As the white sun rose again over the grey-toned landscape, he tried to gather his thoughts. Had this anything to do with Dolfi Jensen's disappearance? It certainly indicated that the man had a secret life, a shadow side. Had he suffered some sort of nervous breakdown? As the result of some irresolvable conflict between his bourgeois persona and his inner self? The drunken accident scenario was still the most plausible explanation. But then, a confused man, half-mad, only half-knowing who and where he was, wandering around Vienna for several months … One would have imagined that the probability of someone who knew him running into him and recognising him was not negligible. But possibly not. Vienna was a big city; and there was no easier place to disappear than in a teeming metropolis. One saw lost men every day, wandering the streets, idling in the parks, determinedly drinking themselves into oblivion with cheap Gypsy schnapps from earthenware bottles, disappearing at night into Vienna's multitude of dosshouses – or into the city's sewer tunnels. But then there were the two ten-*Krone* notes he'd had on him when he'd been washed up out of the Danube. It was hardly a sum that one expected your average down-and-out to have on his person. And neither were brandy and artichokes standard evening fare for your average Viennese tramp. His clothes had been in the water for a week or so – and then laundered – so it was impossible to tell what condition they had been in originally.

The mystery woman appeared on the screen again. It was not so much that the act was outrageous, but rather the seeing of it performed. Every imaginable sexual act – *natural* and *unnatural* – had been depicted in one form or another at some time or another: on Grecian vases, on the walls of Indian temples; and there were those gargoyles with gaping female genitalia on old Celtic churches. And now the erotic imagination was being re-formed by technology, by the pornographic moving picture – and by Fromm's reusable rubber condom and Mensinga's rubber diaphragm. Yet still, the chances of seeing an overtly sexual act in reality was actually quite small; unless, of course, one was willing to pay for the pleasure.

He waited until a reasonably sharp and recognisable image of her face appeared and then flicked the lever that Winterkorn had told him would stop the film at an individual frame. The image on the screen disappeared, just as Winterkorn said it would. He looked into the frame viewer. But he hadn't been fast enough. The frame the film had stopped at was of her turning away from the camera lens, of her pale back and the full round curves of her young woman's buttocks: an erotic form all the more powerful for its abstract grey-tone simplicity, even in miniature, and upside-down. Now he realised, of course, why Winterkorn had suggested he might 'want to linger' and wondered if Winterkorn had himself lingered; and what Anja Jensen might look like revealed in her nude white fleshiness. Would her body, he wondered, be a version of brother's, but rounder, fleshier, and with breasts. Michelangelo's nudes were reputed to be male nudes with female breasts grafted on. He wondered vaguely what it would be like to have sex with a man who inhabited the body of a woman, and thought of the question that had been written in of Dolfi Jensen's copy of *Psychopathia Sexualis*: *Is this what makes everything so complicated?*

It took him a few attempts, running the film backwards and then forwards again, before he managed to catch a frame that showed her more or less looking directly into the camera. The image in the frame viewer was small, but it was definitely the woman he had seen at the funeral, no doubt about it. The expression on her face seemed almost unnaturally carefree, yet there was also a vulnerability there.

He wondered where Winterkorn was. Perhaps in the canteen. He switched off the projector and decided to go and look for him. But he was in the corridor, smoking one of his Nils. The smell of Indian hemp and whatever other herbs they put in the things was quite pungent.

'Done, sir?' he asked, that grin on his face again.

'Not quite,' Pechstein said, pretending not to notice the technician's none too subtle attempt at innuendo, but thinking that there was perhaps a bit of the voyeur in every inquisitor, as they went back into the laboratory. 'I want you to do something for me. If it's possible, that is.'

Pechstein showed him the image of the mystery woman's face in the frame viewer.

'Can you make a photograph of that image?' he asked.

'No problem, sir,' Winterkorn said. 'It won't be as sharp as the original but it'll be sharp enough. I can have it ready for you tomorrow.'

'Good,' Pechstein said. 'Do it. Had the film already been developed?'

'Yes,' Winterkorn said. Which meant that someone else would have had already looked at it. 'And edited …'

'I don't understand,' Pechstein said, adding, without thinking, 'I'm a bit of a technical ignoramus, I'm afraid,' and immediately regretting it. He was the man's superior, and should not be explaining himself.

'The first half of the film has been edited,' Winterkorn explained. 'That basically means the film was cut, the badly filmed parts taken out, and then the good parts spliced together again.' He unwound some of the film from the reel and showed Pechstein the splice marks. 'The second part of the film is uncut. There are no splices. But you can also tell by the quality of the camerawork. All those badly focused and badly lit sections would all normally have been cut out. A bit like what we do in our heads, in a way.'

'I'm afraid you've lost me there.'

'Our memories. If you think of our eyes as camera lenses – and our brain as a kind of recording device. We get rid of what we don't need. Or what we want to forget. I read somewhere that's what dreams are, a sort of nightly editing session. After all, from a scientific point of view, we are biological machines.'

Pechstein wondered if the future belonged to men like Winterkorn, to men for whom electricity, chemistry and mechanics held no mysteries; and to whom duty was duty and schnapps was schnapps.

***

'Her name is Sigrid Kupfer,' Anja Jensen told Pechstein when he showed her the photograph Winterkorn had developed. 'Why?'

'It was among your brother's papers,' he lied, wondering if the S in the Krafft-Ebing book stood for Sigrid? 'I saw her at the funeral. Can you tell me anything about her?'

'She was a friend of Dolfi's. She works at that Mundaneum place. I don't know much more about her. But I can give you her address.'

As she wrote out the address on a blank postcard, he asked her how she was 'bearing up'. It was not the best choice of words.

'Have you ever lost somebody, somebody who was an essential part of your life?'

'Not really,' he said. 'My parents of course, but somehow one is prepared for that.'

'First there is shock,' she said. 'Then there is waking up into a dark, desolate place, to a world emptier than one could ever imagine it could be … But … one sleepwalks on … and sometimes one half-forgets …'

She handed him the postcard with the address on it.

'The shaman called on me a few days ago.'

'The shaman?' he repeated, taken aback, thinking of a Red Indian witch-doctor.

'Sorry. Joke. The pastor who officiated at the funeral. But in a way, when one thinks about it, isn't he a sort of shaman? Except he wears an ecclesiastical robe rather than animal skins and doesn't have feathers in his hair.'

'Or a bone in his nose,' he joked.

'He was not exactly what one would expect, though I'm not sure what one expects from pastors or priests these days. He said that God never forgets anything or anyone. That all that exists, exists in the mind of God, and thus exists eternally.'

'That is one way of looking at it,' he said.

'But it does rather presuppose that God exists.'

7

Instead of seeking out Sigrid Kupfer at her Mahlerstraße apartment, Pechstein decided to go to the Mundaneum which, he recalled from the *Prager Tagblatt* article he'd read in the hotel in Preßburg, was in a converted paraffin lamp factory in the Favoriten district. He could have telephoned first but decided not to.

The Herr Direktor Doktor Frederick Brockhaus, a neatly dressed man in his middle forties, was wearing a thin silk tie and starched standing collar, and sporting an English moustache. The only thing missing was a monocle or a pince-nez. When he'd introduced himself, he'd joked about his name being the same as that of one of the world's most prestigious encyclopaedias. There was a near life-size portrait of the emperor in the blue and gold dress uniform of a prestigious regiment, posing in front of a gleaming new AEG aëroplane, its eight wings painted in the Habsburg colours, hanging on his office wall. Karl I was a monarch who liked to project an image of both tradition and modernity.

'Stability, continuity, progress,' Brockhaus said, noticing Pechstein staring at the portrait. He was sitting behind his Bakelite-topped desk. 'No stability, no continuity, no progress. It's what the Mundaneum is about.'

He said Sigrid Kupfer was 'on an errand' but was expected back any minute. While they waited, Brockhaus suggested he give him a tour of what he called 'our information factory'.

'Our ultimate aim,' he explained, 'is to extract all the *facts* buried in books and scientific and scholarly journals, and catalogue them in an easily-accessible and cross-referenced archive.' Several women were consulting a row of card index cabinets – which Pechstein recognised from the photograph in the *Prager Tagblatt* – while others were busy at Mercedes Elektra electric typewriters. 'These cabinets will eventually contain more than a hundred times the information in a full set of my namesake, or in the *Britannica* or the *Larousse*.'

One of the typists smiled at Pechstein.

'In a way,' Brockhaus went on, 'we are constructing a sort of colossal arithmometer, except that instead of computing numbers, we are computing facts. Otlet's Universal Decimal Classification System is based on the Dewey card index system – the one used in libraries – but it is much more effective, and enables us to locate a card on any particular subject far faster. One day, for the price of a stamp or a telegram, men will have any piece of information they require delivered to them in a couple of days. Someday, we hope, all our various international branches will contain all the books ever published – but in photographic form.'

Sigrid Kupfer appeared a few minutes later. Pechstein recognised her immediately, though her flaming ginger-red hair took him back for a moment, he had assumed from the photograph it would be a shade of brown. She was wearing bicycling knickerbockers. Assuming they knew each other, Brockhaus disappeared back into his office, leaving them alone with each other. Which was just as well; Pechstein was not sure how exactly he would have introduced himself in the Direktor's presence. He mentioned Anja Jensen, Dolfi and the Agency, said something about 'tidying up legal loose ends' and asked her if there was somewhere they could perhaps talk more privately.

***

The Blumenthaler was a remnant of the nineteenth century: dark-wood colours, armchairs rather than straight-backed chairs, brass chandeliers, paintings of hunting scenes and a stag's head on a plaque – typical Alpine kitsch – except for the near-life-size wooden statue of three Afro-American musicians paying a silent tune on their wooden trumpets. The place was empty. It was half past five: the working day over, the evening not yet begun; and it was already beginning to get dark outside.

'There's a film,' Pechstein said after they'd ordered a pot of coffee. 'It was found among his things. *The Age of Aquarius.*'

'And you've watched it?'

Her reaction was not at all what he had anticipated. There wasn't a hint of anything besides curiosity in her voice.

'It's rather ...' – he searched for a euphemism – '... French.'

She laughed.

'Is it good?' she asked. 'I haven't actually seen it. It was made at a place called Monte Verità, an artists' and *Lebensreform* colony near Ascona. In Switzerland.'

He realised she knew nothing about the last part of the film, about what the camera had filmed after the dance ritual.

'I've heard of it,' he said, avoiding the question as to whether he thought the film was good. 'I think I might have seen a photograph of one of the buildings there. Rather impressive. With a lot of those yin-yang symbols.'

'That would be the sanatorium. The whole thing started off as a sort of diffuse *Landkommune* sometime around 1900,' she said. 'I've changed my mind. I will have some of the apple tart after all.'

Pechstein caught the Chinese waiter's eye and ordered two portions – with cream.

'The film was made by an Englishman, one of those archetypically eccentric Englishmen. An occultist. Calls himself a magician. A much-travelled man. Ceylon, the Himalayas, China, Egypt. In fact, he'd just come back from Mexico and the United States. He's known as Meister Therion in occultist circles. He also paints, and not badly.'

'Therion?'

The apple tart arrived on two warm, white plates.

'Greek for "beast",' she explained, 'something to do with one of the beasts in the Book of Revelation. He believes that we are currently experiencing what he calls the birth pangs of a new aeon.'

'One does not particularly have to be an occultist to believe that.'

'The whole idea also has something to do with the sun moving into the sign of Aquarius.'

'As above, so below.'

'Therion's universe consists of what he called interpenetrating spheres of different categories of being. We exist in the lowest, in the most material sphere, as embryonic souls wriggling about in a worm-world, blindly burrowing about in base matter, unaware of the sublime and glorious meadows and blue skies above us …'

He wondered just how much credence she lent to any of this eccentric Englishman's occult ideas. He tried to remember what Freud called it … the swamp of the esoteric?

She finished her apple tart and extracted a hand-rolled cigarette from a green enamel cigarette case. Pechstein took out his cigarette lighter to light it for her but it took him several attempts before he managed to produce a flame. He lit a Sphinx for himself.

'A yearning for faerieland is at the root of all our desires,' she added, exhaling the smoke leisurely.

'So what was the purpose of the ritual?' Pechstein asked, thinking of his own faerieland imaginings. But then, the varieties of imagined erotic paradises were numberless: Gothick castles, Moorish palaces, 'strict French lady teachers', even public toilets. Doktor Freud would no doubt classify them all as pathological perversions of the sexual drive. Doktor Jung would see misdirected mystical yearnings.

'The hocus-pocus?'

'If you like,' he said.

'It was more of a dance really. Dance is thought of highly at Monte Verità – and naturism is not considered, as the name implies, anything but natural. It was supposed to be an exercise in re-sacralising nature, creating a magical space. In our minds. What's inside is outside. That sort of thing. Didn't Kant say something like that? That even space and time is inside our heads.'

'But why film it?' he asked. 'Isn't it a bit like making a cinematographic film of a High Mass? All one does is make a moving image of its outward form.'

'To make art perhaps. The magical acts of the new aeon need to be works of art. And vice versa. Though it's probably bad art. It was an experiment. Everything at Monte Verità is an experiment.'

'How did you get involved?' he asked her.

'I was working as a computer at Bohemian Assurance. Doing endless calculations on the statistical risks of what can go wrong, to whom, and where; deaths, accidents, fires ... The Bohemian applies Adam Smith's – or is it Henry Ford's? – theory of the division of labour to the human brain. There were fifty or so of us. Females to a man, needless to say. The men do the science and the women do the arithmetic. The incessant clickety-clackety-click of the Brunsvigas was enough to drive you mad.'

'Brunsvigas?'

'Mechanical calculating machines. German contraptions. I was looking for something more interesting, I suppose. As for Monte Verità, there was an advert in *Der Naturfreund* for a sort of retreat.'

'You were close to him? To Dolfi Jensen, I mean.'

'Once,' she said. 'For a while.'

She took a sip of coffee. Her blue-grey eyes stared at him over the rim of the cup for a moment.

'Fraulein Jensen believes there is a connection between her brother's disappearance and his death.'

'One thing did follow the other.'

'That does not mean that they were directly connected with each other. What kind of man was he?'

'Unpredictable. He had a habit of becoming obsessed with ideas. Ideas which are kind of interesting ... and then discarding them. He had a bit of a religious streak, always searching for some ultimate meaning.'

'A religious streak?' Pechstein repeated. He remembered the Lutheran pastor's eulogy and his impression that the man had known Dolfi Jensen. Then there had also been that copy of *The Idea of the Holy* among his books.

'In a way, yes. It's what attracted him to Therion, I think. Monte Verità was about possibilities. The air of the place radiated possibilities. Everyone whom the seas of providence and chance washed up on the slopes of Monte Verità – I could never make out who lived there and who was a visitor – possessed a profound dissatisfaction with bourgeois civilisation and all its works and were, I suppose, seeking a utopian alternative to it all. Dolfi also had what some would call it an exaggerated sense of right and wrong, or what he thought was right or wrong. Personally, I think most things simply mostly are. Neither right nor wrong very much. And being wrong feels exactly like feeling one is right. He could be an insufferable moralist at times, to tell the truth. But what do you think? Do you think there is a direct connection between Dolfi's disappearance and his death?'

He thought for a moment.

'If I had to hazard an informed guess, I'd be inclined to say no, not really, and that his disappearance was the result of some mental breakdown. I imagine him in an acute state of disorientation, living on the streets, sleeping in dosshouses, drinking … and then one evening …'

He should have asked Żuławski to check the public dosshouses after Anja Jensen had come to him that first time, to do some ferreting around in that particular underworld, the sad habitat of Viennese society's detritus. It could still be done. Though that scenario hardly fitted with Frau Doktor Dobrovodská's description of Jensen's final meal. Nevertheless, he made a mental memo to have a word with Żuławski about it.

'But?' she said.

'His disappearance was sudden, unexpected. Though that is usually the nature of disappearances. It was seemingly out of character I suppose I'm trying to say. Nobody, as far as I have been able to ascertain, ever laid eyes on him again. Which would be understandable, of course, if he had left Vienna. But there is no reason to think that he did. But if his disappearance was the result of some mental breakdown of some kind, one would have expected somebody to have come across him on the street or something.'

'Dolfi was a sensitive soul,' she said. 'Said he was allergic to tinned foods, insisted on eating only things that were in season, and sort of thing. In fact, he sometimes came across as – how shall I put it? – *as a feminine soul, heaving in male bosom*!'

He thought he'd recognised the quote. It was from Krafft-Ebing, except it was the other way around: *A masculine soul, heaving in female bosom*! He was on the verge of asking if that was what had made everything so complicated, but didn't.

'Go on,' he said.

'There are men who cannot stand the very idea of that.'

'You mean that someone might have assaulted him for that reason?'

'It's possible … But there was also something else.'

He raised his eyebrows in surprise but said nothing.

'I need your assurance that this will go no further than you and I.'

'I give you my word. If I follow up on any information you give me, I will never mention your name in connection with it.'

'There was another side to Dolfi. Or rather, sort of. I never knew how real it was. It wasn't unreal … but … maybe he was exaggerating its significance …'

Pechstein remained silent.

'He used to do work for the Castle.' Both the Evidenzbüro and the StaPo – the Staatspolizei – operated from the War Ministry building on the Stubenring, or 'the Castle', as it was called by both those who approved of its activities and those who did not. 'Occasionally. Or at least he said he did. He did translations for them. Scientific papers, technical stuff. He used to joke about it. I could never tell how serious it all was.'

'Go on,' he said.

'A few weeks before he disappeared, perhaps a fortnight before, he came to see me. He said it was about work. He wanted to know if the Mundaneum needed any translating work done. I told him it was quite possible and said I would ask. There was some work and I wrote him a card about it.'

So that *S* did stand for Sigrid.

'I even called around about it a little later but he wasn't there,' she continued. 'I think he'd only been missing for a couple of days then, so I thought nothing of it. But anyway, when he came to see me that time, he also asked me if I could safekeep something for him. He told me he had some papers, personal documents, and he didn't feel comfortable – that was the word he used – having them in the Girardigasse. Which I can't say surprised me. Every Tom, Dick and Harry and God knows who else is in and out of the place all hours of the day and night. There's some sort of mad party every week.'

'Who actually owns the house?' he asked. He hadn't thought to ask Anja Jensen.

'Viktor Polanyi. You might have seen him at the funeral. Railway workers' overcoat, rimless eyeglasses, unshaven, Hungarian, with a predilection for cheap vodka and apocalyptic visions of revolution. Though he can be quite the charmer when he's of a mind to be.'

'I've made his acquaintance,' Pechstein said.

'He inherited the place, somehow. The result of a serendipitous series of distant relatives dying intestate and the idiosyncrasies of inheritance laws. He also owns that gallery, the Crimson Cockatoo. It has one of those swinging signs over the front door with a red cockatoo on it. Gives rather rousing lectures on and off. At the Crimson Cockatoo mainly. And in the Herzen. But he's more bark than bite. He does a sort of an ad-lib music-hall comedian act. Very funny – hilarious even – yet serious in its way. He can be rather fascinating to listen to at times.'

Pechstein had heard of the Herzen; it was named after some

Russian socialist. He'd seen it more than once mentioned in police reports.

'What sort of lectures does he give? What are they about?'

'The necessity of the social revolution. And that nothing that does not contribute to the struggle to achieve a higher life is worth a whit.'

'I see,' he said noncommittally.

'He's married to an Italian woman. An heiress. Papa made a considerable fortune in the jig-saw puzzle business of all things. The Italian press used to call him the Jigsaw King. She came to Vienna to do a course at Berlitz. As dull as doornails, but then she met Polanyi – God knows how! – and then metamorphosed over overnight into ...' – she paused for a moment – '... well, a rather minxy *femme fatale* ...'

For a moment he wondered vaguely if she was trying to find out how shockable he might be.

'... which I mean in the nicest possible way of course,' she added.

'Of course,' he said.

She would no doubt get to the point in her own good time. Informants – if she could be described as that – often revealed most when digressing from what they thought one wanted to know.

'... and a futurist suffragette,' she continued.

The word *futurist* was being increasingly used to refer to any sort of political agenda that envisaged some kind of utopian future.

'She lives in Italy these days,' she added. 'Can't say I blame her. Polanyi is – how shall I say? – a bit of a challenge.'

He was getting the distinct impression that – in some inexplicably female way – she admired Polanyi.

'Anyway, Dolfi left me his envelope of documents. His reasons sounded plausible but, to tell the truth, I thought he was just being his usual over-imaginative self. I didn't think much of it at the time. But then he disappeared ...'

'And things appeared in a slightly different light?'

'No, not really. Not then. As I said, the simple fact of him simply dropping out of view without telling anyone why did not surprise me overly. Dolfi was not your average eight-to-five man. He was erratic at the best of times. I thought his sister was being somewhat melodramatic about it all. She called around on the day of the emperors' funeral to tell me he'd disappeared. We heard that Egyptian's bomb go off. Though we didn't know it was a bomb, of course, not until later.'

She was silent for a moment. The espresso machine hissed in the background.

'I opened the envelope after the funeral. But it didn't contain what he said it did. The documents were in an unrecognisable foreign language – or seemed to be. It looked like gibberish even. Or a private language he'd made up, or a sort of imaginary language.'

She extracted another hand-rolled cigarette from her cigarette case. He put another Sphinx in his mouth. He made to light hers first but this time his lighter refused to ignite at all.

'I have some matches somewhere,' he said and started to rummage around in the pockets of his overcoat, which was hanging over the back of his chair. He eventually found the matchbook he had purloined from Dolfi Jensen's room.

'The Café of Electric Delusions,' she said, reading the lettering on it.

'It's the Café Griensteidl, that arty place, isn't it? I thought it was quite clever of them.'

'I don't understand.'

'Using their nickname like that. The Café of Electric Delusions, that's what everyone calls the Griensteidl, isn't it?'

'You are getting mixed up. The Griensteidl is called the Café of Grand Delusions. There's a new place called the Café of Electric Delusions. That's its actual name. It's on the Beatrixgasse. It opened up a couple of months ago. I've been there a few times. They do cabaret, dance. Wigman did a performance there a few weeks back. Polanyi's even given a couple of his ad-lib lectures there. It has a big multicoloured neon electric sign outside which flashes on and off. Electric lamps and telephones on the tables. Which is all the rage in Berlin these days, I'm told. Makes the Griensteidl feel positively eighteen-ninety-something. And this place positively mediæval.'

'When did you say it opened?' he asked her.

'October, November,' she said. 'I'm bad with dates. The week the Italians aëroplane-bombed Constantinople.'

Which would have been around the end of November. So Dolfi Jensen could not have been in the Café of Electric Delusions – the real one, the one the matchbook came from. Somebody else must have been in his room, searched it. Polanyi would most likely have a key.

'Those documents are not mine,' she continued. 'To be honest, I feel uncomfortable possessing them. By right they're his sister's. I have my own memories of him. That's all I need. I don't want to be reminded of his crazy ideas or whatever else he was up to, or imagined he was up to. That's not the way I want to remember him.' She stubbed out her cigarette, half-smoked. 'But to tell the truth, I would feel a bit odd about just giving them to her ... having to explain ... after all that's happened. Could you give them to her? I could put them in the post to you.'

'Best not in the post,' he said. 'I can send one of our people around to collect them. Just to be on the safe side. At a time that's convenient for you, of course. I'm sure Fraulein Jensen will appreciate it.'

'Send somebody to me at work,' she said. 'Tomorrow if you like.'

Their conversation over, he called for the bill, paid, and offered to escort her to her tram stop. He'd left her bicycle at the Mundaneum.

The billboards at the newspaper kiosk were all about the gas attack: GASSED CITY EVACUATED – OTTOMAN CASUALTIES HIGH. He bought a copy of the *Neues Abendblatt* and stuffed it into his pocket.

'The Mundaneum sounds like an interesting place to work,' he said as they waited in the cold under the electric streetlights.

'In its way. Though sometimes I think that attempting to gather all human knowledge in one place is all rather ...' – she searched for a word – '... anally retentive.'

'As opposed to anally expulsive,' he said without thinking but she showed no visible sign of being taken aback by the comment.

'The Bohemian crunches numbers. The Mundaneum crunches facts and references. I think imagination is as important as mechanical reasoning. A world made up solely of dry facts does not leave much room for—'

'For magic?'

'Or poetic truth.'

'There was somebody at the funeral,' he said. 'Long hair. Beard. German speaker. Carpathian accent. Or so somebody told me. Sort of character that sticks in your mind ... a *Naturmensch* type.'

'What about him?'

'Just wondering who he might be. Idle curiosity.'

'A hazard of your profession?'

He laughed.

'At Monte Verità they called him the Transylvanian Daoist,' she said. 'Dolfi used to call him Siddhartha. He called himself Gusto, from his Christian name Gustav – if Daoists can be said to have Christian names. He lives in a cave there when not wandering around Mitteleuropa in a ramshackle self-built caravan with his wife and at least half a dozen offspring. He was one of the founders of the Monte Verità *Landkommune*. He must have been in Vienna and seen the death notice in the newspapers or something.'

The tram pulled up. There was an advertisement on the sides of several of the carriages, in bright yellow Latin lettering, for HOUSEHOLD REFRIGERATION – NEW FROM AMERICA.

'Don't be so suspicious,' she said to him she climbed aboard. 'Sometimes there is a sort of symmetry in things. That's all.'

She waved oddly, almost shyly, as the tram pulled out and disappeared into the icy Viennese evening. Pechstein wondered if the Agency had anything on Polanyi in the Basement.

***

The next morning Pechstein sent one of the Agency clerks to the Mundaneum to collect the documents from Sigrid Kupfer, and when he came back up from his lunch in the canteen, the envelope was on his desk.

He opened it with his pocket knife. Inside there was another envelope, cardboard-backed and already opened, which contained ten sheets of closely typed A4 sheets of paper, or rather photostats of them; they still smelled vaguely chemical. She hadn't told him they were photostats. A few of them were stapled together as if they were reports of some kind. The text was all lower case, unpunctuated, each line just a long stream of letters. Perhaps they were in a foreign language but it was none that looked even vaguely familiar. It could be a code of some sort. He doubted very much if it was a made-up imaginary language. Each stapled-together set of pages had what looked like a title, underlined. However, these were not in code, or at least didn't seem to be. One began with the word projectbeowulf, followed on the next line by a six-digit serial number consisting of both letters and numerals. There was also a projectmordred, a projectwayland and a projectfraoch. The word beowulf rang a bell but he couldn't place it. It sounded Anglo-Saxon or Scandinavian, as did the others. In any case, he was sure he had heard it before. And mordred also sounded familiar. It would be easy enough to look them up in the office Brockhaus.

Photostat machines were few and far between. There was one at the university library. Werner had even been muttering about purchasing one for the Agency. Whatever the reports were about must have been important enough to justify the effort involved in making photostat copies of them. The longer he looked at the incomprehensible lines of unpunctuated text and numerals, the more he became more convinced that it was a code of some kind. A private cipher perhaps? To which only Dolfi Jensen himself held the key? But, if they were something Dolfi Jensen had written himself, why make photostat copies?

8

Stanislaw Lachmann's office smelled of stale pipe smoke. The view through the leaded windows behind his desk was of the Vienna skyline and the Danube. Otherwise, the only notable feature was a glass display cabinet containing about a dozen mechanical devices that looked – to Pechstein – like various types of calculating machines, and a rather ancient-looking abacus.

'I have something to show you,' Pechstein said.

'Always happy to be of service to the Agency.'

Pechstein laid out the photostats on Lachmann's large desk.

'I think it might be in code,' he said.

'Could well be,' Lachmann said after about a minute. 'Too ordered to be merely random nonsense. But not regular enough to be merely some mechanically produced sequence of letters.'

Pechstein nodded as if he had understood, but Lachmann could see that he hadn't.

'Information – or data – is a sequence of symbols,' Lachmann explained. 'There is information in any regular pattern. For example, in the movement of the moon. Its path across the sky, its waxing and waning, tells us that the Earth is spinning and that the moon is orbiting around the Earth. But there is no intentional message. It's ordered and repetitive, an ordered natural phenomenon. On the other hand, if you listen to a wireless that has not been calibrated to receive a transmitting signal, that hissing howling noise you hear is the opposite of information: just chaos, the chaos of the ether, pure randomness, devoid of any message, intentional or otherwise. Then there is information which does contain an intentional message—'

'How can you tell which is which?' Pechstein asked him.

'From the patterns, their irregularities and regularities. The irregularities of their regularities. The regularities of their irregularities. The way the letters and numerals repeat and don't repeat. Intuition.'

It was not too often that the Agency had cases that involved ciphers and cryptograms, but when it did, it availed itself of the services of Stanislaw Lachmann. Pechstein had never had much cause to speak to him before. All he really knew was that Lachmann – a prematurely balding man in his late twenties, with large Bakelite-framed eyeglasses – besides being a lecturer at the university and an authority on an obscure branch of mathematics, also did jobs for the banks and the finance houses setting up systems to do with encrypting money transfers sent over the telegraph wire system. Werner said he used him because he was fairly sure he had no Castle connections, that the authorities had their own men for this kind of thing. The Agency did more than a few odd jobs for the Castle but that did not mean that it wanted the Castle poking around in its affairs. Werner described him as 'a virtuoso when it came to numbers' but, more to the point, also that he was the 'soul of discretion'.

'Where did you get these?' Lachmann asked.

'One of our clients,' Pechstein half-lied.

Lachmann gave him a short, silent but intense look.

'Confidential, I'm afraid,' Pechstein added. 'You know how it is.'

'Of course,' Lachmann nodded, and resumed his examination of the photostats. 'Any idea what the word *beowulf* and these other project names refer to?'

'Beowulf is the name of a dragon slayer in an Anglo-Saxon legend,' Pechstein said. 'The others are also the names of figures from ancient legends.'

'Ancient legends?'

'Wayland is a sort of Anglo-Saxon Vulcan. Mordred is the illegitimate son of King Arthur – even gets a mention in Dante's *Inferno*. Fraoch is another dragon slayer, an Irish one. Can you tell what the language it might have been in originally? Our client believes it could be English or French, or even Danish, if it's not German.'

He knew Dolfi Jensen had translated from English and French, but he would also have been able to translate from Danish.

Lachmann shook his balding head.

'Impossible to even guess. The no spaces between the words and everything in lower case does not help. Celtic monks were the first to put spaces between words. In Latin anyway. Not common knowledge. Not that that has anything to do with anything.'

'Can it be decoded?' Pechstein asked.

'Deciphered. Only with the key.'

'As in A equals B, and B equals C and so on.'

'Something like that. Except that A might equal B plus X minus Y if A is the first letter of the word. But if A is the second letter of the word, then A might equal C plus X minus Y … and so on.'

'I see,' Pechstein said, a nebulous mental image of the mathematical process Lachmann had described forming in his mind.

'These are a professional job,' Lachmann said.

'How professional?'

'Very,' Lachmann said, adding, 'As far as I can see.'

'Are you sure?'

'As much as I can be. Could even have been done with some kind of cryptographic machine.'

'Such things exist?'

'Oh, yes. Did your client find anything else along with these, a book perhaps with some words underlined? A bible or some classic work of literature is a favourite. A slim volume of Goethe? Or Schiller perhaps?'

'No,' Pechstein said, shaking his head.

'It's usually not something obvious,' Lachmann said. 'Something reasonably commonplace, easy to overlook. It could even be a phrase written on a slip of paper, a few words on a postcard.'

'No, definitely not.'

'I see,' Lachmann said. 'It is theoretically possible of course – without the key – to decipher a coded text by going through every possible possibility. One might be lucky, but there is a near-infinite amount of possibilities one could go through, or as near enough for all practical purposes. Think of a thousand monkeys doing the same thousand-piece jigsaw. And how long it would take before one of them completed one. That's the level of probability we are talking about – with any self-respecting encryption job. Of course, one of our simian brothers might be a very lucky monkey and get it right after a hundred years. It could be done mechanically, in theory – which would, in theory, be more efficient – but the principle is the same. I'm afraid that without the key, whatever these documents contain shall remain a mystery,' adding, in mock imitation of an ominous music-hall villain, 'until the end of time.'

'I see,' Pechstein said.

Outside the office window, two large, grey-black, whale-like balloons were slowly ascending into the sky. Each was attached to several thick guy cables originating somewhere below the skyline in the neighbourhood of the Imperial Palace.

'What in God's name are those?' he asked.

Lachmann turned around and looked out the window to see what Pechstein was looking at.

'Barrage balloons,' Lachmann explained. 'Protection against enemy aëroplanes. Exercises. Precautionary. For The Day. For Armageddon. Should it ever come to pass.'

'They look like something out of *The War of the Worlds*.'

'The idea – in the eventuality – is to float a ring of them around the centre of the city. Each one held in place by a dozen or so steel cables with the cables crisscrossing each other and forming a sort of steel net. By the time an airman sees it, it's a bit late and boom-crash. The things can go up as high as four kilometres.'

For a moment the two men looked at the scene unfolding in

the sky in silence.

'I sometimes think men yearn for times,' Lachmann said, 'when they – or we – can all somehow feel we are partaking in something greater and more profound than ourselves, something that transcends the mundanities of ordinary life … something historic … some sort of Götterdämmerung.'

'History with a Hegelian H,' Pechstein suggested.

'Something like that.'

'War has become impossible,' Pechstein said, not wanting to contemplate what should not be contemplated, though he knew there were men that did. 'It's all bluff. Berlin, London, Paris, Vienna, Rome, Saint Petersburg, they'd all be gas-bombed, laid utterly to waste.'

'Accidents happen.'

Lachmann turned around again.

'Are you sure that your client is kosher?' he said.

Pechstein looked at him, not quite understanding.

'Being above board with you? Not up to any tricks? On the right side of the law?'

Pechstein waited for Lachmann to elaborate.

'Telegraphic money transfers are encrypted. But also other information. To know the price of bonds on the New York, Tokyo or Calcutta stock exchanges has its advantages, or the price of gold on the Witwatersrand a few hours before anybody else. It's valuable information and is often transmitted in cipher. Information like that is big business. That's the legal stuff. But there is also commercial information of a more questionable nature being transmitted over the telegraph wires these days.'

For an instant, Pechstein imagined the house in the Girardigasse – a bohemian dosshouse inhabited by assorted anarchists, sundry artists and occultists – as the centre of an international financial conspiracy with Dolfi Jensen in his room masterminding secret communications to all corners of the globe … a ludicrous idea. The man had only barely managed to keep his head above water financially.

'I'm sure,' he said, 'it has nothing to with anything like that.'

'There is another possibility,' Lachmann said.

'Espionage?' Pechstein suggested half-jokingly. That the documents had something to do with the work that Jensen had been doing for the Castle had crossed his mind.

'Let's just say,' Lachmann said, 'I would tread carefully. I'm sure there is no need to spell it out.'

'No,' Pechstein said. 'There isn't.'

'I'm sure the Agency has excellent relations with the authorities but all the same …'

Pechstein nodded slowly.

Lachmann handed him the photostats.

'I haven't seen these,' he said as Pechstein took them from him. 'If anyone should ask. I hope that is clear.'

Pechstein nodded again.

'Very clear,' he said.

He walked back to the Agency. The empire's capital was finally emerging into spring. The daffodils were in bloom. At Judenplatz, an organ grinder with a monkey, dressed in a sailor's hat and uniform, was plying his trade on the pavement in front of the colonial wares shop. The tune was something from the previous century with a vaguely operetta-maritime hint to it. The man, who was cajoling the passing crowd to drop coins into an enamel cup, had a look of forced jollity on his unshaven face and was wearing what was supposed to be a ship captain's peaked cap. There was something odd about the scene but it took Pechstein a few moments to realise what. Usually it was the other way around: the man ground the organ and the monkey collected the money.

'He did translations for them,' Sigrid Kupfer had said. 'Scientific papers, technical stuff.' But the idea that Dolfi Jensen's disappearance and death had something to do with the Castle was fantastical, the stuff of boys' adventure annuals. Or was it?

***

A brown folder containing information on Polanyi was on Pechstein's desk when he got back to his office. There were several sheets of paper in it, some handwritten and some typewritten, each with a reference card stapled to it so that it could be returned to its original place in the Basement's filing system. There was also a gallery catalogue. It was more than he had expected.

The Schiele Affair, as the yellow press had dubbed it, had been about a semi-legal – though some would say, from the Austro-Hungarian point of view, entirely legal – scheme to smuggle paintings into the Russian Empire. But it had incurred the displeasure of the authorities. The Agency had become involved at the tail end of 1916. By pure chance, Pechstein had been in Werner's office – a much more spacious affair than his own, and on the top floor – when the bespectacled, bowler-hatted and pipe-smoking Maximilian Eisenstein of the Vienna StaPo, or 'Max, the faceless man from the government' as Werner called him, popped around to have a cosy chat and enlist the Agency's services in the matter. In radical circles, Eisenstein was often referred to as the Man in the Iron Mask; the reason being that not many people knew what he looked like, though his name – and reputation – was a byword for the Castle's surveillance activities. It wasn't a nickname that really made that much sense, but incongruous nicknames often stuck. He was also high up in the Evidenzbüro; which, strictly speaking, was responsible for 'foreign affairs', while the StaPo was responsible for 'home affairs'. Pechstein did not particularly like him. Perhaps it had something to do with the dichotomy of the power the man wielded and his apparent ordinariness. He had a villa somewhere in Döbling, named – of all things – Arcadia.

'Our Russian brothers have a penchant for the decadent and the abstract,' Eisenstein had said. 'Perhaps it's the Asiatic influence, the mysticism of the steppes ... But it's got a little out of hand, so much so that it has become a matter of state. Some of the dealers are making small fortunes.'

Eisenstein had been sitting across from them at the other side of Werner's immaculate desk, with Werner's gaudily decorated Christmas tree behind him.

'Saint Petersburg has very strong feelings about Futurist art. It believes it could put democratic ideas into the heads of the bourgeoisie, of people like our good ourselves, and, more to the point – which is a rather ludicrous proposition – into the heads of their unwashed masses. Personally, I think all this modern stuff is a sort of safety valve, a way for neurotic artists to channel their nervous energies into a sometimes disturbing but generally futile activity. And if those with more money than sense want to buy the stuff, well, what's the problem? But be that as it may, Saint Petersburg wants the flow of Austro-Hungarian avant-garde genius into Holy Russia stopped. Which is impossible of course. But we need to be seen – discretely – to be throwing a spanner in the works. Demonstrate a degree of good faith, as it were. The feeling at the Castle is that it needs to be handled sensitively, privately. The press and the liberals would make a dog's dinner out of us if we were seen to be cuddling up too much to the *dreaded* Okhrana.'

A couple of months later the whole business had imploded, or rather exploded, resulting in egg on quite a few faces, making Egon Schiele – 'Europe's most shameless, outrageous, degenerate painter', as the yellow press called him – into a household name; though only some of the paintings were in fact by Schiele. Werner, via his nefarious contacts, had managed to avoid any public mention of the Agency's involvement. Then there had been the fire, perhaps a fortnight after the Agency had ceased being involved in the case, that had incinerated a warehouse in the suburbs wherein, as one newspaper put it, were stored several dozen 'controversial paintings executed in the Futurist style'. Werner had said that Eisenstein had suggested it might have been the work of the *dreaded* Okhrana, the Czarist secret police, but then, as he put it, 'that was a very convenient explanation'. Needless to say, if the StaPo had a hand in it, they would not have done it themselves; but there was no shortage of desperate low life in the back alleys of Vienna who would burn down the Stephansdom itself if provided with a box of matches and an envelope of ten-*Krone* notes. He'd said that Eisenstein had been uncharacteristically vehement in his denials – he was usually a cool-headed paragon of *Homo bureaucraticus* – when he, Werner, had suggested – in utter jest, of course – that it had been a rather convenient conflagration. When the gutted shell of the warehouse had been deemed safe to enter, a corpse had been found in the ashen debris. The newspapers had dutifully informed the public that the police believed that the corpse was that of the arsonist – hoist with his own petard, as it were – but that it had been so badly incinerated as to make any definite identification impossible.

Pechstein went through the papers in the folder. There were six in all, one with a newspaper cutting gummed to it.

Two of them were lists. One of these was of dealers and gallery owners who were known to buy and sell Futurist art generally. The other, made later, at the conclusion of the Agency's investigation, was a list, or rather two lists: one of persons who were most definitely involved in smuggling paintings and one of those who were possibly involved. Polanyi was on the list of those possibly involved.

The third sheet was simply a report on Polanyi's gallery, the Crimson Cockatoo, giving the kind of details anyone could pick up just by visiting the place and noting the address, and stated that Viktor Polanyi, a Hungarian national, was the proprietor.

The fourth sheet was simply entitled 'Viktor Polanyi – Movements, 17 February 1917'; it listed his time of arrival at the Crimson Cockatoo on the day, a lunch break at a vegetarian eating house, the purchase of a bottle of vodka and cigarettes, his return to the gallery and then a visit to 'a subversive bar called the Herzen' from whence he retired to his domicile, Girardigasse 13, at ten past three the next morning. It was signed by Żuławski.

The sheet with the newspaper article gummed to it had only

the name of the newspaper, *Der Sozialist*, and the words
'Gustav Landauer, Socialist Federation' written on it. The
article itself was a brief account of a lecture Polanyi had given,
again in February 1917, on 'Anarcho-cosmism and the
Common Man' at the Crimson Cockatoo. It said nothing about
what he had said, beyond noting that 'futurist-proletarian ideas'
had been 'proposed and discussed, at times passionately, and at
times humorously', adding that the lecture had been 'well
attended', and that the exhibition running at the time was by the
Dachau Expressionist Grove.

The sixth and final sheet was headed 'Viktor Polanyi –
Personal Details' and gave a brief curriculum vitae: Born
5.6.1889, 'various Buda-Pesth schools' from circa 1894 to
1907; circa 1907 to 1913, worker at Kogutzki Typesetters and
Printers Co., Buda-Pesth; then circa 1913, relocation to Vienna,
art gallery proprietor, exporter of 'paintings in the so-called
Futurist style', with long-standing connections to 'socialist,
nihilist and socially disruptive circles', and 'connections to
similar circles in Italy', 'known to have literary ambitions,
reported to be writing a Futurist novel' and 'known among his
associates as a heavy drinker with a violent temperament when
under the influence of strong spirits'. That too was signed by
Żuławski. The catalogue was for a 'mystical-realist' exhibition
called The Lost Cause – of lithographs and paintings by a
British artist by the name of Austin Osman Spare. The cover
image was an intense self-portrait of the satyr-like artist 'felling
the last tree on Easter Island'.

9

Weber had never met either of the two tweed-suited men facing him across his desk in the book-lined study – his Holy of Holies, as he called it – of his large Berggasse apartment. But he knew who they were, or rather where they were from, and whom they represented. Their 'letter of introduction' – signed by Eisenstein himself, and which they had been very careful to make sure he handed back to them – had made that crystal clear. They had also politely informed him that they were unable to tell him their names.

'We're sure he's well-meaning, doing what he considers his job and all that,' the fat one said. 'It's just that we feel he's got the wrong end of the stick …'

'… and that could lead to some embarrassment,' the thin one added.

'The wrong end of the stick?' Weber repeated.

'Seems to have got the idea into his head that there was foul play involved,' the fat one said. He reminded Weber of a well-fed imperial railway inspector. The only thing missing was a gold-braided uniform and a shiny peaked cap. 'Which of course there wasn't.'

'At the time,' Weber said, 'it was simply a matter of a disappearance. I had no reason to think it had anything to do with anything.'

'And it didn't,' the thin one said quietly.

'Jensen's sister asked me to help her,' Weber said. 'The lady is a colleague. A close colleague. She was distraught. Jensen wasn't the most stable of men. I suspected he'd had some mental breakdown of some kind. She needed someone who could provide professional assistance. Pechstein seemed a good choice. I'd assumed that when Jensen's body was found that had been the end of his involvement.'

'What exactly is your relationship to Pechstein?' the thin one asked. He was an inordinately tall, gaunt man, and he was wearing a black wig. It was so obviously a wig, it was ridiculous. He reminded Weber of an undertaker.

'Our social circles overlap. I knew he would be discreet …' Weber said, 'and thorough.'

'His thoroughness has transformed itself into a misguided excess of wrong-headed zeal.'

'You should have come to us,' the undertaker added.

Weber nodded. Perhaps he should have. But he hadn't.

'Has he spoken to you about the case?' the imperial railway inspector asked.

'No.'

'Has the sister?'

'In a general sort of way.'

They waited for him to elucidate.

'Fraulein Jensen is a friend,' was all he felt like saying.

'Of course, he's wasting his time,' the railway inspector said. 'He's on a wild-goose chase.'

'All the evidence, the police report, the necropsy report,' the undertaker added, 'says it was an accident.' Weber sensed that the undertaker was the imperial railway inspector's superior. They were like a comedy music-hall duo, but one exuding an aura of unspoken intangible menace. 'Tragic accidents happen.'

That Dolfi Jensen's disappearance and death had nothing to do with whatever work he did for the Castle was most probably the case. He knew Dolfi did translations for them now and again, and possibly other odd jobs – but he'd hardly been a master spy. It had probably been an accident, but why were they being so adamant about it? Was it possible that there was more to it? But if there were, they were hardly going to tell him.

'So how can I be of assistance?' he asked.

'Do you have any influence with Herr Pechstein?' the undertaker asked him.

It was Weber's turn to allow them to elucidate.

'If, hypothetically, you were to suggest to him that Fraulein

Jensen was … how shall I put it? … being hysterically paranoid or something like that? Do you think that might dissuade him from wasting his time?'

'From stirring up rumours and the like,' the imperial railway inspector added.

'I think he might already think that,' Weber informed them. 'My repeating it would hardly make him change his mind about anything. Or anything else I should say.'

'So, you have spoken to him about the case,' the undertaker said.

'No, but Fraulein Jensen told me as much,' Weber told them. 'She has suffered a severe emotional shock, as I'm sure you can appreciate. She's looking for some sort of explanation, a way of making sense of what happened. I think she half-realises that herself. I'm sure Pechstein does. But she says Pechstein has agreed to humour her.'

'Those were the words she used?' the imperial railway inspector said. 'Humour her?'

'Yes,' Weber said.

They neither indicated that they believed nor disbelieved him.

'She is a strong-willed woman.' Weber felt compelled to add. 'She'll get over it. The looking for a reason. That part of it. They were twins, you know.'

'We know,' the undertaker said.

'She said he told her that he believed that it was most likely an accident,' Weber said.

Weber's two visitors exchanged glances.

'Most likely?' the undertaker said.

'But, as you said,' Weber added, 'there is nothing to find. He'll realise that eventually.'

It took slightly longer than usual for one of them to reply.

'It's the irresponsible stirring up of rumours we are concerned about,' the imperial railway inspector said.

'So, you are sure that there is nothing you could say to him which would cause him to cease these enquiries?' the undertaker asked.

'No,' Weber said, after an appropriate pause. 'No. I don't think anything I could say would influence him at all.'

'Thank you,' the undertaker said. 'Just a few more questions and we'll be finished'

Weber said nothing.

The undertaker took out a notebook and flipped to a page that seemed to have some sort of list on it.

'Sigrid Kupfer,' he read. 'Does that name mean anything to you? Has it come up in any context whatsoever? Please take your time and think carefully.'

'No,' Weber said. 'Never heard of her.'

'Tobias Donnerstag? Jewish.'

'Who shared an apartment with Herr Jensen?'

'Yes.'

'I know of him. But only that he lives there and that he's a customs inspector or something like that.'

'He was at the funeral,' the imperial railway inspector said.

'I wouldn't have recognised him,' Weber said, surprised that the Castle had thought it important to send someone to observe the grim event.

'Viktor Polanyi?'

Weber shook his head.

'Constance Cohen?'

'No,' Weber said. 'Never heard of her.'

'Siegfried Moses Manga Bell?'

The name sounded familiar, but *Manga*?

'Father from the Protektorat Kamerun. Imports colonial wares, ivory and that sort of exotica. Supplies primitive art to various galleries, including to the aforementioned Viktor Polanyi. Not as black as the ace of spades but close enough.'

'Yes. I know him by sight. I was introduced to him once. He's doing a doctorate of some kind. But not in my faculty.'

In fact, he'd met Bell twice, both times in the company of Dolfi Jensen. But they hadn't exchanged more than a few pleasantries.

'Well, we're finished,' the undertaker said. 'That's all. But I must request you to keep both the occurrence and the content of this conversation strictly confidential. I'm sure there's no need to explain why.'

Weber heaved a sigh of relief once they were out of the apartment door. When he returned to his Holy of Holies, he sat down again and lit a Sobranie. He didn't think they had lied to him but he was sure they had not told him everything. That was obvious. The nature of the game really. It had not been a pleasant experience but he hadn't blotted his copybook. They seemed satisfied with the reason he gave for sending Anja Jensen to Pechstein. So, it was their problem, whatever the problem was. He hadn't run any errands for the Castle for a couple of years and he had no intention of starting again. And he was angry: Eisenstein could at least have had the bloody courtesy to have spoken to him personally, instead of subjecting him to the charade those two underlings had put him through. It had been like something from that fellow Kafka's absurdist novellas … life imitating bad art.

**

Polanyi was in his armchair reading *The Voice of the Ordinary Man* – what the *Beobachter* had recently taken to calling itself. Otherwise, the Crimson Cockatoo was empty.

'France allies herself with Russian autocracy,' he said as he put down the newspaper and took a sip of schnapps from his pocket flask, 'and Germany with Ottoman satrapy … But maybe a bloody catastrophe is exactly what's needed.'

'Wilhelm has called for another international peace conference,' Bell said. 'The British have agreed.'

'The Italians haven't.'

The two Benin bronzes were still in the gallery, two thirty-centimetre-high, troll-like figurines, one male and one female, with oversized heads and large elfish ears, identical except for the conical breasts on the female and the cherub-sized penis on the male.

'I think I have a buyer for them,' Polanyi said.

'Anybody I know?'

'An aristocrat, a Count von Burkheim,' Polanyi said. 'A connoisseur of fine things. Bit of an eccentric. Says he has one of those electric windmills on his country estate. He charges the batteries of an electric boat with it.'

The name meant nothing to Bell.

'I presume you'd like to see the remains of old Zarathustra,' Polanyi said.

'It's been in nearly all the newspapers.'

'That walrus moustache of his is from his insane period,' Polanyi said. 'When he was relatively sane, he had a more modest, dapper thing. Or so they say.'

Bell followed him as he headed through the gallery, which had previously been a basket-weaving workshop. Most of the Futurist paintings – everyone seemed to be calling anything avant-garde Futurist these days – were of multicoloured visions of speed and flight, automobile wheels and aëroplane propellers, architectural forms rising skywards like twentieth-century Towers of Babel, and exuded a muted electric energy. Though a few of the *oeuvres* were collages of various materials: newsprint, cuttings from illustrated magazines and cigarette packets, the paint more a coloured glue to stick them to the canvas than anything else. 'Primitivism for a new sensibility' somebody had called the original Futurist movement, or movements rather; there were many Futurisms and Modernisms. Marinetti's *Manifesti Futuristi*, which was full of the worst sort of chauvinism, had imagined – and proposed – a toppling of everything, a violent apocalyptic upheaval: but the word Marinetti had practically invented had come to be used to describe artistic and political sensibilities that were, more often than not, the opposite of the destructive chauvinism he was enamoured with.

The remains of Dix's Nietzsche bust were in the back room, laid out haphazardly on sheets of newspaper on a low table against the wall. There must have been more than twenty or thirty plaster fragments. Bell picked up a chip the size of a lozenge and examined it. The whole head had obviously just shattered.

'A fragment of his frontal cortex?' Polanyi suggested. 'Or his pineal gland perhaps?'

'A proper mess,' Bell said, as much to himself as to Polanyi, replacing the unrecognisable piece of plaster with the rest of the rubble.

'Indeed,' Polanyi said, shrugging his shoulders. 'And all the King's horses and all the King's men couldn't put Humpty together again.'

'The way it disintegrated like that …' Bell said. 'It's almost as if it exploded from within.'

'Well, it was … in a manner of speaking … Nietzsche's brain!'

Bell tried to imagine what had motivated the mad iconoclast. A case of killing the messenger perhaps.

'He used one of those things they use to get those petrol-engine automobiles started,' Polanyi explained. 'I think it's called a crank handle or something.'

Then for a while they discussed some new artefacts that Bell was trying to get his hands.

'I'm off to Berlin next week,' Bell said when they were done. 'I got a letter from the Imperial Colonial Office. An invitation to an interview.'

'About what?'

'Something about a possible post in sunny climes.'

'Well, I suppose somebody has to take up the white man's burden.'

As Bell left, one of the more apocalyptic paintings caught his eye: a city being engulfed by a fiery conflagration. What could have been a Zeppelin was hovering above the collapsing buildings. It was entitled *Burning City* and dated 1913. He wondered vaguely if it was meant as a warning. Or a manifestation of Wagnerian yearning? There'd been an article in the *Beobachter* earlier that morning about a new gas weapon. The headline had been about how it smelled like mustard.

***

When he had finished reading it, Pechstein deposited
Żuławski's report into his out-tray with a handwritten TO FILE
notice taped to it. The dosshouses had not turned up anything.
The only possible lead Żuławski had come up with was an
Adolf something-or-other, who turned out to be an artist who
sold hand-painted postcards for a living and was still very much
alive.

He decided to have a Buddhist smoke.

Item one: There was no evidence that Dolfi Jensen's death
was not an accident.

Item two: There was no evidence as to the whereabouts and
activities of Dolfi Jensen between his disappearance in July and
his death in January. Had he left Vienna? And if so, why? And
had he then subsequently returned to the city?

Item three: The coded photostats. 'A professional job',
Lachmann had said. But what were they about and why did
Jensen go to the trouble and expense of photostatting them and
then giving them to Sigrid Kupfer? Who had obviously been his
amante at some point. Because he was afraid something might
happen to him? Because he'd got into something over his head?

Item four: That matchbook from the Café of Electric
Delusions. Had somebody searched Jensen's room after he had
disappeared? Had it been Polanyi? A man with a 'violent
temperament' and involved in all sorts of subversive activities,
according to Żuławski. Polanyi certainly had the opportunity.
The Kupfer woman had said Polanyi frequented the Café of
Electric Delusions.

Other items: Had Sigrid Kupfer told him everything? Was
there something she knew but didn't know she knew? Did this
Donnerstag have anything to do with anything? And then there
were Dolfi Jensen's possibly ambiguous sexual inclinations.
'There are men who cannot stand the very idea of that', Sigrid
Kupfer had said. Had she been hinting that it was something
that he himself could not stand? That he might have taken his

own life because of it? He had not thought of that when she'd said it. If he had been murdered, the perpetrator, or perpetrators, might not have known him – and it had simply been a robbery or a random act of violence – or … on the other hand, if the perpetrator, or perpetrators, had known him …

So what did he have, he asked himself. The distinct possibility that Jensen's room had been searched sometime after his disappearance. And the indecipherable coded photostats. Not a lot. But enough to prevent him from consigning the whole thing to the Basement files.

There was a knock at the office door.

It was Żuławski.

'Come in,' Pechstein said. He had been expecting him. 'Take a seat.'

Żuławski was one of the Agency's hands-on men, the men who did the unsavoury work, the following of adulterous spouses, the bribing of concierges, and the steaming open of letters, the stuff barely on the right side of the law.

'So the dosshouses were a dead end?' Pechstein said.

'Afraid so,' Żuławski said.

He was a sharp-featured man, a particular type that one found scattered among the range of racial types that made up the German, clever-looking rather than intelligent-looking. But the appearance was deceptive. Pechstein had more than once wondered if he was related to Jerzy Żuławski, the Polish author of the scientific moon-romance trilogy – called *The Silver Globe* or something – but had never got around to asking him. It was probably unlikely.

'So be it. But I have another job for you. There is a man I want you to keep an eye on. In fact, it's two men, but one in particular, somebody with whom you're already acquainted with.'

Pechstein slid the file containing the Basement report on Polanyi across the desk. Żuławski picked it up and opened it.

'Viktor Polanyi,' Żuławski read. 'I remember him. A funny fish.' He lit a Roth-Händle. He knew Pechstein loathed them, so he didn't offer him one. 'What exactly are we looking for?'

'I don't quite know.'

Pechstein did not expect Żuławski to ask him for more information than was required for the job. And he did not.

'Suggested modus operandi?'

'Spend a few days on him over the next month or so. A random sample of his movements. Spread it out. Get a feel for him, what he might be up to. Look for anything …' – he searched for the right expression – '… out of character, anything you would not expect the type of man he seems to be to be up to, or any contacts that don't quite fit. I know it sounds like looking for a needle in a haystack and I'm not even sure there is a needle.'

'Might it not be better to stick to him like glue for a couple of weeks?'

'I don't think Werner would be too happy with me taking you off that Salzburg job to send you on a wild-goose chase with possibly no wild goose at the end.'

'True enough,' Żuławski agreed.

'This Polanyi. What was your overall impression of the man?'

Żuławski grimaced, the way he usually did when he wanted to indicate that he needed to think, a disconcerting habit if one was not used to it.

'He's an odd bird,' he said eventually. 'That's for sure. Fingers in quite a few pies. Some perhaps not very kosher. And that place of his in the Girardigasse … packed to the seams with oddballs of all types. There's even an old geezer in one of the ground-floor rooms who claims he was a Paris Communard. And a Russian who claims he was on the Potemkin.'

'His politics?'

'Calls himself an anarcho-cosmist.'

'Which is?'

'The Russian cosmist Nikolai Fyodorovich Fyodorov advocated what he described as a solar economic system. Coal is the product of solar energy. Men should not spend their lives labouring away in mines digging out the stuff. Solar energy should be harnessed directly. Anarcho-cosmists believe that a prerequisite to achieving this state of affairs is a proletarian social revolution.'

'You are well-informed!'

'My line of work obliges me to keep up to date on tendencies in contemporary radical thought.'

Pechstein vaguely remembered once reading something about a British scheme to irrigate the Egyptian desert with some sort of pumping system using mirrors to concentrate the sun's energy – he presumed, in order to generate steam – and a similar German scheme in Mesopotamia.

'And his involvement in the Schiele Affair?'

'Officially we said he was *possibly involved* but the truth is that he was most certainly involved. The scandal hit the press before we could prove anything definitively. All we ever managed to do was a bit of asking around. Even Polanyi's curriculum vitae consists of educated guesses. Your brother asked me to make it look good. You know how it is. That fire … If I remember correctly, it happened after the Agency had been pulled off the case.'

'What about it?' Pechstein asked.

'A bit too neat and tidy wasn't it,' Żuławski said. 'Arsonist burns down building. Destroys a load of paintings that have become a pain in the arse for the powers that be. Said arsonist incinerates himself beyond recognition in the process. If it was a him. They couldn't even tell the sex of the remains. No witnesses. No evidence of anything. All frightfully convenient … to one of a suspicious turn of mind … A fair few of Polanyi's hoard of degenerate masterpieces were stored there. They were probably worth a fair bit. A lot of this Futurist art can fetch a pretty pfennig in these decadent times.'

'Surely the place was insured?'

'The place was, but not the contents. The building was insured by the owner. But the paintings weren't. Funny thing was that Polanyi's reaction was—'

'Fury, I would imagine.'

'Yes and no. From what I can gather he simply more or less locked himself in his room in that communal Girardigasse madhouse of his and proceeded to attempt to drink himself into an early grave. As if he was grieving …'

'Grieving?'

'Perhaps the body they found was not of the arsonist but somebody Polanyi knew, somebody he knew well, somebody he was quite close to. Or maybe he was actually there on the night and something went wrong … Wild speculation on my part. But—'

'But what?'

'Word in the anarchist back alleys was that he believed the StaPo was behind it – not an unreasonable assumption, some might think. He even made a few speeches to that effect in the Herzen, said that one day the Man in the Iron Mask would have a face and *vengeance would be ours* … He can be quite the firebrand when he gets going.'

'I see,' Pechstein said, though he really didn't.

'You know they have a sign behind the bar that reads: *We are not the doctors. We are the disease.*'

'Where?'

'In the Herzen. One of Aleksandr Ivanovich Herzen's more notable aphorisms. Allegedly.'

'And what does it mean?'

Żuławski shrugged.

'Who is the other man you want me to check out?'

'He lives in the same house as Polanyi. A customs officer. A Tobias Donnerstag. See what you can find out about him too.'

10

'To date, the fossil remains of four of the precursor species to the various now-existing races of *Homo sapiens* have been found.' Weber was speaking in the Kaiser Rudolf Auditorium at the Natural History Museum, Vienna's nineteenth-century temple to the Empire of Science. He had a strong voice and the acoustics were near excellent. Beside him on the podium, there were six plinths, the objects on them shrouded over with green baize clothes. 'Java Man, Piltdown Man, Heidelberg Man, Neanderthal Man and Cro-Magnon Man. With the exception of the Neanderthal, all are believed – by the various factions in the palæoanthropological community – to be our distant ancestors.'

Anja Jensen was in the audience, at the back of the auditorium. Weber did not know she was there.

'Putting these versions of man – or proto-man – in their correct chronological order is no easy task. Palæoanthropology is a maze of complexity in which anatomy, zoology, geology and archaeology converge. And each of these disciplines has its preferred method, or mixture of methods, for dating finds. Archaeologists, for example, date human remains by a presumed association with any artefacts found in its adjacency. But the further back we go, the rate at which a new technology – a flint tool or a type of pottery – replaces a previous technology is very slow; the process takes generations. Dating finds – by archaeological methods – from pre-history, from the unimaginably distant past, is fraught with difficulties. But so are other dating methods.'

He whisked the green baize cloth from the object on the plinth nearest him and revealed a bone-coloured plaster-cast skull.

'Java Man. *Pithecanthropus erectus.* Upright ape-man. Believed to have inhabited the jungles of the Dutch East Indies between seven hundred thousand to a million ago. At the most, an ape with some vaguely human characteristics. Discovered by the Dutchman du Bois in the early 1880s in some caves in Java. He found cranium fragments, jawbones and other assorted bones at various locations, enough to fill a few crates. We can tell from its skeletal structure that the creature walked on two legs. The skull and brain cavity are considerably smaller than that of a modern *Homo sapiens*. And as one would expect from such an early specimen, the forehead is much more rounded, and the jaw protrudes in an ape-like manner, as do the eyebrow ridges.'

He unveiled the second plinth to reveal another skull.

'Piltdown Man, *Eoanthropus dawsoni*. Dawson's dawn-man. The pride of Anglo-Saxon palæoanthropology. Dates from about five hundred thousand years ago. Considered perhaps by the majority in the scientific community to be the best candidate for what the popular press calls the missing link. The first mineralised skull fragments of the creature, along with a surprisingly well-preserved mandible with teeth intact, were unearthed seven years ago in the South of England. Initially, many were rather sceptical and suggested that, though the skull was human and old – but not that old – the mandible might be that of a prehistoric chimpanzee-like ape, and that the vagaries of time and earth movements had fortuitously brought both together. But subsequent discoveries have confirmed its authenticity. In 1915, the Piltdown Man II fossils were discovered in the same area – skull fragments mainly, and a molar. And a fossilised cranium found in Australia, the Talgai skull, known as the Antipodean Piltdown Man, seems to be closely related to the English Piltdown Man.'

Weber uncovered the next skull, clearly enjoying playing the showman to the erudite audience.

'Heidelberg Man. *Homo heidelbergensis*. The current consensus is that he post-dates Piltdown Man. But alas, by how much, it is hard to tell. Perhaps he existed a hundred thousand years later. The only dating method that can be used with most of these very early specimens is to extrapolate from the geological strata in which a fossil is found – a method complicated by the fact that though geologists agree on the sequence of the various strata, they do not necessarily agree on their relative durations. How well the anatomy of a specimen fits into the evolutionary tree – as we currently understand it – also has to be taken into account. There are a few chemical tests available now but these really only prove that something is not very recent. The Heidelberg mandible – and it was mainly a mandible – was discovered twenty years ago by Schoetensack in a gravel quarry outside Heidelberg. This reconstruction – based on some skull fragments and a few teeth, all from a single individual – is a work of the scientific imagination. To date the find, Schoetensack made use of every available modern analytical tool, including Röntgen rays. His conclusion was that the mandible was that of a *Pithecanthropus*, a later version of Java Man, and definitely pre-Neanderthaloid.'

Weber whisked the green baize covering off the next plinth and revealed another plaster skull, perhaps one-third bigger than the others.

'Neanderthal Man. Originally called *Homo primigenius*, though now called *Homo neanderthalensis*. Discovered sixty years ago, in 1856 – three years before Darwin published his *On the Origin of Species by Means of Natural Selection*. The Neanderthal probably came on the scene perhaps a hundred and fifty thousand years ago. And became extinct only as little as twenty thousand years ago. The cranium capacity is slightly greater than that of the skull of a contemporary European, though the forehead is more retreating than in any of the existing human races of *Homo sapiens*. It is now generally agreed, though not universally, that he is a branch or race of the main *Homo sapiens* branch – alongside whom he existed for perhaps even as much as a hundred thousand years. Eighty skeletons found in a cave near Krapina – that's in Croatia – a few years ago indicate that at least some of this race were cannibals: cut marks on bones, burning consistent with cooking, and percussion marks consistent with the bones being crushed to extract marrow. But then, some races of *Homo sapiens* are also eaters of their own kind. A sad fact well documented in Wilfrid Powell's descriptions of the tribes of Kaiser-Wilhelm-Land.'

The fifth plaster skull was about the same size as the Neanderthal skull, perhaps slightly smaller, and under the electric stage lighting looked like that of a modern human.

'And then we come to our most recent ancestor: Cro-Magnon Man. To the untutored glance, indistinguishable from modern man. And he is considered to be a species or race of *Homo sapiens*. But to the professional craniologist ...' – he picked the skull up and, Hamlet-like, held it in front of him, pointing out some of its features – '... note the slightly retreating forehead, the faint eyebrow ridges. The cranial cavity is marginally larger than that of a modern human. Five skeletons were found in a cave in the Dordogne in 1868. More specimens have since been uncovered. He probably first emerged at the about the same time as the Neanderthal, and eventually replaced him.'

The stage lighting dimmed and an image – beamed from a projector at the back of the auditorium – of a group of bison and a deer drawn on what seemed to be an uneven surface appeared on the screen behind him.

'These cave paintings are believed to be the work of Cro-Magnon Man,' he continued. 'Of an extraordinary quality and aesthetic sensibility, I think you will agree. They were discovered in Altamira, Spain, in 1880. Yet – despite the incongruity of his having a slightly larger brain cavity than a modern man – Cro-Magnon Man was obviously a primitive, comparable perhaps the most primitive races still extant today. Like the Neanderthal, the Cro-Magnon too, in his turn, was replaced, though not completely extinguished. Traces of the Cro-Magnon cranium form can be found among the Berbers of North Africa and among the peasants of the Dordogne. It is believed that the now-extinct Guanches of the Canary Islands – a light-skinned, blue-eyed race – were largely of Cro-Magnon stock.'

Anja remembered the conversations she and Weber used to have at Das Grab. Once they had talked for a whole evening about when an ape – or an ape-man – could be said to have become a man. Was it the discovery of fire, tools, bipedalism? Or was it burial of the dead, or language, or art? Or shamanism, religion, music, reasoning ability, or memory? The ability to tell lies? The ability to laugh? And if the latter, what did the first man, or woman for that matter, who laughed, actually laugh at? Was it a sudden outbreak of something approaching joy? Or was it at some cruel torture inflicted on a fellow or some animal? Or did the primeval ape become man when he realised that he was fated to die, and all his fellows too? When and where did the transition take place? On a particular day, hour, minute somewhere in the vast stretch of prehistoric time? Was it like a sudden awakening from a long sleep or was it a process so gradual as to be imperceptible to those beings undergoing it?

Weber replaced Cro-Magnon Man on his plinth, went to the last one and unveiled what Anja immediately recognised as the Yorick cranium.

'*Homo sapiens*. A creature far superior to all his predecessors. Uncovered last year at Das Grab, in the course of my excavations at the Celto-Romano-Germanic settlement there. Biologically, a modern European of the *Homo sapiens alpinus* type. Gone entirely are the protruding mandible and those Cro-Magnon eyebrow ridges. The highest form of human to date. Believed to have emerged more or less at the same time the Neanderthal emerged. The five or six branches of *Homo sapiens* now existing are believed to have separated from each other in Lower Palaeolithic times in Asia. The estimated date of this particular specimen is somewhere between 600 and 800 AD.'

He picked up the cranium, again Hamlet-like, and held it with its eyeless face towards the audience.

'Which, in the larger scheme of things, is only yesterday. As are the skulls from the ancient world which we possess: the mummified heads of pharaohs, the relics of martyrs. One diocese, which shall remain unnamed, proudly boasts half a dozen John the Baptist skulls in its reliquaries.'

A laugh of sorts, that of intellectual men who had put away childish things, rippled through the auditorium. For a moment Anja though he was going to say that was a joke he'd made up himself, but he didn't.

'What we see here is the same cranial form we see in the sculptures of the ancient Greeks,' he continued. 'If the glass sarcophagus of Alexander the Great in the Soma Mausoleum in Alexandria had not been vandalised and his mummified body cast into the waters of the Nile by Theophilus' Parabolani, it is such a skull that we would see. But a closer look will show us that there is something rotten in the state of Denmark.'

He turned the skull around and showed them a gaping *Krone*-sized hole in the back of the cranium.

'The death of this individual was caused by an act of violence. By a penetrating blow to the head of some crude but nonetheless lethal dark-age weapon. But delivered by whom? A raider? By a member of his own tribe in the course of a feud? By an executioner carrying out a sentence of death? Or was he a victim of racial competition. The Tasmanian, or *Homo sapiens tasmanianus*, was hunted to extinction a mere eighty years ago by Anglo-Saxon settlers. A cruel fate to befall any people, and a tragic loss for science. Though it is a fate which Darwin believed will be the eventual and inevitable fate of all the primitive races.'

He put *Homo sapiens alpinus* back onto its plinth.

Anja, for a moment, tried to imagine a world in which Neanderthals had survived until the modern era. How then, she wondered, would our perception of what was human and what was non-human be?

'Several hundreds of thousands of years separate Piltdown Man from ourselves. Endless years of evolutionary progress. The result of the, by definition, aimless workings of Darwin's law of natural or circumstantial selection? Yes. Without a doubt. But is that all? Or are there other forces at work? Forces as yet only glimpsed at through a glass, darkly? Darwin's and Wallace's theories are true but is there more to it? Just as Newton's theories are true, and Einstein laid bare a deeper level. He did not falsify Newton. And Wallace himself was not convinced that natural selection alone could produce the human mind.'

He paused for a moment.

'There are many questions that it might be fruitful to ponder. Is the progress in evolution generated merely by the mindless reproduction of variety? Or is it the slow generation – via natural selection – over the vast aeons of geological time of higher forms of life, a somehow *mindful* movement towards greater ordered complexity, more complex nets of life, and higher forms of consciousness. Does evolution have an inbuilt tendency to progress not from the merely different to some other configuration of the merely different but to the higher from the lower? Is the progress from inanimate matter to the biological and to mind, from atoms to galaxies to planets to life to man – or, as Vernadsky puts it, from geo-sphere to bio-sphere to noo-sphere – merely the result of random mechanism?

'Or is the process what Bergson calls creative, a machinery for the making of gods? De Chardin argues that evidence for directionality in the process of evolution – which he compares to a flow, seemingly chaotic, but in a general forward direction towards levels of greater ordered complexity. It can be glimpsed, he says, in what is known as parallelism, the development of similar traits and physical characteristics in populations of animals geographically isolated from one another and with no common ancestors, such as in the beaks of birds and cephalopods or octopi. He sees the universe as evolving towards a maximum state of complexity and consciousness, an Omega Point, a final state of the cosmos which is luring – if one can call it that – all creation towards it, via an undefined time-transcendent mechanism. Morality, ethics, the unique human awareness that there is right and there is wrong, cannot be explained by the Darwinian notion of natural selection. The meek and the humble are the hardly the fittest, hardly more likely to survive – and thrive – than the strong and the ruthless. Yet Christianity teaches us that meekness and humility are the essence of the highest concepts of morality. There are few animals that do not spend near half their life asleep and defenceless. But what is the evolutionary advantage of sleep in the schema of the survival of the fittest? Surely not having to sleep would give any animal a greater chance of survival than its fellows.

'The history of mankind is also evidence that could lead one to conclude that the tendency to progress from the lower to the higher is inherent within nature. There have been setbacks and relapses into dark ages, but in the long run we progress, we become better. There are currently near to one and a half thousand million human beings inhabiting our planet – there are few blank spaces on the map now – and yet not all is relentless struggle, red in tooth and claw. We modern men are obsessed with reforming this and that, and with suppressing all sorts of abuses that we have inherited from the past. In short, we grow more civilised.

'To conclude, I shall leave you with one final thought. And that is that while there may be no white spaces on the map of the world any more, there are vast white stretches of time – and a vast cosmos – to explore. There is so little we know. And in those vast white spaces there are endless discoveries to be made. We are, I like to think, but at the beginning of human history?'

The applause was enthusiastic.

The obligatory closing speech was given by Henning, one of the Museum's assistant directors. He was in his early thirties, which was rather young for the semi-august position he held, Weber mused as he listened. The depressingly bland tweed suit he was wearing was just like those worn by the emissaries from the Castle who had recently paid him a visit.

Henning's words of obligatory praise were greeted by another round of applause. Then the crowd made its way down the stairs to the spacious atrium below, where, under the sightless eyes of a marble pantheon of past generations of natural philosophers and natural historians, refreshments were being served.

Weber was engaged in conversation with a journalist from the *Telegraf* when he saw Anja Jensen, standing beside a glass display cabinet containing half a dozen stuffed Brazilian parrots, cup and saucer in her hand, sipping coffee, alone. He extracted himself from the pressman's questions and made his way through the chattering crowd towards her.

'Good to see you out and about,' he said.

She smiled awkwardly.

'The Yorick article will be in the next edition of the *Mitteilungen*,' he told her. 'They say your photographs will print well. It shall be noticed and no doubt soon forgotten. The Fertile Crescent, Mesopotamia is where the action is these days. The cradle of civilisation and all that. And Egypt of course. A Celto-Romano-Germanic settlement in Eastern Europe might be academically respectable but it's hardly Ur.'

'Your lecture was well-received,' she said.

'Palæoanthropology is not exactly my field of expertise but Piltdowns and Neanderthals do sell tickets. Part of the modern fascination with the primitive Other. Which, I dare say, also accounts for this current Tarzan craze.'

'But no mention of Herr Marx's social evolutionary theories.'

'One doesn't want to overdo it,' he laughed. 'I've just been talking to a fellow from the *Telegraf*. He says the noble gazette might well be interested in an article on Piltdowns and Neanderthals. *Quelque chose* for the weekend illustrated supplement. What they call a popular science article. If you're interested, I'm sure we could cobble something together from my lecture notes. The facts and the chronology would need checking. A day at the university library should sort that out. I have my notes. They'd need ordering, polishing up. And some drawings would not go amiss. A little exposure in the non-academic world does no harm, as long as one doesn't overdo it.'

'I don't see why not,' she said.

'But more to the point,' he said, changing the subject, 'how have you been doing?'

They'd met once – or perhaps twice, she couldn't quite remember – in the weeks following the funeral. She had not heard from him since. But then, some people were embarrassed by grief, being around anyone whom the Grim Reaper had touched; perhaps out of a semi-unconscious belief that tragedy was infectious. She half-expected him to offer some kind of polite explanation but he didn't.

'You seem ...' – he searched for a word – '... somewhat recovered.'

She had the distinct impression that there was something particular on his mind but perhaps it was simply the awkwardness of the situation. They had, once, even been lovers of a sort.

'Sometimes it feels like yesterday,' she said, 'sometimes like a very long time ago.'

'Time and memories are funny things. Has that private investigator fellow, Pechstein ...' he began to ask, seemed to suddenly to have second thoughts, but then decided to ask anyway – 'Is he getting anywhere?'

She wondered how Weber knew that Pechstein was continuing his investigations, if they could be called that. Perhaps Pechstein had told him. And if he had, she wondered what else he might have told him.

'Not really,' she said.

'I see ...' He hesitated for a moment, obviously thinking about what he was going to say next. 'When Charlotte passed on – so suddenly like that – I was distraught. Lost. The boys were only eight and six at the time.' His wife had died – it must have been a decade ago – of meningitis. He'd told her about it once. 'I blamed the doctors, the whole of the medical establishment. But now, in the remorselessly cold light of day, I can see that I was just trying to make sense of it all, grasping at straws ... Eventually one just has to accept ... It sounds heartless but it's not, you know. It's what she would have wanted. I know that now. Accidents, infectious diseases. They just happen. There's no sense to them – not any sense that is any consolation.'

Maybe Pechstein had been talking to him.

She was on the verge, for some reason, of telling him of Gusto Grass visiting her. Weber would have surely remembered him from the funeral; he was pretty unforgettable with his long hair and beard, and his mediæval habit, which he'd also worn when he'd called on her. But she decided not to. Besides, what he had said – if she could even remember it well enough to repeat it – would probably sound banal.

'Bell, Siegfried Bell,' he said just as he was about to take leave of her, 'that black German … he was a friend of your brother's, I believe.'

'Of us both,' she said. In fact, she hadn't seen Bell since the funeral. He'd called once but she had not been in. He'd left a note but she had been too distraught to reply.

She sensed something subtly disingenuous in his manner – nothing she could put her finger on but it was there all the same – but maybe it was simply her imagination.

'Is he still in Vienna?'

'No. He's in Berlin.' He had written to her before he'd left, but again she had not replied. 'But I don't think he'll be there for long. He's been offered a position in Africa. Something to do with that German Jewish scheme.'

'I see,' Weber said and nodded thoughtfully.

***

'Chinatown?' Pechstein repeated and looked at Żuławski in bewilderment.

'He usually spends his days sitting in that gallery of his or in some coffee house scribbling away. But he goes there. The only odd thing he does really.'

Vienna's Chinatown had only taken form three or four years earlier. Now there was even a Chinese temple, a multicoloured building with a pagoda roof decorated with a pantheon of fierce and simultaneously comical-looking demon-gods. Most of the immigrants, officially, were from the Tientsin concession, a patch of Chinese soil barely covering more than a square kilometre and which had become part of the empire as compensation for Austria-Hungary's contribution – dispatching four small cruisers – to aid in the suppression of the Boxer Rebellion. Pechstein had seen photographs of the place; its cobblestoned streets and architecture would not have been out of place in Vienna, and it possessed a bathhouse that would not have looked out of place in Buda-Pesth.

'So, what does he get up to there?' Pechstein asked. 'Some form of sex thing?'

'The thought did cross my mind,' Żuławski said. 'But he's got a bit of a reputation in some circles as a purveyor of very good quality Turkish delight. I'm fairly sure that is where he gets his supply. I have only managed to follow him there twice. The first couple of times, I lost him. He always goes there at rush hours and hops from tram to tram. He's more agile than he looks. I don't think he knew he was being followed. I think he was just being careful, taking precautions in case somebody was following him. But the third time I was able to keep up with him.'

'Hashish might be frowned upon in certain quarters but it's hardly illegal.'

'No, but not paying your taxes is. He might be selling a lot of the stuff.'

'Go on,' Pechstein said.

'There's a rather opulent opium den. The place is in a ground-floor backhouse. It actually has a sign over the entrance saying 'Opium Teahouse' – though it is in Chinese. The next time I followed him I lost him again. But I went there and I waited and, sure enough, that was where he had gone, and an hour later he emerged. I saw him shake hands with a Chinaman as he left. They seemed to know each other quite well.'

'What else did you manage to find out?'

'Not a lot. But I did find somebody who says she might know

something.'

'A she?'

'A Madame Hsiung-nu.' Żuławski pronounced it as if he could pronounce Chinese words correctly, which was hardly likely; but one never knew with him, perhaps he could. 'Somebody for whom I did a favour once put me onto her. A complicated story.'

Pechstein decided not to ask who the somebody was and what the favour might have been.

'She's a petty crook. Peddles a bit of opium, pimps a bit, gambling, that sort of thing. Says she knows something. Said she's quite willing to talk. But for a price.'

Żuławski told him how much.

'No mean sum,' Pechstein said, imagining this Madame Hsiung-nu as some kind of a female version of Doctor Fu-Manchu.

'Something tells me it might be worth it. That's just a hunch, of course. But sometimes one does not have anything else to go on.'

A hundred *Kronen* was not pocket money. The information that this Madame Hsiung-nu said she had might be nothing of any significance.

'There's something else,' Żuławski added, reaching into his jacket pocket and extracting a cheap-looking paperback book. 'This is the Futurist novel Polanyi was writing.'

Pechstein examined the cover. It was unillustrated. Nothing indicated what it might be about.

'*Primroses in December*,' he said, reading the title, 'by Lishny Chelovek Kalashnikov?'

'It's a *nom de plume*. Made-up. Lishny Chelovek means *superfluous man* in Russian, from the title of a novella by Turgenev – I think. Kalashnikov is just a common or garden Russian surname.'

Pechstein flipped through the pages and glanced at some of the rather bizarre-sounding chapter headings.

'Have you read it?' he asked.

'It's a sort of scientific romance. Not much of a plot. A bit of a mishmash. Misquotes philosophers and then misinterprets the misquotes – and you don't know whether he's doing it deliberately or not. Not really my sort of thing. More a collection of tenuously connected short stories than a novel. A novel – in my humble opinion – should be true to the minute facts of the everyday world, deal with the possibilities – if not the probabilities – of human experience. Should be plausible. If you can just make up anything you like, I don't see the point.'

Żuławski's answer took him by surprise. He had not expected him to have strong opinions on matters literary. Pechstein's own preferred definition of a novel was, as somebody once said, a long work of something made-up with something wrong with it, and sometimes with a lot wrong with it.

'And Donnerstag?' Pechstein said. 'Did you manage to find out anything about him?'

'Goes around in his customs officer uniform most of the time but somehow manages to look like a tramp. Involved in occult nonsense. But otherwise as clean as a whistle, as far as I could make out.'

11

Madame Hsiung-nu was lighting incense sticks in front of a gold-coloured idol – of ambiguous sex – on a dragon-decorated altar when Pechstein entered the temple. She was a tall, thin woman – the word *willowy* came to mind – aged between thirty and forty. Her oriental face was difficult to read. She wore a jacket with braided collar and cuffs, and trousers – what Pechstein assumed was some sort of traditional Chinese dress – which made her seem even taller.

'Just put your tribute on the altar,' she said.

It took Pechstein a moment to realise that she was referring to the hundred *Kronen*. He extracted the brown envelope containing the cash from the inside pocket of his coat and placed the envelope in front of the idol.

She indicated to the sturdy, big-muscled, pigtailed man – a bodyguard of some sort; his dress was European – that she wished to be alone with Pechstein. He went quietly outside.

The temple was built entirely of wood. It might have been oak but perhaps it was an Asian hardwood. The beams supporting the roof were as solid as those in an old man-of-war; in fact, there was something distinctly ship-like about the whole structure. A profusion of carvings of all kinds of Chinese figures, symbols and characters filled every nook and cranny, and nearly everything was painted in a cacophony of garish synthetic colours. Pechstein had expected an atmosphere similar to that of a church or a synagogue – he had removed his hat, as he would on entering any place of worship – but it was nothing like that. The silence of the place was a lack of noise rather than the hush quiet of a sacred space. The smell of the smouldering incense sticks evoked a sense of the exotic rather than the holy.

'To Chinese sensibilities, a Christian church would also be exotically alien,' she said as if reading his mind. 'So you are investigating the activities of Herr Viktor Polanyi?'

'Yes,' he said.

She spoke German with a Hungarian accent. Had she married some Hungarian in China? But then, these days, with such large tracts of the globe which had previously been left to themselves so firmly incorporated into the European empires, millions were uprooting themselves and crossing oceans and continents in search of opportunities to live modern lives. The most unlikely people were ending up in the most unlikely places.

'Well,' she said, picking up the envelope containing his *tribute* and inserting it into an inside pocket of her jacket, 'here is Herr Polanyi in person to tell you what you wish to know,' and then simply made her way towards the open temple doorway.

Polanyi entered as she left.

He was wearing a straw hat, a grubby silk waistcoat, and equally grubby black corduroy workman's trousers – and was unshaven.

'No doubt I'm the last person you expected to see here,' he said.

'You could say that,' Pechstein said, trying to think.

'Well, relax. My bark is worse than my bite. Most of the time anyway. Take a pew!' He pointed at one of the carved wooden benches. 'I'm sure we can have a civilised conversation about all of this.'

Pechstein accepted the invitation and Polanyi sat down opposite him.

'But before we do that,' Polanyi said. 'I would like to know why you have been poking your policeman's nose into my affairs.'

'I'm not a policeman.'

'That's arguable. I don't like policemen, of the state or the private variety. You're all cut from the same cloth as far as I'm concerned. You haven't answered my question.'

Pechstein sensed Polanyi would see through anything untrue he told him, not that he could think of any untruth that might even sound half-plausible.

'I'm investigating the death of Dolfi Jensen,' he said.

'Which is why you were rummaging through his things that day.'

'Yes.'

'I thought the powers that be had decided that it was an accident?'

'There are some loose ends,' Pechstein said.

'And I'm some sort of suspect or something?'

'We are following various avenues of enquiry. It's all rather routine really.'

'You seem to be going to a lot of trouble for something rather routine. And who's paying for your illustrious services, may I ask.'

'I'm afraid that's confidential.'

Polanyi laughed.

'Would those loose ends have anything to do with the fact that he did odd jobs for the Castle?'

'That might have some bearing on the case,' Pechstein said, then he wondered if that was something Polanyi had only suspected but which he had now inadvertently confirmed. 'But how do you know that he did odd jobs, as you call them, for the Castle?'

'A little bird. So why are you not poking your nose around in the affairs of the Castle? Or are you? You suspect the Castle might have something to do with his demise?'

'The police – even the secret police – do not go around killing people willy-nilly,' he said, but then backtracked: 'Not that I'm saying there was any foul play involved.'

'Do they not?'

'No, they do not.'

'Spoken like a fully paid-up lackey of the ruling class,' Polanyi laughed again. But it seemed to be genuine amusement, not a jeer.

'I'll tell you what I know on condition that you keep your nose out of my life – and forget that you ever knew anything about me. Agreed?'

'That does rather depend on what you tell me.'

'I'll take a chance on that.'

'I'm all ears,' Pechstein said.

Polanyi began to roll a cigarette.

'I doubt if these Chinese demons will mind,' he said as lit up. 'Not your tight-arsed Catholic saints, this lot. Besides, they like smoke.' He indicating the smouldering incense sticks. 'I like these Eastern deities. They are all so unredeemedly ridiculous-looking. Beer-bellied Buddhas. Gods with the head of elephants and monkeys.'

The smell of hashish-filled the air.

'The gods of the Egyptians were also animal-headed,' Pechstein said. 'I think it's a case of essentially tribal deities – animal gods, animist spirits, totems – simply being retained even though the Egyptian society had progressed beyond the tribal stage, become city-based. But then, religion – if it is to be any sort of a metaphoric description of the ultimate nature of reality – must partake of the ridiculous as well as the sublime.'

'Our oriental brothers certainly appreciate the former.'

'What do you have to tell me?' Pechstein asked, resisting the temptation to continue to discuss the origin and function of religious belief systems with the bearlike creature sitting opposite him.

Polanyi blew out a lungful of hashish-scented smoke.

'He was recruited at the university.'

'How do you know?'

'He told me. He used to joke about it. At first it was all a bit of a laugh, a bit of interesting cloak-and-dagger. But I think he was also somewhat enamoured with the idea that he was somehow privy to the scheming of our masters.'

'What exactly did he do for them?'

'He translated stuff. Statistics. Tonnes of prussic acid produced per quarter, where, by whom. Import statistics.

Rubber and the like, countries of origin of same, price per tonne et cetera, et cetera. Stuff to do with trade. Or so he said. On the face of it, nothing particularly exciting. Nothing I imagine that one wouldn't find in the business pages of *The Times* of London or even *Le Figaro*.'

Pechstein lit a Sphinx.

'Then – it was maybe six months before he disappeared – he began to have serious reservations – I think one could call them that – about the whole business.'

'Did he tell you that?' Pechstein asked.

'Yes. But he did not tell me exactly what was giving him second thoughts about it all, just some vague stuff about how it was all a rotten business. And he did go on about it. At first I didn't take it too seriously. I thought it was one of his moods. He was temperamental at the best of times. I thought it would pass. But it didn't. He started talking about spilling the beans on the bastards. I suggested he simply walk away from it, make some plausible excuse and drop it all, and not to go making his life more complicated than it seemed it already was. He talked about causing a scandal of some sort. I told him that all that would come out of it – if he went to the newspapers with whatever it was, which he was threatening to – would be some printed words on newsprint that would end up being used to wipe somebody's arse the next day. At the most, some bureaucratic nobody might end up having to resign on full pension. The usual scenario. And to what end? Only to antagonise the authorities – who, unlike the gentlemen of the press, can have very long memories, and do not like having their undergarments washed in public. Not worth the candle, I told him.'

'How did he react?' Pechstein asked, trying to imagine Polanyi doing the ad-lib comedian act Sigrid Kupfer had said he did.

'He said it was bigger than that.'

'Bigger than what?'

'He refused to elaborate. It made me nervous.'

Polanyi stubbed out the butt of this cigarette on the lid of his tobacco tin. He wondered what Polanyi was not telling him.

'But he didn't go to the newspapers,' Pechstein said.

'No, but I think he intended to.' Polanyi handed him the lid of his tobacco tin to use as an ashtray. 'There was a seriousness about him, a sort of determination that I'd never seen in him before.' And began to roll another cigarette. 'There's an ancient Chinese curse which runs—'

'May you come to the attention of the authorities!'

Polanyi lit his cigarette but his time there was only the smell of burning tobacco.

'I am not a man who likes to come to the attention of the authorities,' he said.

Pechstein didn't doubt that. Żuławski had shown him one of Polanyi's political tracts, a rambling pamphlet entitled 'The Crimes of the Bourgeoisie'. The gist of it was, in reasonably lucid prose: man had deified money, and money's encroachment into every nook and cranny of life was the real terrorist in our midst; but what he called the money-civilisation was a doomed civilisation because social evolution was an unstoppable force that would eventually bury it. There were quotes from Kropotkin, and from Engels's *The Part Played by Labour in the Transition from Ape to Man*, and an appendix-list of the crimes (a sorry list of them) of the money-civilisation: German atrocities in South West Africa, British atrocities in South Africa, Leopold's rape of the perversely named Congo Free State – for rubber for bicycle and automobile tyres. The thing did have a logic to it, though the average respectable citizen would no doubt dismiss it all as the febrile rantings of an anarchist madman.

'So what did you do?' Pechstein asked him.

'I decided to do a little sniffing around.'

'And how did you go about doing that?'

'I searched his room, went through his papers. It was easy enough. I have a master key.'

'Did you find anything of interest?'

'Half a dozen pages of something written in a code of some kind.'

'In code?' Pechstein repeated, looking deliberately puzzled.

'He'd seemed to have decoded some of it,' Polanyi continued. 'About half a page. But had not got around to translating it.'

Pechstein said nothing.

'It took me a while to figure it out. But I'm fairly sure the document he was decoding was in English. He had to decode it first and then translate it into German. The half-page he'd decoded was still in his typewriter – in English. I don't read English but I know enough to recognise it.' Polanyi reached into an inside jacket pocket and extracted a sheet of A4 typewriter paper, unfolded it and handed it to Pechstein. 'This is not the original. I made a copy and typed it up later. I was careful but I was in a rush. There are probably a few transcription errors.'

Pechstein examined it. All the letters were lower case and there were no spaces between the words – just like in the documents Sigrid Kupfer had given him. The first four lines read:

<u>projectcolman</u>
24november1915
sciofficercapthitchens
tosciallocationscom

The rest of the text was incomprehensible; though he thought he recognised some of the words; it might be possible to tease some sense out of it with the help of a dictionary.

'You didn't make a copy of the original, the coded document?' Pechstein asked. 'What it was decoded from?'

'No.'

'Do you know have any idea what it's about?'

'I'm not so sure I want to know what it's about.'

Pechstein wondered if that was entirely the truth.

'Not now, anyway,' Polanyi continued. 'After having given the matter due consideration, one might say. But at the time I was naturally rather curious. So I decided to do a little more sniffing. I followed Jensen to one of his rendezvouses …' – Pechstein was sure he deliberately mispronounced the word; perhaps he was a man who liked others to underestimate his intelligence – '… with whomever he was in contact with from the Castle.'

Again, Pechstein said nothing and just let him continue.

'I knew he had the habit of disappearing every other Sunday around noon – and I knew it wasn't to church – so I took a chance and followed him. I imagined he would take the tram or an omnibus to some coffee house or something like that, but he didn't. Not that time anyway. He walked to the end of the street and took a horse cab. But I was in luck. There was another one nearby. So I got into it and simply told the coachman to follow.'

Life imitating art, Pechstein thought sardonically – or, in this case, one of those American Nick Carter detective magazines.

'And where did he go?'

'To the planetarium.'

'It was easy enough following him in the cab,' Polanyi continued, 'but it was a bit trickier once I got there. The place was packed. That show about the Andromeda Nebula was on.' Pechstein remembered reading about that. Öpik's more or less definitive proof that the Andromeda Nebula was another galaxy – only one of a dozen or so others – was all over the newspapers at the time. 'They met in the garden where that fancy Klimt sundial is. I had to keep a fair bit away from them – I couldn't risk getting close to them – but I managed to get a good look at Jensen's mysterious interlocutor.'

'Description?' Pechstein asked.

'Short, bald, thin, clean-shaven, glasses. In his late forties, I'd say, maybe even early fifties. But agile, fit-looking for his age. A pipe smoker.'

'There's fifty thousand men in Vienna whom that description would fit'.

'The man had Castle written all over him. I have a nose for

sort of thing. I could hear nothing of what they were saying to each other, but they were arguing about something. Jensen seemed to be very angry. The Castle man looked as if he was trying to calm him down.'

Pechstein tried to imagine the scene: the Klimt Jugendstil sundial, a summer Sunday afternoon, two men arguing, Polanyi observing them from a distance. Though he wondered for a moment if Polanyi might be actually making it all up.

'They didn't speak to each other for long, perhaps ten minutes at the most, and then they both went their separate ways. Jensen took a cab again. The Castle man took a tram. It was him I followed then. It was easy enough to blend into the Sunday crowd. After his third change of tram, I realised he was taking precautions against being followed. But I was fairly sure he didn't think he was being followed; it was too mechanical, too practised. At one stage I took a chance and got into the same carriage he was in and managed to get a better look at him. He was trying to be invisible, reading a book, or rather trying to or pretending to ...'

'What was the book?' Pechstein asked out of curiosity.

'That *Tarzan and the Monkeys* thing. By that American. what's his name? Edgar something-something-or-other.'

'Burroughs, I think. And its *apes*.'

'Anyway, he looked like a man with a lot on his mind, agitated, worried. And it was obvious that he didn't think he was really being followed. No furtive glances over his shoulder or anything like that. It was just after that I lost him. He simply disappeared. One minute there, the next not a sign of him.'

'And where was that?' Pechstein asked him.

'In leafy Döbling.'

Werner was in the process of buying a modest villa in leafy Döbling. The apartment on the Franz-Josefs-Kai, overlooking the Danube and, its spaciousness notwithstanding, it was a bit cramped with six growing children.

'Do you think he lives there?'

'It's possible. He'd already changed trams near half a dozen times by then. I hardly think he was going to keep changing trams ad infinitum. Which – if he does live there – would indicate that he was a man of some substance, an alpha-animal, despite the way he was dressed.'

'How was he dressed?' he said. He should have asked him earlier.

'Like your common-and-garden petty bourgeois. A shabby grey suit, leather patches on the elbows, jacket sleeves a bit too long, and a bowler that had seen a few summers – and winters.'

'Could have been a disguise.'

'That thought did cross my mind.'

'So what did you think was going on?' Pechstein asked.

Polanyi rolled another cigarette and lit it.

'This is speculation, but I think Jensen either told our mysterious Castle man he was going to divulge all, as it were, about whatever was going on, or threatened to do so. And that was why the Castle man looked so worried after their meeting.'

'Plausible,' Pechstein admitted.

'There's something else. Speculation again, and based on the assumption that our Castle man is indeed a high-up alpha-animal.'

'Go on.'

'In the normal course of things, with these sorts of shady dealings, would one expect somebody like Jensen – who was most definitely not an alpha-animal – to be meeting up with some underling rather than some high up. They knew each other. I'm sure of it. It was not their first meeting.'

'What are you trying to say?'

'Two possibilities. Either whatever the whole thing was about was so important that it had to be dealt with personally by someone high up in Castle pecking order—'

'Or?'

'That whatever was going on between them was not, let us say, strictly official.'

'I don't understand.'

'Perhaps it was something personal.'

'When exactly did this meeting take place?' Pechstein asked. Polanyi was proving to be more astute than he had expected.

'About a fortnight before Jensen disappeared. Is that enough for you and your Agency to get your noses out of my life?'

'Yes,' Pechstein said, deciding not to add that only if what Polanyi had told him was the truth.

'There's one other thing,' Polanyi said as Pechstein got up to leave.

'Yes?'

'Jensen's pistol did a Houdini at about that time. Don't quite know when exactly.'

'Jensen's pistol?'

'He had a revolver pistol, some sort of Danish military thing. And ammunition for it. Said it was a family heirloom or something. Not exactly a collector's item but quite unusual. He kept it in one of the drawers in his desk. A few weeks after he disappeared, I searched his room again,' Polanyi said.

'And?'

'As I said, it had done a Houdini. Disappeared. It wasn't there any more.'

On the electric tram back to the Agency, Pechstein observed the bustling streets of summertime Vienna through the glassless window. Women's dresses were shorter again this year. Bourgeois adolescent boys were wearing airmen's suits rather than the now old-fashioned sailor suit. And there were noticeably more electric and petrol automobiles and fewer horse-drawn carriages than there had been even two years earlier. But, resisting the temptation to speculate on the *Zeitgeist*, he set about mentally digesting what Polanyi had told him. Why would Dolfi Jensen have been decoding documents for the Castle? Translating them, yes – that made sense. But decoding them? That was surely something the Castle was more than capable of doing itself, and would want to do itself – for obvious reasons. But it could make sense if – as Polanyi had suggested – the whole thing had been *personal* in some way.

When he reached the Salvatorgasse, he bought a copy of *Die Presse* from the tram stop newsboy. The headline was ITALIAN MARINES ROUTED IN THE DARDANELLES. Ten minutes later he was back in his office at the Agency and there was a note on his desk from Werner reminding him to look at some affidavits to do with another tedious divorce case.

***

'Give me a minute,' Lachman said. He was on the telephone. 'Just listening to the four o'clock news.'

Vienna's telephone 'newspaper' had only just started operating. The one in Buda-Pesth had been running successfully for years.

'The university has an institutional subscription,' Lachman explained as he replaced the telephone on its stand a minute later.

Pechstein showed him the typewritten page Polanyi had given him.

'I've underlined what I think the separate words are,' Pechstein said. He'd gone through the text with the help of a dictionary and had been able to decipher about half of it; there were several words which he thought were chemical formulae. 'My guess is that it's part of a description of some chemical process.'

Lachmann looked at it.

'My English is rudimentary but you could be right.'

'Is it possible to use this to decipher the other documents,' Pechstein asked, 'the ones I showed you a while back?'

'We would need to know what the original encoded text was. Which we don't. If we did, we could use it to help figure out what the key might be. Without the key it's practically impossible to break a code like this. What we have here cannot be used to find the key. For that, we would need to know which encoded page it is actually a decoded version of. So, the short answer is no.'

Then he noticed it. It was among the strange devices in Lachmann's glass display cabinet. He didn't understand how he'd missed it before – but maybe it hadn't been there. The object was almost an exact replica of that bizarre cylindrical device with the letter-discs he had found at the back of Dolfi Jensen's desk drawer, except this one seemed to be made out of some sort of white Bakelite rather than metal.

'What is that?' he asked Lachmann, pointing at the mysterious device.

'It's a so-called Bazeries cylinder – invented by a French military man of that name around thirty years ago – a mechanical device for encoding and decoding messages. Bought it a few weeks ago. Bit of a collector's piece.'

'How does it work?'

'The sender encodes the message using a specific configuration of the discs. If the recipient knows the configuration, he just carries out the same procedure in reverse. Not easily breakable.' Lachmann attempted to explain the theory behind it but the mathematics of it was beyond Pechstein. 'Checking every possible disc arrangement is near impossible – even with just ten discs, you still have over three million possibilities, and this one has twenty discs – though there are some tricks one can use to get around that.'

It was a bit of coincidence finding a near-exact replica of the device that Jensen had used in Lachmann's office. What had Sigrid Kupfer said? Something about their sometimes being a sort of symmetry in things? Something like that. But then, where else was he likely to come across something like it?

'It's cumbersome,' Lachmann added. 'Not state of the art but still used.'

'So, what is the state of the art these days?'

'The Enigma electromechanical rotary cipher machine,' Lachmann said, opening a cupboard adjoining the glass display cabinet to reveal what at first sight looked like a cross between a typewriter and a cash register.

'From ChiMaAG,' Lachmann informed him. 'In Berlin. It's only been possible to buy them this year. The future of sensitive commercial correspondence, of sensitive correspondence of any type. The wars of the future will be fought on the bond markets and stock exchanges … if you ask me, which nobody does.'

Lachman closed the cabinet.

'So,' Pechstein said, 'there is no way any of what I've shown you can be deciphered?'

'Not without a key,' Lachmann said. 'Or the original coded text.'

1920

12

'That Adolf what's-his-name. The fellow they found in the Danube at Preßburg two years ago.'

It was Binswanger's voice on the telephone.

'Dolfi Jensen,' Pechstein said.

'Yes, that's it. Jensen. Well, something odd has come up.'

'Odd?'

'Yes. It's … complicated. Awkward to explain on the telephone. Delicate.'

'Then, let's meet,' Pechstein said.

'Tomorrow, the usual place? One thirty?'

'The schnitzels are on me.'

***

The usual place was the Phaffenhof, a restaurant off the Wiedner Hauptstraße that serviced the midday culinary needs of uniformed civil servants and the clerks who toiled for their daily bread in the counting houses of the city's numerous financial institutions. The large dining salon smelled of sauerkraut, potatoes, roast meat, beer and tobacco smoke. As usual at lunchtime, it was crowded.

Binswanger was already there when Pechstein arrived, seated at a table for two near the window, reading the *Beobachter*. He was a big man, red-cheeked and weathered, with a full head of grey hair, and a grey handlebar moustache. When in his full police uniform, he looked like a caricature jolly hussar. But usually, as was the case today, he was dressed in an immaculate grey suit, the brass chain of his pocket watch hanging across his prosperous and well-fed beer belly. He was also wearing a flamboyant American-style necktie, a habit he had picked up recently. Pechstein hung his overcoat and hat – there was a distinct September chill in the air – on the nearby overcoat rack, and joined him.

'It seems Italy is plunging into anarchy and revolution,' Binswanger said, putting the newspaper away. 'Not that you can believe anything you read in this rag. But it's sometimes more important to be informed about what is believed to be true – what is going on in the collective reptilian brain of our glorious empire's citizenry – than what is actually true.'

'Ah, truth …' Pechstein said, lighting a Sphinx, intending to make some erudite or witty quote on the subject, but he wasn't able to think of anything.

A waiter appeared and took their orders.

'So what odd thing has come up?' Pechstein asked after their mugs of beer had arrived.

'As you know, these days my duties involve me liaising with the Castle on a fairly regular basis …' Binswanger had been semi-promoted a few months earlier. He had not been exactly forthcoming with regard to the details, but it was something to do with some new committee to co-ordinate the 'various machinations', as he called them, of the empire's numerous police forces with those of the StaPo. '… as a consequence of which I see things. A week ago I was in the bowels of the beast, as it were, in the office of a personage who shall remain unnamed, and I saw something. A document. Something I wasn't supposed to see.'

Their schnitzel, roast potatoes and turnips appeared. Two large platefuls.

'Anyway, to cut a long story short,' he continued, as he began to tuck into his schnitzel, 'it was from the brothers in Berlin.'

'Berlin?'

Binswanger swallowed a mouthful of schnitzel and washed it

down with some beer before replying.

'Yes, the big brothers. With whom, officially, we co-operate very closely. Which is true of course, but not the whole truth. Little brother also has his own interests. A bit naughty of me ...' – he had a habit of switching into Viennese dialect every now and again, usually when he was a bit uncertain of how to put something – '... casting my eyes upon it, that is.'

'So what did you see, or rather not see?'

'What I didn't see was a teleprint from some nameless bureaucrat in Berlin to a Castle bureaucrat here who shall also remain nameless.'

'A teleprint?'

'The latest thing in tele-communication machinery. A sort of typewriter connected to the telephone lines that prints out messages. Well, two typewriters. You type a message on one typewriter and the typewriter on the other end of the line automatically types it out. It can also be done with radio waves, I'm told. Don't ask me how it works.'

'What *will* they think of next?'

'God knows. In any case, this teleprint that I did not see was from the middle of last year. From a while back. It was a query as to the quote-unquote "legal situation" regarding one Adolf Michael Jensen. Felt like somebody wanting to tidy up something. You know what these Berlin bureaucrats can be like.'

'I see,' Pechstein said.

'I thought it would pique your interest. It also contained a mention of one Constance Cohen. British subject. Jewish extraction. Employed by the War Office in London until up to sometime in 1917. Forty-something. Suspected pacifist. Possible contacts with the British Campaign for Mutual Disarmament, last known residence and so on. Current whereabouts unknown.'

'Was there anything else?' Pechstein said.

'Yes, in fact, there was. Somebody had scribbled some notes at the end of the page.'

'Jensen dash legal situation dash accidental death certified. Cohen dash noted. Weber comma professor dash to be spoken to dash discreetly. The notes were initialled.'

'What were the initials?'

'M E. I have a damned good idea who that might be, but it's more than my job's worth to even whisper the name. I shouldn't be even giving you the initials.'

Pechstein nodded. M E meant nothing to him.

'Cohen? Weber?' Binswanger continued. 'Do those names mean anything to you?'

Pechstein thought for a moment. The name Constance Cohen meant nothing to him. But Weber? Heinrich Weber? There couldn't be that many Herr Professor Webers in Vienna. It didn't make sense.

'Constance Cohen,' he said, forgetting the Weber name for the moment. 'British. What was her last known residence?'

'Somewhere in England. A place called ...' – Binswanger spelled it out – '... M-O-R-D-O-N comma W-I-L-T-S-H-I-R-E. I think that's a county or something. Did either of those names, by chance, come up when you were trying to track down Jensen? Or since?'

He had spoken to Binswanger a few weeks after the funeral, and asked him what he thought about Anja Jensen's speculations or obsessions – he forgot what he had called them at the time. Not suspicions; they had hardly merited being called that. Together they had gone over Dobrovodská's necropsy report and the Preßburg Gendarmerie's official conclusions and their recommendations to the coroner. Pechstein had not told him about the film or the coded photostats.

'No, I can't say they have,' Pechstein said. He decided not to mention the fact that a Professor Weber had recommended him to Anja Jensen.

'Szombathy is more than reasonably competent,' Binswanger continued. 'I'm sure if anything was amiss, he'd have spotted it. Have you come across anything that might suggest he missed something?'

'Let's say I'm following a few lines of enquiry,' Pechstein said.

Binswanger ignored his schnitzel and roast potatoes for a moment and looked at him.

'If something does come up – above and beyond uncovering the usual sins of the dead – I mean anything serious … Well, be sure to let me know. This is not a divorce case. Not that I'm saying it is a case.'

'If something does emerge, I'll tell you,' Pechstein reassured him.

'Do. For your own sake. Secrets will out, in one way or another. Raskolnikovs do not usually walk into police stations to confess their crimes, but somebody always confesses to somebody eventually, and that somebody confesses to somebody else. Though when the tale is finally told, it's usually a somewhat skewed version of what really happened. What I mean is—'

'I understand.'

When they had finished their beers, Pechstein paid the bill and they left together. A roller skater – a clean-shaven young man in a blue suit and bowler, and carrying a briefcase – passed them on the pavement.

'I wonder if that will ever catch on,' Binswanger said. 'I've seen a few about. It's not a bad way of getting around.'

'Anything is possible these days.'

As they exited onto the Wiedner Hauptstraße, they passed a turbaned Gypsy sitting on a stool, playing an accordion. It sounded vaguely like something from Strauss Junior. Binswanger extracted a handful of change from his pocket and dropped a twenty-*Heller* coin into his collecting bowl.

'The Gypsy is the only European nation never to have waged a war,' he said as they walked on. 'A Gypsy in uniform. The Imperial Gypsy Fusiliers! Ridiculous concept. Petty thieves and vagabonds by nature, and skilled in the dark arts. They're despised of course – but it's resentment – we resent them because they remind us of the freedom we *gadjos* have sacrificed to the idols of respectability and illusionary security.'

'But men have never been freer …'

'Hundreds of millions of free men get up freely at the same time every day, go freely to work at jobs they hate …'

Binswanger's personal criminological theory, if it could be called that, was that criminals were as much victims of what they were as they were perpetrators. He maintained he'd rarely come across one who, at some level, was not unhappy with the psychological forces that drove him to commit the crimes he committed. Some embraced their criminality, he said, justifying their criminal acts as acts of resistance against an inherently unjust world. Others tried to change themselves; and it was only there that morality really came into the whole business – wanting to change was the moral act, whether successful or not. 'It's all ignorance of one form or another,' he'd said once. 'Ignorance of the ethical law or whatever one chooses to call it. Ignorance of the mechanisms of their own minds. Even the normal man doesn't know the half of what is going in his head. Jung – or was it Gross? – said that man had achieved more knowledge about the structure of the atom and the shape of space and time than of the contents of his unconscious mind; and that, if we did not find methods of exorcising the monstrosities that sleep deep within us, they would one day awake; that the greatest monsters were buried in the catacombs of unconscious minds of those who on the outside were all petty-bourgeois properness, politeness and *Kaffee und Kuchen*.'

Pechstein wondered, not for the first time, how the man had ended up as a police officer.

They parted at the Naschmarkt cheese stalls.

The whale-like barrage balloons, floating high in the autumn-blue sky, were visible. There were at least two dozen of them now.

As he made his way back to the Agency, Pechstein turned over in his mind what Binswanger had told him. The name Constance Cohen meant nothing to him. He would write to MacLean. A favour or two was owed there. The details

Binswanger had given him just might be enough to go on. As for this mysterious Weber ... he would have to think about that.

***

'Have you found out anything new?' Anja asked him.

The last time Pechstein had spoken to her was at the beginning of the year. He had not told her anything about either the coded papers Dolfi Jensen had given Sigrid Kupfer or what Polanyi had told him. And he had not yet decided how much to reveal to her. She had not told him about Dolfi working for the Castle, but he suspected that was because she had not known about it.

'Does the name Constance Cohen mean anything to you?' he said, avoiding reply to her question.

They were in his office, sitting across from each other at his desk.

'No.'

She looked different, less crushed. There was a bit more colour in her face. But perhaps it was the autumn chill.

'Are you sure? An Englishwoman. Jewish. Forty-something. Anyone with a name like that? Or anyone who might meet that description?'

'No definitely not. Why?'

'You never told me your brother worked for the Castle,' he said, avoiding answering her question.

'I knew he did work for a government department. Translations. Technical documents.'

'Well, that government department was the Castle. And the documents he was translating for them were not exactly – how shall I put it? – technical documents for the Board of Trade.'

'Are you sure?'

'Yes.'

She looked both surprised and angered. He wondered if it was at him or at her dead brother.

'How do you know this?' she asked him.

'Let's just say he was mentioned in dispatches. Confidential dispatches. I know somebody who caught a glance of one of those confidential dispatches. I'm afraid I'm not at liberty to tell you more.'

'I see,' she said.

He said nothing for a while. She was obviously trying to make sense of what he had told her.

'I wouldn't jump to any conclusions,' he said. 'There is no reason to suspect that what happened has anything to do with the work he was doing. In fact, it most probably doesn't.'

'So why are you asking me about this Cohen woman?' she asked.

'She's a name that came up.'

'Just a name that came up?'

'Yes. In a document, a note really, in an internal Castle document.'

'And what was this note about?'

'It was a request for information on the quote-unquote "legal situation" regarding your brother.'

'Regarding his death?'

'Yes. It wasn't quite clear. I wish I could tell you more, but I can't. However, there is something else.'

He got up, walked over to his office combination-locked safe, unlocked it, extracted a light brown folder, opened it and placed it in front of her.

She picked up one of the photostats and glanced through it.

'What is this?' she asked. 'Is it some sort of code or something?'

'Yes, it's a code, which I have been assured is indecipherable without a key. Which, needless to say, we do not have. They're something to do with your brother's work for the Castle. He passed them onto to someone for, let's say, safekeeping – and again I'm not at liberty to say to whom – who passed them onto me. Do you know anything about them?'

'No, nothing,' she said. 'I've never seen them before.'

'It's important that you not repeat any of this to anyone,' he said. 'I mean anyone. No matter how trustworthy you consider them.'

'I won't,' she said.

'And avoid jumping to conclusions of any kind. Austria-Hungary is not Russia. The Castle does not go around murdering people because they are inconvenient. And it is not my intention to imply that something like that could have happened. But I thought you had a right to know.'

He put the folder back in the safe and locked it. He thought she might ask him to give it to her but she didn't.

The second question he wanted to ask her concerned the matter of Weber. He'd spent an afternoon at the university library looking through various yearbooks. He had found several Professor Webers in Germany – the only one he'd heard of was the sociologist Maximilian Weber in Munich who had written something about the Protestant work ethic as the motor of capitalism. There were two Professor Webers in Switzerland but only one in Austria.

'I read your article in the *Telegraf*,' he said as a way of delicately broaching the subject.

'Mine and Weber's. It was a joint effort. I hope you found it readable.'

'I found it …' – he searched for a word – '… thought-provoking. Especially the idea about evolution tending towards biological systems – complex nets of life, I think, you called them – somehow in balance, but dynamic, and capable of further evolution. Rather than merely the survival of the fittest individuals or species. Natural selection getting better at natural selection. Never thought about it like that before. Your brother and Weber … Did they know each other?'

'They were acquainted. But I don't understand. Surely you know that?'

She lit a Waldorf.

'No, I didn't. When Weber told me he'd recommended me to you – when your brother disappeared – he didn't say he knew him. At least, I'm fairly sure he didn't.'

'Odd,' she said, exhaling a cloud of white smoke.

'Odd?'

'Yes,' she said. 'He's asked me a few times how your investigation is going. Not in so many words but that was the gist of it. So I presumed you'd told him … I'd assumed you told him that I had asked you to—'

'To look into the circumstances surrounding your brother's death?'

'Yes', she said. 'And that you'd known that he knew Dolfi.'

'I haven't seen him since. And I've never discussed anything with him. I hardly know him. Though I was at his house on the Berggasse once …'

'I must have misunderstood,' she said.

At some stage he would have to talk to Weber. He didn't relish the prospect. There was something intimidating about the man. Perhaps the best thing was to wait until he heard from MacLean – which he was sure he soon would. The Englishman might be somewhat eccentric in his manners but he was proficient at what he put his mind to – that, at least, was the impression he'd got when they'd worked together that time on the Lloyd's case.

13

The letter from MacLean, in a brown envelope, had no return address or any indication of the sender. It was typewritten, in English, and long:

The details you provided regarding CC were more than enough to go by. M, as you correctly guessed, is a small place. CC's employers (or rather previous employers) have a 'facility' there. The village is typical for that part of England, and to the casual visitor seems a place where the lives of its inhabitants have been barely touched by twentieth-century metropolitan hectic. The excursion was a welcome break. London was experiencing a particularly bad 'peasouper' at the time (one of our frequent yellow-green fogs).

The boarding house where she used to reside was easy enough to find. The landlady (I shall simply call her Mrs X) rents out two rooms and provides evening meals. Her husband runs a small butcher's shop (the relevance of which will become clear below). I introduced myself as a solicitor's agent on a benign mission to track down CC on the grounds that she had been left a substantial inheritance and so on. Mrs X was the talkative type. She described CC as a 'quiet woman', a frequenter of the newly-opened public library, 'a bit posh' and 'a bit fussy about her food' (the relevance of which will also become clearer below).

Mrs X informed me that CC used to work at the facility above mentioned, but that she had left rather suddenly round about mid-1917. She took the early morning Saturday train to London at the beginning of her annual two-week summer holiday, which she had arranged to take in June rather than in August. At the time there was nothing thought to be odd or amiss about this. However, when she did not return, Mrs X informed me that a gentleman from the aforementioned facility called round several times enquiring as to her whereabouts – twice in the company of a policeman (an officer of rank, not a simple uniformed constable). Her rooms were searched, and some items were taken away. Mrs X also told me that CC used to receive regular mail from London – always addressed in the same hand, with a Whitechapel postmark on it. (What would we sleuths do without nosey landladies and concierges!) I assume she told the police this as well. The good landlady was unwilling to let me see CC's room as it had long since been let to a new lodger.

But – and I was surprised the police had not taken them – she said that CC had left some effects. They were in a cardboard box. It wasn't much: a few items of clothes, a pair of rubber Wellington boots, some bottles of perfumes and items of crockery – the latter wrapped carefully in newspaper. At first, I assumed CC had packed it all in the box herself – with the intention of having it forwarded to her or collected – not that that made much sense. But, in passing, Mrs X said that she had packed them herself and said she would be happy if I took them off her hands and returned them to CC when I eventually 'caught up with her'. I was about to demur but said I would without really thinking about it – in hindsight a wise decision.

When I got back to London, I made a discreet enquiry with a reliable source we have in the London Metropolitan Police Service. I wanted to know if CC was any on any wanted list, if there was a warrant for her apprehension. There was no warrant. However, she is on their missing-persons list.

I also had another look at the contents of the cardboard box containing the effects CC had left behind in the boarding house in M. And by the sheerest chance I noticed that the newspaper Mrs X had wrapped CC's perfume bottles and items of crockery was a monthly called the *Vegetarian Clarion*. Odd, I thought, for a woman whose husband ran a butcher's shop to subscribe to a vegetarian newspaper – but then I remembered that she had described CC as 'fussy eater'. Had what she meant was that CC was a vegetarian? Quite possibly, I thought. So, it seemed most likely that the newspaper was CC's and, not imagining that it would be available in M, that she was a subscriber. And if she was a subscriber, was it even remotely possible that she was still a subscriber, and that the *Vegetarian Clarion* might have her new address? A bit of a long shot, as our American cousins say, but I had little else to go on. The *Vegetarian Clarion* is published from an address in Whitechapel.

I am reasonably familiar with Whitechapel, a district of East London. Our company has on several occasions been engaged by the Eurasian Bear to make discreet enquiries among its emigrant milieu there. Most of it is a slum (infamous because of a series of unsolved and particularly horrifying murders that took place there at the end of the last century), a haunt of idlers, Eastern European Jews (you hear as much Yiddish as you do English, if the dialect spoken by the place's natives can be called English), prostitutes, renters, various sub-categories of the criminal classes, sprinkled with a heady seasoning of assorted anarchists, socialists, pacifists, 'life reformers' and band-playing, soup-dispensing, Christian proselytisers attempting to save them from the errors of their ways.

The *Vegetarian Clarion* shares offices in a rather dingy converted workshop with an organisation calling itself the British Indian Rationalist Association. When I called, the only person there was a turbaned chap seated at his desk under a large framed photograph of Sir Rabindranath Tagore (Bengali rhymester, won the Nobel prize for literature a few years back) and the flag of the proposed Dominion of India: a green-white-and-orange horizontal tricolour with a theosophist hooked cross – I think it's called a *svastika* – superimposed on the white, and the Union Jack in the corner. The turbaned chap informed me that the *Clarion* person was out to lunch, so I waited and he appeared about ten minutes later.

Still playing the benign solicitor, I introduced myself to the man – who in truth looked more like a vicar with a cosy country living, a man habituated to regular Sunday roasts rather than plain fare – and made my humble enquiries. I said I had an important letter regarding an inheritance I wished to deliver to Miss CC and so on.

I told him that I had good reason to believe that CC was a subscriber to his worthy publication. He checked his card index box and told me that a lady of that name had been a subscriber but that her subscription had lapsed, and that he was not at liberty to give me her address. He offered to post any communication I had onto her. But I wriggled out of that by saying that it had to be delivered personally, showing him the envelope, which I'd presciently marked 'personal delivery'.

The Whitechapel branch of the CMD – that's what this Campaign for Mutual Disarmament is more commonly known as here – has offices in a building called Levellers House, a haunt of various subversives. There is a printing press is on the ground floor; and upstairs, a workingmen's club and library up above that, and on the top floor is the CMD office.

The walls of the stairway were plastered with posters advertising all the usual causes: equal rights for the gentler sex, the Malthusian League, the International Workingmen's Association, Marie Stopes's Mothers' Clinic for Constructive Birth Control, the Anarchist Society, the so-called Wobblies (the ONE BIG UNION crowd), a Californian periodical called *Mother Earth* and so on.

The offices were larger than I expected: half a dozen desks with typewriters, stacks of *Peace in Our Time* (their periodical), and boxes of leaflets for a big march in the offing. There was a rather spectacular view of the city from the window: a sea of roofs and chimneys that seemed to stretch until the ends of the earth. The river, busy with the trade of the world, and London Bridge were visible. It was an unusually clear day. London in all her shit and glory, as we say. But I digress.

I spoke to a young woman who seemed to be some kind of secretary. I had a feeling that pretending to be a benign solicitor was hardly going to wash, so I posed as a fellow radical and gave a vague story about having recently returned from Italy. I was loud about it. I wanted to be noticed. I was aware that it was unlikely that I would be told much, if anything. But perhaps there would be somebody there who might wonder why I was interested in CC, somebody who knew something about her – bait, as it were.

The secretary lady said the name CC meant nothing to her but then (which I had not expected) she asked the others – there were half a dozen other people there – if anyone knew of her. Her query was met by the shaking of heads and mumbled disavowals. I left and made my way down the stairs. But before I'd reached the front door, one of the characters who had been in the office (and who'd obviously run after me) caught up with me. He was a young man, perhaps in his mid-twenties, poorly but neatly dressed, bowler-hatted, and slightly breathless.

'Did you say CC?' he asked me, the emphasis on the Christian name. From his accent, I judged him to be a member of what we call the 'lower middle classes', as many of these radicals are.

I answered him in the affirmative.

'You've been in Italy?' he asked.

He was obviously – how shall I put it? – checking my revolutionary credentials.

'Yes,' I said. I mentioned Malatesta and Kropotkin. Their antics in Milan are being regularly reported in the newspapers here.

He then introduced himself – I shall simply call him HP – and muttered something about 'man equal, unclassed, tribeless, and nationless'. I think it's a line from Shelley or one of that lot.

'The name does sound somehow familiar,' he said. 'I could ask around. But I can't talk now.' He was looking around him as if he was afraid that somebody might be listening to us, which was patently absurd. The stairway was empty. It was an act of course, but I couldn't have known that at the time. 'Could we meet later? The Lyons teashop in Jubilee Street, off Commercial Road? The day after tomorrow, in the afternoon, at about three?'

Needless to say, I agreed.

Jubilee Street, situated in what is known as the anarchist quarter, is fairly notorious. The Workers' Friend Club is located there: a hornets' nest of Jewish anarchists, and the headquarters of the notorious Rudolf Rocker. (Rocker, a German who pretends to be a Jew though everybody knows he isn't – he picked up Yiddish in Paris – runs the *Der Arbeter Fraint*, a Yiddish insurrectionist rag. A few years ago, during the big garment workers' strike in the East End of the city – he managed to turn it into a daily, which it still is.) Lyons teashops are a bit of an institution here. There's one in every town, more or less – and there must be a couple of hundred of them in London. Small affairs, most of them, cosy in an English sort of way, entirely different to your Viennese coffee houses. Gallons of tea rather than coffee. No free ink and paper, I'm afraid, a fairly limited selection of newspapers, and no encyclopaedia to peruse; and the coffee (or rather tea) is not freely on tap once you've bought your first cup.

HP was waiting for me at a table in an alcove at the back of the teashop – but he was not alone. At this stage I did not know what to think. Was he genuine or a police informer of some kind? Or perhaps even a bit of both. Men do have a tendency to become what they pretend to be.

But it was his companion who spoke.

'Hallo, Mister MacLean, a pleasure to meet you,' he said, folding away the copy of *The Manchester Guardian* he had been reading. It was the Wednesday after Black Tuesday – as we call it here – the day of the Crash; and before I knew it, he was shaking my hand vigorously, as if we were already the best of chums. 'I'm Oscar.'

I was taken aback by the fact that he knew my real name but decided not to let it ruffle me.

'I am given to understand that you are looking for Miss CC,' he continued when we were seated again. His accent was distinctly Welsh.

There was a bit of something of the toad about him, of a very clever and observant toad. He wore thick half-moon glasses, and a tweed jacket with brown elbow patches.

'Do you know where she is?' I asked.

A pot of tea and some buttered scones arrived.

'No,' he said. 'I'm afraid we don't.'

'We?' I repeated.

'The authorities whom I represent,' he said. 'Those responsible for law and order, imperial harmony and all that.'

'The Branch?' I asked. Meaning the Special Branch, our British Okhrana. But he ignored the question.

'George,' he said. 'May I call you George?' He didn't wait for a reply. 'Of MacLean and Sons. Gentlemen investigators. I believe that's what you call yourselves. A very respectable firm, by all accounts.'

He extracted his pipe and a tin of Murray's Erinmore.

'We too are very interested in Miss CC,' he resumed, lighting up. 'We have been looking for her – unofficially – for quite some time now. When we find her – and that's only a matter of time, they always turn up somehow in the end – it may become all very seriously official.' The policeman's belief in his omnipotence, always getting his man, or this his case woman! 'But that's by and by. The crux of the matter is that Miss CC has been instrumental in passing on information to an agent of a foreign power. Which, if you check your law books, is a crime you'll find listed under treason of some sort. Which is a very serious matter. The Official Secrets Act and all that.'

'I know nothing about that,' I said. 'As far as I'm concerned it's a simple missing person case.'

'I have no reason to disbelieve you,' he said. 'But others, my masters, may not be so – how shall I put it? – credulous. Though that is perhaps too harsh a word. We live in unpredictable times. The Dardanelles did it for Italy. At first, it was only a few strikes but then these anarcho-syndicalist councils were sprouting up like mushrooms and now they've got a full-blown revolution on their hands. We Britons are a cool-headed race, unlike the hot-blooded Latin, mercifully – but now ...' – he indicated his copy of *The Manchester Guardian* – '... we too are heading into uncharted waters ...'

The Erinmore smoke had a sweet, faintly tropical smell.

'I am going to make a polite proposition to you,' he said. 'And it's not a proposition it would be advisable to refuse, politely or otherwise.'

'I'm all ears,' I replied.

'I tell you what we know about Miss CC – and what we don't

know – and, when I have finished, you will tell me what you have found out. Are you amenable to that?'

'Yes,' I said. I didn't have much choice.

'Miss CC was an employee of His Majesty's Government at an establishment at a location somewhere in the glorious English countryside,' he said. (This, needless to say, is not quite a word-for-word account of what he said, but as good as for present purposes.) 'There is no need for me to go into the details beyond saying that the work being done at said establishment is of considerable importance to the defence of the empire and all that. She had a rather modest position. Her duties were mainly clerical and secretarial. But it was a position which gave her access to very sensitive information. She started working there in 1914, about the time of all that brouhaha about that Austrian aristocrat being shot at. Prior to that, she had been in other unrelated government departments. And, as far as we can tell, led a normal respectable spinster's life. Yearly holidays in Brighton, sometimes in Wales – in Aberystwyth, lovely place in summer, you should go there sometime – book club member, a mild but generally harmless interest in the National Union of Women's Suffrage Societies.

'But then, at some point, she fell in with some CMD people, with some of its more fanatical adherents. I suppose one could say she was "radicalised" – if that's a word. In particular, she made the acquaintance of a man – Jewish like herself – who called himself Saaldeck. No Christian name. Sounds German or Dutch but could be just made-up. These types like reinventing themselves, giving themselves new names – just like in occult societies – wiping the slate of the past clean, so to speak. But then a lot of these radical organisations do have occult origins. Their emblems are often derived from Masonic and Illuminati symbolism of one kind or another. There may have been a romantic interest, but we are not sure. His real name we have not been able to ascertain. However, we do have some photographs of him.'

He took an envelope out of his pocket and extracted two photographs. They were of a public meeting. I could tell it was on

Trafalgar Square from the statue of one of the lions in the background. There were about half a dozen people, both men and women, on the podium, standing behind a man addressing the crowd. They were standing under a banner which read: DREADNAUGHTS – NO THANKS!

'Saaldeck is the speaker. That's George Bernard Shaw beside him, the one with the nineteenth-century beard.' (Shaw is an Irish playwright, and well known for his wit. His *Forward to Methuselah* is playing to packed houses in the West End at the moment. It's set thirty thousand years in the future, or something like that, when men live as long as Methuselah.) 'And that is ...' he pointed at the other figures on the podium – '... Sir Roger Casement, the Congo-rubber-scandal man, and Bertrand Russell, the mathematician. The woman is Sylvia Pankhurst ...'

(The Female Suffrage Bill is before the House of Commons at the moment and expected to pass – the Mother of Democracies cannot be seen to lag behind the Kaiser's Germany! There are white-green-purple flags and bunting all over the place – the colours of the Women's Social and Political Union – and posters announcing a mass demonstration in Hyde Park which is expected to draw an even larger crowd than the one in '08; they say that was attended by half a million.)

'... and Big Jim Larkin, the Irish Wobbly man. All fairly respectable – with the exception of Big Jim – as far as these things go. The Indian character with the glasses is Ambedkar, the so-called untouchable. As well as being involved with the CMD, this Saaldeck is also a leading figure – behind the scenes, shall we say – in the International Workingmen's Association, the so-called International. After CC disappeared, he too went to ground. Took the mail boat to the continent one dark night, we assume.'

Saaldeck was youngish looking, medium height, had one of those toothbrush moustaches. A bit too intense to be called handsome. He was holding his hat, a peaked cap, in one hand, gesticulating with the other.

'We believe that he was supplying information,' the Welshman continued, 'information that he obtained from Miss CC, to an agent of a foreign power.'

'A German spy?' I suggested. These days the only spies one reads about are German spies – and their number is legion, apparently.

'No, Austrian,' he said. 'Who it's possible was posing as some sort of pacifist or some other kind of social revolutionary. But maybe not. All we know is that they met on several occasions and documents changed hands.'

'What kind of documents?' I asked.

'That I cannot divulge.'

'And this Austrian?' I asked him.

'He went by the name of Wartenheim, Konrad Wartenheim. He was not a member of their diplomatic corps or officially connected with the embassy but he did pop in there a few times. That could have been for some above-board business but we doubt it. We only found out about him because we were keeping a discreet eye on our Mister Saaldeck. Saaldeck also made trips to the continent. We suspect to Vienna. Which we don't think was for the waltzing and the pastry.'

'I see,' I said, though of course, I didn't.

HP ordered another pot of tea. It was the first time he'd spoken.

'Now,' Oscar said. 'Your turn. The whole truth, mind you, and nothing but. Best for all concerned that way.'

I told them what I knew. Which, of course, was precious little.

'You neglected to say who your client was,' he said when I had concluded, filling his pipe again.

'An investigative agency in Vienna,' I said. I could hardly have told him anything else. 'Sometimes our work has an international aspect. Missing persons do hop on the mail boat to Calais. We've worked with them on occasion in the past.'

He exchanged a glance with HP. It was the only time there was really any communication between the two of them during the whole of our conversation.

'By the name of?' he asked.

I told him.

'Tell me more,' he said.

I told him nothing amiss, just said Pechstein and Pechstein were a respectable member of the security and investigative business community, uncoverers of embezzlement and the like, sang your praises.

'A bit of a coincidence, don't you think,' he said, 'them also being Austrian ...'

'I suppose so,' I said, 'but ...'

'You didn't say why these Pechstein and Pechstein chaps were looking for her,' he continued. 'Presumably, they don't just pick names out of a spiked helmet and declare them missing persons.'

'They didn't say,' I said. Which, as you know, is the truth.

'Curious,' he said.

'But, as I said, it was a rather informal request,' I said.

'In response to which you have gone to a considerable effort,' he said.

I told him it was a chance to get out of the office. If he thought I was being facetious he didn't show it.

'Do you have any idea where she might be?' I asked. I felt it was my turn to ask a question. His answer surprised me.

'We are sure she has left the country,' he said. 'We think she's gone to that Jewish colony that Germans are setting up in Africa.'

With that, our conversation more or less came to an end.

But before I left, he said: 'Mr HP followed you from Levellers House. That's how we found out who you are. Oldest trick in the book.' At which HP smiled gleefully at me.

As for CC's motives in all of this: my guess is that she was an impetuous lady driven by misguided pacifist ideals rather than anything else. So, if she betrayed her country, it was most likely not for the love of another, but for an idea. I doubt if her being Jewish, which 'Oscar' had sort of vaguely intimated, had anything to do with it. If this all sounds a little like the convoluted plot of a Gilbert and Sullivan operetta, a farcical tale of spies spying on spies spying on spies, at least these spying games are better than shooting wars.

PS: Managed to get over to Antwerp for the Olympics with some old school chums. Had a spiffing time.

The letter was simply signed GML. Despite being peppered with English idioms that – it was obviously written by a man who did not speak a foreign language – Pechstein had understood the essentials. And as for the MacLean's attempt at opacity: he had little doubt that the British secret police, if they had a mind to, would hardly have much trouble ascertaining the identities of 'Oscar' and 'HP', or 'CC' and 'Mrs X'.

So much for the mysterious Constance Cohen. The German Kaiser's Zion, in the unlikely event that it took off, was a rather adroit political move: a way of cosying up to the Rothschilds, a slap in the face for Russia (from where the majority of the settlers were to come from, in theory), the founding of a German-speaking settler colony, and enhancing the German Empire's pretentions to be seen as a protector of Jewry and non-Christian peoples. Funnily enough, the name Konrad Wartenheim sounded vaguely familiar.

***

Lieber Siegfried,

I am writing to you with a request that will no doubt sound odd to you and which concerns my brothers' disappearance and death.

But first, I would like to say that I remember very well your attending Dolfi's funeral and your kind words to me on that day, for which I have never properly thanked you. And my apologies for not replying to the kind note you left me when you called round some weeks later. How I functioned in the long months that followed I still do not know. The existence of everything seemed relentlessly pointless.

When Dolfi disappeared, I engaged a private investigator to try and find him. Later, when his poor lifeless body was found in Preßburg, I asked this investigator to look into the matter. To date, nothing very substantial has come of this private investigator's queries. But last week he informed me of a woman who might have had some dealings with Dolfi – and perhaps had been in contact with him after his disappearance. This woman is an

Englishwoman by birth, and forty or so years of age. Her name is Constance Cohen and she is believed to have emigrated to the Jewish colony in the Protektorat, perhaps a year or a couple of years ago, perhaps even earlier.

I know none of the details of your duties in the Protektorat, and I realise it is an extensive country, but would it be possible – assuming that you are in a position to do so – if you could perhaps make an enquiry as to if she is resident in the colony? I would be in your debt for any assistance you could give me in this regard. Perhaps there is a central register of settlers or something of that sort.

I don't know if this means anything, but for some reason, I feel compelled to ... Do you remember that strange bearded man in a sort of mediæval habit who stood at the back of the gathering in the churchyard (I don't think he was at the service)? I was only vaguely aware of him. At the time, he was just another apparition in a world of apparitions. But I think I remember seeing you and him in conversation. I vaguely remember him shaking my hand – and offering condolences in a very formal but sincere manner. I do not remember him giving me his name and I was too distraught to even think of asking. Well, a few months ago he came to see me. His name is Gusto Grass. He knew Dolfi from Ascona. (Dolfi used to describe it as a place where 'the contours of a utopia were sometimes visible'. He was a bit of an idealist, as I'm sure you know.) We spoke for a long time. We simply chatted – but somehow, afterwards, I realised (though it did not come up in our conversation) that to find the will and energy to live we need to embrace our lives, not merely accept them – not to do so is to live like a ghost in a ghostly desert of a world. Gusto's visit and this realisation – revelation even – are somehow inseparable in my mind. I do not understand it, but at least now I am finding some inner strength to struggle on. But I am not consoled. I will never find consolation.

(There is a verse somewhere – in the New Testament? – I am not sure – about how angels appear as strangers when least expected, and at moments when those to whom they appear are wandering lost through the valley of the shadow death or some such.)

Please do not think of me as a hysterical woman trying to find sense where there is none to be found. My request, unusual and odd as it may be, is serious. It is a matter which weighs heavily upon me.

I hope this finds you in good health.

Mit lieben Grüßen, Anja Jensen

14

A buxom, blond domestic – she had a Rumanian accent – led Pechstein down the carpeted hallway, knocked perfunctorily on the door to Weber's study and opened it.

The academic was sitting behind a large green-baize-surfaced desk. Pechstein was immediately reminded of the Buddha-bellied demon statues in the Chinese temple where he'd had that extraordinary meeting with Polanyi.

'Welcome to my Holy of Holies,' Weber said, adding by way of explanation, 'My refuge from the world. I call it that. Private joke. Take a seat.'

Pechstein had been in the house only once before – to attend a monthly meeting of the Austrian Society for Psychical Research; his interest had been erratic – but he had not been further than the drawing room.

'They keep that which lies beyond the boundaries of what little we really know at bay,' Weber said, referring to his book-laden bookshelves.

'How many are there?'

'A thousand tomes in all, give or take,' Weber informed him, adding, in a sudden change of tone, 'How can I be of assistance? You were not very specific in your letter.'

'It's about Adolf Jensen,' Pechstein said, deliberately saying no more. He wanted to see Weber's immediate reaction to the statement, without putting it into any sort of context.

Weber nodded, slowly. It was a nod that could have meant that he was totally surprised by the statement, or the opposite.

For form's sake, Pechstein was about to say that Anja Jensen had continued to engage him after Dolfi's body had been found, and had asked him to attempt to 'throw some light on the circumstances of her brother's death' – but Weber spoke first.

'Fraulein Jensen is not wholly convinced that the official version of her brother's death is the whole story?' Weber said.
'And you think I might know something?'

'You did know him? That is correct, isn't it?'

Weber extracted his silver cigarette case and offered Pechstein a Sobranie. Both men lit up from Weber's desk lighter, a device in the shape of a military aëroplane; the flame came out of a machine gun mounted in front of the cockpit.

'Yes, I knew him. A gifted young man. Rather gifted, in fact. But – how shall I put it? – of his age.'

'Of his age?'

'Inexperienced in the ways of the world. But, I suppose, any man with an ounce of life in him is prone to youthful folly of one kind or another. In my experience ...' Pechstein let him continue in this vein for a while. With Weber not knowing what he knew, perhaps he would say something that might provide him an opening of sorts. Pechstein did not relish the prospect of confronting him directly with the fact that he been 'mentioned in dispatches' from Berlin; but if he handled this correctly, perhaps it might not be necessary. Weber's Buddha-like physique and an obviously powerful intellect that gazed out into the world through darting bespectacled eyes made him uneasy. '... beyond the biological fact that he was her twin and male – in more ways than one, her mirror image. Anja, in temperament, tends towards masculine; whereas he is ... or rather *was* ... temperamental, impetuous more often than not, and her inverse in many ways.'

Then he simply added: 'I recruited him for them'.

'For them?' Pechstein repeated, taken aback by the unexpected confession.

'For the StaPo. For the Castle. It's something I used to do.'

'Patriotic duty and all that,' Pechstein suggested half-jestingly, trying to maintain his composure.

'I prefer to think that my ideas are a little more sophisticated than that. The bourgeois state needs eyes – and ears – if it is not to become a lumbering cyclops. It needs to be informed if it is to function efficiently, to play its proper historical role.'

'Which is?'

'Its *mission civilisatrice.* imperfectly discharged thought it may be at times.'

Weber stubbed out the butt of Sobranie in the half-full ashtray on his desk.

'When I was approached by the powers that be,' he continued, 'and asked if I might be inclined to help, to make a humble contribution, I felt – as a member of the bourgeoisie – somewhat obliged, as it were, to oblige. The cloak-and-dagger aspect of it all did rather intrigue me. You look surprised. But surely you know how these things work?'

'Somewhat,' Pechstein said.

'But, as I said, my role was somewhat humble.'

'How humble?'

'I was asked to keep an eye out for possible informants among the studentry, young men on the fringe of various movements.'

'Such as?'

'Oh, the usual suspects. The pan-Germanists, the pan-Slavists, the anti-Semites, the philo-Semites, all that collection of reactionary idealists and anti-modern modernists who haunt the hallowed halls of academia. The various hues of social revolutionaries – who are considered the more dangerous – all these communists, socialists and anarchists loathe private property. And private property is the economic and ethical bedrock of bourgeois civilisation.'

'To which political category was Jensen considered to belong?'

'He had rather eclectic tastes. Dipped his intellectual toes in many waters. The Kropotkin Society. Landauer's Socialist Federation. Went to meetings of Steiner's anthroposophists a lot. The Colonial Society. Even the Aëronautical Society. The mutual disarmament crowd was another of his intellectual-political waterholes. It was his eclecticism that made him particularly interesting. People were used to him popping up at all sorts of meetings and events. That made him potentially a useful informant, I thought. And the Castle agreed. So I had a discreet word with him, put him in touch with some people.'

Pechstein wondered what Weber thought he knew already.

'He was offered translation work,' Weber continued, 'but that was a teaser. The idea was that he would provide more or less regular reports on various groups, on those he was not particularly sympathetic to at first – *de rigueur* when one wants to gradually get a man used to being an informer – but eventually also on the social-revolutionary scene, which was where his political sympathies, vague as they were, seemed to lie. But, I was told, he proved stubbornly old-fashioned about telling tales out of school. So, in the end, he ended up mainly doing translation work – at which he was very good.'

'Any sort of translation work in particular?'

'I was never informed as to the specifics. But I don't think it was anything that top secret. He was always held at arm's length, never entirely trusted.'

'So why did they keep him on the books?'

'Because there's always the future. One never really knows how the ways of the world are going to unravel. Always useful to have a man in place. No need to burn bridges if one doesn't have to.'

'And did something turn up?' Pechstein asked, wondering why Weber had decided to tell him any of this. It was hardly a Raskolnikovian unburdening of the soul, though he seemed to feel a need to justify it for some reason.

'Not that I know of. However, I don't think I was ever told the truth of it all, not the whole truth as they say. But one never is with this sort of thing.'

'Does the name Constance Cohen mean anything to you?' Pechstein asked him. 'Did Jensen ever mention anyone of that name? English. Mid-forties maybe. Unmarried. Jewish.'

'No,' Weber said.

Pechstein decided it was probably the truth.

'Or the name Saaldeck?'

Weber shook his head.

'Or Wartenheim?'

'Sounds vaguely familiar,' Weber said, shaking his head again. 'But no, can't say I have. Definitely not. Is he a real person?'

'A real person?'

'Sounds like a fictional character for some reason. Not that I'm a great fiction reader.'

Pechstein wondered if perhaps 'Wartenheim' might be a pseudonym, based on a character in a book or play. It was plausible.

'After Jensen disappeared, did anyone talk to you about it?'

'You mean from the powers that be? Yes.'

Pechstein waited for him to elucidate.

'I had a visit. But it was last year. From two gentlemen, from the StaPo. They were concerned.'

'Concerned?'

'Only to be expected. Jensen was after all an employee of theirs, of sorts. You're not suggesting that the Castle had something to do with his disappearance or death! For God's sake, man, that's insane!'

'Yes, it would be,' Pechstein said.

Weber looked at him. Pechstein did not feel inclined to reassure him that he really did think that such a thing would indeed be insane.

'But,' Weber said, 'as I told you, I am not involved any more.'

'Why did you stop being involved?'

Weber was silent for a moment.

'A change of *Weltanschauung*?' Pechstein could not resist suggesting. 'Nagging doubts about *la mission civilisatrice*?'

Weber laughed.

'Have you read Karl Marx?' he asked.

'Can't say I have,' Pechstein replied. 'Read about him.'

'He got a lot wrong of course, fell victim to what he himself called ideology, his own. But Karl the philosopher of history got a lot right. He was right, by and large, about the material conditions of life-determining social forms and cultures. Clay pots and flint axes produced Stone Age society. The castle and the armoured horseman produced feudalism. The steam engine and electricity produced bourgeois civilisation. Though it goes without saying that's not all there is to it. He clearly recognised that the bourgeoisie is the engine of civilisational progress.'

Weber got up and extracted a slim volume from one of his bookshelves. He showed the cover to Pechstein. It was a copy of the *Manifesto of the Communist Party*.

'By Marx and Friedrich Engels,' he said. 'Not many outside socialist circles have read it. Some workers read it. But where it really only safely belongs is on the bookshelves of the private libraries of the thinking bourgeoisie.'

Weber began to flip through it.

'The bourgeoisie has been the first class to show what man's activity can bring about,' he said, then began to read, '"It has accomplished wonders far surpassing Egyptian pyramids, Roman aqueducts, and Gothic cathedrals ... Constant revolutionising of production, uninterrupted disturbance of all social conditions, everlasting uncertainty and agitation distinguish the bourgeois epoch from all earlier ones. All fixed, fast-frozen relations, with their train of ancient and venerable prejudices and opinions, are swept away, all new-formed ones become antiquated before they can ossify. All that is solid melts into air, all that is holy is profaned, and man is at last compelled to face with sober senses his real conditions of life, and his relations with his kind. The need of a constantly expanding market for its products chases the bourgeoisie over the entire surface of the globe ... given a cosmopolitan character to production and consumption in every country." End of quote. Capitalism. Imperialism. Science. Can you think of a more exact description of the world we live in?'

'Not really.'

'Though to a large degree it's merely cultural mimesis—'

'Mimesis?'

'Imitation ... a defence mechanism used throughout history when a society comes into contact with another society that is technologically superior to it … though that which is imitated is not always what should be imitated and often profoundly misunderstood.'

'Of course, Marx and Engels believed that the bourgeoisie was sowing the seeds of its own destruction. But I do not see any sign of that. Do you? And that the proletariat – God help us! – should one day initiate a civilisation …'

Pechstein thought of saying that it could very well be argued – and that he believed it was the case – that no small part of the liberties enjoyed by men under the bourgeois regime had been hard fought for by coal miners and factory proletarians, but thought better of it.

'And the Crash?' he said instead. 'Didn't Marx predict that capitalism would collapse?'

'Crashes come and go, and this one will not be the last.'

'But …' Pechstein began to object. A few days previously he'd been walking along on the Bräunerstraße. The rain had been bucketing down from a grey sky and a trio of heavily intoxicated city tramps had taken refuge in the alcove of the Unionbank. One of them, a weather-beaten, bald-headed soul, was squatting with his trousers down, defecating on the doorstep of the august institution.

'But there's always the possibility of catastrophe.' Weber said. 'That's what you were going to say. Isn't it!' It wasn't, but Pechstein let it pass. 'The slightest rumour of war has the stock exchanges of the world going into a downward spiral. The bourgeois world has no intention of destroying itself in some holocaust. The world is being run by the most enlightened societies that have ever existed, run by the most enlightened social class that has ever existed: Bourgeois Man, the product of the Enlightenment, the likes of you and me, and millions like us in our own small ways. Even the social democrats yearn only to turn workers into waged bourgeois. The natives of the tropics are slowly becoming civilised – and in time they too will become bourgeois, of their own volition, once they are shown the way. Admittedly, it can be a messy business, and at times …'

'That's one way of putting it.' Pechstein said. 'And Izmir? Gas-bombing civilians is not particularly civilised.'

'Unfortunate. A temporary reversion. And there was an international outcry.'

Pechstein could not help thinking that the trouble with men with formidable intellects was that they were able to convince themselves of what they wished. Though he did not necessarily disagree with much of what Weber said.

'So, if it wasn't a change of *Weltanschauung*, why did you become uninvolved?'

'I lost … how shall I say? … my taste for it,' Weber said.

Pechstein looked at him, unconvinced.

Weber thought about it for a moment.

'There was an incident … a young man I recruited … whose romantic inclinations ran in what could be called a contrary direction to what is morally and legally acceptable … his Castle handlers put pressure on him to go further in the line of duty than he was inclined to go … It ended rather tragically … but I shall say no more. These things happen. We'll never live in a perfect society. The gentlemen from the StaPo who paid me a call were particularly concerned about your investigations. The StaPo don't like being scrutinised by outsiders, or rumours getting out of hand.'

'So they know about my investigation?'

'Oh, yes. They asked me to have word with you.'

'To what purpose?'

'To advise you of the folly of your inquisitions.'

'But you didn't?'

Weber ignored the question.

'You are being watched. Many eyes, as I said, and many ears … in all sorts of places.'

'You mean at the Agency?'

Weber made a barely detectable affirmative nod.

It made sense, of course. It would have been strange if the Castle did not have someone at the Agency keeping a discreet eye on things. He wondered who it might be. Not that Werner himself did not himself pass information onto them; he was well aware of the necessity of keeping in with the Castle.

'If there was anything amiss about Jensen's tragic death,' Weber continued, 'I am sure it has nothing to do with his activities for the StaPo ... The Castle is not the Peter and Paul Fortress. The StaPo is not the Okhrana. They are secretive, yes. That is the nature of such beasts. One can hardly expect them to make a public announcement in the *Wiener Zeitung* stating that they had nothing to do with the whole affair. It's not for me to tell you that I think you are barking up the wrong tree but ... The police know their business. And as far as I know, they have no reasons for thinking any foul play was involved. I am fond of Fraulein Jensen. I can only think that dragging it all out like this does not help her one iota.'

'Perhaps you are right,' Pechstein said.

Before he left, he asked Weber if he was still involved in the Society for Psychical Research.

'No,' he said. 'I gradually drifted away. Perhaps one day it will be put on some kind of scientific footing. This new physics might give us some sort of theoretical framework. Who knows?'

***

Kaiserliche Königliche Österreichische Post
Von: *herr s bell*
An: *frau a jensen. zedlitzgasse 14. vienna*
Datum: 11. 11. 1920
letter received. making enquiries. siegfried bell

1921

15

None of his four-man audience had ever seen anything quite like the machine – which vaguely resembled a printing machine of some sort – that Brockhaus was showing them.

'The operating principle is simple yet ingenious,' he explained, 'and is not new. French textile manufacturers used punchcards to automise weaving patterns into fabrics in the eighteenth century. But the first to come up with the idea of using them to store information and then retrieve it mechanically was a Russian by the name of Korsakov in the 1830s who worked in the statistics department of Saint Petersburg Police Ministry. And railway conductors have been using punchcard tickets for decades to make punch-"photographs" of passengers. The tickets have columns for, say, hair colour, facial hair, body size and so on. Under the hair colour, holes are punched for dark, brown, blond, grey and bald, and so on. And the same for other physical characteristics.'

Sigrid Kupfer added some of the A6-sized punchcards to a stack already in a rack at the front of the machine and pressed a button. The machine's internal mechanisms made a whirring, rattling sound as it swallowed and sorted them, and spat them out at an impressive speed into another rack at the back of the machine.

'This marvel of engineering is from DEHOMAG – Deutsche Hollerith-Maschinen – in Berlin,' Brockhaus continued. 'Though originally it's an American invention.'

'Fascinating,' Count Wolfgang von Burkheim said. He was a big man with a leonine grey beard and a full head of equally grey and shaggy hair, and was from the Ministry for the Promotion of Science and Industry.

The other three other members of the delegation were Rudolf Jürgens from the Office of Public Health and Hygiene and the Austro-Hungarian Eugenics Association, a Herr Schmidt from the Census Bureau, and a Herr Konrad Wartenheim from a government department vaguely named the Office of Assessments and Surveys.

'And now for Exhibit B,' Brockhaus said.

The four men followed him into another room. There were two new-looking apparatus on a bench: a camera on a stand, its lens facing downwards, and a device that looked like a cross between a lightbox and a microscope with two eyepieces. Beside them were some reels of what looked like miniature cinematographic film.

'This …' – Brockhaus held up a strip of the film – '… is what is called microfilm, and this is the camera that it's used in.' A book, its pages flattened by a small pane of glass, lay open directly below the camera's lens. 'Again, microfilm is not a recent invention. The Paris Communards communicated with Tours using pigeons carrying microfilmed documents. They were read by projecting the images onto a screen with a magic lantern. But these days we use this device here.'

He switched on the lightbox-microscope apparatus. The image of a page from a scientific journal appeared on the glass screen.

'In theory, it's possible to fit at least twenty million words onto a square centimetre of microfilm – which, I'm sure you'll agree, is rather impressive. Indeed, I can foresee the days when it will be possible to print any book on request using some kind of photographic process.'

When the tour was over, Brockhaus led his audience into the Mundaneum's boardroom and passed around a box of Cuban cigars. All the men lit up and aromatic smoke quickly filled the room.

'Otlet and La Fontaine,' Brockhaus resumed as the cognac decanter made the rounds, 'looked into the future and they saw that the day would come – if it has not already come – when scientific advancement would take place at such a rate that scientists would be overwhelmed by the sheer volume of information being produced – unless a new and efficient system for making it accurately, quickly and cheaply accessible was developed.'

Sigrid was jotting down his words in shorthand at a small desk against the wall. Out of sight and out of mind, she could not help thinking, a fly on the wall at the deliberations of the good and the great.

The first one to speak was the small man from the Office of Assessments and Surveys. As to exactly what the function this organ of state performed, Brockhaus had earlier said 'ours is not to pry' and winked.

'So,' Wartenheim said, 'for example, let's say that we had cards for everyone in Austria, with holes in positions indicating the year of birth and residence. And I wanted to find all the people born in Vienna in 1890. You'd run all the cards through the machine and it would select only the cards with the hole positions for 1890 and Vienna. And likewise, with appropriate holes on the cards, one would be able to sort them into male or female, or by nationality, or religious affiliation, and so on.'

'More or less,' Brockhaus said.

Then the blond and blue-eyed Jürgens, the man from the Office of Public Health and Hygiene, spoke.

'How much information can you actually put on one card?'

'It depends on the size of the card. The ones we are using have ten rows and forty-five columns. Which makes for four hundred and fifty discrete items of information. The Hollerith can sort up to three hundred cards a minute. The Americans rate the calculating power of these types of machines in girl hours or kilo-girls.'

Von Burkheim frowned inquisitively.

'Girl hours refer to how long a real girl computer takes to perform a computing operation,' Brockhaus explained. 'And a kilo-girl is equivalent to the machines' horsepower, as it were.'

'Public health policy in the twentieth century will require that the collection of considerable quantities of information on each individual citizen,' Jürgens said. 'A sort of citizenography, one could call it.'

Sigrid noticed that he was wearing a wristwatch.

'Such as?' Schmidt – from the Census Bureau – asked.

'Height, weight, vaccination records, disease records, blood types, and all other sorts of physiological dimensions and the like. Who is descended from whom. Inheritable debilities, both physical and mental.'

The expression on von Burkheim's face as he listened to Jürgens hovered between suspicion and curiosity.

'Modern life, unsanitary conditions, overcrowded cities and slums,' Jürgens continued, 'are all exacting a toll on a species which was not designed for mass urban life. You see the result every day on the streets of any European metropolis you wish to name: racial degeneracy. But it's not an easy task to identify individuals who only appear to be degenerate – due to economic or social reasons – from those who are genetically degenerate and will pass on that degeneracy to their offspring. Natural selection works well in the animal kingdom, but in modern human societies – largely due to progress in medical science – that process needs to be managed. There is also an increasing body of evidence to suggest that moral qualities are largely inherited.'

'Moral qualities?' von Burkheim repeated, now more suspicious than curious.

'Character. Intelligence. An American social scientist called Pearson did a study of four thousand children and their parents – using the latest mathematical methods – and demonstrated quite conclusively that character and intelligence are largely hereditary. All human qualities are measurable if one has the appropriate techniques. Craniometry can tell us a lot about the criminal propensities of individuals. But to carry out such studies on a large scale involves a lot of girl hours, as Direktor Brockhaus called them. And then there's the propensities to dipsomania, sexual inversion and the other psycho-pathologies … many inherited, the result of the genetic mix of two parents, four grandparents, sixteen great-grandparents. It is not possible to construct such detailed individual eugenic trees right now, but in ten or twenty or years' time, with the help of these punchcard machines … Social policies based on science: that is the road to healthier populations – and fewer hospitals, fewer asylums, fewer prisons, and considerably less human misery. And, I believe, to a happier society. Happiness through science.'

Schmidt had a serious of technical questions which Brockhaus answered with ease.

Then, the main business over, Count von Burkheim stood up and began what was obviously a planned closing speech:

'Our time is a time of which it can be said: no other epoch has been so obsessed with the future. The future has become our religion. Some describe what the world is today experiencing as a second industrial revolution, an electric industrial revolution, and that the century before us will be a century of the production line and the conveyor belt – and the cheap availability of vast quantities of manufactured goods.

'When I began my career in the Imperial Civil Service thirty or so years ago, a mere generation ago, the overwhelming majority of men and women lived in the countryside, and the rhythm of their lives was set by the seasons – not, as it is today, by the railway timetable and the factory clock – and yesterday was still a reliable guide to tomorrow. Sons followed largely in the footsteps of their fathers, and the seasons came and went. It was a world of the village and the fields, not of the metropolis and the cinema house. Of course, even then new things came into the world – as they always have – but they appeared slowly, one at a time, and only rarely did they upset the balance of life. Today things just change and change. All this is very exciting, but it is also unnerving. Perhaps, I think, because there seems no end to it. Sometimes I ask myself: will the human race ever know rest again, slow days and the soothing regularity of slowly changing seasons? The medical men tell us the current neurasthenia epidemic is nothing less than nervous prostration caused by not being able to keep pace with the dizzying speed of modern life.

'The miracle of the wind-up gramophone was unheard of in the 1880s. An automobile was still called a horseless carriage because it was such a rarity, we didn't even have a proper name for it. There were no telephones, nor means of communicating with ships out of sight of land. While today, with wireless telegraphy, a message can be sent through the ether to anywhere on the globe at the speed of light. They say that in a few years' time there will even be television machines that will be able to send cinematographic images over the ether. Truly, I sometimes fear that *Homo typographicus* will eventually become *Homo cinematographicus*, a befuddled creature whose perception of the world will be formed – or should I say deformed – by the disjointedness and flickering images projected onto screens rather than by the linear logic of great books. There is hardly a field of human endeavour that is not being transformed. Medicine. Soldiering. The list is endless.

'And nothing appears certain. In one of his novellas, that H G Wells fellow had one of his characters say that all the main things have been discovered, and that all that remained for the scientists of the twentieth century to do was to cross the "t"s and dot the "i"s. But then, low and behold, Rutherford and Einstein appeared among us. It has become impossible to predict what lies ahead. The most we can do is speculate, imagine this and that, and the newspapers and magazines are full of such imaginings.

'No doubt all this brings with it astounding possibilities of organising society and promoting human happiness according to the latest scientific principles. But I sometimes ask myself: who is really steering the ship of human society, all these new inventions or man? Indeed, can the ship be steered at all? And what icebergs lie hidden in the fog that stretches out over the uncharted ocean of the twentieth century? Are we on a *Titanic*? The Crash and the collapse of whole industries – for no rational reasons that I can see – must give us pause for serious thought. The factories and the workers are still there, but large numbers of both are suddenly idle, and nobody – as far as I can see – understands why. Some political economists blame the current situation on what they call overproduction. Yet, the streets of Vienna are chock-a-block with the destitute, which if anything would lead one to conclude that the current situation is one rather of under-production and a rather askew distribution of what is produced.

'On the one hand, for better or for worse, our guide must be the past, the past interpreted wisely. For it is in that, sometimes to modern eyes, strange country that morality and ethics, the result of the collective wisdom of past generations, have their genesis.'

And collective follies, Sigrid could not help thinking.

'However, on the other hand,' von Burkheim continued, 'it is also clear the old ways of doing things need serious reform. Some cry out recklessly for social revolution – and who can deny that many profound changes are required if we are to master the possibilities of the modern world – but revolutions are bloody affairs. No, the only prudent way forward, as the emperor himself so succinctly put it when signing the German-Austro-Hungarian Customs Union Treaty, is social monarchy, the synthesis of modernity, tradition and fair play. The common man has got used to improvements and expects more. And right now, he is severely disappointed. In the modern age, the state needs to meet those expectations. Which calls for the rational organisation of production and distribution of the fruits of men's labours for the public good – but within a solid social hierarchy built firmly on the wisdom that we have inherited from those who came before us, and to whom, in the last resort, we owe most of what we are privileged to enjoy in this modern age.'

His speech was greeted by a hearty and congratulatory round of applause.

Brockhaus stood up again.

'Thank you, gentlemen,' he said. 'And with that thought-provoking contribution from Count von Burkheim our proceedings must unhappily draw to a close. Except for one more thing. I have taken the liberty of engaging a photographer to make a permanent record of our meeting here today. So, if you retrieve your coats and hats, we shall proceed to the courtyard, where the good man has set up his apparatus.'

16

The reply from Siegfried Bell was in a blue envelope, and smelled faintly of somewhere far away. The green postage stamp had an elephant on it, and the letter was typewritten.

There is indeed a central register of settlers here – we are a German Protektorat after all – and a Constance Cohen is listed. There are still only four thousand or so Europeans here now, so it can hardly be any other than the woman you mentioned. Her place of birth is given as Shoreditch, London, her parents as George Cohen (originally Coen) of Hamburg and Mathilde Cohen (née Mayer) of Hamelin, her date of birth as 14 August 1880, and current place of residence being one of the New Judea settlements. I spend most of my days in the office here in Von-Humboldt-Stadt, our modest and dusty regional capital, organising this and that; but a week ago, as luck would have it, I was due to make a 'safari ' (Swahili for 'journey') to New Judea as part of my duties (which consists mainly of typing rather dry reports for the Reichskolonialamt in Berlin).

New Judea is not that far by African standards. But it took us two days to get there – our 'roads' in this far-flung corner of the German Empire are little more than vague tracks – in one of our Mercedes-Knights. There are no private automobiles in the colony but there is a government pool of a dozen vehicles, all petrol-driven. And, for some odd reason, most of the driver-mechanics are Berliners. It is hot at this time of the year: the sun transverses the sky with excruciating slowness and is unforgiving. (I sometimes dream of snow, endless vistas of it; and occasionally yearn to be able to wrap up against the cold.) The country is sparsely inhabited, though along the way we passed several villages, primitive affairs, as yet barely touched by the modern world. The native huts are mud-walled structures with simple straw roofs for the most part, though some of the dwellings of the families of chiefs and headmen have thatched roofs as good as those I've seen in Schleswig-Holstein. Whenever we stopped to pay our respects to the local headman, we would be invariably surrounded by the villagers. The sight of the European and his machines is still rare here. Away from Von-Humboldt-Stadt, there are very many natives who have never seen a European.

When I first arrived here, I had somehow imagined that the Africans would mistake me for a fellow African – though I am lighter in complexion – but they never do. In fact, I do not think they have any concept of Africa as such, for them this is merely 'the world' and we are strange beings from somewhere else. 'Africa' is after all the name of a Roman province which we – twentieth-century Romans that we are – have given to this continent. As for race-thinking among them: I think they see us just as another tribe which, like all tribes, has its idiosyncratic peculiarities.

New Judea consists of three settlements or 'kibbutzim' (a Hebrew word), all three quite close to each other; but 'close' in Africa can mean a drive of several hours. Each settlement is laid out around a central square in the centre of which, invariably, stand two flag poles: one flying the Protektorat's imperial tricolour (with elephant's head on a red shield superimposed), and one flying the Star of David flag. Each has workshops and other types of buildings: a small school, a dispensary–apothecary, a general food store and the like. Life revolves around a communal dining hall – which is also used for meetings and has administrative offices attached to it. The kibbutzniks – as they call themselves – live in spartan huts. The land they have been allocated is held in common, and work is organised on a sort of socialist basis. An elected works council decides what needs to be done and allocates tasks. They grow maize, potatoes and various vegetables, and their cash crops are tobacco, sisal and coffee – though these have not brought in much cash yet. To help them do this, they employ the Africans, with whom they sometimes work side by side. In general, they just manage to more or less to feed themselves; other necessities are purchased from funds they receive from the Reichskolonialamt and Internationalist Zionist Fund.

Constance Cohen lives at the settlement called Ararat. We arrived there as the sun was setting, a red-orange ball sinking below the western horizon. None of the Jews at Ararat are particularly religious. There's no synagogue, though there is a rabbi. Constance Cohen's hut – a tin-roofed shack really, though as neat and tidy as that of a Swabian housewife's – is on the edge of the settlement. She looks younger than her forty or so years; though her face is tanned and weathered by the sun.

I had not been sure how to approach her, so I simply told her what you told me in your letter, how you had reason to suspect that she possibly knew your brother, and of the general circumstances surrounding his death. But she said your brother's name meant nothing to her and had no idea why anyone would think it would. But my impression was that she was shocked by what I had told her, rather than merely surprised; as if, perhaps, my query had resurrected some memories that she had hoped were long buried in the past?

'So, how does an Englishwoman end up living in a Jewish colony in the middle of Africa?' I asked her later, a little impolitely perhaps.

We were sitting on her veranda. The moonlit landscape seemed to extend endlessly into the African night. Every now and again, the primeval cry of an animal or bird would interrupt the constant nightly orchestra of the cicadas.

'I could you ask how does a black man end up as a colonial official dealing with Jewish affairs in Africa?' she replied. Her German is grammatically perfect but she does have more than a trace of an English accent.

'To take up the white man's burden?' I suggested jokingly.

She smiled at that.

'Well, I'm a very subaltern colonial official,' I said. 'But that is a question I ask myself often enough. I was offered the position pretty much out of the blue. I knew nothing of Africa – beyond a few stories my father told me – but somebody in Reichskolonialamt seemed to think I did. Maybe they thought they were sending me to the Kamerun. My mother is Jewish. The inscrutable bureaucratic mind put two and two together and came up with five – or perhaps three. There have also been political changes in Berlin. Or perhaps I am simply an experiment. There are not many positions for atmospheric physicists in Europe right now. But I keep my hand in here with some weather recording and the like. And you?'

'The world I inhabited disappeared one day,' she said. 'Sometimes the threads of one's life end up in a knot that can't be undone. And the knot simply needs to be cut.'

I sensed she was going to say more so I said nothing.

'A few years ago I made some decisions based on idealistic sentiments. It made life very difficult.'

'But you seem not have not lost your idealism?' I said, alluding to her coming to Ararat and this whole Jewish project. But she simply shrugged her shoulders enigmatically.

On my way back to my tent I caught a glimpse of a particularly bright shooting star. Its tail, a streak of copper-green light, must have spanned half the arc of the sky. The African night sky is quite as sharply brilliant as the northern, winter night sky, but the Milky Way with its countless stars is much more clearly visible.

The next day we drove to the next settlement, Babel. Like Ararat, it too is a busy place. But Babel – as one might infer from its name – is a more cosmopolitan place, with a fair few Poles and even Russians of various hues. It is situated beside a small river which has crocodiles in it and whose waters, I have been told, end up in the Congo. They have a small herd of Friesland cattle which they are trying to interbreed with the local cattle in the hope of producing a hybrid which combines the quality of the former with the hardiness of the latter. They also have a small letterpress and produce a four-page newssheet every few weeks called *Dos Shvebele* (Yiddish for matchstick, presumably an allusion to the matchstick that is struck to light the flame of their aspirations).

The day I was there, there was a long queue of Africans in front of the dispensary–apothecary. Alone of settlements it has a qualified doctor, a Polish woman from Danzig. One of my tasks was to deliver a chest of various medicines and medical equipment that had been sent from Berlin by the Zionist Fund. Another was to mediate in a dispute over grazing rights on some savannah alongside the river, which I managed to resolve to the half-hearted dissatisfaction of both parties.

It took us another half a day – driving through a landscape rich in wildlife; we even saw a lone bull elephant – to reach the third settlement, called Gibeon (after the name of the battle at which Joshua commanded the sun to stand). It is the most religious of the three. It has an active synagogue and the settlers – the men bearded and always wearing those black hats and those long black coats, and the women in those distinctive shawls, despite the heat – would not look out of place in a Polish shtetl.

What will become of this whole Jewish project – the Kaiser's playing at being a latter-day Cyrus the Great, saving the Chosen People, not by releasing them from a Babylonian exile, but by enabling them to go into permanent exile – it is impossible to say. The British had a plan to found a Jewish settlement in Uganda at the turn of the century but nothing came of that. Prejudice towards Jews is surely slowly dying out – at least among civilised peoples – for there to be much incentive for emigration on any large scale. But, it must be said, the settlers are determined. The worm in the apple of this whole enterprise is, I suspect, relations with the local Africans.

As for the whole imperial enterprise: I think if there is any 'natural law' that can be discerned in the fog of history, it is perhaps that political power structures abhor empty spaces and inexorably expand into lands where there is no power to resist them. And that the pertinent question is not: should this occur? But how can this inevitable process be somewhat civilised?

Rosa Luxemburg and radical social democrats argue that colonies are nothing but a means for exploiting native peoples, with the profits going to plutocratic capital while the metropolitan

proletariats pay the bill. Which is no doubt the truth, if not all of
it.

To modern ears the very word 'Congo' conjures up an image of
hell: Leopold, King of the Belgians – 'Satan and Mammon in one
person' as he has been rightly called – was one of the greatest
mass murderers in the history of the human race. Hangman Carl
Peters in Ostafrika … the list of outrages is endless. But is not the
Congo better off today as an official Belgian colony than it was as
the private fiefdom of Leopold? And India not better off as a
British possession than subject to the predations of the East India
Company? And, it must be admitted, the bulk of the imperial
enterprise would be impossible without the active connivance of
local elites. How else, for example, could the British rule India, a
subcontinent with a population of three hundred million, with
only 100,000 British civil servants and military personnel? It
cannot be solely explained by evil men taking advantage of
innocent men.

So where personally do I stand regarding all this, I ask myself. I
am convinced that the ideal polity is the multinational state. Only
by living intertangled can the nations and religions of the world
learn to live in peace, and leave their ultimately petty nationalist
and racialist prejudices behind them (of the latter, as you can
imagine, I have some personal experience). As for the idea that all
the tribes of Africa (or of the world for that matter) should have
their own one-tribe states: it would be the Balkans on a global
scale! Such states would be independent in name only, their
destinies shaped by their previous masters, who would no longer
have any legal obligations towards them, and the weak among
them would fall prey to the strong. And the minorities and
territory-less peoples such as the Jews: where would they find a
home in polities which are based on race and religion?

To progress, the backward regions of the world will only acquire
technology and capital if they are legal colonies, with loans and
finance and currency guaranteed by their mother countries. Here,
the wiser of the chiefs know the time of clans and tribes is passing
and that their future security is dependent on being part of a

larger polity. The Protektorat is slowly being modernised. Schools are being built, though not enough. That there is much compulsion involved cannot be denied, and much casual brutality in the administration of regulations and laws. But in time these practices will surely disappear as they have disappeared in Europe. And what polity has not had a bloody birth? The British Empire was founded on slavery and opium. Every country in the Americas is grounded on the near extermination of its original inhabitants. We cannot swim against the tide of history. We can only strive to do some good within the history we are fated to find ourselves. There are many who oppose imperialism yet who do not fall into the trap of nationalism: Luxemburg herself and the Indian Tagore come to mind. No, the non-European peoples have the right to be part of the empires and participate in their progress, and not be relegated forever the status of political white spaces on the world map. It is not impossible to imagine a day when representatives from African and the South Seas sit in the Reichstag alongside the representatives of Bavaria and Silesia. A representative from Senegal already sits in the French National Assembly. And the recent decision to grant India what the British call 'dominion status' can only be lauded.

Perhaps in the end all will be subsumed in a sort of World State – if the state-concept has any meaning if there is only one state. (Ironically, the anarchists may be correct: the 'end of history' may be a state-less world society, a 'voluntary empire' with a 'plateforme' organisation structure. I think it hardly a coincidence that Reclus was, and Kropotkin is, a geographer, men who see the world – this small planet – as a whole.) In my reveries, I envision a future world, maybe sometime towards the end of this century, administered rationally by a world government of some type, a sort of a committee of the empires: a prosperous and educated world, with passenger dirigibles sailing the skies and the continents crisscrossed by high-speed electric trains: a world which has moved beyond classifying men by creed, social class, nationality, caste and race. Tagore wrote somewhere: 'There is only one history – the history of man. All national histories are merely chapters in the larger one.' But that is enough of that.

A curious incident occurred on our return-safari to Von-Humboldt-Stadt, which I feel compelled to describe. An old man – clad in a sort of tartan toga (a common item of dress here) and carrying a walking staff decorated with beads – was standing in the middle of the 'road', motionless, obviously wanting us to stop, which we did, though we could easily have driven around him. We tried to speak to him in German but he didn't understand a word. He pointed to an escarpment or ridge perhaps about five kilometres in the distance; it's hard to judge distances in the midday heat haze. It seemed to me he was trying to tell us that there was something there, or something had happened there. Knoll – my driver, one of the Berliners – was about to drive on, thinking the old fellow what he would probably call 'just another crazy African'; but I decided to have look.

So I invited the old man to get into the back of the vehicle and we headed across the savanna – the ground was flat and easily driveable-on – for about a quarter of an hour, until we were more or less on top of the escarpment. Then, the old man began to make gestures again, indicating that this was where we should stop. Immediately we did so, he got out and gestured for me to follow him. Knoll stayed with the automobile while I went up with him to the ridge, not knowing what to expect … and then suddenly I was standing at the edge of a steep cliff and looking out over the landscape below: a vast plain, simmering in the heat of the early afternoon. I could make out small herds of antelopes and wildebeest through my binoculars. Some large solitary birds, eagles or some sort or vultures, were gliding in circles on the hot air updraughts from the plain below. For a few moments I stood sort of mesmerised there. It was almost as if I was looking back through the epochs and seeing the world as it was at the primeval dawn of time, and thought how mankind and all its works were but a fleeting phenomenon. I turned around to say or gesture something to the old man but he was unexpectedly gone, as if he had vanished into thin air.

As I made my way back to the automobile I wondered if he had simply wanted a free ride to this place because he lived or had some business somewhere nearby, or if it had been to show me what I had just seen. One has no idea what the peoples here really think of us. Perhaps we are to them as Laßwitz's Martians would be to us if they landed their space-ships in a Bavarian town square: sources of infinite bewilderment. But then, the truth is we understand as little of the peoples here as Laßwitz's Martians – who had been landing at the North Pole in their solar-electric space-ships for years and thought the Eskimo language was what all Earthmen spoke – understood the human race.

PS: Gusto Grass: I had met him before, at the university, at an evening organised by one of those theosophist groups – or anthroposophist; apparently, there is some significant difference. Not the sort of thing I usually go to. He was not the speaker – and I'm not sure he approved of the group in question – though he did participate in the discussion following the lecture, which was something along the lines of the *Ursubstanz* of the universe being consciousness, and that in dreams we somehow participate in some timeless/eternal realm, that sort of thing. He is certainly someone who sticks in one's mind. Polanyi once told me that he had heard that he had refused to do military service and had been court-martialled, sentenced to death and spent three days in the death cell; but then – obviously realising there was nothing they could do to make him put on a uniform – they had him declared legally insane and sent to a lunatic asylum. Something like that, I imagine, leaves a mark on a man.

17

'Yes, I remember him,' Sigrid said, looking at the photograph in the copy of the *Telegraf* that Polanyi had handed her. 'He was from some government department, the Office of Assessments and something, or something like that.'

The New Ottoman Bazaar was near-empty except for the last of the late-breakfast crowd. The place smelled of oriental spices and food. A snowstorm, visible through the plate-glass windows, was raging in the streets outside. It had come, seemingly, out of nowhere. The sky had been blue and sunny an hour earlier.

'You sure they haven't got the names mixed up?' Polanyi said.

'Yes. I'm sure, his name is Konrad Wartenheim.'

They were speaking in hushed tones. The acoustics of the place were such that, when it wasn't packed, sounds carried – crystal clear – from one end of the high-vaulted saloon to the other.

'The article does not say much,' he said, 'just the usual blah-blah-blah about government in the modern world, changing times and all the rest of it. Is that all this so-called fact-finding mission was really about?'

'More or less. Not everything is a conspiracy.'

'Oh, no?'

She was wearing a green dress, knee-length, and vaguely Grecian. The colour went with her ginger-red hair, which she'd had cut short since the last time he'd seen her. It suited her, he thought. Short hair and free-flowing shorter dresses were in. Corsets, a garment that ambivalently restricted the female body and accentuated the female form, seemed to be slowing falling out of fashion.

'They talked a lot about a so-called citizenography,' she said.

'And what, pray tell me, is that supposed to be?' he said, pretending to flirt, or pretending to pretend to flirt – or maybe he *was* flirting, or trying to, she thought.

'Something like a library card index system, except for people not books. All cross-referenced. And all done by machine.'

'By machine?'

'Yes, we have this new German machine, a Hollerith machine. It uses punchcards – they have holes punched in them which signify numbers and letters …'

'Enlighten me,' he said.

She described how punchcards worked.

'Sounds like a secret policeman's wet dream! Is that *the* Rudolf Jürgens?' he asked, pointing out a tall figure at the back of the group posing for the camera, 'the eugenicist.'

'Quite good looking, isn't he,' she said, lighting one of her hand-rolled cigarettes. 'A Nietzschean blue-eyed blond beast. He seemed more interested in it all than anyone else.'

'And Wartenheim?'

'He didn't say much.'

'The shy type?'

'More the calculating type, I think. Thinks before he speaks. Like a foreigner who knows a language perfectly but not well enough to speak it without thinking through what he's going to say first. Though he was certainly camera shy. The Direktor had to cajole him into posing for the photograph.'

'A lot of people are,' he said. 'Camera shy, that is.' It made sense that the Herr Konrad Wartenheim might not have wanted to be photographed and have his mug, with name attached, appear in the *Telegraf* for half of Vienna to peruse over as they shovelled down their breakfasts.

'What's this all about?' she asked.

Just at that moment their orders arrived: a 'peasant's fry-up' with beer, and a glass of Coca-Cola with lime juice. The Romanian waiter had no trouble intuiting who had ordered what.

'Dolfi Jensen,' Polanyi said as he sprinkled copious amounts of black pepper and salt onto his plate of diced fried potatoes, onions, carrots and bacon. 'This bacon is gorgeous. Of course, the only ethical position is vegetarianism but the flesh is weak.'

'Dolfi? I don't understand.'

'You are sure you've never seen this Konrad Wartenheim before?'

'Yes, absolutely.'

'Herr Konrad Wartenheim is Castle.'

'StaPo?'

'Our dear departed Dolfi had some sort of relationship with him, a rather intense relationship.'

'Are you sure?'

'Yes,' Polanyi said and continued eating.

There was something inexplicably fascinating about him, she found herself thinking. He exuded unpredictability and had a reputation for general anarchism. And he often came across as a man with a surreptitious agenda all of his own – and God only knew what that could be. She'd read some of the utterly insane stories in that scientific romance of his that was making the rounds. Everybody knew it was by him despite the ridiculous *nom de plume* he'd used. Most of the stories were alternative histories. In one of them, when Pontius Pilate asked the Jerusalem mob to choose between Jesus and Barabbas, the crowd had chanted 'Jesus! Jesus!'. Another of the oddly compulsive, bizarre tales had Okhrana agents travelling forward in time in some Wellsian machine in order to forestall an impending Marxist revolution in Saint Petersburg in 1933 – in Russia for God's sake, a more implausible fantasy than time travel itself – by assassinating the bearded would-be prophet of world social revolution as he penned *Das Kapital* in the reading room of the British Library, a hail of bullets blowing his brains out – described in rather graphic detail – just as he'd finished the first paragraph on commodity fetishism.

'Did you know he worked for them?' he asked.

There seemed little point in not telling him what she knew.

And, she suspected, if she did not, he was not going to tell her what this was all about. So she told him more or less everything while he ate.

'And did Pechstein ever manage to find out what the coded documents were about?' he asked when she had finished.

'Not that I know of?'

Polanyi pushed his empty plate aside, opened his tobacco tin and rolled a postprandial cigarette.

'So now,' she said, 'are you going to tell me who this Konrad Wartenheim really is?'

'Konrad Wartenheim – if that is in fact his real name – was Dolfi's contact with the Castle, his handler – I believe that's what it's called. Shortly before Dolfi disappeared they had some sort of a disagreement.'

'And you think that had something to do with Dolfi's disappearance … even his death?'

Polanyi was silent for a moment.

'Far be it for me to speculate on such matters,' he said eventually.

The chiming and clacking of the cash register behind the bar suddenly reverberated through the high-ceilinged room.

'The sound of the world rotating on its axis,' he said.

'What on earth are you talking about?'

'The sound of money being counted.'

He took another drag on his hand-rolled cigarette and was suddenly silently, looking at her oddly. Despite his looks and his unbelievably shabby dress, and his drinking – though right now he was as sober as a bishop – she had to admit she also found something strangely attractive about the man.

'What are you thinking?' she asked him after a few moments.

***

The Waugh House memory that most often came back to Constance Cohen during the long African nights – and even more so since Siegfried Bell's disquieting visit – was of that gruesome 'little experiment' which Youghal had Dickens perform during his first projector-lecture.

She remembered how Dickens, in his habitual white laboratory coat, had made his way to the blackboard. He looked as if he was in his fifties, but his full head of unruly brown hair, round rimless eyeglasses and a rather dapper pencil moustache lent him an oddly youthful look. The chalk made a squeaking sound as he wrote out the letters: *Cl*.

'Chlorine,' he said, turning to his audience. 'Chemical notation: Cl. A heavier-than-air gas. Colour: pale yellow-greenish. Atomic number: 17. Boiling point: minus 29 degrees Fahrenheit. Lethal to the human organism at a concentration of one part per thousand in air. Smell: a little harder to pin down. Perhaps somewhere between bleach and, oddly enough, something like a mixture of pepper and pineapple. It's not a substance one is inclined to sniff too enthusiastically.'

He had an air of ferrety intelligence about him, and of a man whose natural habitat was the world of Bunsen burners and test tubes.

'Now for a wee experiment, a demonstration,' he said. The 'wee' was an affectation. His accent was distinctly Birmingham.

Then two technicians in blue coats rolled in a wheeled table with a glass cage and some scientific-looking apparatus on it. There was a large fluffy white rabbit in the glass cage. Somebody muttered something about Alice in Wonderland.

'Meet our guinea pig,' he said, 'or rather our guinea rabbit.' The joke elicited some muted guffaws. 'The glass cage in which our rodent here finds himself incarcerated is one hundred percent airtight. The only way air can get in or out is via this valve here.' He indicated a tap-valve.

He then described the purpose of the apparatus beside the glass cage: a small copper cylindrical vessel about a foot high with a tap and a round pressure gauge on top of it, with a copper pipe that fed into the top of the cage.

'The chlorine is in a gaseous state. By opening his tap here, we can feed the gas into the glass cage at a controlled rate,' he said, mimicking opening and closing the tap-valve on top of the cylinder.

The rabbit's eyes, staring obliviously out at them through the glass, had reminded her of a teddy bear's.

'The wee demonstration I am about to perform is to give you an idea of the effect of chlorine gas on the human organism,' he continued. 'But seeing that we don't have a human at our disposal, we shall have to make do with a substitute. Of course, a monkey would have been a better subject – being a closer relative, so to speak – but I'm afraid they were out of simians at the pet shop.'

As the chuckles petered out, she remembered thinking at the time that they might have laughed more – Dickens, in his perverse way, did have 'a way of telling 'em' – but they hadn't; and, funnily enough, the military men least of all. Everybody knew what Dickens was going to do and they were obviously fascinated by the prospect of seeing him actually do it. They were like a music-hall audience watching some Houdini, tied up and incarcerated in a glass tank being slowly filled with water, secretly half-hoping that the escapologist would not actually escape, allowing them – in dubious innocence – the experience of seeing the unspeakable happen. Except, in this case, the demise of the Houdini substitute was absolutely certain.

'But that's enough jaw-jawing for now,' he said. 'Time for our wee demonstration.'

Then he began to slowly open the valve on the top of the gas cylinder. Yellowish-green puffs – like steam slowly escaping from the spout of a teapot – flowed out of the pipe and slowly descended, curling, to the bottom of the glass cage.

'Heavier than air,' he reminded them.

The gas began to settle into a yellow-green foggy layer at the bottom of the glass cage. When it was about nine inches high, he shut the valve off.

The men watched with hushed fascination. Outside the half-open windows, some pigeons were cooing in the chestnut trees.

After perhaps thirty seconds, the rabbit became agitated and to half-hop, half-run around in the swirling yellow-green gas, bashing itself against the glass of its transparent death chamber. Then the rabbit's frantic movements slowed down and it made a few squeaking, asthmatic gasps before, after a couple of spasms, it finally collapsed, and the yellow-green gas began to gently settle at the bottom of the glass cage again.

'Thank you, Mister Dickens,' Youghal said then, making his way towards the lectern, clapping as he did so, with the audience following his cue.

He waited until the relatively short and restrained round of applause had faded before continuing.

'Not exactly the most morally edifying scientific experiment to be obliged to witness. Though I have no doubt that many of you have seen worse on the King's business.'

He glanced at Owen-Sykes but the old warhorse's weathered features were as unreadable as they usually were.

'Mister Dickens's rabbit was undoubtedly innocent of any crime – as no doubt the individual enemy soldier encountered on the field of battle is undoubtedly innocent of any crime. He too serves a higher cause, *his* country, *his* idea of civilisation, as we serve ours. But history is a struggle of civilisations. To the man in the moon the difference between the enemy's idea of civilisation and ours might no doubt appear insignificant, trivial even; and that our ideas of what is right and what is wrong, moral and immoral, mere accidents of birth. But that is a superficial view. No, what appears insignificant is mere outward form. The differences are profound. And if our civilisation turns its back on science, it will become a China: backward, an empty shell of past glories, impotent. The days of Lancelots on white steeds are dead and gone. We live in an industrial age, a scientific age, the age of electricity, an age that calls for a new sense of the heroic, for soldier-scientists. To allow sentimental squeamishness cloud our judgement would be a betrayal of what we are. Tea and biscuits are being served in the games room. That's down the corridor on your left as you go out. Thank you.'

Owen-Sykes had been the first to clap.

18

Several weeks later Anja Jensen received another letter from Siegfried Bell, again in a blue envelope. It was even longer than the previous one.

A few days ago an unexpected visitor turned up on my doorstep – or rather the veranda – of my tin-roofed bungalow here on the outskirts of the European quarter of Von-Humboldt-Stadt. My housekeeper, a large jolly woman by the name of Maria, who goes about her duties singing hymns with a light-hearted enthusiasm that I've never come across in Germany or Austria, was still at the market, so I went to door myself. To my utter surprise, there standing in the doorway, wearing a wide-brimmed pith helmet, was none other than Constance Cohen.

I could tell immediately that it was not a social call but etiquette required us to pretend for a while that it was. So when Maria returned, I ordered tea for us.

'I see Von-Humboldt-Stadt is thriving,' she said.

'It's the railway,' I explained.

The line to the coast was completed a month ago and the station is now nearly finished. The train, a new Prussian P8 steam engine with two passenger carriages and six goods wagons, runs twice a week. The station itself, a red-bricked edifice, though modest, would not look out of place in a small town in Brandenburg.

'It was all planned and contracted for before the Crash,' I added. 'Before Berlin decided to tighten its belt.'

(What follows is an abbreviation of our subsequent conversation, as I imperfectly remember it.)

'I haven't seen a newspaper for months,' she said. 'What is happening in the big wide world?'

I remember telling her: 'The social democrats are demanding

that the Kaiser abdicates. There's been some sort of uprising in Warsaw, with refugees flooding into Germany and Austria-Hungary. Bread marches in Britain. Riots in Paris. Half of Italy's been declared an anarcho-syndicalist republic. An Englishman called Archibald Low has flown a radio-controlled aëroplane across the English Channel. Benedict XV has issued another new encyclical against modernism. And Russian avant-gardists – I think that's what they're called – have taken to wearing radishes on their lapels ...' But, I forget, none of this will be news to you.

'I was in two minds about coming to you,' she said. 'And I am still not sure if I should have. Perhaps I should just go. The sun will be setting soon.'

'Stay for dinner,' I suggested. 'The night watchman will escort you back to the hotel.'

Over stewed African wild pig, the tastiest game animal in my opinion, a spicy groundnut sauce and ugali (a sort of polenta, made from maize), our conversation, by unspoken agreement, was typical colonial fare: the latest Government House gossip, the incomprehensible idiosyncrasies of the Africans, and the like. After our meal, I proposed we take coffee and brandy on the veranda – there are practically no mosquitoes during the dry season.

'I am still not sure if what I came here to tell you will mean anything or make any sense to you at all,' she began when we were comfortably seated. 'And I am not even sure why I feel the need to tell you about it. It's not as if I'm racked by guilt and need a father confessor.'

I said nothing. I merely smiled at her, in an awkward sort of way.

'It began,' she said, 'shortly after the so-called July–August Crisis in 1914. The end of a summer like countless others. A report of a bungled attempt to assassinate the Habsburg Crown Prince in the Balkans on page three of *The Times*. Then a fortnight later the newspapers were about nothing else and everyone had an opinion on the rights and wrongs of it. Some days the air seemed to vibrate with both dread and a sort of excited anticipation ...'

'... that The Day was finally to dawn,' I added, 'and give birth to some glorious modern crusade which would lend significance to our lives, and cast the old decrepit world into the rubbish bin of history ...'

'Half of England seemed to relish the thought that there would be a European war,' she said.

'And half of Germany,' I said.

'I was working in the War Office at the time, as a general secretary and typist, in London,' she said. 'They told me I was to be transferred to a new ministry facility – a scientific research establishment about a two hour train journey from London. I was to pack over the weekend, lodging would be arranged, arrangements would be made to forward my mail ... and secrecy was the watchword.

'The Establishment – that's what it was usually known as – was at a place called Waugh House, a large country mansion with extensive grounds, which had been requisitioned for the "duration" – that was the way people spoke at the time. The place was a hive of activity. Men in all sorts of military uniforms. Scientific types in white coats setting up various types of technical equipment. Civilian technicians in blue and brown boiler suits. Temporary huts and tents being erected on the lawns. There were about three or four dozen secretary-typists like myself. We were all given identity cards – with photographs pasted into them – which we had to show to the Territorial Force sentries. It felt all rather adventurous, at first.

'The purpose of the Establishment, we were told, was to apply scientific and technical methods to warfare. It had existed since the 1890s, housed in some huts somewhere near London and under a different name, but now its activities had suddenly been given a new and unprecedented urgency. I found myself allocated to the department dealing with what they called chemical agents – with gas weapons.

'So suddenly I was at the coalface, as it were. One might think that working at the War Office I had always been in the bowels of the military beast but, in reality, most of us clericals spent the bulk of our time wading through paperwork dealing with the supply of horse fodder, wages and pensions calculations. A modern army is as much a bureaucracy as a fighting machine. The Day never dawned, of course. But the work went on.

'Was I shocked? Yes, at first. Gas was thought of as dishonourable weapon, as something particularly cruel, forbidden by the Hague Convention. But human beings are herd animals. We adapt to the ways of thinking of those with whom we find ourselves alongside and play the roles that circumstances allot us. And sometimes, before we know it, without sprouting tell-tale horns and tails or cloven feet, we are about the devil's work. For a while I simply accepted it all – and lamented in an unthinking sort of way that this was simply the way things were ... that such was human nature.

'The first experiment I witnessed – or rather demonstration; there was never any doubt as to its outcome – was to show the effect of the gas chlorine on an air-breathing animal. They used a white rabbit. A rat or some other vermin would have maybe been less shocking, but perhaps they thought that the perversity of asphyxiating an Alice in Wonderland white rabbit with a noxious gas would somehow obscure an infinitely greater perversity: the asphyxiation of men with a noxious gas. The rabbit was in a specially-built glass cage, into which a horrible little man named Dickens pumped chlorine gas until the creature coughed itself to death. The head of the chemical agents department, Youghal, an equally horrible specimen of *Homo sapiens*, orchestrated the whole affair. The assembled company of those who were to be impressed by this macabre circus trick – military men mainly – applauded on conclusion of the spectacle. I think I simply tried to brush off the experience as one of those occasional horrors one is inevitably exposed to in the course on life – like a child stumbling across a farmer castrating a litter of piglets – and that one banishes to those recesses of one's mind where we bury such things.

'A few weeks later another so-called experiment took place, again orchestrated by Youghal, with Dickens as his trusty assistant. The pair of them enjoyed pretending to be a pair of music-hall-farce villains. It was a particularly sunny and near-windless winter morning. The remains of the previous night's frost were still shimmering on the grass in the field in which the whole sorry theatre was to be enacted, about half a mile away from the main house. "Spiffing conditions," as Youghal said. It involved twenty animals – dogs, cats, sheep, and even a cow – tied to stakes. Several cylinders of a chlorine-phosgene mixture were released and a green-yellow cloud slowly enveloped the creatures. All the animals died, horribly.

'Youghal, in a rare candid moment – he had obviously detected my discomfort during the obscene display – later said to me (his very words, more or less): "I realise this is a gruesome business. I suppose I just assume women are the less squeamish sex … childbirth and all that. But if it's too much for you I can always arrange for you not to witness these unpleasantnesses." That was the word he used: unpleasantnesses. The funny thing is that he was not without some fellow feeling for animals. He had a pet, a cat, a blue-eyed Siamese which he used to bring into work with him in a special basket he had made to fit onto the handlebars of his bicycle. There was always a saucer of milk out for it in a corner of his office. He called it Cúchulainn, after a Celtic Siegfried-type hero. He had a thing about legendary heroes – he named half the projects after them, after figures like Beowulf and so on.'

I always find mention of my mythical namesake slightly embarrassing.

'Then he said,' she continued, 'in a manner of confiding in me: "One has to look at the big picture, the larger canvas. I believe in peace as much as the next man. But don't get me wrong: I'm not posing as an evil scientist who harbours sympathies for vegetarian, Esperanto-speaking, internationalist fanatics. No, I believe, as the Romans said: *si vis pacem, para bellum*. To secure peace, prepare for war. You might think us a right jolly group of Doktor Frankensteins but the peace of the world depends on us being more Faustian than our enemies. The peace depends on what, in a more gentlemanly past – if the past was more gentlemanly, which is very questionable – was called the balance of power. But this is the twentieth century ... and in the twentieth century that balance will be a balance of terror, in comparison with which the terror of nihilist bombs, Fenian bombs and suffragette bombs is but a piddling thing. Effective gas weapons will mean that any general war would be a universal Armageddon. Nobody could win such a thing. A fact that I'm sure even the dimmest politico will realise."

'Youghal had a bit of a way with words. He was brought up in an Irish parsonage. He had what his countrymen call the gift of the gab, apparently acquired by kissing some ancient rock somewhere there. He is not a man of science. He made his career in the Indian Civil Service and has the look of it.

'I could simply have walked away from it, got another job in London. Commerce was booming again after the international situation had settled down. The collective sigh of relief found expression in the form of a mass shopping spree. I fantasised about writing a letter to *The Manchester Guardian* or even *The Times* and exposing it all. But I also imagined the response: the killing of animals in the name of national security is hardly more amoral than that which occurs every day in the country's slaughterhouses to put pork sausages on our breakfast plates. I would have had to write anonymously, of course, if I wasn't to fall foul of the Official Secrets Act. Judges and juries are not inclined to treat traitors with leniency, and traitresses even less so.

'The CMD – the Campaign for Mutual Disarmament – was fairly active at the time. Their mass demonstrations were always reported in the press, usually with either open disapproval or disdain, or at best with a sort of condescension towards what was seen as for the most part the cause of a motley bunch of naive pacifist and vegetarian cranks. But, by and large, they are a rather respectable crowd. The Quakers, men and women of letters – they can even count a couple of bishops in their ranks – and academics considerably outnumber the so-called cranks. Leave arrangements at the Establishment were generous and I had long weekends free every couple of months. So the next time I was in London, I went along to a couple of their public meetings. I had never really attended a political public meeting of that sort before and I'm not sure what I expected. But it was just people giving speeches for the most part, passing motions full of noble sentiments about the brotherhood of man and woman, and the duty of Christians – "of all churches and of none" as one grey-haired Quaker lady put it – to renounce all forms and means of violence. It was all vaguely church-like, in a non-conformist sort of way. A plate was even handed around at the end for donations. But I went back several times, perhaps three in all, before … But I get ahead of myself.'

I was trying to imagine it all as she spoke: a stately country mansion, the English countryside, scientists in white coats experimenting on animals, the whole Luciferian side to maintaining the international order – and a respectable middle-aged woman, a typical product of her country and her class, though undoubtedly more enlightened and progressive than her peers, slowly becoming horrified with it all …

'One afternoon Youghal had all the staff gather in what used to be one of Waugh House's Victorian drawing rooms for what he called "a little cosy tête-à-tête" over cups of tea and chocolate biscuits. It was something he did, not regularly but often enough, usually when he had some sort of announcement to make. He started off, as usual, by thanking us for our "spiffing" devotion to duty and "practical patriotism". "As many of you are already aware," he said, "the recent tests that we have carried out on the efficacy of the Harrison mask have been a resounding success." The Harrison mask is a gas protection mask. It covers the head entirely and has a tube coming out the front – like an elephant's trunk – that goes to a canister worn on a shoulder strap. There are chemicals in the canister that filter the gas out of the air.'

'I've seen a photograph of something like that,' I said.

'A few weeks earlier,' she explained, 'they'd constructed several testing chambers, basically sealed windowless wooden huts with thirty-foot high chimneys so that gas could be safely released after they'd done their tests. A hundred or so Territorial Force volunteers had been brought in. They would go into the gas-filled testing chambers and stay there for different periods of time. There had been a few so-called mishaps – mainly due to masks not being worn properly – but no fatalities. A few of the men had panicked and torn their masks off. A mask for horses was even tested.

'"We can be sure that whatever protective measures British ingenuity can think up," Youghal said, "the Hebrew Fritz Haber and his little helpers in their Berlin den will be busy thinking up a way around them." He was one of those jokey Jew-haters. One never quite knew if he really was an anti-Semite or was just pretending to be one for a laugh – which is the more objectionable I am not quite sure. "Perhaps one day the Prussian dachshund will roll over and let us tickle its tummy," he said, "but I suspect that day lies far in the very misty future. And until that unlikely event happens, we have to keep up with his devilish machinations." He would smirk gleefully at what he called his little jokes. It was as if it were all a game of cricket. But also it was as if part of him was embarrassed by the horrible childishness of it all. "Thus, we need to proceed to a new phase of research," he said. "Chlorine gas needs to be inhaled in order to do its job. The tests with the Harrison mask have shown us that on a modern battlefield, if the enemy is also equipped with such masks – a rational assumption – chlorine and any similar gas would be ineffective. Though no doubt chlorine could prove useful in other situations, against a less sophisticated foe. But never fear, the scientists ..." – he cast an approving glance in the direction of Dickens at back the of the room, puffing silently on his briarwood pipe – "... are now about to embark on testing a novel range of chemical agents, ones which do not have to be inhaled to do their job. The code name of this project is Colman – for reasons which in due time will become apparent." There had been rumours of something "innovative" in the offing. He ended his little sermon with a few words about secrecy. "There is no need for me to remind you all that all of our activities here fall under the Official Secrets Act," he said, "which you have all signed." Putting one's signature to a copy of the Act is evidence that one is aware of its provisions. A formality really, since, as some esteemed justice once pronounced: "ignorance of the law is no excuse". But it is a rather effective formality. "I am sure," he said, "you all abide by its provisions religiously. However, a certain confusion has arisen, though I'm not sure confusion is the word. Anyhow, none of you can have failed to notice that there have been several speculations in the press – and not just in *The Manchester Guardian* – on the subject of chemical warfare in general. These reports have been attributed to what are euphemistically called sources close to the War Office and such like. These nebulous half-revelations – all plausibly deniable – have been deliberate. There has not been a breach of security. His Majesty's Government needs to let foreign powers know – while keeping the details as fuzzy as possible – what His Majesty's Forces are capable of on the battlefield if, so to speak, push should ever come to shove. Our adversary is playing the same game. But His Majesty's Government can hardly come straight out and announce to the world what we are doing here. The new Great Game is as much poker as it is chess. So, I just want it to be clear to you that these leaks of information are not due to anyone here playing silly buggers and talking to reporters. These little titbits that surface in the press … well, they are all part of the divine plan, as it were. So, as far as you personally are concerned, there has been no relaxation with regard to the utter secrecy of what you are doing here. So, mum's the word, as ever."

'A few weeks later the first large-scale Project Colman experiment was carried out. Its purpose was to test one of Youghal's novel range of chemical agents, the Colman gas – they had started calling it that – in the open air. They used a hundred or so dogs and cats, all shaved hairless. The animals were tethered to wooden stakes in one of the fields half a mile or so from Waugh House. I was not there. An officer who saw it told me that the scene was like something from a Hieronymus Bosch depiction of hell. The gas hadn't killed the animals, he said, and they'd had to shoot them to put them out of their misery. He told me it smelled faintly of mustard – hence Colman gas; Colman's is a common brand of mustard in England – and it had a yellowish colour. It doesn't kill outright – and if exposure is not to a high enough concentration, it does not kill at all. And it can take a few hours to take effect, depending on the level of exposure. It causes blindness and corrodes the mucous membranes, the lungs, and blisters the skin horribly. That was why they'd shaved the animals, so they could see the effect it had on their skins. The fact that it caused debilitating injuries rather than simply killed was the point of it. A dead enemy soldier could easily be disposed of but a horribly injured soldier would need to be taken care of, hospitalised, nursed, and thus be a greater drain on an enemy's manpower. The dead animals were thrown into a pit, drenched with paraffin and set alight. The smell of burning flesh hung around the place for days.'

The 'civil defence' leaflets that were being distributed to Berlin households just before I came out here did not mention any such weapon. They recommended purchasing a government-approved gas mask or, failing the means to do that, various home-made and highly ineffective-looking alternatives involving cotton wool soaked in vinegar. I can't say it was particularly confidence-inspiring.

'At the fourth or so CMD meeting I went to I met a man called Sebastian Saaldeck,' she continued. 'That is not his real name. I never learned what that was. But that's the name I knew him by. I don't remember how exactly we fell into conversation. Perhaps it was the workings of that mysterious mechanism by which souls who need each other supposedly recognise each other. I will not bore you with the details of how Sebastian Saaldeck and I became amorously involved. He was younger than me by a few years. He had a beautiful smile at times. Though whether we really needed each other is another question.'

You may be surprised by her frankness – and indeed by my frankness in relating all this – but people can sometimes be astonishing frank out here, far from the mores of what we like to call civilisation.

'"The only things truly worth doing are those we believe are the most important things in the world," he used to say to me. A bit of a cliché. For the most part, I think that what we believe are the most important things in the world is pure chance. It depends on the circumstances we are born into, the age we live in, the social class or religion or country or race we belong to. But there's more truth in clichés than we like to admit. He had a German mind. He spoke English well but in a German way, as if the world was entirely susceptible to linguistic logic. He used to talk about what he called the laws that govern history and how political action was futile if it did not proceed according to those laws. And that he was a follower of a certain Russian in Zurich, a something Lenin, the theoretician of an obscure social-democratic sect – "the Cause", he called it – who believed that history must be given a helping hand.'

Why she had become involved with this Saaldeck seemed to make little sense. But then, affairs of the heart rarely do. She'd obviously seen qualities in him which I could not detect from her description of him.

'He believed,' she said, 'that personal happiness is inconsequential in the larger scheme of things, that one must become what he called an "objective man". By which he meant, I think, to devote oneself to a larger shaping of what he called "objective reality". That one needed to transcend one's ego and desires when they conflicted with that cause in order to give one's existence an objective significance beyond the short and individually insignificant lives we are fated to live. But is it not a fallacy to imagine any sort of objective reality in the relationships between men, between men and women, and in politics? It might exist, but we can never know it.'

Her face was barely visible in the darkness. It was a moonless night and the only light was from the paraffin lamp hanging from one of the veranda-roof beams. But I detected a sort of despair in her expression, a despair tempered by something else: some sort of determination to simply carry on.

'And thus began,' she said, 'by gradual degree, the process by which I became a traitress.' Her emphasis, again, had been on the 'ess'. 'At first it was only talk. I told him things. About the experiments, who was who, how it was all organised. At the time the existence of gases like the Colman gas was not publicly known. Though there had been the odd report in the press about gases which gas masks were useless against, but nothing very specific.'

Then, suddenly, as if changing the subject, she asked me: 'Do you know how the Colman gas was invented, or discovered rather?'

I shook my head. She rolled and lit a cigarette before replying. The nocturnal sounds of Von-Humboldt-Stadt filled the short silence: the barking of a dog, a shout from some servants' quarters, the cry of some night bird.

'An English chemist,' she said, 'by name of Hans Thacher Clarke, working at the Kaiser Wilhelm Institute in Berlin in 1913 dropped a flask or something and ended up being hospitalised for two months.'

'The fruits of international co-operation,' I remarked ironically.

'One day,' she continued, 'on a rainy afternoon in a tea house on Tottenham Court Road, after we'd been seeing each other for a couple of months, Saaldeck said: "We need proof." For a moment I was at a loss. "But the world knows," I said, "that gas weapons are being developed by all the powers. All one has to do is read the newspapers."

'"Men know it," he said, "but don't know that they know it. We are sleepwalking into the abyss. Mankind needs to be woken up."

'I asked him how he proposed to do that.

'"The details must be revealed," he said. "Places, dates, chemical formulae, facts. There is a plan. One could call it a conspiracy even. Its aim is to reveal details of this whole evil business in as much of its evil detail as is possible."

'"There is a man," he told me. "A very well-placed man in Vienna. He is gathering information on chemical weapon research in Germany, France, Russia and Britain. He plans to publish it. It will be information that will surpass all the generally vague and deniable stuff that has appeared in the press to date. It will be published in a neutral country, most probably Switzerland, in several languages. So far it has proved difficult to get detailed information on the British gas programme …" There was no need for him to say much more. "I realise that I am asking you to cross a Rubicon," he said.'

I tried to imagine this conversation: the London teahouse, its petty-bourgeois customers, a rainy afternoon, this talk of treason among teacups, sponge cake, and her motivations, and this Saaldecks's motivations.

'And you agreed?' I said.

'Yes,' she nodded. 'I agreed. Eventually. I went back to work and behaved as usual. I still could have walked away from it all, and the thought of doing so crossed my mind more than once. What he had asked also seemed impossible. Simply purloining some documents and smuggling them out was out of the question. Just to get access to them involved a complicated system of forms to be filled out and get signed and stamped and countersigned. The Establishment's procedures were … Kafka-ish.'

'Then, one morning, Youghal called me into his office. He stood up when I entered and invited me to sit down – though he had to shoo Cúchulainn off the chair first. He had a bronze bust of Oliver Cromwell on his desk; and behind him, on the wall, there was a copy of that Burne-Jones painting of an armoured knight killing an eel-like dragon to rescue or perhaps gain possession of an archetypical nude maiden chained to a rock.' I think Oliver Cromwell was some seventeenth-century English republican. 'He said he had a sensitive task for me, something that required the "utmost discretion".

'"There is a series of meetings coming up," he told me. "Between my good self and various War Office officials and representatives of the very discreet parliamentary committee charged with overseeing the activities of establishments such as ourselves. I will need somebody to take minutes at these meetings. Somebody competent and discreet. I will need to speak freely with all these gentlemen and they will also need to feel that they can speak freely with me. I need someone unobtrusive. The other girls … Well, they can be a bit flirty, a bit of a distraction. I'm sure you know what I mean. These talks will be quite frank. The people I will be meeting with are not – as I believe the Yanks say – middle management. They are people who make important decisions, exercise real political power, and not merely pretend that they do. Sir Beardsley will also be present at times." Beardsley was the overall director of the Establishment, though he spent most of his time in London.

'The meetings took place over the next couple of months. There were four members of Parliament at one. At first they were given a sanitised tour of the Establishment, and then over tea and biscuits they had their little chats with Quentin Youghal Esquire in his office – with me at a small desk in the corner taking minutes and bearing mute witness to their deliberations. It was educational. But not in the way I imagine that Youghal thought it would be. The discussions were frank … and revealing. But they were not quite what I expected. Though I am not sure what I expected. It is so hard to imagine how power is actually exercised, what goes on in the corridors of power, not just what words are exchanged but the texture of them, the nuances, the unsaid … mutual understandings, I suppose. But what I had not imagined was the sheer banality of it. Yes, they were powerful men. And they were men who made decisions that determined the course of lives. But, despite what Youghal had said, it was all also a sort of pretending. But a pretending that made it so. If that makes any sense. Something like that. What the real purpose of the meetings was I never really made out. Internal War Office political shenanigans of some kind most probably. But I was also asked to write what were called "technical summaries", basically descriptions of the most secret weapons projects.'

Most of the projects concerned weapons whose existence is now pretty much common knowledge: the various gas weapons mainly. But there were some that I had never heard of: miniature radio-steered aircraft and dirigibles, even a radio-steered torpedo.

'The descriptions included manufacturing processes and the results of the so-called experiments,' she said, 'and included a lot of numbers and drawings.'

'Enough to provide Herr Saaldeck with regular reports from the belly of the beast?' I suggested.

'Are you shocked?' she asked me.

'Only at the risk you took,' I said.

I wear my loyalty to the German Empire lightly. There are greater causes than the accidents of birth and country. I like to consider myself a cosmopolitan man; but how would I react if ever put to a real test? Some English writer – I forget who – when once asked if faced with an impossible choice, if he would betray his country or his friend, is reported to have said that he hoped he would have the courage to betray his country.

'I never knew to whom Saaldeck gave the documents, or precisely how he passed them on. He had a mechanical device, a cylinder-thing with rows of letters – on rotatable discs. It produced a code that was unbreakable, he said. He told me he didn't use it all the time – it was a laborious process to encode a longish text with it, he said – but he always used it for anything that contained information that might expose us.

'This went on for some months. It was all rather tricky, copying the documents and then smuggling them out. There's no need for me to go into the details. And then … It was one of those rainy spring days in April. I was working late, finishing up something – the others had left – when I heard a noise in Youghal's office, which adjoined the main office. I was wondering if I should go and have a look – I was sure he was not there and the door would have been locked – when it happened again. I should have knocked I suppose but, as I said, I was sure nobody was there. So I turned the doorknob. It was not locked. Youghal was sitting at his desk, with his back to me, staring at his Burne-Jones dragon and nude-maiden painting. The air in the room reeked of that Scottish pipe tobacco he smoked. He seemed not to have heard me. He didn't turn around. I had to pretend-cough two or three times before he heard me and slowly turned around – he had one of those swivel chairs – and looked at me. At first, I did not notice anything amiss, but I saw the bottle of Bushmills Irish whiskey on his desk, half-empty. He was drunk. Very drunk. I had never seen him like that before.

'"Mademoiselle Cohen?" he said. It was almost a question. As if for a moment he was not quite sure who I was.

'I was about to say I thought I'd heard a noise but he spoke again before I could say anything.

'"Fancy a drop of the devil's brew?" he said.

'I was about to politely decline the offer and leave him to it, but before I could say anything, he'd extracted another glass from a drawer in his desk and begun to pour me some of the Bushmills. "We have a rotten apple, a rotten apple in the barrel!" he said as he did so.

'That took me aback. I found myself sitting down. Then he just talked, or rambled on rather, and I listened to him, taking the odd sip from the whiskey.

'"Yes, a rotten apple," he went on, refilling his glass from the half-empty bottle. "A spy. A two-timer. A shyster. A traitor in our midst. But that's the nature of this damned business. Do you know how many German spies there are in this country?"

'"No, sir," I said, rather meekly.

'"Thousands of the bastards according to the *Daily Mail*," he said. 'Ferreted away in God only knows what government departments, in every city, and God only knows how many coastal villages, wandering around dockyards, ports and train stations. Foreign waiters sucking up every crumb of information that might be of use to the Kaiser and his Jews ... like those new-fangled electric floor-cleaning thingies ... What the bloody hell are they called?"

'"A vacuum cleaner," I said, but he gave no sign of having heard me.

'"And now we have one of the buggers in our midst," he ranted on. "Some Yid or Yid brown-noser no doubt. Up to his tricks. Doing it for the bloody money most likely. No principles, some of these people. Anything for a filthy shekel. Our mandarin-masters in Whitehall have informed me that details – bloody sensitive details – have turned up where they should not turn up. Namely, in Berlin. There's a creepy little Austrian involved whose movements are being kept an eye on. Never liked Austrians. Arrogant people. Give me your honest plodder of a German any day."

'He was surprisingly lucid for a man so drunk, though his words were slightly slurred.'

'I've known men to function quite well,' I said, 'or at least well enough not for anyone to notice, on a bottle a schnapps a day or even half a dozen pipes of hashish.'

She continued:

'"Bloody high-ups are having kittens. Litters of 'em," he said. "They want results. They want the traitor on the end of a big barbed hook, safely landed so they can give the bugger a fatal and very painful whack on the skull with the Whitehall equivalent of a fishing priest."

'"What are you going to do?" I asked, again quietly.

'"Flush the bastard out," he said. "Put the fear of God into the bugger. Force him to sweat blood, to make a break for it, to break cover. There'll be two gentlemen from the Special Branch here tomorrow. One of 'em is a Welshman – a bit of charmer when he wants to be – but a man who get results – broken a few Fenians in his time. Everybody will be questioned, every porter, charwoman, clerk and laboratory technician … everybody in this whole accursed shop."

'He was drunk but he still had his wits about him. Nothing he was telling me would not be common knowledge when men from the Special Branch arrived the next day. So he was giving away no secrets. He was obviously angry – both at the fact that there was a so-called shyster in our midst but also at "our mandarin-masters in Whitehall". The Welshman – his name was Burton, Oscar Burton – and his companion arrived the next day.'

'And you were questioned?' I said.

She helped herself to another of my cigarettes and lit it, and inhaled deeply before answering. The smoke hung in the night air, reminding me of the morning mists we often see here. The world she was describing seemed to be on another planet; but, of course, it was not.

'Eventually,' she said. 'It was a rather formal affair. Burton was quite charming and civilised in a way, but you could feel that he took nothing at face value. He looked at my ministry file and just asked me to confirm some details. In the end, he asked me if I had any reason to suspect anyone. "Anything you say will be treated in the utmost confidence," he said. "Not a word of it will go beyond these walls." He held all the interviews in one of the drawing rooms; his companion – I never learned his name – just sat there as silent as Lot's wife throughout. "I am not asking you for proof of anything, more a woman's intuition. Think about it. Take your time." I pretended to think about it; not too quickly and not too long. I could feel him watching me as I did so. It was then I really noticed his eyes. They were – how shall I describe them? – chillingly neutral, and grey. He was one of those men who appear intelligent and curious about the world but really aren't. The curiosity was suspicion. His intelligence was merely cleverness. I told him had no reason to suspect anyone.'

'What happened then?' I asked her.

'Burton and his silent companion left shortly afterwards,' she told me. 'I was one of the last to be interviewed. Youghal said nothing to us about the outcome, if there was any outcome. There was just a hushed silence about the whole thing. It appeared that the whole affair was over, but I suspected it wasn't. And I didn't know if it had had anything to do with the documents I had given to Saaldeck, or if it was about something else entirely.'

'You must have been terrified,' I said.

'I had no idea what I should do,' she said. 'I thought about making a run for it of course. But how, and where to? It would have to be abroad. But that would take money that I didn't have. I knew nobody abroad. And that was what Youghal wanted – for his prey to make a run for it, to break cover, as he put it. I couldn't think straight. I was just about capable of behaving normally. And, of course, I spoke to Saaldeck about it.'

'What was his reaction?' I asked.

'He was even more afraid than I was,' she said. 'He said he would introduce me to someone who could help. He arranged for me to meet him at his place. It was a Sunday afternoon, an unusually warm and sunny day. Sometime around three o'clock there was a knock at the front door and Saaldeck went down and brought him up. He was a small man, not obviously a foreigner until he spoke. His English was rudimentary. I took him to be a German, but he said: "It is not only Germans who speak German."

'He was blunt, to say the least, and direct. The first thing he said, to Saaldeck, was: "So this is the woman." Saaldeck simply nodded. Then he turned to me and said: 'You are not safe. Things are happening. I fear the English secret police are getting closer every day. They smell the fox in the chicken cottage. That is the saying, is it not?' I asked him who he was. "My name is Konrad Wartenheim," he said, "for now, anyway, and while in this country." After that we spoke German. He had an Austrian accent. From which I deduced that he was probably the "creepy little Austrian" Youghal had referred to. I never found out what his real name was. But he knew how to organise things. He had already arranged for me to travel to the Netherlands as a passenger on a cargo steamer. From there I went to Germany. My life was suddenly out of my hands. My coming here was also his idea.

'This Wartenheim was also obviously the "very well-placed man in Vienna" that Saaldeck had told me about. They had known each other for years; I saw that immediately. One look at him – it was so unbelievably obvious – was enough for me to realise that Saaldeck's talk about revealing the "details of this whole evil business in as much of its evil detail as is possible" was not the whole story, if it was the story at all, even if he somehow believed in it himself.'

'So you were dreadfully deceived,' I said without thinking.

She neither agreed nor disagreed.

This strange conversation over, I called Elias, the night watchman. He has a sort of cubby hole by the compound gate. What he does there all night I have no idea. Sleeps, I suspect. Before she left, I gave her an eight-week-old copy of the *Berliner Volks-Zeitung*. From the veranda, I watched them both walk off into the African darkness of Von-Humboldt-Stadt: Elias in his long, vulcanised raincoat and with an African spear over his shoulder, carrying a paraffin lamp; and this woman who had betrayed her country believing she could save the world.

PS: A request on my part, for some books (sorely lacking here). I have taken the liberty of enclosing a postal order – I trust it will be sufficient. I would greatly appreciate it if you could send me some. Perhaps: the novel *Metropolis* by Thea von Harbou; *The Economic Consequences of the Long Peace* by that English economist, Keynes, (I forget his Christian name); the new Albert Schweitzer book, I think it's called *The Primeval Forest*; and something by this Kafka fellow, his new novella if possible, *How Ape became Man* – I think that's what it's called. But anything reasonably intelligent would be appreciated.

PPS: Still on the subject of books: a signed copy of Viktor Polanyi's oeuvre arrived in the post a fortnight ago (with a fictional return address on the envelope: Bakuningasse, Vienna – and obviously from the good man himself). The book, which, though absurd, does pose some interesting questions. In one story Jesus is set free, not Barabbas, giving rise to a rather odd version of Christianity. But a more nuanced treatment of the whole issue of necessity and contingency in history might have been to select a more recent event, one in which the outcome could have more easily gone another way; say, Napoleon winning the Battle of Leipzig, and Waterloo remaining forever nothing more than the name of an insignificant Belgian village; or if – by some slight and subtle chemical imbalance in those early stages of the foetal development in which such things were determined – some significant historical character had been born female rather than male ... Jesus himself, even.

19

'Does the name Konrad Wartenheim mean anything to you?' Polanyi asked.

'Konrad Wartenheim?' Pechstein repeated.

The Café of Electric Delusions was packed and smoke-filled, but they had managed to get a relatively quiet table in the alcove near the bar, directly under the larger-than-life-size portraits of Marcel Proust and the English Lord Byron, the unofficial mascots of the place.

Polanyi pushed a copy of the *Telegraf* across the table.

Pechstein examined the Mundaneum group photograph in the light of the electric table lamp.

'Back row on the left. Bowler hat. The fellow who looks like a cat who's been caught red-handed stealing the milk.'

But Pechstein had already recognised the grainy image of the bespectacled figure. It was Maximilian Eisenstein, looking perhaps not so much like a cat who had been caught stealing the milk as the caricature of a bespectacled bureaucrat; but then, everybody looked like a caricature of themselves in photographs.

'His name is Maximilian Eisenstein,' Pechstein said without thinking, 'not Konrad Wartenheim.'

The expression on Polanyi's face suddenly changed, but to what Pechstein couldn't make out. The man was difficult to read at the best of times.

'The Castle man?'

'Yes,' Pechstein said.

Just at that moment the electric loudspeakers screeched. One of the stage assistants, in a red boiler suit with the words GOD IS UNDEAD stencilled in yellow on the back, was fiddling around with the equipment. The distraction gave Pechstein a moment to think. He shouldn't have said it was Eisenstein, but what was said was said. This was serious. The last thing he wanted was Polanyi going around the coffee houses and bars of Vienna asking questions about one of the Vienna StaPo's alpha-animals and mentioning him in the process – which he was very sure he was capable of doing.

'The Man in the Iron Mask!'

Pechstein nodded.

Polanyi cut up one of the curried meatballs he had ordered and, dipping the pieces in ketchup, began to eat them. But it was obvious that his mind was not on his food.

'Is he the man Dolfi Jensen met at the planetarium?' Pechstein asked. 'The man you followed?'

The air suddenly filled with the sound of raucous fiddle and drum music. Both men turned to look at the stage.

Three women in unidentifiable peasant costumes with fiddles and a male singer in a white woollen pullover with a frame drum had begun to play folk music of some kind, but none that Pechstein was familiar with. It was definitely not Gypsy. But the lyrics were in German.

'It's Irish or Scottish or something,' Polanyi explained. 'They're from Berlin.'

'Well, is he?' Pechstein asked again. 'Is he the man you saw Dolfi Jensen with at the planetarium?'

'The very one,' Polanyi said, as the singer introduced the next song, something about whiskey and highwaymen.

As they listened to the unfamiliar music – it was too loud to converse over – Pechstein remembered that Binswanger had told him that the notes on the teleprint he had seen had been initialled M E. M E: the initials of Maximilian Eisenstein. Suddenly it was all beginning to fit together. Or was it?

'You said that you thought there was something personal going on between him and Dolfi Jensen. What did you mean exactly?'

'Perhaps it was something off the record. Something the

Castle was not supposed to know anything about.'

For a moment Polanyi seemed to be distracted by something. Pechstein turned around to see what he was looking at. The object of his curiosity was a very tall man in a tweed suit at the bar, using one of the in-house telephones. There was something unusual about his hair: it was just too black, coal-black. Pechstein wondered if it were dyed.

'StaPo,' Polanyi informed him when the music finished. 'There's always a few of them hanging out here. One of their favourite watering holes. God knows what they think they are going to find out.'

Pechstein decided it was probably a wig.

Polanyi rolled another of his endless cigarettes.

'But then again, I suppose there is always something to find out,' he went on. 'Every man has some sort of secret tucked away.'

'Indeed,' Pechstein said, absent-mindedly. He was thinking about how absurd all this real-life cloak-and-dagger stuff was, a silly game played by grown men. Then he remembered the matchbook he'd found in Dolfi Jensen's room. Had the StaPo also searched it, and was it one of them who'd left behind a matchbook he'd picked up here?

'And sometimes, I wonder, what yours is, Herr Pechstein?' Polanyi added.

'My what?'

'The secret you've got tucked away.'

For a moment Pechstein was taken aback but then realised from the laughing look in Polanyi's eyes that the man was merely trying to provoke him, not even fishing. But it was true: every man had secrets. And he suspected that Polanyi had – he searched for a word – a voyeuristic streak.

'Do you mind if I keep this?' he said, referring to Polanyi's copy of the *Telegraf*.

'What for?'

'I'd like to read the article properly,' Pechstein said, rather implausibly.

'Afraid not,' Polanyi said. 'I'm going to have a few hundred copies of the bastard's photograph made. They'll be distributed in certain circles.'

'The StaPo will not be happy with that,' Pechstein said, thinking that perhaps the reason Żuławski had had difficulty when following Polanyi was not only because Polanyi wanted to avoid drawing the attention of the tax office to his Turkish delight business, but also out of a well-founded fear that the StaPo were keeping a discreet eye on him.

'No. They will not.'

***

'Siegfried Manga Bell?' Pechstein said, referring to the signature at the end of the letter. His face had been near expressionless while he had been reading through it, except for every now and again when he had pursed his lips in a gesture of intense concentration.

'His father was originally from the Protektorat Kamerun,' Anja Jensen explained. 'The Manga Bells are local royalty. He's vaguely related to them. His mother is German.'

She was wearing dark olive-green lipstick. Her choice of make-up was usually more restrained.

'I remember reading something about a Rudolf Manga Bell a few years back. Something about the expropriation of native lands. There was a court case, I think. How do you know him?'

'Through my brother. He came to Vienna a couple of years ago to do some research for a doctorate. Something to do with carbonic acid in the atmosphere and ice ages.'

'I think I saw him at the funeral.'

'He was there,' she said.

'Well, it all fits.'

This Youghal naming his projects after legendary heroes – Beowulf especially – and the reference to the Colman gas surely proved that the documents that Constance Cohen passed onto 'Saaldeck' and which Saaldeck had in turn passed onto 'Wartenheim' were the documents that Eisenstein had given to

Dolfi Jensen to decode and translate. Saaldeck had obviously coded the documents – or at least some of them – with a Bazeries cylinder given him by Eisenstein, and Dolfi Jensen had decoded them with the one he'd found in his desk when he'd searched his rooms in the Girardigasse house. The ten photostatted pages Dolfi Jensen had given to Sigrid were obviously only some of the documents, ones that Jensen had thought particularly important. And the decoded but untranslated half-page – the one titled projectcolman – that Polanyi had discovered in Dolfi's typewriter matched perfectly with what Constance Cohen had told Bell about the experiments with chemical weapons. Though Eisenstein's using the pseudonym Wartenheim for his activities both abroad and in Vienna was sloppy; which surprised him.

'I do not understand,' she said.

He lay the sheaf of closely typed pages down on his desk.

'There are things I didn't tell you about. Perhaps I should have … but—'

'But what?'

'I managed to find out some things.' He took a Sphinx from his desktop cigarette box and lit it. 'I was not sure they were relevant. I did not want to give you false hopes. I wanted to protect you—'

'False hopes?' she repeated, helping herself from the cigarette box. 'Protect me?'

There was anger in her voice.

'Sorry,' he said, 'I should have offered you one.'

He lit the cigarette for her.

She inhaled once and exhaled.

'I think you had better tell me how it all fits,' she said.

'This Wartenheim that Constance Cohen talks about is in reality a man named Maximilian Eisenstein, a man very high up in the StaPo. He was your brother's contact. The translations your brother was doing for the Castle were most probably the documents that this Constance Cohen was smuggling out of that place in England. Though he was most likely doing other work for the StaPo or the Evidenzbüro too.' He wondered if he should tell her that it was Weber who had originally recruited Dolfi for the Castle but he didn't see the point. 'At the beginning of 1918, or earlier even, Dolfi began to have qualms of conscience—'

'About working for the Castle?'

'More about the contents of those documents,' he said. 'He seems to have threatened Eisenstein that he would go to the press and spill the beans, as it were. I don't know the exact details but they had arguments ... especially during the few weeks before he disappeared. I can't tell you how I found all this out but that's the gist of it. Beyond saying that Polanyi was extremely helpful.'

'Polanyi?'

'Yes. Your brother told Polanyi he was planning to go to the press, cause a scandal. He didn't tell him everything but he told him enough. And it all fits with this Siegfried Bell's account of his conversation with this Constance Cohen woman.'

Pechstein opened the drawer of his desk, extracted the copy of the *Telegraf* with Eisenstein's photograph in it and passed it to her. Polanyi had sent it to him by bicycle messenger a few days after their conversation in the Café of Electric Delusions, with a note saying that the copies of 'our friend's portrait had reproduced better than the original'.

'That's Eisenstein,' he said. 'The man in the bowler. The caption gives his name as Konrad Wartenheim. He lives in Döbling. He has a villa there. It's called Arcadia. An odd choice for the name of a house, but then, life is full of oddities.'

He watched her as she examined the photograph of Eisenstein, as if she were trying to memorise what he looked like.

'So this is the man responsible for my brother's death?' she said after a few moments.

'I wouldn't go that far. In the normal run of things, there's probably a case for an investigation. But that's all. And this does not fall into the normal-run-of-things category. Any attempt to bring any of this out into the open would be the equivalent of kicking a wasps' nest. It would annoy a lot of influential people and it wouldn't achieve anything. And when it comes down to it, it's all hearsay and innuendo, circumstantial at best. Most of it out of the mouths of two of what might not be considered exactly credible witnesses. Polanyi is a notorious malcontent, a man who has spent too many nights in the Herzen downing green faeries.'

'Green faeries?'

'Absinthe. And Bell, a German African who's had a touch too much tropical sun. That's how it would be seen. There's nothing that would hold up in a court of law, not that it would ever be permitted to get that far.'

'But those coded documents? Constance Cohen said this Youghal man used code names based on mythical figures. Beowulf. Mordred. Surely they are some sort of material evidence?'

'Copies of copies. No proof that they are the copies of genuine originals. And they are indecipherable. Even if it could be proved that your brother was working for the Castle in any sort of capacity … Those few sheets of paper prove nothing. The necropsy found nothing amiss. The Preßburg public prosecutor's office didn't even think a full formal inquest was necessary.'

'So, this Maximilian Eisenstein is untouchable.'

'Such men usually are.'

'They walk among mortals as if they were gods,' she said. It sounded like a quote but he had no idea from where.

'I would not go quite that far,' he said. 'In a way, such men are also cogs in the machinery of power. Big cogs, but cogs nonetheless. They merely do what is expected of them.'

'Men can make choices,' she said. 'Constance Cohen made a choice.'

As she left the building, Pechstein observed her from his office window as she crossed the courtyard and disappeared into Vienna's lunchtime pedestrians on the Naglergasse, and found himself again thinking of her muscular white body concealed within her fashionably calf-length dress and navy-blue coat.

'"Men can make choices",' she had said. '"Constance Cohen made a choice."' But there were choices and choices.

But, somehow, he could not imagine her in a paroxysm of sexual desire ... or was it that he dared not? And how would a man – a man like him – go about seducing a woman like that? Would he be capable of it? And if she did somehow fall into his arms, what then?

A lot pointed to Eisenstein having been involved in the death of Dolfi Jensen, having arranged it even. But why? What could the man's motivation have been? If Dolfi Jensen was proving to be a problem, surely there were more than sufficient legal ways of silencing him. A dawn arrest, a court case held in camera, with the prospect of a long prison sentence served in some fortress in the Carpathians. Even the threat of that would be enough to shut most men up. No, it had to be something else. Had Dolfi Jensen been a threat, not to the Castle, but to Eisenstein himself? But nothing in Constance Cohen's confession to Bell indicated that Eisenstein was not simply doing his job. And Polanyi's speculations were just that: speculations. '"Something off the record",' he'd said, '"something the Castle was not supposed to know anything about."' But suppose for a moment that Eisenstein was a double agent of some kind – and Dolfi Jensen had been threatening to expose him, not knowing that what he was decoding and translating for Eisenstein was for eyes other than those of the Castle. That might provide Eisenstein with a motive. But for whom would have Eisenstein been spying? For Berlin, but perhaps also for others. Britain? France? Russia? Italy? Or even Japan or the Ottomans? But why would a man like Eisenstein work for a foreign power? For money? The man was rich, if his villa in Döbling was anything to go by; not that being rich ever seemed to stop the rich from wanting more. Did he have debts? Or was it for an idea, an ideology? Hard to conceive. There were no real differences in the realm of political ideas between the powers. When it really came down to it, France, Britain and Germany were all much of a muchness. They were in fierce competition with each other, but in terms of ideology, they were bourgeois polities with no serious differences between them; their constitutions were parliamentary, their economies were industrial-capitalist, and their foreign policies were nationalist-imperialist. Though, of course, the Russian Empire was another thing entirely: an autocratic and unstable beast. The last time political ideology had played any role in relationships between the states of Europe had been in the wars following the French Revolution. Of course, Eisenstein could have been playing the double spy for some obscure psychological reason.

His thoughts drifted back to when he had first met Anja Jensen. Which had been an autumn day in … it must have been 1918. It was hard to believe that the case had really been going on that long, that so much time had simply slipped by, and with it, all the nebulous – perhaps illusionary? – opportunities that life seemed to offer. Was it his age? Or the age? The twentieth century: the age of new things and fashions every year, and new fads every few months. He remembered how at school they used to move the hand of the classroom clock forward when a teacher had to leave the classroom for some reason … The passage of time had not seemed so relentless then.

But perhaps Eisenstein was not untouchable.

Pechstein returned to his desk and picked up the telephone.

***

Binswanger devoured his schnitzel in his customary methodical way while Pechstein told him more or less everything he knew – taking care not to mention Sigrid Kupfer – amid the familiar smell of sauerkraut, roast meat and beer, and the cacophony of the Phaffenhof patrons tucking into their midday meals. A few times Binswanger stopped, his fork and knife posed momentarily in mid-air, asked a question to seemingly clarify a seemingly minor point – but then got back to his schnitzel as if what Pechstein was telling him was nothing out of the ordinary.

When Pechstein was finished, Binswanger washed down the

last of his meal with a long draught of beer, wiped his mouth with his napkin, and indulged in his habitual postprandial burp. But then he looked directly at Pechstein, his face utterly devoid of its typical Binswanger good humour.

'I don't ever want to be reminded that you told me what you have just told me,' he said. 'This conversation is not taking place.'

'But ...' Pechstein began.

'I'm serious,' Binswanger said.

Pechstein nodded slowly. From the look on Binswanger's face, he could see he was being very serious.

'And your friend Viktor Polanyi is on the blacklist,' Binswanger added. 'Point of information.'

'The blacklist?'

'The list of those to be picked up if things get out of hand,' Binswanger added. 'Unofficial, of course.'

'So writing stories about the industrial revolution starting in Renaissance Italy is considered subversive these days?' Pechstein said. He'd managed to get hold of a copy of *Primroses in December*.

'Depends on the spirit in which they are written. How did the industrial revolution start in Italy?'

'Leonardo da Vinci develops a steam engine based on some rediscovered plans by Hero of Alexander for a steam-powered temple-door opener, and the Medici decide to invest in the thing. But that's beside the point. Are things getting out of hand?'

Every day there seemed to another protest about something or other, and strikes every other day, though most of them were short-lived. The day before yesterday it had been the public telephonists. And there were roadblocks checking vehicles going in and out of the government quarter.

'Let's just say, Italy and the Warsaw Easter Uprising have made a lot of people nervous ... and political passions are running quite high at the moment. Some are fired up by—'

'Visions of a utopian future.'

'And others by visions of a utopian past. The man who is lost tries to make his way back to where he knew where he was, or thought he knew where he was … But now let us talk about more pleasant things.'

Binswanger lit a cigarette, smiled oddly and pretended to pretend that they had been merely gossiping about nothing in particular for the previous half hour.

20

Sigrid and Polanyi were lazing, naked, on Polanyi's Japanese mat – beds were bourgeois, he maintained, more than half-seriously – in his chaotic room on the top floor of the house on the Girardigasse. The walls were covered with theatrical and cinema posters in lieu of wallpaper; and there were three framed von Bayros lithographs, some of the tamer ones. His desk was a clutter of typewritten papers – the product of his nineteenth-century typewriter – handle-less mugs stuffed with pens and pencils, and two overflowing tin-top ashtrays. Some of his threadbare shirts and underwear were hanging up to dry on a clothes-horse precariously attached to the mock-baroque and welcomingly-warm ceramic stove. And his bookshelves – he was currently wading through Gross's *The Taboo on the Public Representation of the Tumescent Phallus* – consisted of half a dozen Jaffa orange crates stacked on top of one another. Though the spring light flooding through the balcony glass doors and the view of the tops of the still-leafless Girardigasse trees outside gave the room a light and airy feel.

'Tell me,' she said as her hand slid up and down his erect and delightfully solid penis, 'what you are thinking?'

His unshaven face was alight with pleasure, his eyes like those of a child anticipating the heaven of a chocolate-sprinkled ice cream cone.

'That there's not enough mindless fucking in the world,' he said.

'There might be more if men were not such pigs.'

'Or women such prudes.'

She pretended to frown.

'Present company excepted,' he added.

'Or if women didn't get pregnant,' she added.

He ejaculated slowly, the sperm bubbling out his cock and onto her hand and his large, hairy belly. Then she lay on top of him, and they both fell into a half-doze, the wet sperm drying from the warmth of their intertwined bodies.

'Italy is only the beginning,' he said about ten minutes later. 'A world of aëroplanes, moving pictures, and women voting ruled by emperors and landed aristocrats with their heads in the Middle Ages is a labyrinth of untenable contradictions.'

She looked unconvinced.

'All these fantasy-ideologies,' he continued, 'these imaginings in the heads of short-sighted clerks stooped over their inky ledgers, of a land of strapping peasant lads and buxom maids dancing at the crossroads as in times of yore, of the world as some epic Wagnerian battle between blond warriors and swarthy dwarfs to be fought on glorious battlefields in exotic climes – but with anaesthetics and flying machines: they're the last feverish dreams of the old order. History cannot be wound back like a grandfather clock. No amount of parades and flag-waving is going to change that. The graffiti is on the walls. It's not possible to stop the onward march of electric gramophones and moving-picture houses.'

He slowly slipped a finger into the wet warmth of her cunt. She flushed at the sudden intrusion, then relaxed to welcome it.

'The global financial system is falling apart,' he continued. 'The old categories of thought and ideological allegiances are breaking down. Something new is inevitable.'

'Like what?' she said.

'An anarchist society perhaps,' he said, unexpectedly thoughtful and momentarily more serious than he usually was.

'Utopia?' she joked.

'Ten thousand utopias. A world ruled by ideas we can now barely conceive of, in which men do not live in fear of being separated from the herd by simply standing still. Who knows what the human mind and spirit are capable of? Water boils and suddenly it's steam.'

'It's called a phase change. And only possible if most people believe that it is not only desirable but also possible. That's what Malatesta says, you said yourself. To remove all coercion and violence from the affairs of men would require an educational effort which we can hardly imagine. I think we have a long way to go before that happens. Things don't always fall apart the way we imagine they will. Only educated men could run your anarchist society. If the status quo merely collapses and freedom is dropped into the laps of the masses, their confusion may well lead them to desire even crasser tyrannies.'

***

The idea was very simple, really, and seemed come to from nowhere. Pechstein decided he would try and flush Eisenstein out, beat the bushes as it were, and see what came running out. And the way to do it was by blackmail or rather, by pretending to blackmail him. The rational part of him told him to let the whole affair die a natural death, that that would be a sensible thing to do, and not try and play some sort of Austrian Nick Carter. Neither was it the case that he thought that if he *got his man* – or whatever the expression was – Anja Jensen was going to deliver her white naked body into his arms to do with as … He'd been obsessed with women before, but it had always been short-lived and somehow … sentimental perhaps, no, not quite … But with Anja Jensen it was more an erotic fascination, not even animalistic lust. Though it was not as if he saw her as a great unobtainable beauty. Most men, he imagined, would pass her in the street and not give her that much of a second look.

He put together the blackmail note in his office after work hours, when the building was deserted except for the cleaners and the night porters, from letters cut out of a copy of the *Telegraf*. The wording he eventually decided on was:

adolf j left a paper trail
it aint a pretty sight
u show up at 1400 on Sunday
at planetarium cafe
if u dont want me to go yappin to newspapers

Then, as an afterthought, he'd added:

the supreme anarchist council

One always had an advantage when one's opponent thought one was slightly unhinged. He read it again several times: it was short, to the point, and it conveyed what he hoped was just the right amount of semi-literate criminality. Just what he wanted. He folded it in two, and put it in the brown envelope, licked the gummed flap and sealed it. He was going to send it to Eisenstein's home address, to his villa in leafy Döbling. He'd got the house number and the street from the Vienna Telephone Directory – he hadn't expected it to be listed but it was. But then he realised that he could hardly send a letter with the recipient's address written in letters cut out of a newspaper. He could type it, but the point of the using the cut-out newsprint-letter was that typewriters – like fingerprints – were traceable; they all made slightly differently shaped letter-imprints. Reluctantly, he decided to handwrite it, but in block letters and with his left hand.

He took the electric tram to the Südbahnhof. He could have used a post box close to the Agency; but he was sure Eisenstein would most probably look at the postmark, though it was extremely improbable that he would be able to deduce anything from it. The tram carriage was half-empty. A group of students at the far end was passing around a bottle of cheap Polish vodka. A young couple was engaged in a hushed intense conversation. And opposite him, a bowler-hatted figure was immersed in a copy of the evening edition of the *Beobachter*. The front-page headline was GREAT POWERS DECLARE WAR ON OBSCENITY, an obvious reference to The Second International Obscene Publications Conference taking place in, of all places, Paris. A Gypsy, in his sixties perhaps, got on at Karlsplatz and played a tune on an antique accordion. Pechstein gave him a ten-*Heller* coin and the man nodded as if it was his due. Perhaps it was, he thought, remembering what Binswanger had once said about them being a people who had never waged a war.

Pechstein got off outside the Südbahnhof and dumped the copy of the *Telegraf* that he had cut the letters from into a litter bin. The air was damp and warm. It had rained earlier and the puddles of water that had collected on the pavement and cobblestoned street reflected the electric lights from the buildings and streetlamps. A large flood-lit poster was advertising the new UFA sensation from Berlin, Fritz Lang's *The Time Machine*, in FANTASTIC COLOUR, the latest *Gertie the Dinosaur* animation film and yet another Karl May Red Indian saga.

The Südbahnhof was packed. There's been a mass demonstration earlier. The demonstrators – a more respectably dressed crowd than one usually associated with street politics, most of them men in suits – were still carrying their SOCIAL MONARCHY placards, their banners and their miniature yellow-and-black flags. Were they last vestiges of the nineteenth century, he wondered, or was the future going to be shaped by some species of reactionary modernism?

Eventually, he managed to reach the post box and slid the brown envelope into the letter slot. Every man has a snapping point, he thought as the letter dropped irrevocably into the imperial postal system: would this be Eisenstein's? But if it did flush Eisenstein out, and somehow got him to betray himself, what then?

                                ***

Pechstein had more than a few second thoughts about going to the planetarium to see if Eisenstein would turn up. The minute he'd put the blackmail note – the *fake* blackmail note? – into the post box amid the commotion at the Südbahnhof, he'd immediately begun to wonder if he had done something unbelievably stupid. But what was done was done. He'd chosen the planetarium because he hadn't been able to think of anywhere else and, he'd thought, it was as good as anywhere. But now, he realised, from the point of view of putting the fear of God into Eisenstein, it had been a good choice. The man would immediately realise that the writer of the note that had dropped so unexpectedly through the letterbox of his Döbling villa knew enough about him to know that he'd used the planetarium, at least once, to meet with Dolfi Jensen, perhaps even for their last meeting. He had dismissed the idea of wearing some ridiculous disguise. Effective disguises were the stuff of Sherlock Holmes novellas. If Eisenstein appeared and recognised him wearing a false beard and sunglasses, dressed like a music-hall comedian, he would have been hard put to provide any sort of plausible explanation.

He arrived twenty minutes before two o'clock. The planetarium café was full. It seemed as if half of Vienna had turned out in their Sunday best – the bourgeoisie and better-off proletarians near-indistinguishable from each other, the men in their dark suits, the women in their ever-shortening dresses – intent on educating themselves about the wonders of the cosmos. He chose an out-of-the-way table in a quiet alcove and concealed himself behind a copy of the *Wiener Sonn- und Montags-Zeitung*. If Eisenstein did turn up and saw him, he would simply have to brave it out, keep cool and put it down to serendipity. While he waited to be served, he pondered the elegant modernity of the Jugendstil decor of the place: clean colours and clear lines, with coffee pots, cutlery and ashtrays designed to match. Large colour-tinted monochrome photographs of the Milky Way, of countless stars adrift in the unimaginable vastness of the cosmos – or as that American William James put it, 'the celestial ocean of ether whose waves are light' – lined the walls; and for a moment wondered how many stars there were in a galaxy – it must be millions. He decided he would wait for just over half an hour. If Eisenstein was going to turn up, he was hardly going to be late.

He ordered a pear tart and cappuccino and attempted to read a long and rather wordy piece on 'Psychoanalysis and the Contemporary Woman' – by Rosa Mayreder of *Gender and Culture* fame – intermittently casting a surreptitious glance in the direction of the entrance and the terrace visible through the open plate-glass windows, and keeping an eye the minute hand on the Jugendstil clock as it slowly edged its way toward half past two. He could not help thinking that it was an unusual choice of venue for Eisenstein's meetings with Jensen; perhaps it had been Dolfi Jensen's idea.

The gist of Mayreder's essay was about how the emancipated woman, the so-called man-woman, and the so-called effeminate man – and prosperous Jews – were perceived as a threat to the 'self-portrait of civilised manhood'; all of which was to do with the 'psycho-sexual dynamics of patriarchal social forms' and 'the crusade against Eros which Christianity has been waging for two millennia'. There was a lot about the iconography of uniforms and what Mayreder referred to as 'militarist psycho-pathology'. Karl Marx was mentioned a few times, and Rosa Luxemburg's new book.

There was also a short article on the outbreak of some new disease in America that they were calling the Kansas influenza.

The Jugendstil clock reached three o'clock. And there was no sign of Eisenstein. Pechstein decided to smoke one more Sphinx. If the Man in the Iron Mask had not appeared by then, then he was unlikely to appear at all. He smoked slowly and then found himself stubbing out the cigarette butt. Eisenstein had not appeared. He decided to pay and go. He raised his hand and caught the eye of one of the waiters.

21

'Meet me in front of your offices in half an hour,' Binswanger's crackly voice said down the telephone line early next morning. 'I'll pick you up. I have something to show you. I think you'll find it of interest.'

Half an hour later Binswanger's new poison-green electric Austro-Daimler, driven by a uniformed constable, pulled up in front of the Agency.

'Do you remember the Redl affair?' he asked Pechstein as they drove up the Währingerstraße. It was a glorious May day. The summer of 1921 was arriving at last.

'Vaguely. Killed himself, didn't he? In '13 or thereabouts. Some sort of spy scandal. I remember reading about it at the time but I can't remember the details.'

'I shall refresh your memory,' Binswanger said. 'It's a story to bear in mind when we get to our destination.'

'I'm intrigued,' Pechstein said. But he was also relieved. He couldn't see how Binswanger could have found out about his note to Eisenstein but the dreadful possibility that he somehow had was lurking in the back of his mind.

'Oberst Alfred Redl was high up in the Evidenzbüro, and the head of the general staff for the Eight Corps in Prague. He'd been selling army secrets to the Russians for years. An invert. Queer as a coot. The *dreaded* Okhrana – who are, as we know, adept in these matters – found out he was having a *thing* with some pretty officer in the Dragoons and got their claws into him. That's the theory anyway. They paid him well though. Ivan can be generous when it suits his nefarious purposes.'

They turned onto one of Döbling's leafy residential streets and into a police roadblock.

'A symbolic gesture,' Binswanger explained, referring to the roadblock. 'There hasn't been any trouble out here. But the good citizens of Döbling need some reassuring that Father State has everything under control. Nothing to do with what I want to show you.'

They were waved through and drove on.

'Over the years the boy became greedy,' Binswanger continued, 'got used to the rather expensive tastes he had developed. Two automobiles. A stable of thoroughbred gee-gees. Country house. A harem of sumptuous cadets.'

Binswanger had been in the Vice Commission for a while, which made him pretty unshockable as regards anything to do with sex or, for that matter, any other weakness human flesh was prone to. He'd spent a year tracking down an eastern Jewish mafia set-up – he was a near-fluent Yiddish speaker – involved in trafficking peasant girls from Galicia, a few hundred of whom had ended up in the brothels of Constantinople, Alexandria and Buenos Aires, and even Batavia. There were fifty thousand full-time and part-time prostitutes in the city, and their clients outnumbered them by ten to one. All made possible, Binswanger maintained, by the hypocrisy of a society which simultaneous both held prostitutes in contempt and pretended that they did not exist, and thus inevitably leaving most of them to eke out their livings in a lawless underworld.

'Eventually, he also offered his services to the Frogs and the Italians,' the policeman continued. 'He was raking in fifty thousand *Kronen* a year, they say. But, as is usually the case, he was found out. Made a full confession. Then they handed him a pistol and told him to do the decent thing. Best for all concerned and all that. Blew his brains out in his Prague apartment a few hours later. Franz Ferdinand had a fit when he learned about it. Convinced Franz Joseph that some heads had to roll. Anyway, that's the quasi-official unofficial version that has come down to us from on high.'

The trees and the shrubs in the gardens of Vienna's *haute bourgeoisie* were in full blossom, and there was the distinct smell of spring in the suburban air.

'Would you?' Binswanger asked.

'Would I what?'

'Do the decent thing? Under circumstances?' But it was not really a question. 'It has always seemed to me such an extremely ambiguous thing. A man commits a crime so terrible, so low. Yet, despite the fact that he has become the lowest of the lowest, he is prepared to annihilate himself – in order to expunge the shame of it. Which is surely evidence of an essentially noble soul.'

They passed a street sign. Pechstein only caught a glimpse of it as they sped by but was able to make out the Gothick lettering: Walnußgasse. Eisenstein's villa was on the Walnußgasse. Suddenly everything, the drive, Binswanger's tale and his talk of doing the decent thing, had become ominous. Pechstein literally felt a chill crawl down his spine.

'Where are we going?' he asked.

'All shall be revealed in due course.'

But Binswanger was being oddly good humoured, Pechstein thought, and for a moment the policeman hummed a few bars of that new song, 'Ja Da, Ja Da, Jing, Jing, Jing!' – for seemingly no particular reason. The thing was total gibberish but surprisingly popular. Pechstein was not reassured.

A few minutes later they sighted a uniformed constable at the gate of one of the villas.

'The residence of the late Maximilian Eisenstein,' Binswanger announced as the automobile came to a halt, but Pechstein had already seen the nameplate on one of the ivy-covered gate posts. '*Et in Arcadia ego*. That's the phrase, isn't it, on the tomb in that Poussin painting?'

The constable stepped forward to open the automobile door for them.

'The late?'

'The housemaid found him yesterday,' Binswanger began to explain as they walked up the gravelled drive to the two-storey villa. 'He doesn't have any live-in staff. Or rather didn't. Which is rather surprising when one considers …'

'Found him? *Didn't?*'

'Found his corpse. In his study. He'd been dead about maybe sixteen hours by then. Twelve at least, we reckon.'

Binswanger had a key to the porticoed front door. They entered and made their way towards a half-open door at the end of a carpeted hallway. Pechstein could not help noticing the paintings on the walls – all Orientalist fantasies – which only added to his sense of ominous disorientation.

'Persian,' Binswanger commented, referring to the carpet. 'And that,' he added, indicating a painting of a smoking female nude in what was presumably a harem, 'if I'm not mistaken, is Lecomte du Nouÿ's *The White Slave*. A copy of course. Thought some of them are originals, I think. There's a Klimt in his bedroom, no doubt a minor work, but all the same …'

The entered Eisenstein's study. For a moment Pechstein had half-expected that the corpse would still be *in situ*. There was a dark puddle-like stain on the tawny-brown leather desk covering.

'Blood,' Binswanger explained. 'The main mess was on the curtains behind him. The bullet took the back of his skull off, smashed one of the window panes. We found a chunk of skull bone in the shrubbery.'

There were no curtains. They had obviously been removed. But the jagged edges of the smashed pane of glass were still in place. The garden outside was bathed in sunlight, and the dandelions on the grass lawn were in their first flush of yellowness. There was an expensive-looking telescope on a tripod beside the window.

'Shot himself in the face. Not a pretty sight.'

Pechstein felt nauseous.

'He probably meant to shoot himself in the mouth – that's the usual practice – and pretty foolproof. But I suppose the pistol went off prematurely.'

'Horrific,' Pechstein said.

God Almighty, he thought, this was not what he had intended … that that insane note of his would push Eisenstein over the edge into insanity. Had Binswanger found the blackmail note? But even if he had, surely he could not possibly know that he had sent it.

'That one is also by Lecomte du Nouÿ,' Binswanger said, referring to another painting, of a reclining oriental on the roof of a house, smoking a long pipe, staring into a starry oriental sky, the white whirls of his pipe smoke forming into a ghostly erotic apparition floating above the background was of a moonlit desert. 'I believe it's called *The Eunuch's Dream*.'

'And you think he was given a pistol and asked to do the decent thing?' Pechstein said, trying to keep his wits about him. He tried but failed to visualise Eisenstein opening the envelope, reading the note, slipping suddenly into nightmarish despair … The thought of it made him feel faint again. But he managed to steady himself. 'Like Redl?'

'From what you told me that day in the Phaffenhof, he left a bit of a sloppy trail of clues behind him,' Binswanger continued. 'If you managed to stumble across them, I'm sure the internal security lads at the StaPo were also capable of doing so.'

'That makes sense,' Pechstein said. It was a possibility, he had to admit, but it was speculation. But at least it seemed that Binswanger had not discovered his blackmail note.

'These are not normal times,' Binswanger continued. 'Not that any times really are normal. It does not take the imagination of a genius to imagine reasons why the clandestine organs of the state would take extraordinary measures to cover up a potential scandal right now. But that's only half the story. Follow me.'

He led Pechstein down the carpeted hallway again and into another room. There was a glass display cabinet containing a collection of various guns. One of the panes of glass was broken.

'He was a gun collector,' Binswanger explained. 'It looks like he smashed the glass to get at the pistol.'

'But surely he would have had a key!'

'One would have thought so, but he obviously didn't use it.'

Pechstein was about to say surely that did not make any sense, but Binswanger spoke again.

'I think the lads from the StaPo did it. Smashed the glass, put the gun in his hand – at the same time terrifying the shit out of him. Who knows how these things are done? Not very prettily, I should imagine.'

Pechstein nodded, not quite convinced.

'There's more,' Binswanger said.

They went into the kitchen. It Binswanger opened a wooden side door beside a large and modern electric stove.

'To the cellar,' he explained, switching on an electric light by a switch just inside the door. 'To the underworld.'

They made their way down wooden steps.

The cellar was large – larger than the kitchen directly above it, though the ceiling was only half as high – and empty except for a chest-like grey metal-framed cabinet about the size of an office desk.

'Have you ever read those Sherlock Holmes stories?' Binswanger asked him.

'A few of them once. Why?'

'In one of them, Holmes says something along the lines that when you have eliminated what's not impossible, whatever remains, however seemingly improbable, must be the truth.'

Pechstein lit a Sphinx, in his agitation forgetting to offer Binswanger one.

'We are faced here with a series of mysteries, three essentially,' Binswanger continued.

'Go on,' Pechstein said.

'One: Dolfi Jensen disappears. Two: Dolfi Jensen is fished dead out of the Danube. Three: Maximilian Eisenstein blows his brains out.'

Pechstein noticed there was a faint humming sound coming from the cabinet.

'We have established that there is a connection – a rather intricate connection – between Dolfi Jensen and Maximilian Eisenstein,' Binswanger continued. 'Would you agree?'

'Yes.'

'Now if we assume that all three events are somehow connected. The question is: how are they connected? So, let us look at the why of each, starting with number three.'

'Why Eisenstein killed himself?'

'Yes. I'm convinced it was a Redl-type job.'

'How can you be so sure?'

'Bear with me. Let's start with first principles. And use a process of elimination.'

'Go on.'

'If a man kills himself, the natural question is what drove him to do it. Rejection in love? Money? Or did he do it while, as the lawyers put it, the balance of his mind was disturbed? But by all accounts, Maximilian Eisenstein was a sane man, not given to moods of Dürerian melancholia – though, judging from his rather Orientalist taste in art, a man who yearned for some timeless erotic paradise, as an antidote to the hectic of modernity perhaps. So, we can probably dismiss the possibility of his mind being temporarily out of sorts. As for rejection in love: well, I think we can safely assume that he was not a middle-aged Young Werther. Which leaves money.'

'It doesn't look as if he was lacking in that department.'

'He might have been up to his eyeballs in debt.'

'True', Pechstein admitted.

'But I don't think he was. Though no doubt we'll find out if he was. Creditors crawl out of the woodwork rather quickly in cases like this. And even if he was in debt, one needs money to get into debt – on any scale in any case. But in a roundabout way it was about money: the money he was getting from selling state secrets. One usually receives a remuneration for that sort of thing. Or rather it was about being found out selling state secrets and the subsequent visit from the men in tweed suits. There must have been a sense of shame, I suppose. And then some skilled psychological manipulation – with a bit of sheer terror thrown in.'

'So you are convinced that was how it happened?'

'Can't be absolutely certain of course. Can't say I've proof positive beyond all doubt but it all hangs together. Rather unlikely to be all just coincidence?'

'Go on,' Pechstein said. He was now certain that Binswanger had not found the blackmail note. Perhaps Eisenstein had destroyed it.

'Bear with me,' Binswanger began. 'Item two—'

'Sorry, is there something I could use as an ashtray.'

'Use the floor.'

Pechstein stamped his cigarette out on the flagstones and fought the urge to immediately light up another.

'Item two,' Binswanger began again. 'Fact: Dolfi Jensen is fished out of the Danube, dead. Question: Was it an accident or was he pushed? And if he was pushed, by whom? The Preßburg police were convinced that it was an accident. But I'm sure that if Szombathy was acquainted with – let us say – all the circumstances, he might have come to perhaps a more nuanced conclusion.'

Pechstein nodded slowly.

'So,' Binswanger continued, 'it is not an unreasonable assumption to assume that Jensen was pushed – or, more accurately, dropped, but I'll come to that in a moment – and that the perpetrator was Eisenstein, or some criminals acting on his behalf. We know of no other suspects and, as you yourself have intimated, he certainly had a motive. Could I have one of your cigarettes?'

Pechstein obliged and also lit another one for himself.

'And item one?' Pechstein reminded him.

'Yes, item one. Dolfi Jensen disappears.'

'But it was months before he was found dead?'

'Cast your mind back to the necropsy report. Cause of death?'

'Hypothermia.'

'Stomach contents?'

'The remains of a rich meal, wine, cognac.'

'And half-digested salami, carrots and artichokes.'

'So?'

'I'll come to that. Do you remember what he was wearing when he was found?'

'There was nothing amiss there. I examined his clothes myself – rather thoroughly.'

'Humour me,' Binswanger said.

'Jacket and trousers from Gerngross's, shirt, underwear, necktie.'

'Footwear?'

'Cheap shoes, brown, in need of repair,' Pechstein said, visualising them.

'When exactly was this?'

'January, 1919.'

'Precisely.'

'What are you getting at?'

'January. The middle of winter. Cold. In fact, very cold that year.'

'I still don't understand,' Pechstein said.

'Hardly the attire of a man in the midst of winter, I would suggest,' Binswanger said, stubbing out his cigarette on the flagstone floor.

'Go on.'

'He was found dead in January. The time of death was estimated to be around then too, give or take a few days. Yet he was not dressed for winter. No sign of a winter coat or a furry hat, or winter boots. On the contrary, he was dressed as he would most likely have dressed when he disappeared, which was in July. For summer weather.'

Pechstein wasn't sure he was really following what Binswanger was trying to say. He lit another Sphinx, this time not forgetting to offer Binswanger one.

'Thanks,' Binswanger said. 'I know this is all a bit convoluted but it will make sense in the end.' He accepted a light and inhaled deeply. 'Now back to the contents of Jensen's stomach. Artichokes, wasn't it?'

'Yes.'

'Not a winter fruit.'

Pechstein was about to point out that they might have been tinned artichokes but then remembered that Sigrid Kupfer had said that Jensen was allergic to tinned foods, though they could have been jarred artichokes – which Binswanger didn't know. He began to see the outline of what Binswanger was driving at … But Binswanger seemed to have guessed what he was thinking.

'But if he was killed in July, when he disappeared,' Binswanger said, 'and his body turned up in January surely it would have been in an unpleasantly advanced stage of decomposition? Or more likely eaten by the fishes?'

'Obviously.'

'Unless,' Binswanger said, 'the body was somehow preserved.'

'But how?' Pechstein asked, quickly trying to think how a body could be preserved. In formaldehyde? Mummification? In a bog, like those grotesque Danish bog bodies preserved at the moment of their strangulation during a barbaric ancient ritual? They'd discovered prehistoric woolly mammoths with the contents of their stomach still undigested in frozen tundra.

'In formaldehyde?' he suggested half-heartedly.

'Possible, but I should imagine any half-decent necropsy would reveal that.'

'Then I'm at a complete loss.'

'So was I until I came down here.'

'I don't understand.'

'It took me a while to figure it out. I was called here yesterday morning. The place was crawling with StaPo clerks packing the contents of Eisenstein's desk and that filing cabinet in his study into cardboard boxes and carting them off to their den. They photographed the body *in situ*, questioned the housemaid, and then more or less disappeared, leaving yours truly to arrange for the city morgue to pick up the remains of the dearly departed. There was no need for a necropsy. The cause of death was rather obvious. Brain death caused by a rather clumsily self-administered lead projectile. Eventually, I was left here alone and started thinking – and looking around. What you told me in the Phaffenhof began to churn itself about in my mind. I was a bit short with you that day, but then, you were delving into waters into which I did not want to plunge. Anyway, as I thought it all over, I remembered the Redl story and, very slowly, it all began to fall into place. I began to see the big picture, as they say. It was fuzzy around the edges … But then reality is like that, is it not?'

'Sometimes,' Pechstein admitted, still wondering what role his blackmail note had played, if any, and if it still existed, waiting to be discovered. But then, he thought, even if it was discovered, what difference could it make? Binswanger could hardly trace it back to him. He would merely revise his theory to make it fit somehow. 'Very well,' he continued, verbalising what he thought what Binswanger was thinking. 'Eisenstein killed Jensen. His masters found out. Wanted to prevent a scandal. So Eisenstein was given a choice between the hangman's rope or taking his own life.'

'Or they merely found out that he was selling secrets to those who would do us harm. That would be enough.'

'But the discrepancy between the time of Jensen's disappearance and his death …' Pechstein left the sentence deliberately unfinished.

Binswanger indicated the grey metal-framed cabinet against the wall.

'Do you know what this is?' he asked.

'A storage chest of some kind,' Pechstein suggested.

'One could describe it as that.'

Binswanger began to open the lid. It remained stuck for a moment but then gave way. A blast of cold air hit them. Pechstein looked inside. It was full up to about halfway with joints of meat and game, all of it frozen solid. The interior compartment was noticeably smaller than the external casing.

'An icebox,' Pechstein said.

'Close,' Binswanger said. 'It's a Frigidaire. From America. They've been producing them for ten years or so now. But they've only been on sale here for a couple of years.'

'I've seen advertisements for them.'

Pechstein touched one of the joints of meat. It was as hard as a rock. Then, he suddenly understood what Binswanger was suggesting. But it seemed absurd.

'You think Eisenstein froze the Dolfi Jensen's body in this thing in order to preserve it?' he said.

Binswanger pointed to three small holes in the side of the lid of the Frigidaire and three similar holes on the side of the casing directly underneath.

'Screw holes,' he said. 'Now when I saw that I wondered what on earth one would screw to the case and lid of something—'

'A lock, a padlock of some kind?'

'Precisely,' Binswanger beamed. 'He kept the body here, frozen ... in the bosom of his cellar, as it were, and under lock and key. Not so easy to find somewhere more convenient, I would have imagined.'

Or perhaps, Pechstein thought, he'd simply kept the Frigidaire locked to stop the cleaner and the garden helping themselves to his prime cuts of meat. But he decided not to voice that thought.

'The contents of his stomach were preserved,' Binswanger continued. 'And it would be consistent with Frau Doktor Dobrovodská's diagnosis of the cause of death as hypothermia. Then when the time was ripe, Eisenstein somehow, unobserved, conveyed it to the banks of the Danube and dropped it into the water. Either personally or via accomplices.'

Seemingly absurd though it was, Pechstein had to admit to himself that there was a certain logic to Binswanger's elaborate theory.

'When you have eliminated what's not impossible,' Binswanger repeated, 'whatever remains, however seemingly improbable, must be the truth.'

Pechstein had found Holmesian logic rather contrived at the best to times, to say nothing of the plots, in which everything fell too implausibly and too neatly into place. He'd read somewhere that the creator of the great detective – he couldn't recall his name, a Sir somebody – had also been involved in photographing faeries hovering above the flowerbeds of English gardens.

'And do you have a theory of how Eisenstein might have actually killed Dolfi Jensen?' Pechstein asked him.

'A bit of a mystery that. No obvious marks on the body. Poison? Perhaps some sort of drug that rendered him unconscious. His being drunk would have helped, which the necropsy report indicated he was. Freezing would have done the rest. However, that is rather academic now. We're never going to find out the details of that, I'm afraid.'

Binswanger shut the lid of the Frigidaire.

'Shall we go up?'

'So, what do you intend to do now?' Pechstein asked.

'Nix. Nothing. Case closed as far as I'm concerned. As I said, these are not normal times. The winds of change are howling. A lot of effort went into covering all this up … There would be some very unhappy powerful people should that covering-up be, as it were, uncovered. When this is all over – things will settle down, they always do – and when that happens, I want to be still in one piece, and so should you.'

As they were about to leave the house, Binswanger excused himself for a moment to go to the lavatory. And it was then that Pechstein saw it: the brown envelope with Eisenstein's address in the awkward block letters he'd written with his left hand on it, the envelope containing his insane blackmail note. It was sticking out from a small pile of other post on a small table by the front door. Pechstein didn't even consider for a moment what to do. He instinctually grabbed it and shoved it into his jacket pocket. Just as Binswanger reappeared.

'Done,' the policeman said, picking up the mail. 'Nearly forget this lot. Meant to pick it up earlier. Though I doubt there's anything of interest in it.'

'Was there a suicide note?' Pechstein asked him as they drove back towards the city centre. 'There usually is, isn't there?'

'Yes, and no. There was a note but—'

'What did it say?'

'I comma Maximilian Eisenstein comma.'

'I don't understand?'

'That's what it said: *I, Maximilian Eisenstein, …*'

'That's all?'

'Yes. Perhaps it was something else. A last will and testament begun and not completed? Who knows? But then he might have started writing a suicide note and couldn't go through with it – or he was fiddling with the gun and it went off. In suicide cases generally … yes, they do leave notes. But in a case like this, when a man wants to cover up his crimes, bury his shame in a deep grave … Who knows what really goes on in another man's most inner thoughts? Especially as he is just about to meet his Creator. Maybe it was some sort of metaphysical statement.'

'Possible,' Pechstein said, for form's sake.

'His fingerprints were on the gun. It was a Danish military revolver, a so-called pinfire. Packs quite a punch. It's a rare weapon. Part of his collection.'

'Danish?'

'Yes,' Binswanger said. 'It was easy to identify. It had KRONBORG GEVÆRFABRIK stamped in capital letters on the barrel. That's the factory in Copenhagen where it was manufactured. It has a very ingenious safety catch. They stopped making them at the end of the last century.' A row of army trucks heading out of the city began to pass them on the other side of the Währingerstraße. 'I have a meeting with the gentlemen of the press next. Can't say I'm looking forward to it. But some sort of official statement is deemed to be required. No doubt they'll be panting for some juicy details – disgusting bloodhounds that they are – but I shall endeavour to do my best to disappoint them.'

'Where do you think they are heading?' Pechstein asked, referring to the army trucks, trying to remember what Polanyi had said about Dolfi Jensen having a Danish pistol.

'Into the Future with a Hegelian F,' Binswanger said a moment later. 'Whatever that will look like. That fossil bird-thing, halfway between a lizard and a bird. What's it called?'

'An archaeopteryx.'

'Sometimes I think that's what we are. Something halfway along the way to what we might eventually be. We're a bit of a mess, what we are right now, all things considering. Don't you think?'

They were approaching the city centre. The grey-black whale-like balloons were still floating motionless above the government quarter, but there were only three of them now, for some reason.

'How do you suppose they began to suspect that Eisenstein was ... not exactly playing by the rules?' Pechstein asked, partly out of curiosity regarding how Binswanger had come up with his theory, and partly because he half-hoped that that was what had happened.

'Maybe it had something to do with that teleprint, the one I never told you about, the one I never saw.'

'Go on,' Pechstein said.

'Why would Berlin know about Jensen? He wasn't working for them. And those initials ... M E meant Maximilian Eisenstein. And it was in his office that I cast my eyes upon the document. Think about it. Maybe somebody noticed that Berlin had no good reason to know that Jensen was working for the Castle. Of course, passing on unauthorised information to Berlin is a serious misdemeanour – it's hardly in the same league as spying for Saint Petersburg or Paris – but, well, one thing leads to another.'

Eisenstein being a spy of some kind would also, of course, mean that the two gentlemen, the StaPo agents, who had paid Weber a call – on a tip-off from the informer in the Agency which Weber had alluded to – had been telling the truth: the StaPo was not directly involved in Dolfi Jensen's disappearance and death. Had Eisenstein sent them there to try and get Weber to get him to stop asking questions? It took a determined act of will to remain outwardly calm until Binswanger dropped him off at the Agency.

***

Pechstein's hands were shaking as he opened the bottle of Danziger Goldwasser he kept – and normally rarely touched – in the drawer of his office desk. He poured himself half a glass and swallowed the vodka in one draught, and then poured himself another. Then he lit another Sphinx. One's life drifts by uneventfully like a boat upon a becalmed sea under a becalmed sky and suddenly a raging storm erupts and every damn thing is thrown into frantic disarray. But at least he'd managed to recover the blackmail letter.

'It had done a Houdini,' Polanyi had said. 'Disappeared.'

Christ, what a nightmare!

He finished off the second half-glass of vodka and poured another, put the bottle back in the desk drawer and shut it. He needed to steady his nerves. And he needed to be able to think.

Eisenstein's death had had nothing to do with his stupid blackmail note, nor with Binswanger's men in tweed suits – and his theory about the pistol going off prematurely was also pure fantasy. He was sure of it. But first, he needed to know what Binswanger going to say to the newspapers. Perhaps it would be in the early morning editions.

22

The previous day's demonstrations and Karl I's address to the joint session of the Austrian Reichstag and the Hungarian Parliament took up the front, second and third pages of the *Telegraf*. The article on Eisenstein was on the fourth page:

TRAGIC DEATH OF LONG-SERVING STATE SERVANT

What Pechstein had been dreading was in the last paragraph:

> Herr Eisenstein, an avid firearms collector, ended his life with a Danish military handgun, a pinfire revolver, a rare weapon last manufactured during the Second Schleswig War but still used by the Danish military, though those now in service have been converted to centrefire. The investigating officers believe the respected administrator committed the tragic act while the balance of his mind was temporarily severely disturbed due to personal circumstances.

Needless to say, there was no mention of either the StaPo or the Evidenzbüro. The reports in the *Wiener Zeitung* and the *Beobachter* were similar, and they both gave the details about the revolver. The chances that Polanyi would not find out were zero. News of the Man in the Iron Mask blowing his head off in his arcadian villa in leafy Döbling would no doubt spread like a wildfire in the radical demimonde.

***

When Pechstein got to the Crimson Cockatoo, just before noon, some sort of lecture was taking place in the backroom. There was a handwritten sign saying AGAINST TOTAL MECHANICALISATION taped to the wall beside the doorway. An about fifty-strong crowd – of men and women – was packed into the classroom-sized space. There were only enough chairs for half of them. People were squashed up two-deep along the walls and some were sitting on the floor. Despite the two wide-open side-windows, a thick fog of tobacco smoke hung in the air. Most of the summer-clad listeners looked as if they had simply absented themselves from their workplaces, something which would not have happened a fortnight ago, or even a week ago.

The lecturer was a tall, unshaven, lanky man dressed in a shabby and ill-fitting Imperial Customs Service uniform – he was even wearing his peaked cap. Pechstein was half-sure he'd seen him somewhere once, but couldn't for the life of him remember where.

'… a photograph of the world is not the world,' he was saying. He had a deep voice and was speaking slowly, giving the impression that he was choosing each word with the utmost care. 'Real knowledge of the world is only achieved when we don't take the world as it appears in the photograph of it produced by our minds – minds numbed by the routines of habit, the factory clock, the mental drudgery of clerical work, the inane *Weltanschauung* peddled by the yellow press, or distracted by the cheap dreams peddled by advertisers and the publishers of romantic novelists.' He had a few pages of notes in front of him on the lectern but was only glancing at them. 'Real knowledge is only achieved when we can perceive the world's invisible structures and dynamics …'

'Material circumstances determine states of consciousness,' a man's voice, Bosnian accent, half-commented, half-shouted. But from where he was standing in the press by the door, Pechstein couldn't see who it was.

'Perhaps, comrade. But perhaps Karl Marx's interpretation of the world was a bit too mechanistic, a bit too physicalist.'

Pechstein could not see any sign of Polanyi, but that bearded

Transylvanian *Naturmensch* who'd been at Dolfi Jensen's funeral and whom Siegfried Bell had described in his letter to Anja Jensen was there. He was sitting on the floor, cross-legged like an Indian yogi, to the left of the lectern.

'What we see of reality is a visualisation,' the unlikely customs officer continued. 'Normally this is a reasonably precise and solid visualisation of the surface of the things perceived, of matter – and matter is, Einstein seems to be suggesting, as far as I can see, in reality a sort of crystallised energy. Sense-information, light-information, is transformed into images in our minds. But some men, under some circumstances, can also visualise mythical forces and elemental spirits – visualisations based on feeling-information rather than on sense-information – in the form of nature spirits, or Paracelsus' elementals, or the trolls, faeries and elves of folklore …'

Pechstein decided to try and edge himself further down the wall. Almost all he could see from where he was were the backs of people's heads.

'… that of course is not a proposition that can be – as we say – proved scientifically. Though is not science itself based on detecting the invisible mechanisms behind and within natural phenomena? But there are ways of knowing other than through the methods of the material sciences. There are other methods and ways of gaining insights into the All. There is the knowing that comes through art. Through the contemplation of natural landscapes – on canvas, or in nature. Through poetry. Through music. Through the beauty of the human form. From the myths of religion. Through the use of magical plants. During the erotic act at its most sublime … These other ways of knowing give us what I call meta-rational insights into the All – which, to slightly misquote an English mediæval mystic, transcends the light of reason …'

Pechstein managed to get himself almost to the front. As he examined the faces in the crowd in search of Polanyi, he could not help thinking how … peculiar? strange? – he couldn't think of the right word – all this, this crowd cramped into the backroom of a futurist-anarchist art gallery listening to an unshaven, peaked-capped officer of the Imperial Customs Service in his scruffy uniform giving a lecture that sounded like something from the pages of the *Theosophische Wegweiser* or the *Zentralblatt für Okkultismus*. He wondered when he was going to get to the Secret Chiefs in the Himalayas?

'And we are to base the restructuring of society on this so-called meta-reason?' a voice shouted. It was the Bosnian again.

'On the contrary,' the unlikely guru replied. 'Reason is essential to public life, to a humane politics. An enlightened society, to somewhat paraphrase Kant, requires what he called "the public use of reason", the ordering of public affairs on the basis of reason. Meta-reason is a private perception of the world, though of course it can be an experience shared with others.'

Pechstein was quite sure – the unlikely guru's paraphrasing notwithstanding – that was not quite what Kant had said. But then it clicked: the lecturer was Tobias Donnerstag. When he'd seen him at Dolfi Jensen's funeral, he hadn't been wearing his uniform. Żuławski's description fitted exactly: 'Goes around in his customs officer uniform most of the time but still manages to look like a tramp. Involved in occult nonsense.'

'… the deepest roots of knowing are vegetal and animal. Trees know things. Birds, bats and fish know things. The genealogy of human knowing began with the first shaman – who was also the first artist, the first medicine man, the first analytical psychologist, the first astronomer, the first botanist, the first meteorologist, the first moral philosopher, the first natural scientist. The agricultural Neolithic revolution and the surpluses it created enabled the first specialisations: priests and warriors, lawyers and astrologers, masons and physicians. Then, as time went on, and with the first and second industrial revolutions, more and more specialisations appeared. And as the tree of knowledge grew over the millennia, all these realms of human knowledge branched out from each other, became separate branches, refined and perfected themselves, and in turn sprouted sub-branches. And even those which were fruitless and withered on the bough, as it were, contain some valuable seed of ways of knowing the All. But none in itself can perceive all aspects of the All.'

Donnerstag's voice was strangely soothing; and, Pechstein had to admit, he did have a gift of hinting at a universe of strange possibilities. Though, he suspected, what the unlikely latter-day neo-shaman was saying would most likely come across as pseudo-mystical God-knows-what if read in cold print.

'… astrology became astronomy, and while alchemy became chemistry, it is now, at least according to Doktor Jung, also in the process of becoming a way for knowing the psychology of the soul. But these kingdoms of knowledge must once again become entangled in our minds – as they are in reality – cross-fertilise each other, not wander off to exist in splendid and sterile isolation, oblivious to each other, in a spiritual desert …'

Pechstein thought of the moonlit desert in the painting in Eisenstein's study.

'… and now, mankind is at a point in our evolution where we have the beginnings of the capability to cause a total industrialisation, a total mechanicalisation of the world, to lock our consciousness into the lower realms of reason, and forever banish what is not visible from our minds. And that will be our fate unless we truly begin to perceive the thin biosphere that envelopes Mother Earth – and in which we exist – as a living thing. We must see that which is invisible to our material eyes, as well as all that is visible. Instead of seeing the woods and forests as merely so much timber – or even as merely as sources of oxygen – we must learn to sense the elemental spirits of the plant world. Instead of seeing our fellow animal creatures as merely so much raw material for our Sunday dinners and our slaughterhouses, we must learn to see them as fellow beings …'

Then, suddenly, Donnerstag had finished and the crowd was clapping, and Pechstein remembered why he was there.

A few minutes later, in the main gallery, he managed to speak to Donnerstag beside a small bronze statue on a plinth: a giant-headed, Bacchus-bellied goblin-creature with an oversized head. It could have been an abstract Futurist work or genuinely African; it was impossible to tell.

'You need to speak to Viktor Polanyi urgently?' Donnerstag said, repeating what Pechstein had said, raising his black shaggy eyebrows, making the statement into a question.

In the background, somebody with a Russian accent was saying 'Perhaps we should live *as if* we are immortal beings.'

'I have nothing to do with the authorities,' Pechstein said. 'If that's what you think.'

Donnerstag looked at him, obviously trying to decide whether he should believe that.

***

Pechstein took a trolleybus to the Philharmonikerstraße and then the electric tram to the Imperial Botanical Gardens. Public transport was running as normal, and with typical Austrian efficiency; though a lot of the carriages were decked out in bunting – mainly red, black, suffragist purple, and green; he had no idea what the latter signified. He was reminded of the week of the funeral of the two emperors, though then – in what seemed another epoch now – it had been funereal black and imperial flags. Most of the newspapers, even the *Beobachter,* now also under what was being called 'workers' administration', had taken to adding colours to their mastheads which best reflected their political sympathies.

The streets were as busy as on any working day. The white-gloved traffic constables were on their podiums and doing their usual semaphore-like gesticulations. But the atmosphere was different, lighter, playful even. Perhaps it was the mixture of the weather, the blue sky and the sun, and giddiness of what was happening politically, in the empire and in Germany and across half the continent. Banners hung from the windows of a surprising number of office buildings. Most of the slogans were ones that had become near-meaningless from overuse, but a surprising number of them – such as REVOLUTION IS THE HOPE-IUM OF THE MASSES or ANARCHISTS NEED TO GET ORGANISED – captured the light-hearted anarchic mood that had overtaken the city. One hanging from the open windows of the Saint Vincent de Paul Shelter for Indigent Men read: THE LUMPENPROLETARIAT HAS NOTHING TO LOSE BUT ITS RAGS! God only knew what was going on in there. But there was also a vaguely unnerving unpredictability in the air. To think that the 'forces of reaction' had capitulated and had simply gone away was delusional, and he suspected that some of them lurked in the banner-strewn office buildings.

No doubt things would settle down again. But into what new social and cultural configuration it was impossible to guess. However, to think that Eisenstein's death – which the Castle must suspect might not have been a suicide, but for some reason were allowing to officially pass as a suicide – would simply be forgotten in the current turmoil would be folly. Police bureaucracies survived political and social upheavals. The traffic constable would continue to direct traffic no matter what constellation of forces wandered the corridors of power or what social reforms were implemented; and so too, he didn't doubt, would the Castle continue, or some incarnation of it, along with the bureaucrats who ran it. But right now, the danger was that Polanyi might, for some reason, decide to let it be known that Dolfi Jensen had possessed a Danish military revolver matching the description of the murder–suicide weapon. Pechstein tried to conjure up the image of Anja Jensen slowly, with malice aforethought, in cold blood, planning to make her way to Eisenstein's Döbling lair – he'd told her where it was and shown her that grainy photograph of Eisenstein in the *Telegraf* – and Eisenstein inviting her into his study and then her simply extracting the handgun from her handbag or a jacket pocket, pointing it at him, pulling the trigger, and then making it all look like suicide … But he couldn't. Or was it that he did not want to?

But why had Polanyi told him about the pistol at all?

He tried to order his thoughts.

Anja Jensen had the motive and means. But didn't Polanyi also have a motive? He remembered what Żuławski had said about that warehouse fire and the unrecognisable body found in the ruins: 'Perhaps the body they found was not of the arsonist but somebody Polanyi knew … somebody he was quite close to. Word in the anarchist back alleys was that he believed the StaPo was behind it … that one day the Man in the Iron Mask would have a face and *vengeance would be ours.*' Then there was Polanyi's reaction that time in the Café of Electric Delusions when he'd found out Wartenheim was Eisenstein. Had Polanyi told him about the Danish revolver disappearing because he wanted to cover up having taken it himself, thinking that … thinking what? The man had all sorts of radical connections. Had Polanyi wanted him to think that Anja Jensen had taken it? What had Żuławski said he called himself? An anarcho-cosmist or something, as fantastical a political philosophy as you can get. Polanyi could easily have found out where Eisenstein lived. He knew what he looked like, so all he would have needed to do was follow him from the War Ministry back to his villa. He had already proved himself adept at following a man unobserved.

Pechstein got off at the city-centre end of the Jacquingasse. Groups of artists were painting the three-metre-high red-brick wall that surrounded the Imperial Botanical Gardens. Some were perched on ladders. Others were squatting on the ground so as to be able to paint the lower part section. There were tins of paint of every conceivably colour all over the place. The whole scene looked utterly chaotic, but despite the fact that various mini-murals were being painted on the wall in a plethora of different styles – Italian Futurist, French Expressionist, German Romantic Realism – there was a sort of thematic unity to the overall image they were creating, though it took Pechstein a minute or two to figure out exactly what it was.

The paint-stained artists were painting figures and objects that looked as if they were breaking through the wall, trying to give the overall impression that the elemental forces that inhabited the greenery of the botanical garden were escaping through breaches in the brickwork. A Jugendstil bare-breasted Marianne, her long blond hair flowing behind her, was emerging through one painted breach, floating out of the painted arboreal background. She had an electric torch aloft in one hand, its light rays stylised lightning bolts, and in the other an unfurling green banner with the word SOLIDARITY written on it. Hovering above her was a five-pointed purple star, like a twentieth-century Star of Bethlehem. A Cubist jumble of a dozen shades of green with the odd primary colour filled another imaginary breach. Pechstein had to look at it for a few moments before he could make out what it was supposed to be. Then he saw it: a Green Man playing a Pan flute. The mythical figure, suddenly visible, was impossible to banish into the greenery again. A mono-wing aëroplane was gliding out from another breach, dropping bouquets of multicoloured flowers instead of bombs.

Eventually, he spotted Polanyi among the commotion. He was wearing a straw hat, knee-length corduroy shorts and walking boots. Pechstein made to traverse the traffic-less street but Polanyi saw him before he was halfway across.

'We are calling it *The Birth of a Garden City*,' Polanyi said. 'It's not a new idea but perhaps an idea whose time has come … Who knows!'

'Imagining the unimaginable,' Pechstein said. The phrase just came to him.

'Colours courtesy of the German chemical industry.'

'You mean the paint?'

'Not that Michelangelo was drab,' Polanyi said. 'Everything will be synthetic eventually, and that's no bad thing. Synthetic rubber saved the buffalo, you know. Machine belts. That's what they used to be hunted for. They used to use their hides for machine belts, mainly. You look like a man on a quest. On a mission.'

'Am I so transparent?'

'Not usually.'

'Is there somewhere we can talk?' Pechstein said.

'That sounds serious.'

'Donnerstag told me I would find you here.'

A few minutes later they were sitting on a bench in the sun outside the main entrance gates, smoking.

'Did you have anything to do with it?' Pechstein asked, deciding to be as vague as possible in the hope that Polanyi might say something unwittingly.

'With what?'

'This Eisenstein business,' Pechstein said.

'You mean him topping himself?'

'I have it from a reliable source that investigations are on-going,' Pechstein lied.

'I got the impression from the newspaper reports that as far as the powers that be are concerned it was all cut and dried.'

Pechstein looked at him.

'Nothing struck you as odd?' he said. 'About the accounts in the newspapers.'

Polanyi dropped the nicotine-stained butt of his hand-rolled cigarette onto the pavement and stubbed it out. Pechstein wondered if it was possible that he had actually forgotten that he had told him about the revolver.

'There are times when the most convenient thing to do is to accept the official account of the way things are.'

Pechstein concluded he had not forgotten about it.

'That fire …' he said.

The expression of Polanyi's unshaven face suddenly changed but Pechstein could not tell what to. Hopelessness? Repressed rage? Or both? He looked at Pechstein for a few moments before speaking.

'I was there that night,' he said.

Pechstein let him go on.

'I saw him in the act, the arsonist … He was a mere youth, probably not sixteen years of age, but big for his age … I only caught a glimpse of him but a good enough one … It wasn't only the paintings, all that oil and canvas … there was all sorts of flammable stuff in the place. I went there to pick up some paintings. I arrived just as he was setting the fire. One of life's vicious coincidences. I could see the glow of the flames through the skylight windows. The main doors were ajar. The silly bugger saw me as I opened them and ran to the far end, to the back. The fire took like nothing you've ever seen. The main doors, where I was standing, were the only way out of the place. I think he was drunk. Probably downed half a bottle of vodka to give him the nerve to do it … and then botched it. I saw him go up like a torch … I'll never forget his screams. Another nameless victim of human madness, or human folly … Call it what you will. I doubt he even knew why he was doing it, or who had put him up to it. He had a life ahead of him … But then, the masters of the world send eighteen-year-olds and younger onto battlefields, *n'est pas*? To be blown to shreds or, these days, incinerated with one of Szakáts's flamethrowers. The StaPo were behind it of course. Though I'm sure the poor idiot didn't know that. Somebody probably arranged some meeting in a back alley somewhere and showed him more money than he'd had hot dinners and … I'm sure you can imagine the scenario.'

Pechstein was on the verge of saying there was no proof of that but remained silent.

'Something like that: it would have to be given the nod high up, very high up. Which, logically, means that Eisenstein approved it … his idea probably, even. Can't quite imagine one of his underlings popping into his office and saying: "I have an idea, sir, let's just burn that warehouse down" ... Can you?'

Pechstein had to admit to himself that that scenario did sound rather implausible.

'But …' Polanyi added, 'in a way, I also felt responsible for it. If we hadn't been involved in smuggling the paintings …

Well, he wouldn't have been there at all. And if I hadn't turned up there when I did … I felt bad about it. Very bad. It had all been a sort of game up till then.'

'And now?'

'I didn't kill Eisenstein if that's what you are thinking. But I think you know who probably did.'

***

Pechstein took the electric tram again, this time heading to the Zedlitzgasse, to where, he supposed, he really should have gone first. As the tram drove past the Modenapark, he saw about two dozen empty birdcages laid out on the grass, their cage doors open, as if the birds had been deliberately set free. He wondered if putting the cages there was an artistic statement of some kind, or if – in some symbolic act – the caged birds had actually been released, and their now-empty cages had been deposited on a public square as evidence of their liberation. Though, Polanyi's garden-city dreams notwithstanding, he doubted the emancipated budgerigars and canaries would survive the winter.

23

Anja Jensen's ground-floor apartment was more spartan, less homely, than he had expected.

'I've sort of been expecting you,' she said, offering him a seat at the dining table.

'Eisenstein—' he began.

'I know. I suppose I had better tell you what happened.'

***

… the front door opened and suddenly – she had not expected him to come to the door in person; though that was what she had hoped, and that he would be alone in the house – Eisenstein, dressed in a quilted-silk oriental dressing robe, an unlit pipe in his mouth, was looking at her. It was obvious from the expression on his unshaven face that he had no idea who she was.

'My name is Anja Jensen,' she said, without thinking.

He gave no indication that the name meant anything to him.

'Come in,' he said.

She followed him down the Persian-carpeted hallway, barely noticing the Orientalist paintings hanging on the walls, her handbag grasped tightly in front of her. The door to one of the rooms was half-open and she caught a glimpse of a glass display cabinet containing about half a dozen pistols. For a moment she thought that was where he was leading her to, but he closed that door and opened another, and she followed him into his study.

'Take a seat,' he said, indicating the chair in front of his desk – he had the manner of a man used to telling people what to do – and sat himself down, his back to the window. There were some tarot cards laid out in the form of a cross on the desk. She caught a glimpse of the colourful images as he cleared them away. The garden at the back of the house was visible through the half-drawn velvet curtains.

'How can I be of assistance?' he asked.

She had gone over what she was going to say to him – and what she was going to do – countless times in her imagination but now, faced with the physical reality of the man, all the scenarios she had imagined dissolved.

'You do know who I am?' she said.

'Adolf Jensen's sister, I presume,' he said.

She was somewhat surprised that he admitted so effortlessly to knowing Dolfi.

'I knew he had a sister,' he added, 'though of course I would not recognise you by sight – though I can see some physical resemblance. And Jensen is hardly a common name. Danish, isn't, originally?'

'Originally,' she said, finding herself momentarily being polite.

'Terrible tragedy. My deepest condolences. I would have gone to the funeral but ...'

She undid the clasp on her handbag and slowly extracted the Schleswig revolver pistol, and pointed it at him, holding it in both hands, her finger in the trigger guard, less than a centimetre away from the trigger.

'It's loaded,' she said.

She had – in her imagination – expected him to immediately react when she actually took out the revolver and pointed it at him, to cover his face with his hands in a futile self-protection gesture, or to start pleading with her. The change of expression on his face was barely detectable, but in his eyes, there was sudden and unmistakable terror, the dreadful look of an animal instinctively sensing it was in mortal danger. But then, suddenly, it was replaced by something else.

'Please put that away, Fraulein Jensen,' he said. 'Firearms are dangerous, and there is no need ... I can understand your distress but this is not the way. We can talk. Please put it back in your handbag …'

'… like a good girl,' she almost heard him add in her imagination.

'How?' she said.

'How what?'

'And why? Why did you kill my brother?'

Her hands were shaking.

'Your brother's death was an accident …' he began but she found herself suddenly saying to him: 'Rubbish. Untrue …'

'The inquest—' he began to protest, but she cut him short.

'My brother was going to expose you.'

'Expose me?'

'Yes. Go to the press—'

'Do you intend to murder me?' he asked her, neither affirming nor denying what she had said, his eyes fixed on the revolver in her shaking hands.

'I want a confession,' she said.

'A confession?' The expression on his face was somewhere between bewilderment, fear and a sneer.

'Written in your hand,' she said. 'Otherwise – I swear to God – I will pull the trigger of this gun—'

'And at the same time put a hangman's noose around your neck?'

'Not if I make it look like you killed yourself.'

'Nobody would believe that.'

'People believe all sorts of things.'

'I'd say you made me sign it. It will not be worth the paper it is written on.'

'So perhaps I should kill you anyway.'

'This is madness!'

'Yes, it is,' she said. 'Pick up one of those pens!'

There was a row of dip pens in a pen holder on his desk, along with an inkpot and a pad of blue writing paper. He picked one up.

'Now write: I, Maximilian Eisenstein …'

He pulled the pad of writing paper towards him and began to

write. But suddenly stopped.

'I can explain,' he said.

Then it happened. The revolver sprang into life with a deafening crack and jumped out of her hand and his face disintegrated and the curtain behind him was instantly covered in blood and fragments of his brain … and, for some inexplicable reason, instead of falling backwards he slowly slumped face-down onto the desk.

She could not remember what happened next beyond her realising that she was suddenly in a different universe. She vaguely remembered standing in the carpeted hallway, approaching the front door, beginning to open it, and then the blinding vastness of the world outside … and the impossibility of even the slightest refuge anywhere in it. She remembered, again vaguely as if in a dream but not in a dream, shutting the door again, the creaking of its hinges as she did so, walking down the Persian-carpeted hallway, and making her way, automaton-like, back to the horror of the study.

Eisenstein's lifeless corpse was slumped over the desk. The air smelled of blood, metallic. But then a new instinct uncoiled within her, also automaton-like, but purposeful. She realised she had to make it look like a suicide. She remembered the glass display cabinet with its collection of pistols on display. She went out of the study and opened the door Eisenstein had closed only minutes earlier – but what seemed like aeons ago. Men usually kill themselves with their own guns, she found herself thinking. She would make it look like that. She would take one of Eisenstein's pistols and substitute it for Dolfi's Schleswig pistol. But the glass doors of the display cabinet were locked. She pulled and rattled them but they wouldn't budge. There must be a key somewhere but she had no idea where, and looking for it could take forever. She would have to smash the glass. But with what? She looked around for something heavy enough. There were two small bronze statues on a side table: a meditating Buddha and a miniature copy of Donatello's bronze David. She decided on Donatello's David. It was heavy, more than heavy enough.

The glass smashed with a single blow. She put her hand carefully into the cabinet, taking care not to cut herself on the remaining jagged glass panes, and took out a gun about the same size as the Schleswig pistol. She recognised the make. It was an American Colt revolver.

She made her way again across the hallway again to Eisenstein's study, and the horrible mess of dead flesh that had been Eisenstein slumped over the leather-inlaid desk. A pool of fresh blood was expanding beneath him, and dripping onto the varnished floorboards. The horrendous rip she had slashed in the fabric of the world suffused the room with an intensity that took every last shred of her will to avoid being totally overwhelmed by.

Bullets, she thought. The Colt revolver was empty. There were no bullets in it. What if the police were able to tell what kind of bullet had killed him? It was possible. The room stank of cordite. The revolver she'd shot him with would be reeking of it. The Colt revolver just smelled of gun oil, had probably not been fired in years. She cursed aloud and tried to think again. She would not substitute the pistols. Instead, she would simply take the Colt revolver away with her. They would think the gun she had used had come from his collection. She picked the revolver up from the floor, and carefully – there were still five bullets in it – wiped the grip and barrel of it clean with the hem of her dress. Then she had gently put the heavy thing in Eisenstein's hand – which was warm and damp and disgustingly lifeless – and held it in place for a few moments that seemed like an eternity. That would make sure his fingerprints were on it, not hers. But should she leave it there, in his hand? No, better on the floor. If he had killed himself, it would have sprung out of his hand as it had hers. So she placed it on the floor, and picked up her handbag – which she'd nearly forgotten – and made her way back down the carpeted hallway and out the front door and into the vastness of the utterly changed universe …

***

'What did you do then?' Pechstein asked her.

'I came back here,' she said.

'What did you intend to do with the confession?' he asked.

She took another Waldorf from the packet on the table. Her hand was trembling.

'I don't know. Eisenstein was right of course. It would have been of no legal standing whatsoever. I could have simply sent it to the *Telegraf* or the *Prager Tagblatt*, even the *Beobachter* – they might have published it. Or to the Central Committee of the Social Democratic Party ...'

He watched her light the cigarette, wondering what it must feel like to have taken a human life – extinguished a consciousness, an entire subjective world, irretrievably and forever, even it had been unintentional.

'But none of that is relevant now, is it?' she continued. 'How did you know? How did you know that it was me?'

He sensed a determination in her to try and somehow reconcile herself to it all, to the horror that the workings of fate – he could think of no other word – had delivered her. Concepts like guilt, remorse, shame and evil came to mind; but they seemed just so many words ... An image flashed through his mind: the sight of a man – Werner was driving him to Linz for some reason – a Christ-like figure carrying a heavy wooden cross and walking along the side of the road determinately, on some personal pilgrimage, performing some act of atonement.

'Eisenstein was a secret policeman,' she added, 'a spy, or whatever you want to call it. Such men usually have many enemies.'

'True,' he said. 'I did consider that. And the police, officially, say it was a suicide. But ... the Danish revolver. It's in all the newspapers. I knew your brother had a Danish revolver. Polanyi told me about it.'

It was as if she were questioning him about something that had happened to somebody else entirely. But there was a logic to that, in a way. She was more victim than perpetrator. She had not initiated the train of events that had brought her to this, to sitting across this table from him in her Zedlitzgasse apartment with its ceramic tiled stove, varnished floorboards, its walls decorated with art and museum exhibition posters, and admitting to having killed a man. He tried to envisage the pistol springing into life and in an instant transforming Eisenstein's bourgeois study with its books and portrait of a dreaming oriental eunuch into a scene of slaughterhouse carnage …

'Eventually I put two and two together—' he said.

'And got four. Me.'

'Something like that.'

'Didn't Chekov write something about that if there a gun is on the mantelpiece in the first act, it will be used by the third act?'

'I believe so,' he said.

'Life imitates art.'

'Sometimes things just happen,' he said.

She lit another Waldorf.

'What are you going to do?' she asked him.

'You mean am I going to go to the police?'

'Yes, I suppose so. Are you?'

'No,' he said.

She nodded slowly. He wondered if she had been expecting that he would.

'What if I told them it was an accident?' she said.

'They might believe you,' he said, lighting a Sphinx. 'But they might not. The revolver *was* loaded. Why?'

'I thought it might be necessary to demonstrate that it was loaded.'

'Fire a warning shot or something?'

'Something like that.' She paused for a moment. 'Or maybe I did intend to kill him?'

But he doubted that she had.

'Eisenstein was involved in all sorts of …' he continued, '… let's say complexities. Right now, the way things stand, it's all neat and tidy. A respectable servant of the state, in a moment of despair and melancholia – it happens to the best, an intrinsic risk of the human condition – takes his own life. There is no scandal beyond that of a personal tragedy, no soiled linen being hung out for all to gaze at. Even if you said it was an accident, there would be a lot of explaining to do. It might be in the interests of some that it was an accident; another explanation might suit others. These are not normal times. And even if they were … Going anywhere near the authorities would be opening a Pandora's box, courting disaster. There'll be some obituaries in the newspapers. His life and death will be summed up – though I imagine quite a few euphemisms will be employed. And then, in a few weeks, with a bit of luck, it will be forgotten. Case closed. It will all be buried safely under the weight of future events—'

'Except?' she said.

'Polanyi put two and two together. He is preoccupied with other things right now and I think the last thing he wants is to become any more of an object of interest to the authorities than he already is. But … someone else may know about your brother's revolver. What did you do with the Colt you took from the gun cabinet?' he asked her.

'I still have it.'

'I think you'd better give it to me.'

'What will you do with it?'

'Drop it discretely into the Danube from the Reichsbrücke, I suppose,' he said, immediately regretting his insensitivity, but she seemed not to have noticed.

'These are strange times,' he said then. 'Things look as if they are falling apart, and maybe they are—'

'But maybe they are not,' she finished the sentence for him.

'You must leave Vienna,' he said, 'go far away, very far away.'

1943

24

Outside the carriage windows, the spring landscape sped by – like time itself, Polanyi could not help thinking, oblivious to human concerns – under a blue-white-grey Pre-Raphaelite sky.

He returned his attention to the copy of the German-language edition of *La Terre moderne* he'd picked up in Köln. The illustrated bimonthly had only started coming out about a year previously; though its use of line drawings rather than photographs gave it a pronounced turn-of-the-century look, despite a good proportion of them being explanatory diagrams, statistical bar graphs and pie charts like the ones in the article he'd read earlier – headlined MADE IN INDIA – on what was being called the Saffron Industrial Revolution. He read a short piece – by Rudolf Jürgens of all people – on a new medical treatment called anti-biotics and how it was replacing Salvarsan as a cure for syphilis, before settling into a long article on the completion of the Cape to Cairo railway, large stretches of which were now electrified. A mention of Von-Humboldt-Stadt made him think of Siegfried Bell.

It must have been fifteen years since he'd last seen Bell. It was sometime after he'd returned from the Protektorat. He'd called into the Crimson Cockatoo. He had resigned from whatever job he was supposed to be doing there, for reasons he was stubbornly reluctant to reveal anything about, though Polanyi doubted it was because he'd helped himself to the petty cash or been found in flagrante with the Governor's lady wife. Bell had always been too proper for that kind of escapade. Polanyi suspected it was something political, but complicated.

The last he had heard of him was a few years later, just after the German Empire had become the German Weltstaatenbund, when Sigrid told him she'd heard on the wireless that Bell had been elected to the Reichstag. It had been around the time when Ludwig Pechstein's policeman friend – Binswanger was his name, he remembered, a paradoxical kettle of fish – had been assassinated, shot several times on the steps of the War Ministry building by some pan-Slavist. There had been a sort of logic to such acts at the time – a logic of the time – but now, in hindsight and with the strange distance of time, though in the larger scheme of things it had only been yesterday, it had all been quite mad. Poison gases. Dreadnaughts. The possibility of Armageddon had always been somewhere in the back of their minds no matter how much they pretended it wasn't. The madnesses of the 1940s seemed less likely to explode into annihilation. And then the sudden and unexpected unravelling of it all, the Social Revolution which had changed much but had not produced ten thousand utopias.

Whenever he remembered his younger self, part of him shuddered inwardly. He had been full of rage at the way the world had been – dangerous rage, understandable rage. That he had survived those years intact in body and soul had been a miracle of sorts. Had Sigrid saved him from himself? Quite possibly. They didn't spend as much time together as they had in what she called 'the old days'; but when they did, the sex was as good and as badly needed as it had been then.

Other memories came and went, seemingly without rhyme or reason: Dolfi Jensen and Donnerstag, the evening they did that Charlie Chaplin double act at one of the Girardigasse parties – or was it in the Crimson Cockatoo? And that grim day they buried Dolfi, a good man, a hero in a way, when one thought about it. And it had been a grim time too when they'd buried Donnerstag, who had died of the Kansas influenza, as had Madame Hsiung-nu and the Schieles. The monstrous thing had swept across the globe like some biblical plague, killing as many as forty million, according to some estimates. Years later Pechstein had told him all he knew about Dolfi's disappearance and death – and about Binswanger's half-implausible theories – but the details of what had really happened remained a fog of facts, half-facts and speculations, now lost in what Bell used to call 'the fog of history'. But then, neat-and-tidiness was the reserve of detective-novel plots and police reports – and perhaps bad history books. But he wasn't sure he wanted to think about the past. The past was the past and existed in … well, in the past, along with the texture of the reality of its time, largely incomprehensible to the present, in its own category of being – even though this journey was, in its way, a more than slightly unnerving journey back into it.

***

There was a marsh along the pathway that ran along the railway track.

'I walk here often,' Anja Jensen said. Though she no longer used that name.

Usually only one train a day went by, a slow electric locomotive with half a dozen carriages which shattered the tranquillity of the estuary as it trundled through the valley; but the silence and the sounds of the landscape always reasserted themselves again as it disappeared inland towards the mountains.

'Strange where we end up,' Polanyi said.

A light mist hung over the expanse of autumn-coloured reeds. It had rained earlier and everything smelled of damp earth and growing foliage.

'Yes, it's never quite where one had imagined,' she said.

He had aged in the last twenty years, she thought, though grey hair strangely suited him. But then, she had too.

'They've got radio-television in Vienna now,' he said, for seemingly no particular reason. 'The devices cost a fortune, but they say it'll get cheaper. And that it'll be possible to transmit

moving pictures in colour – not just black and white – in a few
years' time.'

A pair of crows flew slowly across the sky, coal-black shapes
against the greys of the clouds. The Etruscans saw the flights of
birds as auguries, she'd read once. One of the reasons she was
drawn to this place was that it evoked such thoughts and a
feeling that there might be some invisible meaning behind the
surface of the world; which was not exactly an antidote to her
inclination to melancholy, but it helped. Though Polanyi, it
seemed, had developed a more cheerful disposition over the
decades. Earlier he had been enthusing about the von Braun
rocket, and also prophesising that before the end of the century
the Germans would land a man on the moon.

'So how did you find me?' she said.

She had intended to ask him when he had turned up the day
before – unannounced – but somehow, the right moment never
quite seemed to present itself.

'Pechstein gave me your address,' he said.

She turned and faced him. The expression on her face wavered
between surprise and confusion.

She knew Pechstein – or Ludwig, rather, she couldn't
remember when she had stopped thinking of him as Pechstein –
had inexplicably developed a friendship with Polanyi years ago.
He had said more than once, in the beginning, that she should
feel under no obligation to reply to his letters, but she had. After
a while, they had settled into writing long meandering missives
to each other several times a year, a silent conversation between
two souls across space and time. At first, until things had
changed, they had used bland pseudonyms, false return
addresses, and coded references decipherable only to
themselves. That their correspondence had been going on for
about twenty years, two decades, when she thought about it,
made her think how unreal the passing of time sometimes
seemed. But that Pechstein would have informed Polanyi, of all
people, of her whereabouts seemed odd. But then, the Polanyi
of twenty years ago had been a different man in many ways to

the one standing before her now.

'Pechstein passed away two months ago,' he said. 'I'm sorry. I meant to tell you yesterday but …'

Somehow, she managed to let the words – and their irrevocable meaning – sink in, and to keep thinking.

'Tell me what happened while we walk,' she said.

They continued down the pathway.

'It was sudden,' he said. 'Not sudden-sudden, not out of the blue. Something to do with his heart. The doctors gave him a few months.'

Polanyi was surprised by her self-possession. But then, experience had taught him that how men and women reacted to life's dismal events was unpredictable.

'He never said anything to me,' she said.

Polanyi was obviously aware that they had been in correspondence.

'He had his reasons,' he said. 'Though I was not privy to them. Perhaps he thought the doctors were wrong or—'

'Or?'

'Sometimes men see their own dying as a sort of personal failure … but maybe he just wanted to spare you the worry … which would have been unnecessary if the doctors were wrong. They sometimes are.'

There was much, she thought, that she, too, had kept to herself over the last twenty years. Though for other reasons.

Polanyi continued: 'There is some money – he never married, but you know that – that he wanted you to have. Simply leaving it to you by name in his will – all legal and proper – would have been … awkward. Though, to tell the truth, I think, after all these years …'

'That my continuing *disappearance* – if one can call it that – has long ago since become unnecessary. Ancient water under ancient bridges.'

'Yes, something like that.'

Of course, he was probably right, she thought. But it had not only been from the authorities she had wanted to disappear. And besides, had she not since become somebody else?

Polanyi began to fill his pipe. He used to smoke self-rolled cigarettes – and Turkish hashish – if her memory served her correctly.

'It's not a large sum,' he said. The House of Pechstein had never really recovered from its fall from glory during the Social Revolution. 'Werner managed to tuck some money away, but Ludwig was never the calculating type – when it came to money, anyway.'

After she had left Vienna, Pechstein had arranged for her and Dolfi's trust fund to be transferred through several bank accounts and lawyers' offices so that it had become untraceable. He had been calculating then. She had lived from it – more or less – ever since.

'It's in a numbered account,' he said. 'It can be withdrawn by you telegraphically. In Switzerland.'

'Some things never change.'

'But much has. For the best and for the worse.'

'One wonders if what happens is all inevitable or if there are real choices along the way. If it could have been a lot better, or a lot worse.'

'That, I'm afraid, is something we will never know.'

'No, I suppose not.'

There was a group of children flying a red kite, clearly visible against the clouds, on the far side of the river.

'I was up in an aëroplane once,' he said. 'It was early in the morning. The sun had just come up and was shining through the clouds. It was astonishingly beautiful. Impossible to describe in words. Almost enough to make one religious.'

'Religious?'

'Not in any sectarian sense … But who knows what our lives are really about? No matter how much we think we know. The chances of living at a time whose view of the essential nature of the universe is correct is rather statistically low.'

The children's voices echoed across the water but it was not possible to hear what they were shouting about. They stopped and looked at them for a few moments. She had never had children. But she knew Polanyi had had a daughter – Ludwig had told her that a few years back – by his Italian wife. They had never properly lived together but had not divorced either.

'They are the future,' he said, referring to the kite-flying children.

'Yes,' she said. 'Life goes on.'

She remembered a moonlight evening, a long time ago, at Das Grab, gazing at the ruins of a distant mediæval church on a hillside further down the valley, trying to visualise generations of men and women who had flickered in and out of existence over the centuries … and wondered what had become of Constance Cohen.

'Strange what we remember,' she said.

'Yes, I suppose it is.'

NOTES

Most of the references in the text to historical figures, books and technologies are based on fact, though they have been put in the context of an alternative history. And most of the institutions mentioned also existed – such as Universal Bibliographic Repertory or the Mundaneum, the Evidenzbüro, the StaPo and the Kaiser Wilhelm Institute. The 'Establishment' is loosely based on Porton Down in England, which opened in 1916 as the War Department Experimental Station. The description of the gas experiments is based on real experiments that took place during the First World War. France was the first to use gas – teargas – in the First World War, in August 1914. The first major poison gas attack, at Ypres, on April 22, 1915, was by the Germans – chlorine was used. There were 1.3 million casualties caused by chemical weapons in the First World War, including 100,000 fatalities, primarily from phosgene. Fritz Haber won a Nobel prize for chemistry in 1919. *A Higher Form of Killing: The Secret History of Chemical and Biological Warfare* by Robert Harris and Jeremy Paxman, 1982, provides an excellent history of chemical weapons.

Some historical details relating to the historical period and mentioned in the novel:

Alfred Redl – The account of Redl's espionage activities and suicide is based on the historical record.

Ambedkar – Bhimrao Ramji Ambedkar (1891–1956) was an Indian jurist, economist, politician and social reformer who inspired the Dalit Buddhist movement and campaigned against social discrimination towards the so-called untouchables (the Dalit caste), and also supported the rights of women and labour. He was the principal architect of the Constitution of India. He had doctorates from both Columbia University, USA, and the London School of Economics, UK.

Anti-Semitism – For an incisive history and analysis of European anti-Semitism, see Hannah Arendt's *The Origins of Totalitarianism*. It is probably safe to assume that the Nazi and Stalinist totalitarianisms that came about in Europe during the first half of the twentieth century would hardly have occurred if the First World War had not taken place.

Biosphere – The word *biosphere* was coined by geologist Eduard Suess in 1875. It is usually defined as the total global ecological system containing all forms of life, but can also be any closed, self-regulating ecosystem.

Carbonic acid, effect on the atmosphere – The reference is to the work of the Swede Svante Arrhenius, a Nobel laureate, who in 1896 first described how increases in atmospheric carbon dioxide would increase Earth's surface temperature through the greenhouse effect.

'Century of peace' – while Europe could be said to have enjoyed a relative 'century of peace' between 1815 and 1914 in comparison with the twentieth century, in that there was no general war between the European powers, it is worth recalling just some of the major wars of that period (estimated deaths include civilian deaths and deaths from non-combatant causes):

Taiping Rebellion, China, 1850–64, 20–30 million deaths;

Crimean War, 1853–56, 500,000 deaths;

Indian Mutiny, 1857–58, 800,000 deaths;

American Civil War, 1861–65, 1,000,000 deaths;

Boxer Rebellion, China, 1899–1901, 100,000 deaths;

Second Boer War, 1899–1902, 60,000 deaths;

Anglo–Zulu War, 1879, 9,000 deaths;

Herero Wars, German SW Africa, 1904–08, 65,000–70,000 deaths;

Maji Rebellion, German E Africa, 125,000–175,000 deaths.

Cosmism – often referred to as **Russian Cosmism**. A good introduction to this fascinating set of ideas is George M. Young's *The Russian Cosmists – The Esoteric Futurism of Nikolai Fedorov and His Followers*. Young describes cosmism as an important line of Russian thought, which runs from the mid-nineteenth through to today, that emphasises that we are inhabitants of the cosmos, not just inhabitants of a single planet or a single country, and that we should not only be intellectually aware of this but actually feel it. Prominent 'cosmists' include Konstantin Tsiolkovsky (1857–1935), the pioneer of theoretical space exploration and cosmonautics, and Vladimir Vernadsky (1863–1945), who developed the notion of noosphere. Many Russian thinkers, writers and scientists have been influenced by cosmist ideas.

Die Waffen nieder! – An anti-war novel by Bertha von Suttner, published in 1889. The English title is *Lay Down Your Arms!* It was extremely successful and translated into many languages. Until the publication of *Im Westen nichts Neues* (English title: *All Quiet on the Western Front*) in 1929. it was considered the most important German-language literary work concerning war. Von Suttner received the Nobel Peace Prize in 1905 for the book.

Electric automobiles and trains – In 1900 in the USA, 38% of automobiles were powered by electricity, 40% were powered by steam, and 22% by gasoline/petrol. Clara Ford, the wife of Henry Ford, drove a 1914 Detroit Electric. The German Kaiser Wilhelm II had three electric automobiles. The first electric train locomotive was built in 1837 by chemist Robert Davidson of Aberdeen, Scotland, and it was powered by galvanic cells (batteries). An AEG and Siemens electric train reached a speed of over 200 kilometres an hour in 1903.

Enigma machines – The Enigma mechanical cipher machine was invented by Arthur Scherbius (1878–1929). He patented it in 1918. The first commercially available machine was produced by Chiffriermaschinen-Aktiengesellschaft (ChiMaAG) in Berlin in 1923.

Eugenics – Eugenics ideas were very widespread during the first half of the twentieth century. The typical concern was with improving one's own 'racial' stock. Winston Churchill proposed the sterilisation of 100,000 of the 'feeble-minded' when he was a Secretary of State for the Home Office in 1911–12, but no such legislation was passed. Eugenics is usually associated with the

Nazis these days, but many eugenicists had ideas which today would be considered very advanced and enlightened. The Swiss scientist August Forel, a co-developer of the theory that neurons are the basic elements of the nervous system, was just one of many such eugenicists. His book *Die Sexuelle Frage* was banned by the Nazis for its liberal attitudes toward homosexuality, contraception, and abortion.

Flamethrowers – The flame thrower was invented by Hungarian Gábor Szakáts. It was first used by the German army in the First World War.

Goethe's Correspondence with a Child – Epistolary novel by Bettina von Arnim, published in 1835. She was linked to the socialist movement, was an advocate for the oppressed Jewish community, and a friend of Beethoven. The Encyclopædia Britannica says of her: 'In the diversity of her talents and interests, she exhibited the universality that has been regarded as the hallmark of the German Romantic spirit.'

Gusto Grass is loosely based on Gustav (Gusto) Arthur Gräser (1879–1958), a German-speaking alternative lifestyle advocate, peace activist, artist, poet, and one of the founders of Monte Verità in Ascona.

Herzen, Alexander Ivanovich – Herzen (1812–1870) is often referred to as the 'father of Russian socialism'. He spent time in London organising with the International Workingmen's Association, and was acquainted with revolutionary circles, including Bakunin and Marx. Isaiah Berlin called his autobiography, *My Past and Thoughts*, as 'one of the great monuments to Russian literary and psychological genius … a literary masterpiece to be placed by the side of the novels of … Tolstoy, Turgenev, Dostoevsky …'. The words 'we are not the doctors, we are the disease,' which he is reputed to have addressed to some anarchists who were plotting to overthrow the Czar, have been interpreted variously.

Hollerith machines – An excellent history of Hollerith punchcard machines can be found in *IBM and the Holocaust: The Strategic Alliance between Nazi Germany and America's Most Powerful Corporation* by Edwin Black.

Ja Da, Ja Da, Jing, Jing, Jing! – This is a real song. It was composed in 1918 by Bob Carleton, and was a 'jazz standard' for decades.

Kansas influenza – This is a reference to the Spanish influenza or the 1918 pandemic. In the alternative timeline of the novel, this pandemic occurs a few years later and spreads more slowly. Estimates as to how many people died range from 17–50+ million. There is disagreement as to its origin. Historian Alfred W. Crosby, author of *America's Forgotten Pandemic: The Influenza of 1918* and *The Columbian Exchange*, believed that it originated in Kansas. Claude Hannoun, the leading expert on the 1918 influenza at the Pasteur Institute in Paris has asserted that the precursor virus was likely to have come from China, and that it then mutated in the United States and from there spread to Europe. The Wikipedia article on the Spanish influenza lists several possible origins. Egon Schiele and his spouse, Edith, the model for most of his female figures and who was six months pregnant at the time, both died from the Spanish influenza in 1918.

Lebensreform – (life reform, German), a social movement promoting a more nature-related lifestyle, health foods, alternative medicine, nudism and sexual freedom.

Lishny Chelovek – While Turgenev did write a novella entitled *The Diary of a Superfluous Man*, a *lishny chelovek* is a fairly common literary character type in nineteenth-century Russian literature. He is usually a dreamy idealist, often an aristocrat, full of goodwill but incapable of meaningful action.

Mother Earth (1906–1917) was an American anarchist journal, edited by Emma Goldman. Contributors included Kropotkin, Errico Malatesta, Élisée Reclus and Rudolf Rocker. In 1917, *Mother Earth* began to call for opposition to US entry into the First World War and resistance to military conscription. The journal's offices were searched by the US Justice Department, using the Espionage Act (passed in 1917). Goldman's US citizenship was revoked and, along with 258 others, she was deported to the Soviet Union in 1919.

Mussolini – Benito Mussolini's (1883–1945) political roots are controversial and complex. His father was an anarchist and he was involved in the Italian socialist movement for many years. He served a term of imprisonment for taking part in a riot against the Italo-Turkish War in Africa, which he described as 'nationalist delirium tremens'. He was an admirer of the writings of Errico Malatesta (whom he knew personally), Friedrich Engels, Karl Marx and Nietzsche. He was expelled from the Italian Socialist Party for supporting Italy's entry into the First World War. One can only speculate as to what his political biography would have been had the First World War not occurred.

Naturmensch – German, translates literally as 'nature-human', or 'Natural Man'; a group of late 19th and early 20th century Germany and Swiss vegans/vegetarians who wore simple tunics and sandals, their hair long, and they were usually bearded. They were also called Nature Boys. Gustav Nagel ('gustaf nagel') (1874 – 1952), who features in the cover photograph, was a well-known *Naturmensch*, one of the first, and *Lebensreformer* (life reformer), and spent time at Monte Verità in Ascona. In 1943, because of his anti-war activities and his criticism of Nazi anti-Semitism, he was arrested and sent to Dachau concentration camp. In 1944 he was committed to a psychiatric hospital but discharged in 1945. In 1950/51, also for political reasons, he was re-committed to the same psychiatric hospital, then in Soviet-occupied East Germany, where he died in 1952.

Palæoanthropology in the early 20th century – A good source for the state of knowledge at the time is *Men of the Old Stone Age – Their Environment, Life and Art* by Henry Fairfield Osborn, 1915. A PDF copy is available on the Internet Archive. However, the ages that Weber suggests for the various hominoid species also come from different contemporary sources and are not necessarily consistent with those suggested in Osborn's text. It was not until 1953 that Piltdown Man was revealed as being a scientific fraud, although from the outset, some scientists expressed scepticism about the find.

Paper sizes – The A-series paper sizes (A1, A2, A3, A4 etc.) became a German industry standard (DIN) in 1922, though they were in use long before that. In the alternative timeline of the novel this happens a few years earlier.

Plate-forme organisation structure – ('flat form', French, from which the word *platform* is derived). In the text the reference is to a 'flat' form of organisation structure as opposed to a hierarchical structure. Not to be confused with, 'platformism', a strand of anarchism which stresses tight political and organisational unity.

Preßburg – Bratislava, now the capital of Slovakia, was mostly known by its German name of Preßburg or Pressburg up until 1919.

Prostitution in Vienna – For an account of prostitution in Vienna, see *The Red House*, a novel by Else Jerusalem, 1909.

Radio-controlled weapons – In 1898 Nikola Tesla demonstrated a 'wireless' radio-controlled torpedo which he was hoping to sell to the US Navy. Archibald Low, known as the 'father of radio guidance systems', worked on guided rockets and planes during the First World War. In 1917, he demonstrated a remote-controlled aircraft to the Royal Flying Corps and built the first wire-guided rocket.

Rudolf Duala Manga Bell – While Siegfried Bell is a fictional character, the Rudolf Manga Bell mentioned in the text was a real person. His full name was Rudolf Duala Manga Bell. He was the king of the Duala in the Protektorat Kamerun. He attended secondary school in Germany and studied law at the University of Cologne. He was executed by the Germany colonial authorities in the Protektorat Kamerun in 1914 for 'high treason' just after the outbreak of the First World War. His eldest son, Alexander (Alexandre) Douala Manga, was an officer in the German army in France at the time; later, in 1915, he fought at Gallipoli. He was elected to the Constituent Assembly of the French Fourth Republic in 1945 as one of the representatives of Cameroon. A detailed account of Rudolf Duala Manga Bell's life and death is given in *Der gute Deutsche: Die Ermordung Manga Bells in Kamerun 1914* by Christian Bommarius, Berenberg Verlag, 2015. German television also produced a documentary on his life in 1997 titled *Manga Bell – Eine deutsch-afrikanische Familiengeschichte*, which is available on YouTube.

Special Branch – British police unit responsible for matters of national security and intelligence, originally called the Special Irish Branch. 'Irish' was dropped from its name as it expanded its activities, such as the surveillance of Indian activists and anarchist organisations.

Sewers in Vienna – For a photographic and journalistic account of men (mainly) who lived in the Vienna sewers prior to the First World War, see *Durch die Wiener Quartiere des Elends und Verbrechens* by Emil Kläger and Hermann Drawe, 1908.

Teilhard de Chardin – The Jesuit palaeontologist and geologist, Pierre Teilhard de Chardin (1881–1955), describes his ideas regarding the universe evolving towards a maximum state of complexity and consciousness, which he called the Omega Point, in *The Phenomenon of Man*; the book was actually written in the 1930s but only published posthumously. In the timeline of the novel, this occurs somewhat earlier.

Telephone network – The figures given for the average number of telephone calls made in Austria-Hungary and Great Britain at the time are based on historical records. Telephone news services also existed at the time.

Television – The word *television* coined by the Russian Constantin Perskyi in a paper to the International Electricity Congress at the International World Fair in Paris in 1900, which reviewed the then-existing television technology. Dates of first broadcasts:

1928 – WRGB (then W2XB) started as the world's first television station. It broadcast from the General Electric facility in Schenectady, New York State, USA.

1931–32 – The Soviet Union began 30-line electromechanical test broadcasts in Moscow, and produced a commercially available television set.

1936 – The BBC began transmitting the world's first public regular high-definition service from the Victorian Alexandra Palace in London.

1936 – The Berlin Summer Olympic Games televised. Twenty-eight public television rooms were opened for anybody who did not own a television set. The Germans had a 441-line system on the air in February 1937, and during the Second World War brought it to France, where they broadcast from the Eiffel Tower. 1941 – First TV advertisement broadcast in the USA.

Wallace, Alfred Russel – While working as a specimen collector in the Dutch East Indies (modern Indonesia), Wallace conceived the theory of natural section concurrently with Charles Darwin. In 1858, he sent an essay to Darwin entitled *On the Tendency of Varieties to Depart Indefinitely from the Original Type*. This was presented to the Linnaean Society of London on 1 July of the same year, along with a description of Darwin's theory, and subsequently published. This prompted Darwin to publish his own ideas in *On the Origin of Species by Means of Natural Selection* in 1859. Later, Wallace came to maintain that natural selection cannot account for higher mental faculties in humans. The film *The Forgotten Voyage: Alfred Russel Wallace and His Discovery of Evolution by Natural Selection*, directed by Peter Crawford, 1983, is a very good dramatisation of Wallace's life in the Far East.